L

# Temptation
## IN PARADISE

# Temptation
# IN PARADISE

LYNNE
**GRAHAM**

CLARE
**CONNELLY**

ANGELA
**BISSELL**

MILLS & BOON

TEMPTATION IN PARADISE © 2021 by Harlequin Books S.A.

The publisher acknowledges the copyright holders of the individual works as follows:

THE BILLIONAIRE'S BRIDAL BARGAIN
© 2015 by Lynne Graham
Philippine Copyright 2015
Australian Copyright 2015
New Zealand Copyright 2015

First Published 2015
Fourth Australian Paperback Edition 2021
ISBN 978 1 867 23751 8

THE GREEK'S BILLION-DOLLAR BABY
© 2019 by Clare Connelly
Philippine Copyright 2019
Australian Copyright 2019
New Zealand Copyright 2019

First Published 2019
Second Australian Paperback Edition 2021
ISBN 978 1 867 23751 8

DEFYING HER BILLIONAIRE PROTECTOR
© 2016 by Angela Bissell
Philippine Copyright 2016
Australian Copyright 2016
New Zealand Copyright 2016

First Published 2016
Third Australian Paperback Edition 2021
ISBN 978 1 867 23751 8

Published by
Harlequin Mills & Boon
An imprint of Harlequin Enterprises (Australia) Pty
Limited (ABN 47 001 180 918), a subsidiary of
HarperCollins Publishers Australia Pty Limited
(ABN 36 009 913 517)
Level 13, 201 Elizabeth Street
SYDNEY NSW 2000 AUSTRALIA

MIX
Paper from /
responsible sources
FSC® C001695
www.fsc.org

Printed and bound in Australia by McPherson's Printing Group

# CONTENTS

# The Billionaire's Bridal Bargain
## Lynne Graham

**Lynne Graham** was born in Northern Ireland and has been a keen romance reader since her teens. She is very happily married, with an understanding husband who has learned to cook since she started to write. Her five children keep her on her toes. She has a very large dog, which knocks everything over, a very small terrier, which barks a lot, and two cats. When time allows, Lynne is a keen gardener.

### Books by Lynne Graham

#### Harlequin Modern

*The Secret His Mistress Carried*
*The Dimitrakos Proposition*
*A Ring to Secure His Heir*
*Unlocking Her Innocence*

#### The Legacies of Powerful Men

*Ravelli's Defiant Bride*
*Christakis's Rebellious Wife*
*Zarif's Convenient Queen*

#### A Bride for a Billionaire

*A Rich Man's Whim*
*The Sheikh's Prize*
*The Billionaire's Trophy*
*Challenging Dante*

Visit the Author Profile page
at millsandboon.com.au for more titles.

# CHAPTER ONE

CESARE SABATINO FLIPPED open the file sent by special delivery and groaned out loud, his darkly handsome features betraying his disbelief.

There were two photos included in the file, one of a nubile blonde teenager called Cristina and the other of her older sister Elisabetta. Was this familial insanity to visit yet another generation? Cesare raked long brown fingers through his luxuriant black hair, frustration pumping through every long lean line of his powerful body. He really didn't have time for such nonsense in the middle of his working day. What was his father, Goffredo, playing at?

'What's up?' Jonathan, his friend and a director of the Sabatino pharmaceutical empire, asked.

In answer, Cesare tossed the file to the other man. 'Look at it and weep at the madness that can afflict even one's seemingly sane relatives,' he urged.

Frowning, Jonathan glanced through the sparse file and studied the photos. 'The blonde's not bad but a bit on the young side. The other one with the woolly hat on looks like a scarecrow. What on earth is the connection between you and some Yorkshire farming family?'

'It's a long story,' Cesare warned him.

Jonathan hitched his well-cut trousers and took a seat. 'Interesting?'

Cesare grimaced. 'Only moderately. In the nineteen thirties my family owned a small island called Lionos in the Aegean Sea. Most of my ancestors on my father's side are buried there. My grandmother, Athene, was born and raised there. But when her father went bust, Lionos was sold to an Italian called Geraldo Luccini.'

Jonathan shrugged. 'Fortunes rise and fall.'

'Matters, however, took a turn for the worse when Athene's brother decided to get the island back into family hands by marrying Luccini's daughter and then chose to jilt her at the altar.'

The other man raised his brows. 'Nice...'

'Her father was so enraged by the slight to his daughter and his family that Lionos was eternally tied up in Geraldo's exceedingly complex will.'

'In what way?'

'The island cannot be sold and the two young women in that file are the current owners of Lionos by inheritance through their mother. The island can only be regained by my family through marriage between a Zirondi and a Luccini descendant and the birth of a child.'

'You're not serious?' Jonathan was amazed.

'A generation back, my father was serious enough to propose marriage to the mother of those two girls, Francesca, although I would point out that he genuinely fell in love with her. Luckily for us all, however, when he proposed she turned him down and married her farmer instead.'

'Why luckily?' Jonathan queried.

'Francesca didn't settle for long with the farmer or with any of the men that followed him. Goffredo had a narrow escape,' Cesare opined, lean, strong face grim, well aware that his laid-back and rather naive father could never have coped with so fickle a wife.

'So, why has your father sent you that file?'

'He's trying to get me interested in the ongoing, "Lionos reclamation project",' Cesare said very drily, the slant of his wide, sensual mouth expressing sardonic amusement as he sketched mocking quotations marks in the air.

'He actually thinks he has a chance of persuading *you* to consider marriage with one of those two women?' Jonathan slowly shook his head for neither female appeared to be a show-stopper and Cesare enjoyed the reputation of being a connoisseur of the female sex. 'Is he crazy?'

'Always an optimist.' Cesare sighed. 'In the same way he never listens when I tell him I haven't the smallest desire to ever get married.'

'As a happily married man and father, I have to tell you that you're missing out.'

Cesare resisted a rude urge to roll his eyes in mockery. He knew that, in spite of the odds, good marriages *did* exist. His father had one, after all, and evidently Jonathan did too. But Cesare had no faith in true love and happy-ever-after stories, particularly not when his own first love had ditched him to waltz down the aisle with an extremely wealthy man, who referred to himself as being seventy-five years young. Serafina had dutifully proclaimed her love of older men all the way to the graveyard gates and was now a very rich widow, who had been chasing Cesare in the hope of a rematch ever since.

Cesare's recollections were tinged with supreme scorn. He would never make a mistake like Serafina again. It had been a boy's mistake, he reminded himself wryly. He was now far less ignorant about the nature of the female sex. He had never yet lavished his wealth on a woman who wasn't more excited by his money than by anything else he offered. A satisfied smile softened the hard line of his wide, expressive mouth when he thought of his current lover, a gorgeous French fashion model who went to great lengths to please him in bed and out of it. And all without the fatal suffocating commitment of rings or nagging or noisy kids attached. What was not to like? It was true that he was an extremely generous lover but what was money for but enjoyment when you had as much as Cesare now had?

Cesare was less amused and indeed he tensed when he strolled into his city penthouse that evening to receive the news from his manservant, Primo, that his father had arrived for an unexpected visit.

Goffredo was out on the roof terrace admiring the panoramic view of London when Cesare joined him.

'To what do I owe the honour?' he mocked.

His father, always an extrovert in the affection stakes, clasped his son in a hug as if he hadn't seen the younger man in months rather than mere weeks. 'I need to talk to you about your grandmother...'

Cesare's smile immediately faded. 'What's wrong?'

Goffredo grimaced. 'Athene needs a coronary bypass. Hopefully it will relieve her angina.'

Cesare had stilled, a frown line etched between his level ebony brows. 'She's seventy-five.'

'The prognosis for her recovery is excellent,' his father told him reassuringly. 'Unfortunately the real problem is my mother's outlook on life. She thinks she's too old for surgery. She thinks she's had her three score years and ten and should be grateful for it.'

'That's ridiculous. If necessary, I'll go and talk some sense into her,' Cesare said impatiently.

'She needs something to look forward to…some motivation to make her believe that the pain and stress of surgery will be worthwhile.'

Cesare released his breath in a slow hiss. 'I hope you're not talking about Lionos. That's nothing but a pipe dream.'

Goffredo studied his only son with compressed lips. 'Since when have you been defeatist about any challenge?'

'I'm too clever to tilt at windmills,' Cesare said drily.

'But surely you have some imagination? Some… what is it you chaps call it now? The ability to think outside the box?' the older man persisted. 'Times have changed, Cesare. The world has moved on and when it comes to the island you have a power that I was never blessed with.'

Cesare heaved a sigh and wished he had worked late at the office where pure calm and self-discipline ruled, the very building blocks of his lifestyle. 'And what power would that be?' he asked reluctantly.

'You are incredibly wealthy and the current owners of the island are dirt-poor.'

'But the will is watertight.'

'Money could be a great persuader,' his father reasoned. 'You don't want a wife and probably neither of Francesca's daughters wants a real husband at such a young age. Why can't you come to some sort of business arrangement with one of them?'

Cesare shook his arrogant dark head. 'You're asking me to try and get round the will?'

'The will has already been minutely appraised by a top inheritance lawyer in Rome. If you can marry one of those girls, you will have the right to visit the island and, what is more important, you will have the right to take your grandmother there,' Goffredo outlined, clearly expecting his son to be impressed by that revelation.

Instead, Cesare suppressed a groan of impatience. 'And what's that worth at the end of the day? It's *not* ownership, it's *not* getting the island back into the family.'

'Even a visit after all the years that have passed would be a source of great joy to your grandmother,' Goffredo pointed out in a tone of reproach.

'I always understood that visiting the island was against the terms of the will.'

'Not if a marriage has first taken place. That is a distinction that it took a lawyer to point out. Certainly, if any of us were to visit without that security, Francesca's daughters would forfeit their inheritance and the island would go to the government by default.'

'Which would please no one but the government,' Cesare conceded wryly. 'Do you really think that a measly visit to the island would mean that much to Nonna?' he pressed.

'The right to pay her respects again at her parents'

graves? To see the house where she was born and
where she married and first lived with my father? She
has many happy memories of Lionos.'

'But would one short visit satisfy her? It's my belief
that she has always dreamt of living out her life there
and that's out of the question because a child has to
be born to fulfil the full terms of the will and grant
us the right to put down roots on the island again.'

'There is a very good chance that clause could be
set aside in court as unreasonable. Human rights law
has already altered many matters once set in stone,'
Goffredo reasoned with enthusiasm.

'It's doubtful,' Cesare argued. 'It would take many
years and a great deal of money to take it to court and
the government would naturally fight any change we
sought. The court option won't work in my lifetime.
And what woman is going to marry and have a child
with me, to allow me to inherit an uninhabited, un-
developed island? Even if I did offer to buy the island
from her once we were married.'

It was his father's turn to groan. 'You must know
how much of a catch you are, Cesare. *Madre di Dio*,
you've been beating the women off with a stick since
you were a teenager!'

Cesare dealt him an amused look. 'And you don't
think it would be a little immoral to conceive a child
for such a purpose?'

'As I've already stated,' Goffredo proclaimed with
dignity, 'I am not suggesting you go *that* far.'

'But I couldn't reclaim the island for the family
*without* going that far,' Cesare fielded very drily. 'And
if I can't buy it or gain anything beyond guaranteeing
Nonna the right to visit the wretched place one more

time, what is the point of approaching some stranger and trying to bribe her?'

'Is that your last word on the subject?' his father asked stiffly when the silence dragged.

'I'm a practical man,' Cesare murmured wryly. 'If we could regain the island I could see some point of pursuing this.'

The older man halted on his passage towards the door and turned back to face his son with compressed lips. 'You could at least approach Francesca's daughters and see if something could be worked out. You could at least *try*...'

When his father departed in high dudgeon, Cesare swore long and low in frustration. Goffredo was so temperamental and so easily carried away. He was good at getting bright ideas but not so smooth with the follow-up or the fallout. His son, on the other hand, never let emotion or sentiment cloud his judgement and rarely got excited about anything.

Even so, Cesare did break into a sweat when he thought about his grandmother's need for surgery and her lack of interest in having it. In his opinion, Athene was probably bored and convinced that life had no further interesting challenges to offer. She was also probably a little frightened of the surgical procedure as well. His grandmother was such a strong and courageous woman that people frequently failed to recognise that she had her fears and weaknesses just like everyone else.

Cesare's own mother had died on the day he was born and Goffredo's Greek mother, Athene, had come to her widowed son's rescue. While Goffredo had grieved and struggled to build up his first business and establish some security, Athene had taken charge of raising Cesare. Even before he'd started school he had been playing chess, reading and doing advanced maths for enjoyment. His grandmother had been quick to recognise her grandson's prodigious intellectual gifts. Unlike his father, she had not been intimidated by his genius IQ and against a background of loving support Athene had given Cesare every opportunity to flourish and develop at his own pace. He owed his *nonna* a great deal and she was still the only woman in the world whom Cesare had ever truly cared about. But then he had never been an emotional man, had never been able to understand or feel truly comfortable around more demonstrative personalities. He was astute, level-headed and controlled in every field of his life yet he had a soft spot in his heart for his grandmother that he would not have admitted to a living soul.

A business arrangement, Cesare ruminated broodingly, flicking open the file again. There was no prospect of him approaching the teenager but the plain young woman in the woolly hat and old coat? Could he even contemplate such a gross and unsavoury lowering of his high standards? He was conservative in his tastes and not an easy man to please but if the prize was great enough, he was clever enough to compromise and adapt, wasn't he? Aware that very few people were cleverer than he was, Cesare contemplated the startling idea of getting married and grimaced with distaste at the threat of being forced to live in such close contact with another human being.

'You should've sent Hero off to the knackers when I told you to!' Brian Whitaker bit out in disgust. 'Instead you've kept him eating his head off in that stable. How can we afford that with the cost of feed what it is?'

'Chrissie's very fond of Hero. She's coming home from uni next week and I wanted her to have the chance to say goodbye.' Lizzie kept her voice low rather than risk stoking her father's already irascible temper. The older man was standing by the kitchen table, his trembling hands—the most visible symptom of the Parkinson's disease that had ravaged his once strong body—braced on the chair back as he glowered at his daughter, his gaunt, weathered face grim with censure.

'And if you do that, she'll weep and she'll wail and she'll try to talk you out of it again. What's the point of that? You tried to sell him and there were no takers,' he reminded her with biting impatience. 'You're a bloody *useless* farmer, Lizzie!'

'That horse charity across the valley may have a space coming up this week,' Lizzie told him, barely even flinching from her father's scorn because his dissatisfaction was so familiar to her. 'I was hoping for the best.'

'Since when has hoping for the best paid the bills?' Brian demanded with withering contempt. 'Chrissie should be home here helping you, not wasting her time studying!'

Lizzie compressed her lips, wincing at the idea that her kid sister should also sacrifice her education to their daily struggle for survival against an ever-increasing tide of debt. The farm was failing but it had been failing for a long time. Unfortunately her father had never approved of Chrissie's desire to go to university. His world stopped at the borders of the farm and he had very little interest in anything beyond it. Lizzie understood his reasoning because her world had shrunk to the same boundaries once she had left school at sixteen.

At the same time, though, she adored the kid sister she had struggled to protect throughout their dysfunctional childhood and was willing to take a lot of grief from her father if it meant that the younger woman could enjoy the youthful freedom and opportunities that she herself had been denied. In fact Lizzie had been as proud as any mother when Chrissie had won a place to study Literature at Oxford. Although she missed Chrissie, she would not have wished her own life of back-breaking toil and isolation on anyone she loved.

As Lizzie dug her feet back into her muddy boots a small low-slung shaggy dog, whose oddly proportioned body reflected his very mixed ancestry, greeted her at the back door with his feeding bowl in his mouth.

'Oh, I'm so sorry, Archie…I forgot about you,' Lizzie groaned, climbing out of the boots again to trudge back across the kitchen floor and fill the dog bowl. While she mentally listed all the many, many tasks she had yet to accomplish she heard the reassuring roar of a football game playing on the television in the room next door and some of the tension eased from her slight shoulders. Watching some sport and forgetting his aches and pains for a little while would put her father in a better mood.

Her father was a difficult man, but then his life had always been challenging. In his case hard work and commitment to the farm had failed to pay off.

He had taken on the farm tenancy at a young age and
had always had to work alone. Her late mother, Francesca, had only lasted a few years as a farmer's wife
before running off with a man she deemed to have
more favourable prospects. Soured by the divorce that
followed, Brian Whitaker had not remarried. When
Lizzie was twelve, Francesca had died suddenly and
her father had been landed with the responsibility of
two daughters who were practically strangers to him.
The older man had done his best even though he could
never resist an opportunity to remind Lizzie that she
would never be the strong capable son he had wanted
and needed to help him on the farm. He had barely
passed fifty when ill health had handicapped him and
prevented him from doing physical work.

Lizzie knew she was a disappointment to the older
man but then she was used to falling short of other
people's expectations. Her mother had longed for a
more outgoing, fun-loving child than shy, socially
awkward Lizzie had proved to be. Her father had
wanted a son, not a daughter. Even her fiancé had left
her for a woman who seemed to be a far more successful farmer's wife than Lizzie could ever have hoped to
be. Sadly, Lizzie had become accustomed to not mea-
suring up and had learned to simply get on with the
job at hand rather than dwell on her own deficiencies.

She started her day off with the easy task of feeding
the hens and gathering the eggs. Then she fed Hero,
whose feed she was buying solely from her earnings
from working Saturday nights behind the bar of the
village pub. She didn't earn a wage at home for her
labour. How could she take a wage out of the kitty
every week when the rising overdraft at the bank was

a constant worry? Household bills, feed and fuel costs were necessities that had to come out of that overdraft and she was dreading the arrival of yet another warning letter from the bank.

She loaded the slurry tank to spray the meadow field before her father could complain about how far behind she was with the spring schedule. Archie leapt into the tractor cab with her and sat panting by her side. He still wore the old leather collar punched with his name that he had arrived with. When she had found him wandering the fields, hungry and bedraggled, Lizzie had reckoned he had been dumped at the side of the road and, sadly, nobody had ever come looking for him. She suspected that his formerly expensive collar revealed that he had once been a much-loved pet, possibly abandoned because his elderly owner had passed away.

When he'd first arrived, he had hung out with their aging sheepdog, Shep, and had demonstrated a surprising talent for picking up Shep's skills so that when Shep had died even Brian Whitaker had acknowledged that Archie could make himself useful round the farm. Lizzie, on the other hand, utterly adored Archie. He curled up at her feet in bed at night and allowed himself to be cuddled whenever she was low.

She was driving back to the yard to refill the slurry tank when she saw a long, sleek, glossy black car filtering off the main road into the farm lane. Her brow furrowed at the sight. She couldn't picture anyone coming in a car that big and expensive to buy the free-range eggs she sold. Parking the tractor by the fence, she climbed out with Archie below one arm, stooping to let her pet down.

That was Cesare's first glimpse of Lizzie. She glanced up as she unbent and the limo slowed to ease past the tractor. He saw that though she might dress like a bag lady she had skin as translucent as the finest porcelain and eyes the colour of prized jade. He breathed in deep and slow.

His driver got out of the car only to come under immediate attack by what was clearly a vicious dog but which more closely resembled a scruffy fur muff on short legs. As the woman captured the dog to restrain it and before his driver could open the door for him Cesare sprang out and instantly the offensive stench of the farm yard assaulted his fastidious nostrils. His intense concentration trained on his quarry, he simply held his breath while lazily wondering if she smelt as well. When his father had said the Whitaker family was dirt-poor he had clearly not been joking. The farmhouse bore no resemblance to a picturesque country cottage with roses round the door. The rain guttering sagged, the windows needed replacing and the paint was peeling off the front door.

'Are you looking for directions?' Lizzie asked as the tall black-haired male emerged in a fluid shift of long limbs from the rear seat.

Cesare straightened and straight away focused on her pouty pink mouth. That was three unexpected pluses in a row, he acknowledged in surprise. Lizzie Whitaker had great skin, beautiful eyes and a mouth that made a man think of sinning, and Cesare had few inhibitions when it came to the sins of sexual pleasure. Indeed, his hot-blooded nature and need for regular sex were the two traits he deemed potential weaknesses, he acknowledged wryly.

'Directions?' he queried, disconcerted by the disruptive drift of his own thoughts, anathema to his self-discipline. In spite of his exasperation, his mind continued to pick up on the fact that Lizzie Whitaker was small, possibly only a few inches over five feet tall, and seemingly slender below the wholly dreadful worn and stained green jacket and baggy workman's overalls she wore beneath. The woolly hat pulled low on her brow made her eyes look enormous as she stared up at him much as if he'd stepped out of a spaceship in front of her.

One glance at the stranger had reduced Lizzie to gaping in an almost spellbound moment out of time. He was simply...*stunning* from his luxuriant black hair to his dark-as-bitter-chocolate deep-set eyes and strong, uncompromisingly masculine jawline. In truth she had never ever seen a more dazzling man and that disconcertingly intimate thought froze her in place like a tongue-tied schoolgirl.

'I assumed you were lost,' Lizzie explained weakly, finding it a challenge to fill her lungs with oxygen while he looked directly at her with eyes that, even lit by the weak spring sunshine, shifted to a glorious shade of bronzed gold. For a split second, she felt as if she were drowning and she shook her head slightly, struggling to think straight and act normally, her colour rising steadily as she fought the unfamiliar lassitude engulfing her.

'No, I'm not lost... This *is* the Whitaker farm?'

'Yes, I'm Lizzie Whitaker...'

Only the British could take a pretty name like Elisabetta and shorten it to something so commonplace, Cesare decided irritably. 'I'm Cesare Sabatino.'

Her jade eyes widened. His foreign-sounding name was meaningless to her ears because she barely recognised a syllable of it. 'Sorry, I didn't catch that…'

His beautifully sensual mouth quirked. 'You don't speak Italian?'

'The odd word, not much. Are you Italian?' Lizzie asked, feeling awkward as soon as she realised that he somehow knew that her mother had been of Italian extraction. Francesca had actually planned to raise her daughters to be bilingual but Brian Whitaker had objected vehemently to the practice as soon as his children began using words he couldn't understand and from that point on English had become the only language in their home.

'*Sì*, I'm Italian,' Cesare confirmed, sliding a lean brown hand into his jacket to withdraw a business card and present it to her. The extraordinary grace of his every physical gesture also ensnared her attention and she had to force her gaze down to the card.

Unfortunately, his name was no more comprehensible to Lizzie when she saw it printed. 'Your name's Caesar,' she pronounced with some satisfaction.

A muscle tugged at the corner of his unsmiling mouth. 'Not Caesar. We're not in ancient Rome. It's Chay-zar-ray,' he sounded out with perfect diction, his exotic accent underlining every syllable with a honeyed mellifluence that spiralled sinuously round her to create the strangest sense of dislocation.

'Chay-zar-ray,' she repeated politely while thinking that it was a heck of a fussy mouthful for a first name and that Caesar would have been much more straightforward. 'And you're here *because*…?'

Cesare stiffened, innate aggression powering him

at that facetious tone. He was not accustomed to being
prompted to get to the point faster and as if the dog
had a sensor tracking his mood it began growling soft
and low. 'May we go indoors to discuss that?'

Bemused by the effect he was having on her and
fiercely irritated by his take-charge manner, Lizzie
lifted her chin. 'Couldn't we just talk here? This is the
middle of my working day,' she told him truthfully.

Cesare gritted his perfect white teeth and shifted
almost imperceptibly closer. The dog loosed a warning snarl and clamped his teeth to the corner of his
cashmere overcoat, pulling at it. Cesare sent a wing-
ing glance down at the offending animal.

'Archie, *no*!' Lizzie intervened. 'I'm afraid he's
very protective of me.'

Archie tugged and tugged at the corner of the overcoat and failed to shift Cesare an inch further away
from his quarry. To the best of his ability Cesare ignored the entire canine assault.

'Oh, for goodness' sake, Archie!' Lizzie finally
exclaimed, crouching down to physically detach the
dog's jaw from the expensive cloth, noting in dismay
that a small tear had been inflicted and cherishing little hope that the damage would not be noted.

Whoever he was, Cesare Sabatino wore clothing
that looked incredibly expensive and fitted too well
to be anything other than individually designed for
its wearer. He wore a faultlessly tailored black suit
below the coat and his highly polished shoes were
marred only by the skiff of mud that continually covered the yard at damp times of the year. He looked like
a high-powered businessman, tycoon or some such

thing. Why on earth was such a man coming to visit the farm?

'Are you from our bank?' Lizzie asked abruptly.

'No. I am a businessman,' Cesare admitted calmly.

'You're here to see my father for some reason?' Lizzie prompted apprehensively.

'No…I'm here to see you,' Cesare framed succinctly as she scrambled upright clutching the still-growling dog to her chest.

'*Me?*' Lizzie exclaimed in astonishment, her gaze colliding with glittering eyes that gleamed like highly polished gold, enhanced by the thick black velvet fringe of his long lashes. Below her clothes, her nipples pinched almost painfully tight and a flare of sudden heat darted down into her pelvis, making her feel extremely uncomfortable. 'Why on earth would you want to see me? Oh, come indoors, if you must,' she completed wearily. 'But I warn you, it's a mess.'

Trudging to the side of the house, Lizzie kicked off her boots and thrust the door open on the untidy kitchen.

Cesare's nostrils flared as he scanned the cluttered room, taking in the pile of dishes heaped in the sink and the remains of someone's meal still lying on the pine table. Well, he certainly wouldn't be marrying her for her housekeeping skills, he reflected grimly as the dog slunk below the table to continue growling unabated and his reluctant hostess removed her coat and yanked off her woolly hat before hurriedly clearing the table and yanking out a chair for him.

'Coffee…or tea?' Lizzie enquired.

Cesare's entire attention was still locked to the wealth of silver-coloured silky hair that, freed from the woolly hat, now tumbled round her shoulders. It was gorgeous in spite of the odd murky brown tips of colour that damaged the effect. Dip-dying, he thought dimly, vaguely recalling the phrase being used by one of his team who had showed up at the office one day with ludicrously colourful half-blonde, half-pink locks. He blinked, black lashes long as fly swats momentarily concealing his bemused gaze.

'Coffee,' he replied, feeling that he was being very brave and polite in the face of the messy kitchen and standards of hygiene that he suspected might be much lower than he was used to receiving.

In a graceful movement, he doffed his coat and draped it across the back of a chair. Lizzie filled the kettle at the sink and put it on the hotplate on the ancient coal-fired cooking range while taking in the full effect of her visitor's snazzy appearance. He looked like a city slicker who belonged on a glossy magazine cover, the sort of publication that showed how fashion-conscious men should dress. To a woman used to men wearing dirty, often unkempt clothing suitable for outdoor work, he had all the appeal of a fantasy. He really was physically beautiful in every possible way and so unfamiliar was she with that level of male magnetism that she was challenged to drag her eyes from his lean, powerful figure.

Dredging her thoughts from the weird sticking point they had reached, she went to the door of the lounge. A businessman, she reminded herself doggedly. Successful businessmen—and he looked *very* successful—were cold-blooded, calculating individuals, ready to do anything for profit and divorced from sentiment. He certainly emanated that arrogant vibe with his polished image that was so totally inappropriate for a male visiting a working farm. 'Dad? We have a visitor. Do you want tea?'

'A visitor?' Brian Whitaker rose with a frown from his chair and came with shuffling, poorly balanced steps into the kitchen.

Lizzie removed mugs from the cupboard while the two men introduced themselves.

'I'm here about the island that Lizzie and her sister inherited from your late wife,' Cesare explained calmly.

The silence of astonishment engulfed his companions. Lizzie studied him wide-eyed while her father turned his head towards him in a frowning attitude of incredulity.

'It's a rubbish inheritance...nothing but a bad joke!' Lizzie's father contended in a burst of unrestrained bitterness. 'It stands to reason that an inheritance you can't use or sell is worthless... What use is that to anyone? So, that's why you're here? Another fool chasing the pot of gold at the end of the rainbow?'

'*Dad!*' Lizzie exclaimed in consternation at the older man's blatant scorn.

She wished she had guessed why the Italian had come to visit and scolded herself for not immediately making the association between his nationality and the legacy left to her and Chrissie by their mother. Over the years the island that couldn't be sold had been a source of much bitterness in her family, particularly when money was in such short supply. She lifted the kettle off the range and hastily made the drinks while she wondered what on earth Cesare hoped to achieve by visiting them.

'I'll put your tea in the lounge, Dad,' she said, keen to remove her father from the dialogue, afraid of what he might say in his blunt and challenging way.

Brian Whitaker stole a glance at the Italian's shuttered dark face, not displeased by the effect of having had his say. 'I'll leave you to it, then. After all, the only reason *he* could be here is that he's coming a-courting!' he completed with a derisive laugh that sent a hot tide of colour flaring below Lizzie's pale skin. 'Good luck to you! Lizzie was ditched by the neighbour a couple of years ago and she hasn't been out on a date since then!'

# CHAPTER TWO

LIZZIE WANTED THE tiled floor to open up and swallow her where she stood. Being humiliated in front of a stranger felt even more painful than the snide comments and pitying appraisals from the village locals that had followed the ending of her engagement to Andrew Brook two years earlier. A month later, Andrew had married Esther, who had already been pregnant with their son. She stiffened her facial muscles, made the tea and the coffee and even contrived to politely ask if the visitor took sugar.

Wide, sensual mouth set in a grim line, Cesare surveyed Lizzie's rigid back view, noting the narrow cut of her waist and the slender, delicate curves merely hinted at by the overalls. Her father had been cruel taking her down like that in front of an audience. Not a date since, though? He was astonished because, unflattering as her clothing was, Cesare had immediately recognised that she was a beauty. Not perhaps a conventional beauty, he was willing to admit, not the kind of beauty that set the world on fire but certainly the type that should make the average male look more than once. What was wrong with the local men?

'Sorry about Dad,' Lizzie apologised in a brittle

voice, setting the coffee down carefully on the table in front of him, catching the evocative scent of some citrusy cologne as she briefly leant closer and stiffening as a result of the sudden warmth pooling in her pelvis. Never had anyone made her feel more uncomfortable in her own home.

'You don't need to apologise, *cara*,' Cesare parried.

'But I should explain. My parents resented the will—personally, I never think about it. Unfortunately, the island was a sore point in our lives when I was a child because money was tight.'

'Have you ever visited Lionos?'

'No, I've never had the opportunity. Mum went once with one of her boyfriends and stayed for a week. She wasn't too impressed,' Lizzie revealed ruefully while she scanned his lean, strong face, taking in the high cheekbones, straight nose and hard, masculine mouth before involuntarily sliding her gaze upward again to take another sweep of those absolutely devastating dark golden eyes of his. 'I think Mum was expecting luxury but I believe the accommodation was more basic.'

'The will endowed the island with a trust and I understand a caretaker and his family live nearby to maintain the property.'

Lizzie cocked her head to one side, her shattered nerves slowly stabilising at his lack of comment about her father's outburst. Pale, silky hair slid across her cheekbone and Cesare looked up into those wide hazel-green eyes framed with soft honey-brown lashes, and suddenly he was aware of the heavy pulse of heat at his groin and the muscles in his broad shoulders pulled taut as ropes as he resisted that sirens' call of lust with all his might.

'Yes. But the trust only covers maintenance costs, not improvements, and I understand that the house is still firmly stuck in the thirties. Mum also assumed that the caretaker would cook and clean for them but instead the man and his wife told her that they weren't servants and she had to look after herself,' Lizzie volunteered wryly. 'All in all she found it a very expensive jaunt by the time they'd paid someone to take them out to the island and deliver food while they were there.'

'Naturally you want to know what I'm doing here,' Cesare murmured smoothly.

'Well, I don't think you've come a-courting,' Lizzie fielded with a shrug that dismissed her father's gibe but completely failed to hide her discomfiture at that crack.

'Not in the conventional sense,' Cesare agreed, lean fingers flexing round the mug of coffee. It was barely drinkable but he doubted if she expended much concern when it came to the domestic front, which was hardly surprising when it was obvious that she was struggling to keep the farm afloat single-handedly. She was leaning back against the cooking range with defensively folded arms, trying to appear relaxed but visibly as tense as a bow string. 'But I do think we might be able to come to a business arrangement.'

Lizzie frowned, dragging her wandering gaze from his lean, extravagantly handsome features with a slight rise of colour, scolding herself for her lack of concentration, questioning what it was about him that kept her looking back at him again and again, long after curiosity should have been satisfied. 'A business arrangement?'

'I don't think your sister enters this as she's still a teenager. Obviously as co-owner of the island, you would have to confer with her, but I'm willing to offer you a substantial amount of money to go through a marriage ceremony with me.'

Her lashes fluttered in shock because he had knocked her for six. Inexplicably, his cool sophistication and smooth delivery made the fantastic proposition he had just made seem almost workaday and acceptable. 'Seriously? *Just* a marriage ceremony? But what would you get out of that?'

Cesare told her about his grandmother's deep attachment to the island and her approaching surgery. As she listened, Lizzie nodded slowly, strangely touched by the softer tone he couldn't help employing when talking about the old lady. His screened gaze and the faint hint of flush along his spectacular cheekbones encouraged her scrutiny to linger with helpless curiosity. He was not quite as cold and tough as he seemed on the surface, she acknowledged in surprise. But she could see that he was very uncomfortable with showing emotion.

'Isn't circumventing the will against the law?' she prompted in a small voice.

'I wasn't planning to publicise the fact. For the sake of appearances we would have to pretend that the marriage was the real deal for a few months at least.'

'And the "having a child" bit? Where does that come in?' Lizzie could not resist asking.

'Whether it comes into our arrangement or not is up to you. I will pay generously for the right to take my grandmother to the island for a visit and if we were to contrive to meet the *full* terms of the will, you and your sister would stand to collect a couple of million pounds, at the very least, from selling Lionos to me,' he spelt out quietly. 'I am an extremely wealthy man and I will pay a high price to bring the island back into my family.'

*Millions?* Lizzie's mouth ran dry and she lost colour, eyes dropping to focus on the long, lean brown fingers gracefully coiled round the mug of coffee. For a split second she saw her every hope and dream fulfilled by ill-gotten gains. Her father could give up the farm tenancy, and she and Chrissie could buy him a house in the village where he would be able to go to the pub quizzes he loved and meet up with his cronies. Chrissie would be able to chuck in her two part-time jobs, concentrate on her studies and pay off her student loans. Being freed from the burden of the farm would enable Lizzie to go and train for a job she would enjoy. Archie could get some professional grooming and a new collar and live on the very best pet food…

It became an increasingly stupid dream and she reddened with mortification, hands clenching by her side as she suppressed her wild imaginings in shame at how susceptible she had been when tempted by the equivalent of a lottery win.

'I couldn't have a child with a stranger…or bring a child into the world for such a purpose,' she confided. 'But if it's any consolation, just for a minute there I wished I was the sort of woman who could.'

'Think it over,' Cesare suggested, having registered without surprise that the suggestion of oodles of cash had finally fully engaged her in their discussion. He rose fluidly upright and tapped the business card he had left on the table top. 'My cell number.'

He was very big, possibly a foot taller than she was, with broad shoulders, narrow hips and long, powerful legs.

'Yes, well, there's a lot to think over,' she muttered uneasily.

He reached for his coat and turned back to her, dark eyes bright and shimmering as topaz in sunshine. 'There are two options and either will bring in a profit for you.'

'You definitely talk like a businessman,' she remarked, unimpressed by the statement, ashamed of her temporary dive into a fantasy land where every sheep had a proverbial golden fleece. Could it really be that easy to go from being a decent person to a mercenary one? she was asking herself worriedly.

'I am trying to negotiate a business arrangement,' he pointed out drily.

'Was it *your* father who once asked my mother to marry him?' Lizzie could not stop herself from enquiring. 'Or was that someone from another branch of your family?'

Cesare came to a halt. 'No, that was my father and it wasn't a business proposal. He fell hard for your mother and they were engaged when she came over here on holiday. Having met your father, however, she preferred him,' he advanced without any expression at all.

But Lizzie recognised the unspoken disapproval in the hard bones of his lean, strong face and she flushed because her mother had been decidedly changeable in her affections and there was no denying the fact. Predictably, Francesca had never admitted that she had actually got engaged to their father's predecessor. But then every man that came along had been the love of Francesca's life until either he revealed his true character or someone else seized her interest. Her mother had always moved on without a backward glance, never once pausing to try and work on a relationship or considering the cost of such continual upheaval in the lives of her two young children.

'I'm afraid I'm not a sentimental man,' Cesare imparted. 'I'm innately practical in every way. Why shouldn't you make what you can of your inheritance for your family's benefit?'

'Because it just doesn't seem right,' Lizzie confided uncertainly. 'It's not what my great-grandfather intended either when he drew up that will.'

'No, he wanted revenge because my grandmother's brother jilted his daughter at the altar. My great-uncle was in the wrong but plunging the island into legal limbo simply to keep it out of my family's hands was no more justifiable,' Cesare countered with complete assurance. 'It's been that way for nearly eighty years but I believe that we have the power to change that.'

'The ethics involved aren't something I've ever thought about,' Lizzie admitted, resisting the urge to confess that the island still seemed no more real to her than that fabled pot of gold at the end of the rainbow that her father had mentioned.

Cesare smiled with sudden brilliance, amused by her honesty and her lack of pretence.

His smile almost blinded her, illuminating his lean, darkly handsome face, and she wanted so badly to touch him for a disconcerting moment that she clenched her hands into fists to restrain herself. She was deeply disturbed by the effect he had on her. Indeed, she feared it because she recognised her reaction for the fierce physical attraction that it was. And nobody knew better than Francesca Whitaker's daughter how dangerous giving rein to such mindless responses could be for it had propelled her mother into one disastrous relationship after another.

In the smouldering silence, beautiful, dark golden eyes fringed with velvet black held hers and she trembled, fighting reactions she had never experienced so powerfully before.

'My offer's on the table and I'm willing to negotiate with you. Discuss it with your sister and your father but urge them to keep the matter confidential,' Cesare advised smoothly, staring down into her upturned face, attention lingering on the lush contours of her lips as he wondered what she would *taste* like. 'We could go the full distance on this... I find you appealing.'

And with that deeply unsettling comment, Cesare Sabatino swung on his heel and strode back out to the limousine sitting ready to depart. The driver leapt out to throw open the door for his passenger and Cesare lowered his proud dark head and climbed in.

*Appealing?* Lizzie pushed her hair back off her brow and caught her surprised reflection in the small age-spotted mirror on the wall. He was really saying that he could go to bed with her and conceive a child with her if she was willing: that was what he meant by the word *appealing*. Her face flamed. She was *not* willing. She also knew the difference between right and wrong. She knew that more money didn't necessarily mean more happiness and that a child was usually better off with a mother *and* a father.

Yet the image of the tiny boy she had glimpsed cradled in her former fiancé's arms after the child's christening in the church had pierced Lizzie with a pain greater than that inflicted by Andrew's infidelity. Lizzie had always wanted a baby and ached at the sight of infants. When Andrew had left her for Esther, she had envied Esther for her son, *not* her husband. What did that say about her? That she was as cold at heart and frigid as Andrew had once accused her of being? Even remembering that hurtful indictment, Lizzie winced and felt less than other women, knowing that she had been tried and found wanting by a young man who had only wanted a warm and loving wife. Lizzie knew that, in choosing Esther, Andrew had made the right decision for them both. Yet Lizzie had loved Andrew too in her way.

Her eyes stung with moisture, her fingers toying with the ends of the brown-tinted hair that Andrew had persuaded her to dye. The dye was growing out, a reminder of how foolish a woman could be when she tried to change herself to please a man...

But where on earth had her strong maternal instinct come from? Certainly not from her volatile mother, who in the grip of her wild infatuations had always focused her energies on the man in her life. Lizzie had not been surprised to learn of the impetuous way Francesca had evidently ditched Cesare's father to marry Lizzie's father instead. Hard Yorkshire winters and life on a shoestring, however, had dimmed Brian Whitaker's appeal for her mother and within weeks of Chrissie's birth Francesca had run off with a man who had turned out to be a drunk. His successor had been more interested in spending Francesca's recent legacy following the death of her Italian parents than in Francesca herself. Her third lover had been repeatedly unfaithful. And the fourth, who married her, had been violent.

Lizzie had always found it very hard to trust men after living through her mother's grim roll call of destructive relationships. She had struggled to protect the sister five years her junior from the constant fall-out of moving home and changing schools, striving to ensure that her sibling could still enjoy her childhood and wasn't forced to grow up as quickly as Lizzie had. Almost all the happy moments in Lizzie's life had occurred when Chrissie was young and Lizzie had the comfort of knowing that her love and care was both wanted and needed by her sibling. When her sister left home to go to university it had opened a vast hole in Lizzie's life. Archie had partially filled that hole, a reality that made her grin and shrug off her deep and troubled thoughts with the acknowledgement that it was time to get back to work and concentrate on what really mattered.

'Marry him and stop making such a production out of it!' Brian Whitaker snapped at his daughter angrily. 'We don't have any other choice. The rent is going up and the bank's on the brink of calling in our loan!'

'It's not that simple, Dad,' Lizzie began to argue again.

But the older man wasn't listening. He hadn't listened to a word his daughter had said since the letter from the bank had delivered its lethal warning. 'Simple would have been you marrying Andrew. He would have taken on the tenancy. I could still have lived here. Everyone would have been happy but could you pull it off?' he derided. '*No*, you had to play fast and loose with him, wanting to *wait* to get married!'

'I wanted to get to know him properly, not rush in. I wanted our marriage to last,' Lizzie protested.

'You might as well have parcelled him up for Esther and handed him over. Andrew was our one chance to keep this place afloat and you threw him away,' he condemned bitterly. 'Now you're mouthing off about all the reasons why you can't marry a man and have a child just to improve *all* our lives!'

'A lot of women wouldn't want to do it!' It was Lizzie's parting shot, tossed over her shoulder as she stomped back into the yard with Archie dancing at her heels. A week had passed since Cesare Sabatino's visit and her father had reasoned and condemned and outright ranted at her every day for her reluctance to accept Cesare's proposal.

Hopefully, Chrissie would not be singing the same tune, Lizzie reflected ruefully as she drove her father's ancient, battered Land Rover Defender down the lane to collect her sister off the train. She had told Chrissie all about Cesare's visit on the phone and her sibling had urged her to follow her conscience and refuse to pay heed to her father's grievances.

That was, however, proving a much more major challenge than she had expected, Lizzie acknowledged heavily. Almost insurmountable problems were forming ahead of her like a string of dangerous obstacles. They could not afford to pay a higher rent when the tenancy came up for renewal and that reality would render them homeless. They could not even afford to live if the bank demanded that the loan be repaid as they were threatening to do. And *where* would they live, if the worst came to the worst? Her father had no savings. Yes, it was all very well following her conscience, Lizzie conceded wretchedly, but right now it was no good at all as a blueprint for economic survival.

Sadly, the stress of the constant arguments and anxiety was taking the edge off Lizzie's usual happy anticipation at the prospect of having her sister home for a couple of days. Chrissie, pale silver hair caught up in a sensible ponytail, blue eyes sparkling with affection, was waiting outside the station, two big cases by her side and a bulging rucksack on her slender shoulders.

'My goodness, you've brought back a lot of luggage… but it's not the end of term,' Lizzie remarked in bewilderment, thinking out loud while Chrissie concentrated on giving her a fierce hug of welcome.

'I've missed you so much,' her sibling confessed. 'And I'm going to ask you all over again—why have you still not had your hair dyed back to normal?'

'I haven't had the time…or the cash,' Lizzie muttered, hoisting a heavy case and propelling it across to the Land Rover.

'No, you're still punishing yourself for not marrying Andrew.'

'They're teaching you psychology now on your English course?' Lizzie teased.

Luggage stowed, Lizzie drove back home. 'I should warn you…Dad's on the warpath.'

'He wants you to marry the Italian and make our fortunes, right?' Chrissie groaned in despair. 'Dear old Dad, what a dinosaur he is. He tried to pressure you into marrying Andrew for the sake of the farm and now he's trying to serve you up on the altar of that stupid island! Well, you don't need to worry, you're not going to come under any pressure from me on that score. We've lived all our lives without the excitement of being rich and what you don't have, you don't miss!'

In spite of her stress level, Lizzie managed to smile. After an unrelieved overdose of her father's reproaches, Chrissie, with her positive outlook, was like a little ray of sunshine. 'You're right,' she agreed even though she knew that her kid sister was not very grounded. Chrissie had always been a dreamer, the creative one with the fluffy romantic and idealistic ideas.

In fact, while she watched Chrissie hurtle across the yard to pet her elderly pony, Hero, and feed him an apple from her pocket, her heart sank from so bald a reminder of her sister's tendency to always look on the bright side even if there wasn't one. Didn't Chrissie appreciate that if they lost their home, Hero would be one of the first sacrifices?

'I've got a surprise for you…' Chrissie told her, almost skipping back to Lizzie's side to help her unload her luggage. 'I'm home for good!'

Lizzie turned incredulous eyes on the younger woman. 'What are you talking about?'

'I'm dropping out of uni…I'm coming home,' Chrissie proffered, her soft mouth set in an unusually firm and purposeful line. 'Even with the two jobs and the student loan, I can hardly afford to eat and my overdraft is *massive*, Lizzie. I'm fed up with it, especially when I know you're slogging away here every hour God gives and still barely scratching a living. I'm going to get a job and help you whenever I can. I'm all grown up now—it's past time I pulled my weight on the home front.'

Shock was reverberating through Lizzie, closely followed by dismay. Much as she missed her sister, the very last thing she wanted was to see Chrissie throw away her education to come home and vegetate. In any case, it was a moot point that they would even have a home to offer her sibling in a few weeks' time. 'I didn't realise that you were having such a struggle.'

'I didn't want you worrying,' Chrissie confided. 'But I've learned a lot. I'd no idea it cost so much just to live. I can't possibly work any more hours, though. I've already had a warning from my tutor about my standard of work slipping… I'm so tired I'm falling asleep in lectures.'

And that was the moment when Lizzie reached her decision. What security her family had was vanishing fast but it was within her power to change everything for the better. How could she stand by and simply do nothing for her family while their lives fell apart? At the very least she should go through with the wedding to enable Cesare to take his grandmother back to the island for a visit. Whatever he paid her for that service would surely settle their outstanding bills and enable her to find a rental property in the village. But how could she go further than that? How could she have a child with him so that he could legally buy Lionos and resolve all her family's financial problems?

The answer came to Lizzie in a blinding flash of

light and she could barely credit that she had not seen the solution sooner. Cesare had said he was very practical and the answer she came up with would not only make the threat of intimacy with a stranger unnecessary but would also be a supremely sensible approach. Suddenly the sensation of weighty responsibility and dread on her shoulders and spine evaporated and she straightened, even cracking a brief smile at the heady prospect of finally being in full control of her life again.

'You're going back to university on Sunday, young lady,' Lizzie told her kid sister firmly. 'You will quit your part-time jobs and concentrate on your studies. I will ensure that you manage.'

'You can't marry the guy, Lizzie!' Chrissie gasped in horror. 'You simply *can't*!'

Lizzie thought fast and breathed in deep before she sat down at the kitchen table. 'Let me be honest with you. I've spent eight years working round the clock on this farm. I've had no time for friends and I've had very little social life. I have no decent clothes or jewellery and I don't even know how to put on make-up properly.'

'But that doesn't mean you have to give way to Dad and make a sacrifice of yourself.'

'Has it occurred to you that maybe I *want* to marry Cesare and have a child? He's a very handsome man and you know how much I've always wanted a baby. I also would like to have enough money not to worry myself sick every time a bill comes through the letter box!' Lizzie declared, her heart-shaped face taut with vehement composure as she watched Chrissie frown and suddenly look unsure of her ground.

'I'm deadly serious,' Lizzie continued with dogged determination. 'I *want* to marry Cesare. It's the best thing for all of us and, believe me, I'm not the sacrificial type.'

'I never thought…I never dreamt…' Bemused and uncertain of such an explanation from the big sister she had always loved and admired, Chrissie shook her head, frowning at her sibling. 'Are you sure, Lizzie? Have you really thought this through?'

No, Lizzie hadn't thought it all through and was determined not to run the risk of doing so before she had tied the official knot. Whatever happened she was going to marry Cesare Sabatino and miraculously sort out her own and her father's *and* Chrissie's problems. No other action now made sense. So, it would be scary and would entail deception—well, she would get braver and she would learn some new skills. My goodness, hadn't she just told a barefaced lie to the sister she loved?

She walked into her bedroom and lifted the business card Cesare had left behind. Before she could take fright, she tapped out the number on her mobile phone and then studied the blank message space.

Will agree to marry you. Talk about the rest when we next meet.

Cesare blinked down at the text and then glanced across the dinner table at Celine, whose sleek blonde perfection had entranced him for longer than most women managed. In his mind's eye, however, he was no longer seeing the French fashion model, he was seeing a slender platinum blonde with luminous green eyes surrounded by soft brown lashes. Surprise was cutting through his satisfaction, perhaps because he had had the weirdest conviction that Lizzie Whitaker would say no to the temptation of the cash he had offered. He wondered why he had thought that, why he had assumed she would be different from any other woman.

Women liked money and he liked women: it was a fair exchange in which neither of them need feel used or abused. Hadn't he learned that a long time ago? Athene would be able to return to her childhood home for a visit at the very least. Was Lizzie Whitaker planning to meet the *full* terms of the will? Raw anticipation of an entirely different kind infiltrated Cesare and he frowned, bewildered by the flood of undisciplined hormones smashing his self-control to pieces. He was thinking about Lizzie Whitaker, *only* thinking about her and he was as aroused as a teenager contemplating sex for the first time.

'You seem distracted,' Celine remarked tentatively.

Cesare studied her without an iota of his usual lust, exasperated by the games his body was playing with his usually very well-disciplined brain. 'A business deal,' he proffered truthfully.

Goffredo would be overjoyed at the news of the upcoming wedding while Cesare was simply stunned at the prospect of getting married, whether it was a business arrangement or not. *Married!* The delicious food on his plate ebbed in appeal. Dense black lashes screened his gaze. It was rare for him to take a night off and somehow Lizzie Whitaker had contrived to kill any notion he had had of relaxing with Celine. What was it about her that unsettled him? After all she was a pretty standard gold-digger, willing to do virtually anything to enrich herself, and how could he criticise her for that reality when he had baited the hook?

# CHAPTER THREE

'I DON'T KNOW what the arrangements are likely to be,' Lizzie told her father while she paced the kitchen, a slim figure clad in jeans and a sweater and workman-like boots. 'Look, I've got a few things to check outside. I might as well keep busy until Cesare arrives.'

'What sort of a name is that he has?' Brian Whitaker scoffed.

Lizzie dealt the older man an impatient glance as she put on her jacket because he had no excuse to be needling her or disparaging Cesare. But everything, she told herself in an urgent little pep talk, was *good* in her world. Chrissie had returned to university and soon she and her father would no longer need to worry about rent rises and bank debts they couldn't cover. 'It's an Italian name, just like mine and Chrissie's and Mum's and it's completely normal. Let's not forget that Cesare is about to wave a magic wand over our lives.'

'Even the Garden of Eden had the serpent,' her father countered with a curl of his lip and his usual determination to have the last word.

Lizzie drank in the fresh air with relief and walked to the stone wall bounding the yard to check the sheep in the field. Lambing hadn't started yet but it wouldn't be long before it did. If she had to leave home before then, Andrew would probably take the ewes, she was reasoning in the detached state of mind she had forged to keep herself calm since she had sent that text to Cesare. There were no successes without losses, no gains without costs and consequences. In the middle of that sobering reflection while she watched the lane for a car arriving, she heard a noise in the sky and she flung her head back in the fading light to look up.

A helicopter was coming in over the valley. As she watched it circled the top of the hill and swooped down low to come closer and then noisily hover. For a split second, Lizzie was frozen to the spot, unable to believe that the helicopter was actually planning to land in a field with stock in it. The craft's powerful lights splayed over the flock of fast-scattering sheep, which ran in a total panic down the hill. Lizzie ran for the gate, Archie at her heels, and flew over it like a high jumper while shouting instructions to her dog to retrieve the flock.

Heart pounding, she ran down the hill at breakneck speed but was still not fast enough to prevent the sheep from scrambling in a frantic escape over the wall at the foot and streaming across the next field towards the river. Sick with apprehension, she clambered over the wall and ran even faster while watching as Archie herded the frightened ewes away from the water's edge. The noise from the helicopter unluckily intensified at that point because the pilot was taking off again and the sheep herded close together and then took off terrified again in all directions.

Someone shouted her name and she was relieved to see Andrew Brook racing down the hill to join her. Struggling desperately to catch her breath, while wondering anxiously where Archie had disappeared to, she hurried on towards the riverbank to see if any of the animals had gone into the water. Andrew got there first and she saw him stooping down in the mud over something, whistling for his sheepdog. One of the sheep had got hurt in the commotion, she assumed, hurrying down to join him.

'I'm so sorry, Lizzie. He's hurt. He was too little to handle them in a panic like that,' Andrew told her.

Lizzie looked down in horror at the small prone body lying in the mud: it was Archie and he was whimpering. She knelt in the mud. *'Oh, no...'*

'I think it's only his leg that's broken but there could be internal injuries. He was trodden on,' Andrew, a stocky dark-haired man in his late twenties, reminded her.

'That *crazy* helicopter pilot! Are people insane?' Lizzie gasped, stricken, while Andrew, always resourceful, broke a small branch off a nearby tree, cut it to size with the knife in his pocket and splinted it to Archie's leg, wrapping it in place with twine.

'Nobody should land in a field with animals in it,' Andrew agreed. As Lizzie comforted her pet with a trembling hand he unfurled his mobile phone. 'We'd better get him to the vet. I'll ring ahead to warn Danny.'

Andrew's dog had retrieved the sheep and on the walk back uphill they were returned to the field from which they had fled. Lizzie was in shock and wildly dishevelled by the breakneck pace of her downhill marathon, sweat breaking on her brow, tears trickling down her cheeks as she held Archie's small, shivering body as gently as she could to her chest. Back in the yard, Lizzie went straight to the Land Rover and settled Archie on the front passenger seat.

'I'll come with you,' Andrew announced. 'I know how you feel about that daft dog.'

'Thanks but I can manage,' Lizzie assured him with a warm smile that acknowledged how comfortable she could still feel with her former boyfriend.

'That's the ex-fiancé—Andrew Brook, our neighbour,' Brian Whitaker informed Cesare, who was stationed beside him outside the back door of the cottage. 'They grew up together. I always thought they'd make a match of it but then he met Esther and married her instead.'

Cesare told himself that he had no desire for that information. He was already irritated that Lizzie hadn't been waiting to greet him—didn't she appreciate what a busy man he was? Now watching her smile beguilingly up at her ex-boyfriend, who was an attractive, stalwart six-footer, he was even less impressed. When she looked at the other man like that and squeezed his arm with easy intimacy it made him wonder why they had broken up and that dart of inappropriate curiosity set his even white teeth on edge, sending another wave of annoyance crashing through him.

'Lizzie!' her father called as Andrew strode back home across the couple of fields that separated their properties.

Lizzie turned her head and focused in bewilderment on the tall, darkly handsome male poised by her father's side. Her heartbeat suddenly thudded like a crack of doom in her ears and her throat tightened. Sheathed in an immaculate grey pinstripe business

suit worn with a white shirt and scarlet tie, Cesàre
looked very much at odds with his surroundings but
he still contrived to take her breath away and leave
her mind briefly as blank as white paper. 'Good grief,
when did you arrive? I didn't see a car.'

'I came in a helicopter...'

Lizzie, the Land Rover keys clenched tightly in one
hand, froze. She blinked in fleeting bewilderment and
then headed towards Cesare in a sudden movement,
rage boiling up through the cracks of anxiety and concern for her dog and her flock. '*You're* the bloody idiot
who let a helicopter land in a field full of stock?' she
raked at him incredulously.

In all his life, nobody had ever addressed Cesare
with such insolence. A faint frown line etched between
his ebony brows, he stared at her as if he couldn't quite
believe his ears. Indeed he was much more concerned
with the reality that, in spite of her awareness of his
visit, his bride-to-be still looked as though she had
strayed in from a hostel for the homeless. A streak
of dirt marred one cheekbone and her clothes were
caked in mud and displaying damp patches. But when
he glanced higher and saw the luminous colour in her
cheeks that accentuated her hazel-green eyes and the
contrast of that tumbling mane of admittedly messy
white-blonde hair, he registered in some astonishment
that even had she been wearing a bin liner it would
not have dampened her physical appeal on his terms.
His usual high standards, it seemed, were slipping.

'What's the problem?' Cesare enquired with perfect
cool, reasoning that some sort of cultural misunder-
standing could have provoked her sudden aggressive
outburst.

*'The problem is...'*

'Don't shout at me,' Cesare sliced in softly. 'I am not hard of hearing.'

'Your pilot landed that helicopter in a field full of sheep...and he should be shot for it!' Lizzie framed rawly. 'They were so terrified they fled. All of them are pregnant, only days off lambing. If any of them miscarry after that crazed stampede, I'll be holding *you* responsible!'

For a fraction of a second, Cesare recalled the pilot striving to persuade him to land a couple of fields away but the prospect of a time-wasting muddy trek to the cottage had exasperated him and he had insisted on being set down as close as possible to his destination. 'The mistake was mine, not the pilot's. I chose the landing spot,' Cesare admitted, startling her with that confession. 'I know nothing about farming or the care of animals. Naturally I will compensate you and your father for any loss of income that results.'

'Well, the man can't say fairer than that,' Brian Whitaker cut in, sending his furious daughter a warning glance. 'Let that be the end of it.'

'Archie was *hurt*!' Lizzie protested fierily, shooting Cesare a seething look that warned him that even admitting his mistake was insufficient to soothe her. 'The flock trampled him at the river. I'm taking him to the vet now for emergency treatment and I haven't got the time...or the patience...to deal with you!'

Cesare watched in disbelief as his future bride unlocked the rusty vehicle several feet away and began to climb in.

'You've done it now. She treats that stupid dog like her firstborn!' Brian Whitaker muttered impatiently and retreated back indoors, bowing out of the situation.

With the split-second timing that matched Cesare's lightning-fast intellect, he strode forward and opened the passenger door of the Land Rover to take the only step left open to him. 'I'll accompany you to the vet's,' he informed her flatly.

Very much disconcerted by that announcement, Lizzie flicked him a frowning appraisal. 'You'll have to hold Archie.'

Cesare, so far out of his comfort zone that he already felt as if he were trapped in something of a nightmare, finally noticed that it was a two-seat vehicle and that the scruffy dog lay comatose on the only seat available for his own use.

Lizzie leapt back out of the car. 'I'll move him and *then* you can get in,' she told him, racing round the back of the vehicle to scoop up Archie in trembling hands and usher him in.

'I could drive,' Cesare pointed out drily.

'You don't know where you're going and I know where the potholes are,' Lizzie told him incomprehensibly as she very gently rested Archie down on Cesare's lap. 'Please make sure he doesn't fall.'

Tears were choking Lizzie's throat. Archie was so quiet and he had never been a quiet dog. Right at that very minute, he could be *dying*, his brave little life and loving spirit ebbing away, and that was why she wasn't going to waste time arguing with Cesare Sabatino about anything.

'Is he still breathing?' Lizzie demanded, turning out onto the road.

'I can feel his heart beating,' Cesare proffered quietly, blocking out his uneasy awareness that the vehicle stank of animals and was far from clean. He stroked the still body for want of anything else to do and was startled when the dog twisted his head to lick at his hand.

'He trusts you,' Lizzie informed him.

'He doesn't have much choice in the matter,' Cesare fielded, reckoning that he had been sent to Yorkshire solely to suffer. In his opinion she drove like a maniac. He had spent the day travelling and his day had started at six in the morning in Geneva. Now it was eight in the evening and, not only had he not eaten for hours, but he was also convinced that many more hours would pass before he could even hope for the opportunity. He knew she had no idea that he had planned to take her out to dinner and, since he didn't have a woolly fleece and cloven hooves, it would never occur to Lizzie to feed him.

Unaware of her unwelcome passenger's thoughts, Lizzie rammed the Land Rover to an abrupt jolting halt in a small car park. Carefully carrying Archie, Lizzie stalked into the surgery, leaving Cesare, a male who was unaccustomed to being ignored, to follow her. An older man greeted them and carried the dog off to be X-rayed, leaving Lizzie and Cesare in the small, dull waiting room.

In consternation, Cesare watched Lizzie fighting off tears again. Driven by a desperate masculine urge to shift her thoughts to what he viewed as more positive issues, he murmured, 'So, we're getting married?'

Lizzie marvelled at his lack of compassion and understanding. Did he really think she was in any frame of mind to discuss that while she was waiting to hear whether Archie would live or die? 'Yes, but it won't really be a marriage,' she parried, striving not to look at him because he really had the most stunning dark golden eyes and every time she looked she ended up staring and she didn't want him to notice her behaving like a silly schoolgirl.

'We're not going for gold, then,' Cesare assumed, referring to the requirement for a child in the will while surveying her down-bent head with a sense of deep dissatisfaction that took him aback. Why was he feeling that way? Common sense suggested that he should settle for taking Athene for a visit to Lionos and think himself lucky to have gained that much from the exchange.

A tangle of silvery hair brushed the delicate cheekbones of Lizzie's heart-shaped face and she glanced up through the silken veil of her lashes, green eyes clear and direct. 'Well, yes, we are. I've thought of a way round that.'

'There's no way round it,' Cesare informed her impatiently, marvelling at the luminous quality of those tear-drenched eyes.

'AI,' she declared quietly.

His straight ebony brows lifted. 'AI?'

'Artificial insemination. We use it with the stock and we can do it that way too,' Lizzie muttered in an undertone, trying not to succumb to discomfiture because he was *really* staring at her now as if he had never heard of such a process. 'I mean, that way there's no need at all for us to get up close and personal. We can both conserve our dignity.'

Cesare was staggered by the suggestion. 'Dignity?'

he queried thinly, his first reaction being one of male offence until his clever brain examined the suggestion. For him, it would be a win-win situation, he acknowledged grudgingly. He would not have to sacrifice his freedom in any field because the marriage would be a detached charade from start to finish. That *was* the civilised sensible approach because there would always be the risk that sexual involvement could muddy the waters of their arrangement. But while his intellect reinforced that rational outlook, he discovered that he was curiously reluctant to embrace the concept of a child fathered in a lab rather than in the normal way and equally reluctant to accept that Lizzie Whitaker would never share his bed.

'Well, obviously neither one of us would want to be put in the position where we would have to have sex with a stranger.'

Without warning, unholy amusement burnished Cesare's lean, darkly handsome features. 'I don't think you know much about the average male.'

Colour flared like a banner in Lizzie's cheeks. 'And if that's the sort of man you are, I don't think you should be boasting about it!' she snapped pointedly.

Cesare breathed in slow and deep and resisted the urge to ask her if she ever lightened up. It was something of a shock for him to discover that there was a woman alive utterly impervious to his looks and charisma. He didn't believe in false modesty and had been well aware since the teen years that he could attract women in droves, a success rating that had only been enhanced by his gradual rise to billionaire status. Lizzie, however, put out no encouraging vibes and was not remotely flirtatious.

Watching the cool forbidding expression spread across his lean bronzed face, Lizzie took fright and said, 'I'm sorry…I'm too worried about Archie to mind what I say. I didn't intend to be rude but you must understand that two people with as little in common as we have really do need a get-out clause when it comes to having a baby,' she framed with a shy upward glance. 'And if I agree to that, there would be additional safeguards I would require.'

'Such as?'

Lizzie breathed in deep. 'You would have to agree to take on the role of acting as a father to the child until it grew up. Obviously we'll marry and then divorce… whenever.' Lizzie shifted an uncertain hand. 'But a child has specific needs from a parent and those needs must be met with love and security from *both* of us. That would be quite a responsibility for you to take on for the next twenty years and I need to be sure that you're willing to accept that.'

A very faint darkening of colour across Cesare's spectacular cheekbones highlighted his discomfiture. He had assumed that Lizzie was planning to discuss the financial rewards for her willingness to fulfil the terms of the will and her true, infinitely more responsible and caring angle of interest had pierced him with a rare sense of guilt. 'Why are you so willing to take on that responsibility?' he prompted.

'I've always wanted a child of my own,' Lizzie responded, quite comfortable and secure in making that admission. 'But I don't really want a man to go *with* the child, so the arrangement you suggested would probably suit me best of all. At the same time I don't want to raise a fatherless child, so an occasional father such as you would be is even more acceptable.'

Cesare was quietly stunned by those statements. The women he socialised with were never so frank about a desire to conceive either now or in the future. He wondered if she was still in love with her ex or simply some sort of man-hater because it was unusual for so young a woman to decide that she wanted to live her life alone. And then in dawning dismay he heard himself say, 'Are you gay?'

Lizzie turned bright pink but recognised why he had interpreted her words in that light. 'No, that's not the problem,' she responded stiffly, determined to keep her reasons for her solitary choice of lifestyle strictly private. There was no requirement whatsoever for her to explain herself to him and she was grateful for the fact.

'If we had a child together, I would hope to meet all your expectations of a father,' Cesare informed her with quiet conviction. 'As it happens, I have a very good father of my own and appreciate the importance of the role he plays.'

Lizzie nodded. 'That was my only real concern… Oh.' She hesitated but there was no way of avoiding the most pressing requirement. 'If we're to proceed with this I'm afraid I'll need some money from you upfront. I have to be honest—we are all stony broke. My sister needs some cash to stay on at university and I'll have to rent a property in the village for my dad because when I leave, he'll be relinquishing the tenancy of the farm.'

Absorbing the fluctuating expressions of embarrassment and apprehension skimming her heart-shaped face, Cesare sent her a soothing smile. 'Naturally it's not a problem. I expected something of the sort.'

'You knew how we were fixed...*before* you visited?' Lizzie queried in surprise.

'I never enter a situation blind,' Cesare countered unapologetically.

Danny the vet appeared in the doorway. 'Archie will be out in a minute. My nurse is just finishing up with him. His leg's broken and he's had a blow to the skull, which means he's a little woozy, but other than that he seems fine.'

After the vet had explained his treatment and proffered medication for the coming days, Archie emerged in the nurse's arms, a cast attached to one small leg and a balloon collar round his neck to prevent him from nibbling at it. Lizzie gathered him close, tears tripping from her eyes again as she huskily thanked the older man while Cesare insisted on taking care of the bill.

'I'm very attached to Archie,' Lizzie explained, dashing tears of relief from her eyes with her elbow. 'You can drive back if you want. The keys are in my pocket.'

Cesare fished out the keys and unlocked the car. 'I was hoping you would fly back to London with me tonight.'

'*Tonight?*' Lizzie exclaimed in disbelief. 'That's impossible!'

'We have a tight time schedule. I have everything arranged. Is it really impossible?' Cesare prompted drily. 'You appear to have no presentable clothes and can't need to pack much.'

'But I have to sort out somewhere for Dad to live and move him out of the cottage.'

'I have staff who will hire professionals to deal with those tasks for you,' Cesare told her with complete cool. 'You've had your say. I have agreed to your terms and now I need you to come to London.'

It was bite-the-bullet time, Lizzie registered, angrily colliding with brilliant dark eyes as hard as jet. He was being unreasonable. Surely there was no excuse for such haste? But what choice did she have? The arrangement having been agreed, he was now in charge of events. 'I'll have to call in with my neighbour to ask him to look after the flock.'

'Andrew Brook?'

Lizzie stiffened. 'Yes.'

'Why did you break up?'

'That's private,' Lizzie told him waspishly.

Cesare gritted his teeth. 'We'll go and see him now, so that you can make your preparations.'

Lizzie left Archie asleep in the Land Rover. Esther opened the door and her look of dismay mortified Lizzie, although she had always been aware that Andrew's last-minute exchange of would-be wives had caused Esther almost as much heartache and humiliation as it had caused Lizzie. People had condemned Esther for sleeping with a man who was engaged to another woman. They had judged her even harder for falling pregnant and thereby forcing the affair into the open and some locals had ignored Esther ever since.

Andrew sprang up from the kitchen table while Lizzie carried out introductions whereupon Cesare startled her by taking charge. 'Lizzie and I are leaving for London tonight—we're getting married,' he explained. 'Lizzie wants to know if you'll take her sheep.'

Lizzie saw the surprise and relief darting across Esther's face and looked away again, her own colour high. Esther would be glad to see her leave the neighbourhood and she didn't feel she could really blame the other woman for that, not after the way people had treated her.

'This is a surprise and it calls for a celebration,' Andrew pronounced with genuine pleasure. 'I didn't even know you were seeing anyone, Lizzie.'

Home-made peach wine was produced. Cesare found it sickly sweet but he appreciated the sentiment while he watched and read his companions and made certain interesting deductions. Andrew Brook appeared fond of Lizzie but no more than that. Indeed his every look of warmth was for his wife, who was a rather plain, plump young woman who couldn't hold a candle to Lizzie in the looks department. Lizzie, on the other hand, Cesare could not read at all. She chatted but was clearly eager to leave as soon as was polite.

'Are you planning to enlighten me yet?' Cesare drawled when they returned to the Land Rover, his Italian accent licking round the edges of every syllable in the sexiest way imaginable.

Lizzie was bitterly amused by that stray thought when she didn't do sex or even know what sexy was. That had lain at the heart of her disastrous relationship with Andrew when she had learned that she was simply one of those women who did not like to be touched. She had assumed—*wrongly*—when she agreed to marry him that her own response would naturally change as time went on and they became closer. But that hadn't happened and her feelings hadn't changed.

'Andrew had an affair with Esther while we were engaged and she got pregnant. We broke up six weeks before our wedding day and he married her the following month. They're very happy together,' Lizzie explained flatly. 'That means I've got an unused wedding gown in my wardrobe, so I'll bring that down to London.'

'*No!*' Cesare sliced in with innate distaste. 'I will buy you another dress.'

'But that's silly and wasteful when there's no need for it!' Lizzie reasoned in bafflement.

'If we are trying to persuade my family that this is a genuine marriage, you will need a designer gown with all the usual trimmings.'

'But how could anyone possibly believe it was genuine? We're chalk and cheese and we only just met.'

'You'll be enjoying a full makeover in London and only my father knows when we first met. By the time I'm finished with you, they *will* believe, *cara*,' Cesare insisted.

'And what if I don't want a makeover?'

'If you want to be convincing in the role you're being paid to take, you don't have a choice,' Cesare told her softly. Of course she wanted a makeover, he thought grimly, unconvinced by her show of reluctance. She was willing to do just about anything for money. Hadn't she already demonstrated the fact? She was prepared to become a mother simply to sell the island to him. But then to be fair, he acknowledged, he was willing to become a father to buy Lionos although, in his case, he had additional and far more presentable motives.

What was the use of working so hard when he had

no heir to follow him? What easier way could he acquire a child to inherit his empire? He had seen too many marriages explode into the bitterness and division of divorce, heard too many stories about children traumatised by their parents splitting up. The will had given him a chance to avoid that kind of fallout *and* the imprisonment of taking 'for ever after' vows with one woman. A marriage that was a marriage only on paper and a child born prior to a low-key civilised divorce would suit Cesare's needs very nicely indeed.

Out of Cesare's response, only one phrase assailed Lizzie: *you're being paid*. It was an unwelcome but timely reminder and she chewed at her full lower lip, restraining a tart response. Hopefully within a couple of months he would have no further use for her and she would get her life back and, even more hopefully, a life that would stretch to include the sheer joy of becoming a mother for the first time. When that time came, maybe she would be able to find some sort of work training course and accommodation near Chrissie. Or maybe that was a bad idea, she reflected uneasily, suspecting that her sibling had the right to her independence without a big sister hovering protectively somewhere nearby.

'A moment before we go inside...' Cesare breathed, striding round the bonnet of the rusty farm vehicle.

A frown drew Lizzie's brows together as she hovered by the back door. When he reached out and tugged her close, Lizzie was so taken aback that she simply froze. His hands came up to frame her cheekbones and she gazed up into glittering golden eyes that reflected the lights shining out from the farmhouse windows, her nostrils flaring on the faint fresh scent of his cologne and the underlying hint of clean, fresh man.

At that point while she was mulling over why he smelled so good to her, Cesare lowered his proud dark head and kissed her. Lizzie stopped breathing in shock, electrified by the sensation and taste of his firm sensual mouth on hers with her heart hammering and her pulse racing as if she were riding a Big Dipper at an amusement park. He nibbled her lower lip and thunder crashed in her ears, the earth literally moving when he swiped his tongue along her full lower lip in an erotic flick that made her quiver like a jelly.

Forbidden warmth burst into being inside her, swelling her breasts, tightening her nipples, spearing down between her legs in a twin assault on her senses. A hard urgency now laced the passionate pressure of his mouth on hers and her head fell back, lips parting by instinct to welcome the deeply sensual dart of his tongue. He pulled her closer, welding her to every powerful line of his lean, powerfully masculine body with a big hand splayed across her hips to hold her in place and in spite of their clothing she felt his arousal, the hard, unmistakeable ridge between them. With almost superhuman force of will because she was on the edge of panic, Lizzie pressed her hand against his shoulder to push him back from her and, to be fair to him, he freed her immediately.

'That's enough,' she framed unevenly, her breath rasping in her tight throat as an ache of what she knew could only be dissatisfaction spread at the heart of her. 'Why the heck did you do that?'

'If we intend to fool people into crediting that we are a genuine couple, we have to be able to behave like a couple…at least, occasionally,' Cesare delivered with an audibly ragged hitch in his breathing.

'I don't like being touched,' Lizzie told him in a small flat voice.

*You could've fooled me,* Cesare thought in disbelief, still tasting the sweetness of her soft, lush lips and struggling to suppress the rush of hungry excitement that had lit him up like a burning torch.

She was out of bounds, he reminded himself stubbornly. He was not planning to bed her. She didn't want it and *he* didn't want it either. Regrettably his body was out of step with his brain, though, and somehow she exuded all the allure of a juicy hamburger to a very reluctant vegetarian. But, Cesare reminded himself stubbornly, he could get sex anywhere. He had Celine for uncommitted sexual satisfaction. He wasn't about to risk screwing up his marital arrangement with Lizzie by flirting with that kind of intimacy. It would blur the boundaries and she might start behaving like a real wife and even start thinking that she could attach strings to him.

'So, it was just a sort of test?' Lizzie gathered in relief, assuming that it was an approach that was unlikely to be repeated very often.

'You won the gold medal for excellence, *bella mia*,' Cesare quipped, striving to will his libido back down to a manageable level but that was a challenge while all he could think about, all he could see in his head, was Lizzie spread across a bed, stark naked and not only willing but also wild. The imagery didn't help, nor did it help that he knew he, who prided himself on his detachment in business situations, was indulging in a deeply improbable but very male fantasy.

Two hours later, Lizzie was seated in a limousine with Cesare in silence. Her case was stowed, Archie was asleep on her knee and Cesare was working on his laptop. She was still thinking about that kiss, wondering what magic spark Cesare had that Andrew had so conspicuously lacked. Was it truly just a case of physical chemistry?

Frustration filled Lizzie to overflowing. There had been very few men in her life, very few kisses and she was still a virgin. Andrew had repulsed her, yet he was a young, attractive man and she had loved him. Naturally, she had assumed that she simply wasn't a very sexual woman. But within seconds of Cesare kissing her, fireworks had gone off inside her in a rush of excitement unlike anything she had ever felt. And now, for the very first time in her life, she was studying a powerful masculine thigh and the distinctive bulge at the crotch and wondering what a man looked like naked. Colour washed in a veil to her hairline and she studied Archie instead, fondling a shaggy ear as the dog slept.

It was sexual curiosity, that was all. Silly, immature, she labelled with growing embarrassment, but nothing to really worry about. After all, nothing was going to happen with Cesare. And as for that moment of panic in his arms? One kiss and she imagined she was about to tumble into an adolescent infatuation as easily as her mother had once done? No, she was much too sensible for that, she told herself soothingly. Cesare was gorgeous and well-off and arrogant and he probably slept around as such men reputedly did. He was not her type at all…

Absolutely *not* his type, Cesare was reflecting with

satisfaction. One dynamite kiss didn't alter the fact that she dressed like a bag lady, had poor manners and barely a feminine bone in her body. Or that she treated him rather like a lost umbrella someone had left behind on a train seat...

# CHAPTER FOUR

THE MAKEOVER, ALONG with the shopping and the ultra-grooming at a very fancy beauty salon, shook Lizzie to her very depths.

She was transformed and she knew it and was surprised by how very much better it made her feel to see herself polished to glossiness, with that awful brown dye gone from the last few inches of her pale silvery hair. Every time she had seen that dye in the mirror it had reminded her of Andrew and the bad times, so it was a relief to be finally rid of it and stop wondering if he ironically had tried to change *her* into Esther, who had mud-brown hair of no great distinction. She regarded her long, glittery nails with positive girlish delight because she had never known such beauty tweaking could transform her work-roughened hands. The calluses were gone as well, her entire skin surface buffed and moisturised to perfection. There was no doubt about it: it made her feel like a new woman, a woman of greater assurance than she had been when she first slunk through the doors of the salon, feeling like a crime against femininity in her untouched, unpolished state.

How would Cesare view her now?

Her cheeks flushed at the thought. Why should that matter to her? What was his opinion worth? Presumably without the polishing he wouldn't have wanted to be seen out with her in public and that was a lowering reflection, she acknowledged ruefully. She had been transformed and she appreciated it, best not to think too deeply beyond that, she decided wryly. And now all dressed up to the nines she felt more armoured to cope with the hen party ahead even if it was without the support of her sister.

Sadly, Chrissie had an exam the next day and there was absolutely no way she could join Lizzie and Cesare's sisters. Lizzie was disappointed. She liked Cesare's friendly siblings very much but they were still strangers and somewhat more uncomfortably, strangers she had to keep a front up with. They thought it was a normal wedding with a bride and groom in love and happy. Unfortunately, living up to that false expectation was a strain even on a shopping and beauty trip.

'You mean, you really *aren't* pregnant?' Sofia, Cesare's youngest half-sister, gasped as she watched Lizzie down a vodka cocktail with every sign of enjoyment. 'Cesare told us you weren't but we didn't believe him.'

'This conversation is not happening,' Paola groaned in apology, the eldest of the trio of sisters, a teacher and married woman and rather more circumspect than her single, fun-loving sisters in what she chose to say. 'I'm so sorry, Lizzie.'

Lizzie smiled, masking her loneliness and chagrin. 'It's all right. I'm not offended. I know you're surprised that your brother's getting married in such a hurry—'

'When we never thought he'd get married at all,' his third half-sister Maurizia slotted in frankly.

'Obviously he's nuts about you!' Sofia giggled. 'That's the only explanation that makes sense. When I sent him that photo of you all dressed up to go out tonight, he wasted no time telling me that he wanted you to stay at home and that he saw no reason for you to have a hen night.'

Of course Cesare didn't see any reason, Lizzie reflected ruefully, glugging her drink because she didn't know what to say to his very accepting and loveable sisters or indeed to his pleasant stepmother, Ottavia, none of whom had a clue that the wedding wasn't the real thing. She had guessed, however, that his father, Goffredo, was simply playing along with their pretence but she found that same pretence stressful and knew it was why she was drinking so much and living on her nerves. Luckily Cesare had not been required to put on much of an act, she conceded resentfully, as he had taken refuge in his city apartment, after marooning her in his unbelievably luxurious town house with his family, before flying off to New York on urgent business.

Apparently it was the norm for Cesare to move out of his flashy and huge town house into his exclusive city apartment when his family arrived for a visit. Lizzie had found that strange but his family did not, joking that Cesare had always liked his own space and avoided anything that might take his main focus off business, which evidently involved socialising with his family as well. Lizzie thought that was sad but had kept her opinion tactfully to herself.

He was *so* rich: in spite of the limo and the driver and the helicopter, she had had no idea *how* rich her future fake husband was. Lizzie was still in shock from travelling in a private jet and walking into a house the size of a palace with over ten en-suite bedrooms and innumerable staff. She had then done what she should have done a week earlier and had checked him out on the Internet, learning that he was the head of a business mega-empire and more in the billionaire than the multimillionaire category.

Indeed the house, followed by the experience of being literally engulfed by his gregarious family, had only been the first of the culture shocks rattling Lizzie's security on its axis. Two solid days of clothes shopping followed by a physical head-to-toe makeover had left its mark. For that reason it was hardly surprising that she should be at last enjoying the chance to relax and have a few drinks in good company for the first time in more years than she cared to count.

Seated on his jet, furiously checking his watch to calculate the landing time, Cesare enlarged the photograph on his tablet and scrutinised it with lingering disbelief.

Don't you dare take Lizzie out dressed like that to a club! he had texted his half-sister Maurizia, with a confusing mix of anger, frustration and concern assailing him in a dark flood of reactions that made him uncomfortable to the extreme.

He still couldn't take his eyes off the photograph: Lizzie smiling as he had never seen her and sheathed in an emerald-green, 'barely there', strappy short dress with perilous high heels on her shapely legs. It was an amazing transformation. A magic wand had been waved over the bag lady. She looked fantastic and would outshine every woman around her now that her natural beauty had been polished up and brought to the fore. Her glorious mane of hair had been restored as he'd instructed, *not* cut. It gleamed in a silken tumble of silver strands round her delicately pointed face, green eyes huge, pouty mouth lush and pink. Cesare swore under his breath, outraged by his sisters' interference and the hen-party nonsense. Lizzie was no more fit to be let loose in a London nightclub than a toddler and now he would have to go and retrieve her!

'You're not supposed to be here… This is *her* night!' one of his sisters carolled accusingly as soon as he arrived at the women's table.

'Where is she?' Cesare ground out, unamused, while he scanned the dance floor.

Looking daggers at her big brother, Sofia shifted a reluctant hand to show him. 'Don't spoil her night. She's having a whale of a time!'

Cesare centred his incredulous dark gaze on the sight of his bride-to-be, a pink hen-night sash diagonally dissecting her slender, shapely body as she danced, arms raised, silvery hair flying, feet moving in time to the fast beat. What infuriated him was the sight of the two men trying to attract her attention because she appeared to be dancing in a world of her own. Suddenly Lizzie teetered to a stop, clearly dizzy as she swayed on her very high heels. With a suppressed snarl of annoyance, Cesare, ignoring his siblings' wide-eyed disbelief at his behaviour, stalked across the floor to hastily settle steadying hands on Lizzie's slim shoulders.

'Cesare…' Lizzie proclaimed with a wide, sunny smile because it only took one lingering glance to remind her how tall, dark and sleekly gorgeous he was. He towered over her, lean bronzed face shadowed and hollowed by the flickering lights that enhanced his spectacular bone structure, stunning dark golden eyes intent on her. She was really, *really* pleased to see him, a familiar reassuring image in a new world that was unnervingly different and unsettling. In fact for a split second she almost succumbed to a deeply embarrassing urge to hug him. Then, luckily remembering that hugging wasn't part of their deal, she restrained herself.

'You're drunk,' his perfectly shaped mouth framed, destroying the effect of his reassuring presence.

'Of course I'm not drunk!' Lizzie slurred, throwing up her hands in emphasis only to brace them on his broad chest while she wondered why her legs wanted to splay like a newborn calf's trying to walk for the first time.

'You are,' Cesare repeated flatly.

'I'm *not*,' Lizzie insisted, holding onto his forearms to stay upright, her shoe soles still displaying a worrying urge to slide across the floor of their own volition.

'I'm taking you home,' Cesare mouthed as the deafening music crashed all around them.

'I'm not ready to go home yet!' she shouted at him.

Lizzie couldn't work out what Cesare said in answer to that declaration. His deep-set eyes glittered like banked-down fires in his lean, strong face and he

had bent down and lifted her up into his arms before
she could even begin to guess his intention.

'Think we're going home,' Lizzie informed his sisters forlornly from the vantage point of his arms as he
paused by their table.

'You *didn't* look after her!' Cesare growled at one
of his sisters, in answer to whatever comment had
been made.

'What am I? A dog or a child?' Lizzie demanded,
staring up at him, noticing that he needed a shave because a heavy five o'clock shadow outlined his lower
jawline, making it seem even harder and more aggressive than usual. It framed his wide, sensual mouth
though, drawing attention to the perfectly·sculpted
line of his lips. He kissed like a dream, she recalled
abstractedly, wondering when he'd do it again.

'Think we should kiss so that your sisters believe
we're a *real* couple?' Lizzie asked him winningly.

'If we were real, I'd strangle you, *cara*,' Cesare
countered without hesitation. 'I leave you alone for
three days and I come back and you're going crazy on
the dance floor and getting blind drunk.'

'*Not* drunk,' Lizzie proclaimed stubbornly.

Cesare rolled his eyes and with scant ceremony
stuffed her in the back of the waiting limousine. 'Lie
down before you fall over.'

'You're so smug,' Lizzie condemned and closed her
eyes because the interior of the limousine was tele-
scoping around her in the most peculiar way.

Cesare consoled himself with the hope that such
behaviour was not a warning sign of things to come.
How could he blame her for wanting some fun? He
had a very good idea of what life must have been like

for her on that farm with her misery of a father, always there at her elbow, keen to remind her of every mistake and failure. For the very first time in his life he realised just how lucky he had been with Goffredo, who saw everything through rose-tinted, forgiving spectacles. In comparison, Brian Whitaker's view of life was seriously depressing.

Lizzie opened her eyes. 'Do you want to kiss me?' she enquired.

Cesare skimmed his disconcerted gaze to her animated features, taking in the playful grin she wore. 'Do you *want* me to kiss you?'

Lizzie flushed and shifted on the seat. 'You're not supposed to ask that.'

'You expect me to act like a caveman?'

Lizzie thought about that. She had rather enjoyed being carried out of the club. Was that weird? She scolded herself for that enjoyment while mustering up a dim memory of her mother giggling and tossing her hair, eyes sparkling at the latest man in her life. Inwardly she cringed a little from the comparison she saw.

'Only when you're sober and you know what you're doing,' Cesare extended infuriatingly.

'You believe I could only want to kiss you when I'm drunk?'

Cesare suppressed a groan and studied her. If truth be told, it would take very little encouragement for him to flatten her along the back seat and take inexcusable advantage of her delightfully feminine body. 'We have a business arrangement,' he reminded her doggedly, cursing the hot swell of the erection disturb-

ing his poise because just the thought of doing anything to her turned him on hard and fast.

Her honey-brown lashes flickered. 'I'm open to
negotiation.'

'*No*, you're not,' Cesare informed her grimly, lean
bronzed face set in forbidding lines, mobile mouth
compressed. 'There will be absolutely no negotiation
on that score tonight.'

Was it so wrong, Lizzie asked herself, that she
should want to experience just once what other women
commonly experienced? She had always wanted to be
normal, to *feel* normal. Was that wrong? Indecent?
Her cheeks burned. Naturally she had picked him.
*That* kiss... Somehow he had become her forbidden
object of desire. How had that happened? Treacherous heat curling in her pelvis, Lizzie breathed in
slow and deep.

Cesare watched her feathery lashes dip and the
sound of her breathing slow as she slid into a doze.
Well, he wouldn't be letting her loose around alcohol
again. Sex, drink and business arrangements did not
make for a rational or successful combination. And he
was a *very* rational guy, wasn't he? Here he was being
a saint and protecting her from doing something she
would regret. Or would she? he wondered with inbred
cynicism. She was a gold-digger, after all, and sure to
be on a high after the orgy of spending that had centred on her in recent days.

He was acting against his own nature, he acknowledged grudgingly. In reality, he wanted to fall on her
like a sex-starved sailor on shore leave and keep her
awake all night. Instead he was likely to spend half the
night in a cold shower. He should have made more of

an effort to see Celine. Clearly, it was the lack of regular sex that was playing merry hell with his hormones.

Lizzie awakened as Cesare half walked, half carried her into the town house only to stop dead as Goffredo and his stepmother, Ottavia, appeared in the doorway of the drawing room.

'Your daughters are still partying,' Cesare announced. 'Lizzie was falling asleep, so I brought her home early.'

'Cesare is a party pooper,' Lizzie framed with difficulty.

Goffredo grinned and Ottavia chuckled and the older couple vanished back into the drawing room.

At the foot of the stairs, Cesare abandoned the pretence that Lizzie could walk unaided and swept her up into his arms.

'I like it when you do this,' Lizzie told him. 'It's so…so…masculine.'

'We are lucky you don't weigh more,' Cesare quipped, barely out of breath as they reached the top of the stairs.

A sudden lurch in the stomach region made Lizzie tense and she crammed a stricken hand to her mouth, mumbling, 'Cesare…'

To give him his due, Cesare was not slow on the uptake and he strode through the nearest door at speed and deposited her in a bathroom.

Lizzie was ingloriously ill. He pushed her hair out of the way, gave her a cloth, extended a toothbrush, which he unwrapped, and politely ignored her repetitive apologies for her behaviour. When she couldn't stand up again, he removed her shoes for her and supported her over to the sink.

'I don't make a habit of this,' she declared, rinsing her mouth several times over while hanging onto the vanity unit.

'I should hope not, *bellezza mia*.'

'What does that mean? The Italian bit?'

And he told her that it meant 'my beauty'.

'But that's a downright lie,' she protested, studying her bleary-eyed reflection in dismay. The make-up girl's artistry and the hairdresser's skill were no longer apparent in the flushed face, smudged eyeliner and tousled hair she now saw in the mirror.

'You need to lie down,' Cesare asserted, lifting her again so that the bathroom spun and then the bedroom that followed.

Lizzie lay flat and dead still on the bed, afraid to move lest her surroundings began revolving again. 'Where's Archie? I want Archie.'

'Archie stays downstairs.' Cesare reminded her of the household rule, announced by Primo, his imperturbable manservant, on the day she moved in.

'But that's just mean… He always sleeps with me,' she mumbled.

Cesare almost groaned out loud. She lay splayed across his bed, clearly trusting him when he didn't trust himself because she was displaying a wanton amount of bare slender thigh.

'If I can't have Archie for company, I'll have you,' Lizzie muttered. 'Lie down.'

Cesare snatched up the phone and issued a terse instruction. Within the space of a minute, Primo arrived at the door with Archie. Cesare clasped Archie and carried him over to the bed, whereupon the dog curled up obediently at Lizzie's feet with his head resting across her ankles.

'You should get into bed…you can't sleep in your clothes,' Cesare told her.

'Why not?'

Cesare released his breath in an exasperated hiss and came down on the bed beside her to run her zip down.

'What are you doing?' she whispered curiously as he smoothed the straps of the dress down off her slim shoulders.

'Making you more comfortable.' Business arrangement, *business* arrangement, bloody business arrangement, Cesare was dutifully repeating inside his head as he eased her out of the dress to expose a filmy and provocative bra and panties set in turquoise lace. He wasn't looking, he wasn't reacting, he told himself doggedly while his dark golden gaze clung of its own volition to the surprisingly full, plump curves swelling the lace cups, revealing pale pink nipples that made his mouth water and the shadowy vee at her crotch. He yanked the sheet over Lizzie's prone length so fast that she rolled and, having been disturbed and crammed in below the sheet without warning, Archie also loosed a whimper of complaint.

Lizzie stretched out a searching hand, her eyes closed. The room was going round and round and round behind her lowered eyelids and she felt lost and nauseous. 'Where you going?'

Weary after a day spent travelling and his last-minute sprint to deal with Lizzie, Cesare surrendered to the obvious. If he left her alone, might she wander off? Sleep on the floor? Have an accident? Stumble into the wrong bedroom? And what if she was sick again? 'I'm not going anywhere.' He stripped down to his boxers and lay down on the other side of the bed. A small, callused hand closed over the thumb of his right hand and held on tight. He wasn't used to sharing a bed and he liked his own space.

Lizzie settled up against a warm solid shape while Archie tunnelled below the sheet to settle down by a less restive set of feet.

Lizzie wakened with a desperate thirst at some timeless hour of the night while it was still dark. She slid her feet off the side of the bed, her soles finding the floor, and slowly straightened. A wave of dizziness immediately engulfed her and she compressed her lips hard, sober enough now to be furious with herself. Despite having hardly eaten all day she had foolishly downed all that alcohol and got carried away by the party atmosphere. Suppressing a groan of frustration, she fumbled for the switch on the bedside light and then stared in bewilderment round the unfamiliar room before focusing on the male sharing the wide bed with her.

Cesare was half naked and lying on top of the sheet she had been lying beneath. He was beautifully built with a broad bronzed torso and corded abdomen that rippled with lean muscle. One long, powerful, hair-roughened thigh was partially raised, the other flat. Unshaven, he exuded a rough, edgy masculinity that made her breath hitch in her throat as she peered down at him in the lamplight. His lashes were like black silk fans and almost long enough to touch his amazing cheekbones.

She remembered asking him if he wanted to kiss

her, absolutely angling for his attention, and she almost screamed out loud at that demeaning memory.
She headed for the bathroom with hot cheeks and a
frustrated sense of self-loathing and shame that she
could have been so silly. Had she asked him to stay
with her as well? For goodness' sake, it was obviously
his bedroom and he had only brought her there the
night before because it was the nearest option when
she felt sick. Now he had seen her in her underwear
and she was mortified, although not as mortified as
she would have been had he removed that as well.
Her head throbbing, she drank about a gallon of cold
water and freshened up as best she could without her
own toiletries. She crept out of the bathroom in search
of something to wear so that she could return to her
own room.

Tiptoeing like a cat burglar, she opened the door
into a massive wardrobe and eased back a sliding door
to yank a man's white shirt off a hanger. The bra was
digging into her midriff and she released the catch and
removed it and the panties, wondering if she dared
go for a shower. Donning the shirt, she rolled up the
sleeves and buttoned it.

Being around Cesare made her feel out of control
but was that so surprising? She hadn't dated since
Andrew, hadn't seen the point, and before him there
had only been a handful of unremarkable men. In
recent times, she had had no social outlets and had
only occasionally left the farm. It cost money to so-
cialise and there had been none to spare. Being with
Cesare's light-hearted sisters had been so much fun
that she had forgotten to monitor how much she was
drinking. One glimpse of Cesare when she was in that

weakened condition had had the same effect on her as a hit man shooting her directly between the eyes. He was a very good-looking male, that was all. Noticing the fact simply meant she was female and alive and not that she wanted to pursue anything with him.

Hovering by the bed, Lizzie tried to work out how to get Archie out from below the sheet without either hurting him or waking Cesare.

'What are you doing?' Cesare husked as she yanked at the sheet to try and reach her dog. Blinking up at her with frowning dark eyes, he lifted a muscular arm to check the gold watch he still wore. '*Inferno!* It's three in the morning.'

'I should go back to my own room.'

'Don't wake up the whole household. Stay and go back to sleep,' Cesare advised her drily, flipping onto his side in a display of indifference that made her grit her teeth.

Would she wake anyone up? Stifling a sound of frustration, Lizzie doused the light and snaked back below the sheet.

Early morning was sending pale light through the blinds when she next surfaced, feeling considerably healthier than she had earlier but decidedly overheated. An arm was draped round her ribcage and she was locked intimately close to a very male body, a very *aroused* male body. A surge of heat that had nothing to do with his higher temperature pooled in Lizzie's pelvis. She eased over onto her back and looked up unwarily into heavily fringed eyes the colour of melted bronze. Her throat ran dry, her breathing ruptured.

'You're a very restless sleeper, *cara mia*,' Cesare

censured softly, his breath fanning her cheek. 'I had to clamp you in one place to get peace.'

'Oh…' Lizzie framed dry-mouthed, entranced by her view of his lean, darkly handsome features in the golden dawn light, even her hearing beguiled by his melodic accent.

'Archie, on the other hand, sleeps like the dead and doesn't move at all,' Cesare quipped. 'I've never had a dog in my bed before.'

'There's a first time for everything.'

'First and *last*,' he stressed. 'Unfortunately you wouldn't settle without him last night.'

'I'm sorry I drank too much.' Colour slowly rose to drench her porcelain skin as he stared down at her 'Was I really awful?'

Long fingers stroked her taut ribcage, making her violently aware of the breasts swelling mere inches above. 'No, you were bright and breezy until the alcohol took its toll.'

Her breathing pattern fractured as she felt her nipples pinch tight while a hot, achy sensation hollowed between her legs. 'I'm not used to drinking like that,' she muttered jaggedly.

His golden eyes smouldered down at her and a wicked grin slanted his shapely lips, ensuring that the rate of her heartbeat accelerated. 'Don't make a habit of it.'

'Of course, I won't,' she began with a frown, tightening every muscle in an urgent, almost panic-stricken attempt to smother the sexual responses trickling through her and awakening every skin cell.

Cesare, who planned everything in Machiavellian detail, had not planned to kiss Lizzie. Having decided not to touch her, he fully expected to abide by that prohibition because he virtually never gave way to impulses. Unhappily for him, the burning desire to pin Lizzie to the bed and have wild, sweaty sex with her had no rational base: it was driven by pure instinct. And when she shifted her hips below the shirt that had most definitely ridden up to ensure that bare skin met bare skin, Cesare was lost.

One minute, Lizzie was drowning in dark golden eyes framed by lashes longer than her own and downright jealous of the fact, and the next Cesare brought his mouth crashing down on hers with the kind of raw, driving passion that she was defenceless against. It was glorious and the taste of his tongue delving deep into the moist interior of her mouth was unsurpassable and an intoxication in its own right.

He traced the pointed bud of a straining nipple and her spine undulated of its own accord, sensation piercing straight to her pelvis. Her breasts had suddenly become achingly sensitive to the palms cupping them and the fingers tugging gently on the prominent tips. That felt amazingly good. A stifled gasp was wrenched from low in her throat and her spine arched, her body rising up to cradle his in an involuntary move of welcome as old as time. He skated his fingers along a slender thigh to discover the hot wet core of her, sliding between the delicate folds to moisturise the tiny bud of thrumming nerve endings above with a skilled fingertip.

Lizzie tore her lips from his to cry out, hungry beyond bearing for that sensual touch and plunging her fingers into his tousled black hair to hold him to her. She was no more capable of thinking about what she was doing than she was of stopping breathing on command. Her heart was thumping, her ragged gasping breaths audible, her entire body was tingling madly with seething heat and need. With his free hand, he ripped at the buttons of the shirt. The shirt fell partially open, exposing the rounded fullness of a breast crowned by a pale pink nipple. He closed his mouth there, teasing the distended bud with the flick of his tongue and the graze of his teeth while his fingers stoked an erotic blaze at her feminine core. She shuddered, talon claws of fierce need biting into her, shock assailing her that anything physical could feel so intense that she could neither fight it nor control it.

'I love the way you respond to me, *mi piace*,' Cesare growled with satisfaction while switching his attention between her pouting breasts and sending fantastic ripples of ravishing sensation right down to her unbearably hot core.

Lizzie couldn't find her voice, her breath or a single functioning brain cell. Her entire being was welded to his every caress, wanting, needing more. And kissing an erotic path down over her flat, quivering stomach, Cesare gave her much more and she didn't have the strength of will to deny him.

With ruthless cool he zeroed in on the tender heart of her with every weapon in his erotic mastery, stroking delicate flesh with his tongue and his mouth and his expert fingers. Lizzie careened into shock at the intimacy and then moaned below the onslaught of wicked, delirious excitement. Intense pleasure followed, sweeping her up into a wild, yearning climb towards a peak that she felt she would never reach. But that climb was unstoppable. Suddenly her body wasn't her own any more and she was flying like a comet into the sun in a climax so powerful it brought shaken tears of reaction to her eyes.

Still ragingly aroused, Cesare sprang out of bed, his fists angrily clenched. What the hell had he been thinking of? No matter how great the temptation, he should *never* have touched her. They had a business agreement and a planned marriage of convenience ahead of them. They were not lovers, not friends with benefits. He did not want to muddy the waters with the kind of physical intimacy that women often assumed meant more than it did. If he wasn't careful, he might find himself more married than he had ever wanted to be, he acknowledged grimly.

Paralysed by a crazy sense of peace in the aftermath of orgasm, Lizzie closed her eyes, her body still trembling from the sweet aftermath of agonising pleasure. The mattress gave but she didn't open her eyes again until a phone rang, shattering her dream state. The phone fell silent in answer to a man's voice speaking Italian. Her lashes lifted then and she stared at Cesare while he paced the floor, mobile phone clamped to his ear. He still wore his boxers and his state of arousal was blindingly obvious. An almost painful tide of colour burned her face.

He tossed the phone down by the bed. 'Do you want the shower first?'

That prosaic question made Lizzie frantically pull the edges of the shirt she wore closed and she sat up in an agony of discomfiture. 'I'll go back to my own room.'

As she scrambled out of bed and reached for Archie, Cesare murmured without any expression at all, 'We made a mistake and we won't repeat it.'

Clutching Archie in an awkward hold, Lizzie attempted to pick up her discarded clothing one-handed. 'Is that all you've got to say?' she prompted shakily.

'It was just sex…nothing worth fussing over,' Cesare opined in a tone that was as cold as a winter shower on her overheated skin. 'Look, I'll see you downstairs in an hour. I have some papers you have to sign before I leave.'

'You're going away again?' she asked in surprise, fighting the roar of temper rising from a secret place deep down inside her.

'We have forty-eight hours to go before the wedding and I intend to use it,' he advanced calmly, deep-set dark eyes hooded, wide, sensual mouth clenched hard.

*Just sex…nothing worth fussing over?* Lizzie mulled that putdown over while she showered. She wasn't hurt by his dismissal, of course she wasn't. *A mistake that would not be repeated.* Didn't she feel the same way as he did? What had happened shouldn't have happened. It was much more sensible if they stayed uninvolved and detached. So, if he had left her feeling a little crushed and foolish, it was her own fault for acting like an idiot and inviting such a denouement. If she couldn't quite shake off the sense of intimacy he had imbued her with, it was only because she had been more intimate with him than she had ever been with anyone else but that was a secret not for sharing…

# CHAPTER FIVE

LIZZIE FASTENED THE cropped trousers and straightened the lilac cashmere sweater she wore with it. Her feet shod in flat ballerina pumps, her face lightly made up, she bore not the smallest resemblance to the woman she had been a mere week earlier.

Of course she was now in possession of a vast wardrobe and owned a choice of outfits for every conceivable occasion. Most probably many of the garments would never be worn because she could not imagine Cesare taking her sailing or out to dinner or indeed to the kind of dressy venue where she would require a full-length gown. The wardrobe was totally wasteful in its size and probable expense but she had already learned that once Cesare had instructed his underlings that she was to be dressed from head to toe in designer fashion, his orders were carried out without question.

A pity she was a little more rebellious in that line, Lizzie acknowledged wryly. A lifetime of counting the pennies meant that extravagance made her feel guilty. Breakfast in bed made her feel even guiltier although, to be honest, any excuse to escape the ghastly prospect of having to breakfast alone with Cesare had been extremely welcome.

After all, she had made a huge fool of herself the night before, hadn't she?

Lizzie inwardly cringed, colour marking her cheeks afresh. It would be a very long time, if ever, before she contrived to forget how she had writhed in ecstasy in Cesare's bed. But mercifully, they hadn't actually got as far as having full sex, she reminded herself bracingly, and she assumed that that reality would make it a little easier for her to reinstate normal boundaries between them. She was no natural wanton, never had been, had simply let alcohol, curiosity and temptation steer her briefly in the wrong direction. She wasn't like her mother either because she was not prone to sudden blinding infatuations. For years, there had been no other man for her but Andrew, a reality that had made the slow death of their relationship all the more painful to endure because it had started out with such high hopes.

It offended her sense of decency, however, that the intimacy she had shrunk from exploring with Andrew, whom she had loved, could be so very tempting when offered by a male like Cesare Sabatino, who had no respect for her at all. Cesare didn't give two hoots what happened to her or how she felt about any issue. Cesare merely wanted to *use* her to regain the island of Lionos and he thought that paying her richly for the privilege should take care of any doubts she might have.

'Mr Sabatino is in the office at the end of the corridor,' Primo informed her as she reached the foot of the grand staircase.

Almost sick with self-consciousness, Lizzie found the door ajar and walked in without knocking. Cesare's arrogant dark head flew up from his laptop, subdued fire flaring in his dark, glittering eyes at the interruption until he realised who his visitor was. A well-bred smile lightened his darkly handsome features and curved his hard mouth as he leapt upright, his attention automatically pinning to the lissom curves revealed by the casually elegant outfit she wore. In startling comparison a pink and white X-rated image of Lizzie splayed across his bed erupted at the back of Cesare's mind and he ground his teeth together as his body leapt in response to the provocation. Not for the first time he regretted the interruption that had left him burning with sexual frustration.

When he had last called Celine, he had grasped that he had a problem he had not foreseen. Aware that he was getting married, his French lover no longer wished to be seen in his company. Celine guarded her reputation because the clients who paid her a small fortune to advertise their exclusive perfume were conservative and Cesare had perfectly understood her determination to put her career first. It was, nonetheless, a challenge for him to work out how he was to cope for the next few months being married and *not* married at the same time.

He had not gone without sex for more than a couple of weeks since he was a teenager. Was he now supposed to sneak around seeking a discreet outlet? Without a doubt, he would have to avoid being seen consorting with any woman other than his wife or their marriage would appear dubious and, after going to such lengths to bring about the marriage, that was not a risk he was prepared to take. Whether he liked it or not and whether anything came of it or not, Lizzie was his only option for the foreseeable future, he acknowledged grudgingly.

'You look terrific, *cara*,' Cesare told Lizzie truthfully, politely tugging out a chair for her to use. The jasmine scent of her perfume flared his nostrils and before he could suppress the memory he recalled the wild, hot sweetness of her response. No man could easily forget that kind of passion, he reasoned, exasperated by his stubborn libido and the effect those turbulent hormones had on his usually cool intellect.

'Thanks but it's all fancy packaging, not really me,' Lizzie parried uncomfortably, because he was towering over her and close enough that she could smell the citrusy cologne that overlaid the erotic undertones of clean, warm male. Her colour fluctuating, she sat very straight-backed in her seat.

'Learn how to accept a compliment gracefully,' Cesare advised softly. 'You have a great figure, gorgeous hair and a beautiful face. Clothes merely provide an effective frame for the looks that nature gave you.'

Lizzie dealt him a pained half-smile. Unlike her, he was a master of the ready word and the right thing to say and had probably never been stuck for a quote in his entire gilded life. She evaded his shrewd gaze because she felt vulnerable, almost naked in his presence, stripped as she was of her usual working clothing and countryside assurance because his privileged world was so foreign to hers. She loved the way good clothes that fitted perfectly made her feel, but she wondered if he would still want her without that superficial gloss, a thought that made her feel inadequate and a little pathetic. In short, the spectacular luxury of his home, the costly garments and the preponderance of staff made Lizzie feel out of her depth and drowning. All she had required to crown her discomfiture was that ill-judged sexual episode that morning. 'I want you to sign these documents.' Evidently impervious to the unease afflicting Lizzie, Cesare extended a slim sheaf of papers. 'I need your permission to make alterations to the villa on Lionos.'

Her brow furrowed in surprise. 'Alterations? But you haven't even *seen* the house yet.'

'Because we won't be married until Friday,' Cesare pointed out drily. 'While we're on our honeymoon in Italy, my grandmother will be having her surgery and recuperating. As soon as she is strong enough we will fly out to Lionos and stay in the villa with her.'

'I didn't realise we were having a honeymoon.'

'It will only be a honeymoon in the eyes of the outside world,' Cesare qualified wryly.

'And your grandmother falls into that category too?' Lizzie checked.

'I've already explained that,' Cesare reminded her. 'For all that Athene's strong, she's an old lady. I don't want her to guess that our marriage is a fake. If she knew the truth she'd feel responsible and unhappy.'

'I can understand that.' Lizzie studied him uneasily. He emanated sleek, expensive elegance in a black business suit that outlined his broad shoulders, narrow hips and long, powerful legs to perfection but, unfortunately for Lizzie, she was still seeing him in his form-fitting boxers, an energising image of him half-naked and rampant with masculine potency. She chewed hard at the soft underside of her lower lip, fighting her awareness and her disobedient and thoroughly embarrassing thoughts.

'Before we can stay at the villa, however, some improvements must be made to the accommodation and for that I require your permission as the property belongs to you and your sister.'

'What sort of improvements?' Lizzie prompted with a frown.

'I want to send Primo out to the island immediately with a team of kitchen and bathroom specialists. The house needs to be brought up to date before we can live there and I want to ensure that Athene enjoys her stay.'

'But won't she be sentimental about changes being made to the house where she grew up?' Lizzie asked in surprise.

'That's a fair point but times have changed since she was a girl and I believe she'll recognise that. She's a practical woman and she likes her comforts.'

'From what my mother said, most of the soft furnishings will need to be replaced as well,' Lizzie told him in wry warning. 'Drapes, beds, sofas. I don't think it's possible to achieve so much within such a short time frame and if you don't watch out...once you start removing fitments, the villa will quickly become uninhabitable.'

His supreme assurance untouched, Cesare dealt her an amused smile. 'Believe me, if I'm prepared to throw enough money at the problem, someone will accept the challenge, *cara*.'

Lizzie shrugged because it was immaterial to her what he chose to have done to a house that she had never seen and would only briefly visit. But it was a painful reminder that Cesare only wanted her because she owned the island and could sell it to him if he married her and nobody, but nobody, could make a relationship out of that, she told herself wretchedly. None of her anxious feelings showing on her face, she dutifully scribbled her signature in the indicated places and provided her sister's address for the documents to be couriered to her.

A wholehearted smile softened her taut mouth when Archie poked his head round the door and trotted across the polished wooden floor to greet his mistress.

Cesare watched the dog receive a warm welcome and decided it was educational. Archie looked pathetic with only three working legs and the fourth in a cast and the dog played his advantage for all he was worth, rolling his tummy up in the air to be petted and then struggling pitifully to get up off the floor again. Cesare bent down to lift the terrier and help him upright again. In reaction to his sudden proximity, Lizzie rammed her chair back out of the way, her nervous response setting Cesare's teeth on edge as he straightened again.

Lizzie collided with stunning dark golden eyes fringed with black velvet lashes and forgot how to breathe, feverish tension snaking through her every muscle as she rose hurriedly from her chair again and moved towards the door, keen to be gone.

'Your father and your sister will be attending the wedding?' Cesare sought confirmation.

'Yes…' Lizzie coughed to clear her convulsed throat. 'And I'll ring Chrissie now to explain about the papers she has to sign.'

'I doubt if I'll see you again before we meet at the church on Friday,' Cesare imparted softly. 'Somehow try to practise not leaping away when I come close. It's a dead giveaway that our relationship is a sham.'

Lizzie flushed with mortification. 'Then practise keeping your distance,' she advised.

Well, that was telling him, Cesare conceded grimly. She was angry with him. He had been less than diplomatic after that phone call that interrupted them earlier that day. He ground his even white teeth together. He had only told the truth. Did women always punish men for telling the truth? If their arrangement was to work, however, he would need to make more of an effort to sustain their relationship, he acknowledged grudgingly. Women were emotional creatures. Her anxious, uneasy attitude towards him had just under lined that unwelcome reality.

Furthermore, Lizzie might be a gold-digger who had chosen money over ethics when given the choice, but how could he blame her for that when she had lived in poverty for so many years? It was not a crime for her to seek to better herself. And how could he fault her avaricious streak when, without it, she would have sent him and his proposition packing? It was unjust of him to view her in the same unforgiving light as the many mercenary women who had shared his bed, he conceded wryly. Serafina, after all, had made a straight-up choice to ditch Cesare and marry a man who had been much wealthier, even though he was also much older. He had to be less judgemental and more generous to Lizzie. In any case, as his wife and potentially the future mother of his child, Lizzie was also the equivalent of a long-term project. Somehow he would have to make her happy and *keep* her happy, because if he didn't all his plans could still come to nothing.

* * *

'You look totally amazing!' Chrissie exclaimed as Lizzie spun to show off her wedding gown, slender shoulders and arms sheathed in the finest see-through lace, her tiny waist accentuated by the fullness of her skirt.

'My brother's a closet romantic. He's going to love that dress,' Maurizia forecast as a knock sounded on the door and she and Sofia went to answer it.

'I'm having so much fun. I wish I hadn't put that exam ahead of attending your hen do,' Chrissie lamented, a slight willowy figure in the topaz-coloured bridesmaid dress that she and Cesare's sisters all wore.

Lizzie gazed fondly at her sister, thinking that she was the real beauty in the family with her perfect features and superior height.

'A pressie for you from Cesare,' Sofia announced, placing a jewel case in Lizzie's hands.

A gloriously delicate diamond necklace and drop earrings met Lizzie's stunned appraisal and a chorus of admiration rose from her companions. Of course, Cesare was playing to the gallery, assuming the role of besotted bridegroom for his siblings' benefit, Lizzie guessed. She put on the necklace and the earrings and realised that she was rather pathetically wishing that her wedding were the genuine article. She loved Cesare's family and would have given just about anything for them to be her family as well. Instead she had to live with the unlovely truth that she was deceiving them and would soon be deceiving Cesare's grandmother as well.

'You're really sure about doing this?' Chrissie whispered in the church porch as she made an unnecessary adjustment to Lizzie's gown while their father hovered, looking irritable. 'Because it's not too late to change your mind. All I have to do is call a taxi and we're out of here.'

'Are you trying to cause trouble? Of course, she's not going to change her mind!' Brian Whitaker declared in exasperation. 'That Sabatino fellow has to be the best thing that ever happened to her! At least he has an ounce of sense between his ears.'

'*We* certainly think so,' Paola piped up without hesitation. 'But sometimes the bride does get cold feet.'

'Not this one,' Lizzie countered steadily, smoothing over the awkwardness that had settled over the bridal party with her father's tactless words.

Cesare turned to look at Lizzie only when she reached the altar. Eyes the colour of melted bronze assailed her and she stopped breathing, gripped by the ferocious force of will in that appraisal. He had no doubts, she interpreted. He knew exactly what he was doing, had come to terms with the drawbacks and was concentrating on the end game. She had to do the same, she told herself urgently. She had to stop trying to personalise their relationship and stop wondering whether or not he would kiss her after they had been pronounced man and wife. Such treacherous thoughts were far removed from businesslike behaviour and utterly inappropriate, she scolded herself in exasperation.

'You look fantastic,' Cesare murmured softly while he threaded the wedding band onto her finger and she followed suit, copying his manoeuvre with less cool and more nerves.

Indeed, Cesare was taken aback by just how fabulous she looked. The effect she had on him was ever so slightly unnerving. It was his libido, he told himself impatiently. As long as he stuck to his rules of never getting tangled in anything that smacked of an emotional connection, he would be fine and perfectly happy.

And then the deed was done and they were married and there was no kiss, nor indeed any instruction to kiss the bride. Her hand trembling on Cesare's arm, she walked down the aisle, seeing a sea of smiling faces on every side of her. It was not her idea of a small wedding because the big church was crammed with guests. Out on the steps, Cesare escorted a tiny woman with vibrant brown eyes set in a round wrinkled face to meet her.

'Athene…meet Elisabetta, known as Lizzie,' he murmured quietly. 'Lizzie, this is my grandmother.'

The two women stood chatting about nothing in particular for several minutes beneath Cesare's watchful eye. Athene grinned at Lizzie. There was an astonishing amount of mischief in that unexpected grin and she squeezed Lizzie's hand. 'We'll talk later,' she promised cheerfully.

Later became much later once the bridal merry-go-round took over. The bride and groom greeted their guests at the country house hotel chosen to stage the reception, dined in splendour while being entertained by a famous singer, listened to the speeches and danced the first dance with Lizzie stumbling over her own feet. In the circle of Cesare's powerful arms and surrounded by so many well-wishers, Lizzie had to struggle to remember that their wedding was a fake.

In fact when Cesare lowered his darkly handsome

head and kissed her, Lizzie was so unprepared for the move and so taken back by it she fell into it like a child falling down a bottomless well. His mouth moved on hers and his tongue darted across the roof of her mouth and excitement leapt so high inside her she felt dizzy and intoxicated, her head tilting back, her hands tightening round his neck, fingertips flirting with the silky strands of his black hair. It was heavenly and devastating; heavenly to glory in her womanhood and appreciate that she had now discovered her sensual side and devastating to register that the wrong man was punching her buttons, simply to impress their audience.

In passionate rejection of that belittling image, Lizzie jerked her head back and pressed him back from her. 'Enough…' she muttered unsteadily.

'*Dio mio*, not half enough for me, *bellezza mia*,' Cesare rasped in a driven undertone. 'I want you.'

Lizzie had become as stiff as a board. 'We talked about that and decided that it wasn't sensible.'

'To hell with being sensible!' Cesare shot back at her with smouldering dark golden eyes framed by black velvet lashes, so breathtakingly handsome in that moment that he took her breath away. 'Passion isn't sensible…don't you know that yet?'

No, but he was teaching her what she had never wanted to know. Experimentation was acceptable to Lizzie as long as she remained in control. She didn't want to be out of control, didn't want to risk getting hurt or making a fool of herself again. Suddenly all her worst fears were coalescing in the shape of Cesare Sabatino and she had only gone and married the guy!

Sofia approached her. 'Athene wants you to come

and sit with her for a while. I expect she wants to get to know you... Cesare is by far her favourite grandchild.'

Lizzie rolled her eyes in sympathy. 'He's the only boy.'

'She practically raised him—that's why they're so close,' Sofia explained. 'Cesare was only four when our mother married his father and although he was supposed to come and live with our parents straight away, he and Athene kept on putting it off and Papa didn't like to interfere too much. Cesare's never been easy—he and Papa are so different.'

'Goffredo is a pet,' Lizzie said warmly. 'You're so lucky.'

'Cesare's too clever for his own good,' his sister opined. 'Papa was in awe of his brain and he was such an argumentative little boy.'

A smile of amusement tilted Lizzie's mouth. 'I can imagine. He likes everything his own way.'

Athene patted the comfortable armchair beside her own. 'Tell me about yourself. I'm a typical nosy old lady,' she confided. 'You talk and I ask the questions.'

Naturally there were questions about Lizzie's mother, whom Athene had met while Goffredo was dating her.

'My son could not have made her happy.' Cesare's grandmother sighed with regret. 'Francesca was always dissatisfied and she was disappointed that Goffredo already had a son. I wasn't that surprised when she broke off the engagement.'

'She wasn't happy with anyone for very long,' Lizzie admitted quietly.

'That must have been very difficult for you and your sister when you were growing up. The things that happen when you're young leave scars,' Athene remarked wryly. 'I believe that's why it's taken so long for Cesare to put Serafina behind him where she belongs...'

'Serafina?' Lizzie queried tentatively, wondering worriedly if this was some family story that she should have been acquainted with and if her ignorance would strike the older woman as suspicious.

'I didn't think he would've mentioned her to you,' Athene told her with a wry smile. 'Cesare hides his vulnerabilities very effectively.'

Lizzie resisted the temptation to admit that she hadn't believed he had any.

'Cesare fell in love with Serafina when he was a student. He wanted to marry her but she said she was too young,' Athene related, her wise old eyes resting on Lizzie's absorbed expression. 'In her first job, she met a very rich man in his seventies and within weeks they were wed.'

Lizzie froze in consternation. 'That must've been devastating for him,' she muttered ruefully, thinking that she had unkindly misjudged Cesare when she had assumed he simply had no heart and no room in his life for anything but business and profit.

'But today I know that he has finally put Serafina back where she belongs in the past,' his grandmother proclaimed with satisfaction and patted Lizzie's hand. 'Today I am joyful that Cesare has married you and changed the whole course of his life for the better.'

Lizzie suppressed a groan of disagreement. She was discovering where Goffredo's optimistic outlook came from—he had inherited it from his mother. It was a source of wonder to her that Cesare had grown up surrounded by people with such sunny natures and yet contrived to retain his cold, unemotional attitude to life. Yet he was also careful to maintain a certain distance from his loving family, she conceded reflectively, wondering if he secretly feared that his family loving softness might dull his own ruthless cutting edge.

A couple of hours after that, Lizzie boarded Cesare's private jet. Her feet, shod in spindly high heels, were killing her. Even the short walk through the airport had been too much and she collapsed into her leather upholstered seat and kicked off her shoes with intense relief.

'You did very well today,' Cesare pronounced, disconcerting her as he took his own seat opposite. 'I don't think anyone suspected the truth.'

'Your father knows,' she reminded him uncomfortably.

'He'll believe the truth for all of ten minutes. Give him a few weeks and he'll persuade himself that we fell madly in love within hours of getting married,' Cesare forecast with sardonic bite. 'That's the way Goffredo functions.'

'You have a lovely family,' Lizzie countered, colour springing into her cheeks. 'Don't be so critical. They love you very much and they aren't afraid to show it.'

Cesare stiffened until he recalled his father-in-law's behaviour throughout the day. Brian Whitaker had turned down the opportunity to make a speech, had kept to his own company in the midst of the crowd and had steadfastly managed not to smile even for the photographs. 'Your father's...different,' he conceded quietly. 'Not the demonstrative type.'

'When my mother left him, it soured him on life,' she muttered ruefully. 'And life has been tough for him ever since. He'll be more content living in the house he's hoping to rent in the village. I think it will be a relief for him not to be looking out of windows at the farm and fretting about the jobs I'm not getting done.'

'Isn't it a relief for you as well?' Cesare prompted, thinking of the long and gruelling hours of work she must have endured while she endeavoured to keep the farm going without help.

Lizzie compressed her lips and frowned reflectively. 'From dawn to dusk I worried about everything and anything and I'm not sorry to be free of that stress. The bank threatening to withdraw the loan was our biggest fear but then the rent was raised...and, that was a body blow, totally the last straw,' she confided honestly. 'That was followed by Chrissie announcing that she was going to drop out of uni and come home because we were having such a struggle. I couldn't let that happen. She *needed* to get her education.'

Cesare was listening intently. 'So that's why you suddenly changed your mind and agreed to marry me?' he breathed in a tone of disconcertion. 'I had no idea that you were under that much financial and emotional pressure.'

'But you said you *knew* our situation,' she reminded him in surprise. 'I assumed you'd used a private investigator to check us out before you came to visit.'

Level dark eyes gazed back at her, a frown line pleating his ebony brows. 'No, I didn't. I didn't know about the bank loan, the rent rise or your sister's plans to drop out. I only knew about your father's ill health and that you were trying to keep the farm afloat on your own.'

'Well, you know the whole story now,' Lizzie commented mildly. 'I was ready to sell my soul for thirty pieces of silver.'

*'No,'* Cesare contradicted, his sibilant Italian accent vibrating in the silence to send a current of awareness travelling down her slender spine. 'You were desperate to protect your family, regardless of what it might cost you personally. That's loyalty and I admire that trait.'

As the silence stretched, Cesare went back to work at his laptop. Driven by something stronger than he was, he found himself glancing up to watch Lizzie leaf through a glossy fashion magazine, pulling faces whenever she came on a picture of any garment she considered too extreme while absently fondling Archie's ear beneath his balloon collar. She was so very natural. What you saw was what you got from Lizzie Whitaker and he had totally misunderstood her. It was a sobering discovery for a male who prided himself on his ability to read others. He had made all too many assumptions about Lizzie, not least that she was a gold-digger, and now that he had discovered that she had been driven more by desperation than greed his innate curiosity about her was finally set free.

'Why did you dye your hair brown?' he asked her abruptly.

Lizzie twined a shining silver strand round a self-conscious finger and winced in evident embarrassment. 'Andrew didn't like my hair. He thought it attracted too much attention and that it looked white and made people think I was an old lady at first glance,' she told him uncomfortably. 'I could see his point.'

'Did you really want to please him that much?' Cesare pressed. 'Your hair's beautiful, unusual but undeniably beautiful, *cara*.'

Lizzie shrugged but her face glowed at the compliment. His lean, darkly handsome features held her intent gaze and she switched her attention back to the magazine, a pool of liquid heat gathering in her pelvis that made her squirm with chagrin. He was so very, *very* good-looking, it was natural for her to stare a little, she told herself ruefully, but she had to keep her feet on the ground and learn to distinguish between what was real and what was more probably fake.

The limousine that collected them from the airport in Italy wended its way along winding roads and through some spectacular scenery. It was late spring and the fields were green with fava beans and wheat dotted with yellow broom. Medieval villages in picturesque hilltop locations were ringed by vineyards and olive groves while the rolling hills were covered with groves of cypresses and umbrella pines. Lizzie was enchanted and plied Cesare with questions.

'You still haven't told me where we're going,' she complained.

'We're almost there.'

Lizzie stared out at the rustic stone farmhouse on the ridge of the hill and blinked because it was not what she expected. Cesare was so sophisticated that she had been convinced that they were heading for some exclusive spa. 'It just doesn't look like your style,' she breathed helplessly.

'I love old buildings. When I first saw it I was a

student out hiking with friends. The roof had fallen in, the first floor had gone and the end wall had collapsed. We took shelter in the barn during a thunderstorm,' Cesare explained as the driver turned down a dirt track that steadily climbed the hill. 'I watched the sun go down over the valley and swore I'd buy it with my first million.'

'Your first…*million*?' she exclaimed.

'It was a money pit,' Cesare told her cheerfully, his dark eyes gleaming with rueful amusement. 'I learnt that the hard way.'

The car drew up in a paved courtyard ornamented with urns full of tumbling flowers. As they climbed out, a rotund little woman in an apron hurried out to greet them. Her name was Maria and she was the housekeeper and, seemingly, Cesare's biggest fan. Ushered into a great vaulted hall, Lizzie looked around herself with keen interest, glancing through to a gracious drawing room rejoicing in a vast pale stone fireplace and an array of vibrant turquoise sofas. The outside might be antique and rustic but the inside was all contemporary elegance.

Maria led her upstairs and into a glorious light-filled bedroom with a window overlooking the valley below. Lizzie fingered the fine white linen bedding and admired the beautifully draped bed while wondering where Cesare was planning to sleep. The driver brought their cases up, closely followed by Cesare, lean and lithe in khaki chinos and an open-necked shirt that screamed Italian designer style.

'Where's your room?' Lizzie asked quietly.

'We *share*,' Cesare told her without skipping a beat.

'I'm not sharing a bed with you!' Lizzie gasped in consternation.

'We're supposed to be married. Let's stay in role,' Cesare fielded. 'Having gone this far, it would be stupid to take risks by using separate bedrooms.'

Lizzie kicked off her shoes and mulled over that argument. 'Maria's not going to talk.'

'She's not the only member of staff with access to the upper floor,' he shot back drily.

'OK...' Lizzie stood at the foot of the bed, prepared to admit that it was huge, but she was still doubtful that she could lose him in it. 'But you have to stay on *your* side of the bed.'

'Are we five years old now?' Cesare quipped, studying her with incredulity. 'You're making a fuss about nothing.'

Lizzie settled glinting witch-green eyes on him. 'I'm not used to sharing a bed. It's not nothing to me.'

'We'll discuss it over dinner,' Cesare decreed.

Lizzie threw her arms wide in emphasis, her temper mounting. 'I don't want to discuss it...I just don't want to do it!'

'Only forty-eight hours ago, you *did*,' Cesare countered, lean, strong face hard, dark golden eyes smouldering with recollection and unforgotten hunger.

Lizzie reddened. 'I was wondering how long it would take you to throw that back in my face. I was drunk, for goodness' sake,' she protested.

'At least you know what you want when you're drunk,' he riposted.

Lizzie slammed shut the door lest they be overheard arguing. 'That's a horrible thing to say!'

'Whether you like it or not, it's the truth. You want

me every bit as much as I want you. You just won't admit it.'

Lizzie was so enraged by that arrogant statement that she walked into the bathroom and closed the door behind her to escape him. The fixtures took her breath away. An antique tub took up prime position by the window while rustic stone walls and a pale marble floor provided an effective frame.

'And hiding in the bathroom isn't going to persuade me otherwise!' Cesare completed loudly outside the door.

Lizzie threw open the door again and marched out with compressed lips to drag one of the cases across the beautiful oak floor. 'I was *not* hiding.'

Cesare snatched up the case and planted it on the bed, helpfully springing the locks for her.

Lizzie hovered, her colour high, her eyes veiled.

Cesare stalked closer like a predator about to spring and she tensed from head to toe. 'Look at me, *bellezza mia*,' he urged.

Almost involuntarily, Lizzie lifted her head, platinum hair flying back from her heart-shaped face. 'Why?' she said flatly.

Lean brown hands lifted to frame her cheekbones and turn her face up. A muscle pulled taut at the corner of his wide, sensual mouth. 'I want to make a baby with you the normal way. I don't want to use artificial insemination. If we're going to become parents, let's try the natural approach first.'

He had taken her entirely by surprise. Her entire face flamed and even worse the heat darted downward to engulf her whole body. 'But that's not what we agreed.'

'We didn't agree anything. You made a suggestion. I didn't like it but I wasn't prepared to argue about it at that point and turn you off the whole idea of marrying me,' Cesare admitted without hesitation.

His sheer honesty bemused her and then touched her deep. *I want to make a baby with you.* The very words made Lizzie melt and she tried to squash her reaction and deny it. It would not be safe or sensible to have actual sex with Cesare Sabatino because it would smash the barriers she had carefully erected. But the prospect of undergoing some cold scientific procedure in a fertility clinic was, she suddenly appreciated, even less attractive to her.

'I'll think about it,' Lizzie mumbled half under her breath. 'Now, if you don't mind, I'd like to get changed into something more comfortable.'

'I'll go for a shower,' Cesare told her, peeling off his shirt without an ounce of inhibition.

Her heart hammering, Lizzie averted her gaze but the enthralling image of his bronzed, muscular torso was still seared across her vision. She pulled an outfit out of the case, nothing fancy for she had had her fill of fancy outfits that day. She caught an accidental glimpse of Cesare striding naked as the day he was born into the en suite and she almost groaned out loud. They were so different, so ill matched. He had seen it all, done it all, while she had only dreamt of the seeing and the doing. If she slept with him, she would develop feelings for him and she would get hurt because he wouldn't respond. Or maybe she would discover that she was the kind of woman who could have sex without getting more deeply involved, she reasoned abstractedly. She might not get attached to him at all, might be grateful to wave goodbye to him after a few months. How could she know how she would react?

When the shower was free, she made use of it and removed most of the heavy make-up she had worn for her big day. Applying only a dash of lipstick and blusher, she pulled on a stretchy maxi skirt and a sleeveless silk top, thrusting her feet into flat sandals. When she reappeared, a maid was in the bedroom hanging their clothes in the built-in closet and Lizzie went straight downstairs.

Cesare strode out to the marble-floored hall. 'Let me show you around before dinner,' he suggested.

'Where's Archie?' she asked.

Cesare held a finger to his handsome mouth in silencing mode and pointed into the drawing room. Archie was stretched out on a shaggy rug, his contented snores audible.

As dusk was folding in fast, Cesare showed her the outside of the house first. Lizzie stood on the covered stone terrace where Maria was fussing over a table covered in a snowy white cloth and admired the stunning view of the valley, which was overlooked by a superlative infinity pool. 'The views are out of this world. I'm not surprised you fell for this place,' she admitted, the tension of the day slowly seeping out of her.

Without warning, Cesare reached for her hand. 'This marriage can be as real as we want it to be, *bellezza mia*,' he pointed out quietly.

Her fingers flexed within the firm hold of his and her colour heightened. Real didn't mean for ever, did it? But then how many marriages truly lasted for ever? They were together now and would stay together until a child was born. The child she longed for, she reminded herself ruefully. Surely the closer she and Cesare became, the easier it would be to share their child both now and in the future?

Her lips parted almost without her volition, green eyes wide and anxious as if she was stunned by her own daring. 'I'll give it a go,' she told him softly. 'But I can't make any promises.'

Cesare smiled. It was a brilliant smile that illuminated his darkly beautiful features and enhanced his stubborn, passionate mouth. 'I'll try to make sure you don't regret it, *cara*.'

# CHAPTER SIX

'MARIA IS WHIPPING out her entire repertoire for this one meal,' Cesare commented in amusement as the lazy meal wound through course after necessarily dainty course of appetising dishes.

Already unable to credit that she had agreed to try being married for *real*, Lizzie was too stressed to eat much of anything. A bite here and there was the best she could do and she proffered fervent apologies to the plump little cook when she came out to the terrace bearing her *pièce de résistance*, a fabulous layered chocolate cake.

They were about to embark on their marriage as if they were a normal married couple. And this was their *wedding night*. All of a sudden something Lizzie hadn't even had to consider in the run-up to the wedding was looming like a concealed tripwire in front of her. If she admitted that she was still a virgin he was sure to think she was a freak. After all, he knew she had been engaged. It would be better to keep quiet, she decided, and hope he didn't notice that there was anything different about her.

'You've barely touched alcohol today,' Cesare commented, wondering why she had fallen so quiet.

Not that she was ever a chatterbox, he acknowledged wryly. In fact there was always a stillness about her, a sense of tranquillity at the heart of her that was disconcertingly attractive.

'In the light of our…er…plans,' Lizzie muttered awkwardly, 'I thought it was better to abstain.'

'You're referring to the alcohol and pregnancy safety debate?'

*Kill me now,* Lizzie thought melodramatically. 'Yes. The argument about what might be a safe level goes back and forth, so it seems wiser just to avoid it altogether.'

'Is that why you made the most of your hen night?' Cesare asked, strong jawline tensing as he remembered her on the dance floor, full of vital energy and playfulness as she cast off her usual restraint.

'No. That wasn't planned. I missed Chrissie,' she admitted, colouring, 'and it had just been a very long time since I had been out like that and I overindulged.'

'Don't beat yourself up about it,' Cesare urged, stunning dark golden eyes shimmering in the candlelight against his bronzed skin.

He was so…hot, he was literally on fire, Lizzie reflected dizzily. And she was married to him, about to share a bed with him…and she was fretting, shrinking, *sighing* over the fact? What was wrong with her? That chemistry he had mentioned was in overdrive, lighting her up from the inside out with a prickling, tingling energy that her body could no longer contain. In an abrupt movement, she rose from the table and walked to the edge of the terrace to study the lights of the fortified village on the other side of the valley.

Her heart was as locked up tight as that village, hidden behind high defensive walls, she reminded herself bracingly. Having sex with Cesare didn't mean she was about to get silly ideas about him and start pining when he was no longer available. She had watched her mother careen blindly from one man to the next, hooked on love, her drug of choice. Lizzie had loved once and learned her lesson. If she couldn't even make it work with Andrew, there was little chance of it working with anyone else. She would have a baby to love though, she told herself in consolation.

'You're very tense, *cara*.' Cesare sighed, stilling behind her and gently resting his hands on her taut shoulders. Her delicate frame was dwarfed by his. 'You don't have to do anything you don't want to do...'

That he could read her nervous tension that accurately mortified Lizzie. In truth the problem was that she wanted him too much and feared the strength of that yearning. He turned her slowly round into the circle of his arms and she looked up at him and her knees went weak and her heart leapt in helpless response.

'I know that,' she asserted valiantly, wondering why he found the sudden change in their relationship so much easier. Were men just built that way? Was he more adaptable than she was? Or more relaxed at the concept of a marriage in which the only glue keeping them together would be sex and the hope of parenthood? *Just sex, nothing worth fussing over*, he had said after he got out of a bed where he had literally rocked her world. It was true that the only pleasure had been hers but his cold-blooded, practical take on what had happened between them had still knocked her for six. Yet she still couldn't drag her gaze from his beautifully shaped, passionate mouth.

Cesare studied her with veiled eyes, black lashes rimming the glint of smouldering gold. Desire was lancing through him with lightning-force potency, sending tiny ripples of tension through his big, powerful frame. He couldn't take his eyes off her lush mouth and the pouting crowns of her small breasts, which stirred softly below the fine silk of her top every time she shifted position.

It was years since Cesare had been so aware of a woman and he loathed the edgy bite of frustrated hunger that made him tense. He wanted to have sex with her and persuade his libido and his brain that, after all, she was just like any other woman he had bedded. He hadn't been with anyone since the day he had first met her and that bothered him. He hadn't wanted Celine when he'd had the opportunity and no other woman had since attracted his attention. Of course the problem was doubtless that his affair with Celine had run its natural course and left him bored. Lizzie was new and different, which had obvious appeal. There was even something strangely, weirdly sexy about the idea of getting her pregnant. He wasn't sure what it was but he knew that just the thought of it made him hard and ready. Given even the smallest encouragement, he would've ditched Maria's wedding banquet of a meal and headed straight for the bedroom.

Shaking off that foolish thought, Cesare gazed down at his bride with the sudden piquant recognition that she was his wife. *His* legal wife, *his* to have and to hold, *his* to protect. Without further ado, he pulled her close and kissed her, a husky growl sounding in the back of his throat when her firm little breasts brushed against his chest. She liked being carried; he remembered that and smiled. He hoisted her up into his arms and Archie scrambled up from his position of repose by the sun-warmed wall and barked in consternation at the sight of them.

'Keep quiet, Archie,' Cesare groaned. 'You can't come between a man and his wife…and I warn you, Lizzie, he's not sleeping with us tonight or any other night.'

Lizzie was challenged enough to think of sleeping with Cesare and her mouth was still tingling from the hungry pressure of his mouth. As he carried her upstairs she decided that she was turning into a shameless hussy. A gasp escaped her lips when she saw the bedroom, which had been transformed into a bower of candlelight and flowers while they had been dining. Candles flickered light from metal lanterns set round the room and lush vases of pristine white flowers completed the magical effect.

'Did you organise this?' Lizzie asked in wonderment when he settled her down at the foot of the bed.

Cesare laughed. 'No. Maria has waited a long time for me to find a wife and I think she's celebrating.'

Sudden shyness reclaimed Lizzie as he gazed down at her, the lights picking out the hollows below his high cheekbones, lending him an enigmatic quality. In that lambent light, he was truly beautiful, sleek and dark, exotic and compellingly male. With sure hands he pushed her hair back from her face, letting the long, silky strands flow down her back. He tipped up her face and claimed another kiss, feeding from the sweetness of her mouth with hungry fervour, crushing her soft full lips below his while her fingers clung to his shoulders.

'I've been thinking about this from the first moment I saw you,' Cesare growled against her reddened mouth, his dark deep voice vibrating down her spinal cord, the very essence of masculinity.

'You do talk nonsense sometimes and please don't tell me that's a compliment that I should gratefully receive. The first time you saw me I was in my dungarees and looked a complete mess!' Lizzie protested on the back of a rueful laugh.

'There's no accounting for taste or the male libido,' Cesare quipped, impervious to her disagreement. 'I saw your face, your skin, your eyes…it was enough, *delizia mia.*'

'I like it when you talk Italian,' Lizzie confided breathlessly. 'You could be reciting the multiplication tables but it wouldn't matter. It's your accent, your voice, the pitch you use.'

Surprised by that unexpected burst of loquaciousness, Cesare grinned, a slanting wicked grin that utterly transformed his lean, darkly handsome face, wiping away the cool vigilance and control that was usually etched there. 'What I like most about you is that you surprise me all the time.'

'Right now I'm surprising me,' Lizzie told him truthfully, uncertainty darkening her hazel eyes as it crossed her mind that she was behaving impulsively, not something she made a habit of after growing up with an impetuous mother. But then she was *not* her mother, she reminded herself squarely, and at the age of twenty-four was surely old enough to make her own decisions.

He took her mouth in a long, intoxicating kiss and sober thought became too much of a challenge. A ten-

sion of a very different kind began to lace her body.
She became ridiculously conscious of the silk rubbing against her swollen nipples and the dampness at
her feminine core. Her body was responding to the
chemistry between her and Cesare with a life of its
own, blossoming like a flower suddenly brought into
bloom by the sunshine. Only chemistry, *just* sex, she
reflected in an abbreviated fashion as she warded off
her insecurities. There was nothing to fear, nothing
to be ashamed of, nothing she need avoid to protect
herself. Dimly she was registering at some level of her
brain that her mother's disastrous affairs had made her
far too reluctant to take a risk on a man.

Her silk top fell in a colourful splash of silk to the
wooden floor and, with a ragged sigh of appreciation,
Cesare closed his hands to the pert swell of her breasts,
his thumbs expertly capturing and massaging the pro-
truding pink peaks until they were taut and throbbing
and the very breath was catching in her tightening
throat. Her hips dug into the mattress beneath her,
seeking to sate the hollow ache tugging at her pelvis.

One-handed, he wrenched at his shirt. 'You see
how I forget what I'm doing when I'm with you, *delizia mia*?' he rasped.

Lizzie only needed that invitation and she tugged
at his shirt, delicate fingers stroking over his taut,
muscular shoulders, adoring the heat and strength of
him. He put his mouth to her neck and skimmed the
tip of his tongue along her delicate collarbone and
then, gently lowering her flat on the bed, he roamed
down over her ribcage, sending delicious little jolts of
desire through her each time he captured the tender
peaks of her breasts.

Passion had claimed Lizzie. Her temperature was rocketing higher and higher, a sheen of perspiration on her brow, and her heart was hammering so fast it felt as if it were at the foot of her throat. Her hand delving into his luxuriant black hair, she pulled him up to her and kissed him with all the urgent hunger racing through her. He pushed her skirt up above her knees and trailed his fingers slowly up her inner thighs. Every inch of her felt stretched taut with the extreme wanting that had taken her over and she gritted her teeth as he anchored his fingers to her knickers and trailed them off. She wanted his touch so bad it hurt and she squirmed in a fever of need.

'I'm trying to go slow,' Cesare bit out raggedly, 'but I feel like an express train.'

'Talking too much,' she told him, her teeth chattering together at the unwelcome pause.

With an almighty effort, Cesare stepped back from the source of temptation. Haste wasn't cool, especially not the first time. He didn't think a woman had ever responded with that much passion to him and it was setting him on fire with overriding need. He told her that in Italian and she gave him a blissful smile, evidently glorying in the sound of his language or his voice or whatever it was that she liked. He stripped off the shirt, unzipped his chinos, pushed off everything in one urgent forceful assault on his clothing. Naked, he came back to her, revelling in the way her eyes locked to him and the sudden blush that warmed her porcelain complexion. He couldn't recall when he had last been with a woman who blushed. And in the bedroom? Never.

Lizzie was transfixed. There he was in all his

glory, her every piece of curiosity answered in one fell swoop. He scooped her up in his arms, pulled off the skirt that was her only remaining garment and settled her down, equally naked, in the centre of the turned-back bed.

Lizzie froze. 'I think we need to put out the candles!' she exclaimed, her entire body burning with embarrassment as she grasped in desperation for the sheet, which was out of reach.

In the very act of surveying her pale slender curves with rapt attention Cesare raised stunning golden eyes to study her in growing wonderment. 'I've already seen you naked,' he reminded her gently.

'That's different…I was too hung-over to be shy!' Lizzie pointed out loudly.

Cesare grinned and with a stretch of a long brown arm flipped up the sheet. 'This is not likely to hold me back,' he warned her.

As the cool cotton settled over her quivering length Lizzie lost some of her tension. Resting on one arm, she found Cesare gazing down at her with slumberous dark golden eyes. He rubbed a slightly stubbled jaw against her cheek in a sensual gesture on his path to her ready mouth.

One kiss melted into the next but as his hands roved skilfully over her, lingering on pulse points and teasing erogenous zones, lying still beneath his ministrations became tougher and tougher. Her nipples throbbed from his attentions, sending arrows of fire down to the tender, pulsing heart of her.

He stroked her and her spine arched. 'You're so wet, so ready for me,' Cesare husked.

A tiny shiver racked her slight frame, all the heat

coalescing in the swollen, delicate tissue between her thighs. She squeezed her eyes tight shut, striving to stay in control and not betray how new it all was to her. But with every ravishing caress, he seduced her away from control. Soft gasps parted her lips, her neck extending, tendons clenching as the stimulation became almost too much to bear.

'You know this will be a first for me, *cara*,' Cesare confided, running the tip of his tongue across a turgid rose-pink nipple.

Lizzie could hardly find her voice. 'What will?'

'Sex without a condom...I've never done that before and it excites me,' he admitted huskily, shifting against her thigh, letting her feel the smooth, hard length of his erection.

Lizzie was trying not to think about the size of him in that department. She was a modern woman, well acquainted with averages and gossip and popular report. Being a virgin didn't mean she was entirely ignorant, she told herself in consolation, striving not to stress as her excitement built and built. Hands biting into his strong shoulders, she lifted her hips upward, succumbing to an almost uncontrollable urge to get closer to him. He toyed with her lush, damp opening, honeyed quivers of sensations rippling through her womb, and circled the tiny bud of her arousal until almost without warning a wild, seething force of irresistible sensation engulfed her like a flood. Her eyes flew wide and she bucked and jerked and sobbed in the grip of rush after rush of intense and enthralling pleasure.

He tipped her up, hooking her legs over his shoulders in a move that unnerved her. He plunged into her tight channel and for a moment she was preoccupied with the sense of fullness, the certain knowledge that this was exactly what her body had craved throughout his teasing foreplay. In fact everything was wonderful until the hot glide of his flesh within hers sank deeper and a sudden sharp, tearing pain made her stiffen and cry out in dismay.

Cesare froze as though a fire alarm had gone off and stared down at her, dark golden eyes like hungry golden flames in his lean bronzed face. 'You *can't* be…'

Enraged by her own bodily weakness and chagrin, Lizzie dealt him a look that would have dropped a grizzly bear at ten paces. 'Well, don't stop now.'

'You're a *virgin*?' Cesare emphasised, his incredulity unconcealed as he held himself at an angle above her, muscles straining in his bulging forearms.

'How's that your business?' Lizzie slung back argumentatively.

Cesare swore long and low in his own language and cursed her stubbornness. He burned for her but he was fighting his hunger with all his might. It struck him as unjust that the hot, tight hold of her body on his gave him pure pleasure while she had only experienced pure pain.

'It's my business,' he told her grimly. 'I think this is my cue to back off.'

'No… No!' Lizzie exclaimed in consternation. 'You don't get to go that far and then *stop*… I want to know what it's like…'

In receipt of that plaintive plea, Cesare groaned out loud, belatedly recognising that marriage was proving a much bigger challenge than he had expected.

She was experimenting with him, he thought in all-male horror.

'*Please...*' Lizzie added, tugging him down to her, pale fingers framing his cheekbones as she reached without success for his beautiful, passionate mouth.

In the mood to be easily encouraged, Cesare shifted his hips, his entire attention nailed to her flushed and expressive face so that he could register the smallest wince she might make. Instead Lizzie smiled up at him with a look of wonderment that was uniquely soothing to his momentarily threatened male ego.

Lizzie closed her eyes again, mortified at the fuss she had made, the lengths she had had to go to to persuade him to continue. She had always believed that a man found it hard to stop in the middle of sex, so the fact that he had offered to withdraw altogether did not strike her as a compliment. But she had wanted to know, had wanted so badly to know what all the fuss was about.

He moved against her and tingling, driving sensation awakened in her pelvis again. She relaxed a little. The slow, almost provocative thrusts became enticing and she relaxed completely, indeed began to arch up to greet him with an enthusiasm she had never expected to feel. His skilled acceleration delivered sensation like nothing she had ever experienced and her excitement soared to delirious heights that climbed and climbed until she reached a peak and soared effortlessly over it and then down and down into the cocoon of lethargy and satiation, exhaustion pulling at her every sense.

Cesare settled her back down on the pillows and smoothed her tangled hair off her damp brow. His hand trembled a little because he was struggling to do two opposing things: firstly treat Lizzie like the bride she was and, secondly, suppress the anger tearing at him. 'Why didn't you tell me I'd be your first lover?' he demanded in a roughened undertone.

His tone, his exasperation, cut through Lizzie in her sensitive state like the sudden painful slice of a knife and she sat up abruptly, clutching the sheet to her chest. 'I didn't see that it was anything to do with you.'

'In other words, you chose to deliberately conceal it,' he condemned, leaping out of bed in one lithe, powerful movement. 'How the hell could you still be a virgin when you were once engaged?'

'Don't you dare raise your voice to me, Cesare Sabatino!' Lizzie yelled back at him furiously, but she was trembling with an innate fear she could not have expressed at that moment. 'As for why I was still a virgin, that's private.'

'You're married to me now, *cara*. I don't think it's unreasonable of me to expect an answer to something so basic.'

'When you have the right to ask me private questions, I'll let you know,' Lizzie slung back flatly, snaking out of the far side of the bed to avoid him and yanking the sheet free of the mattress with a violent jerk to wrap it round her body. 'Now, I'm going for a bath.'

'*Lizzie...*' Cesare ground out in frustration to her rigid back as she reached for the door of the en suite.

'I'm not feeling nice, *wifely* or the slightest bit chatty right now, so please excuse me,' Lizzie breathed icily and stepped into the bathroom, shutting and locking the door behind her within seconds.

Lizzie filled the glorious antique bath to the brim, filled it with bubbles and lowered her body into the warm water. Angry, Cesare could be incredibly intimidating, towering over her, dark eyes glowing with hostility in his lean dark face. She couldn't help that her first reaction to an angry man was to run to the nearest place of safety. Her mother's violent second husband had taught her to get herself and Chrissie out of harm's way fast.

But Lizzie refused to *be* intimidated by Cesare, whom she sensed would never be violent. What did he have to be so angry about? Hadn't their lovemaking been good for him? It had certainly been good for her, apart from the hiccup as such in the middle when she had discovered that her first experience of intimacy could actually be painful. Ironically she was more hurt by Cesare's withdrawal and grim mood in the aftermath, which had made her feel—all over again—inadequate. Why couldn't he have simply let the subject go? Had he no sensitivity? Couldn't he see that she didn't want to talk about it?

Cesare paced the bedroom in fierce frustration. Why hadn't she warned him? Had she been embarrassed about being untouched? He recalled the blushing and gritted his teeth, acknowledging that he was totally unfit to deal with sexual innocence when he had failed to recognise it even though it was right there in front of him. He had screwed up, screwed up even worse when he sprang an immediate interrogation on her.

This was not how he had pictured their marriage kicking off. She was all emotional now, very probably weeping in the bath and regretting their new agreement while wishing she had never laid eyes on him. And yet the sex had been amazing...so amazing he couldn't wait to repeat it. Galvanised into motion by that shameless motivation, Cesare threw on a disreputable pair of jeans and padded downstairs, pondering possibilities to redeem himself in his offended bride's eyes. Before he even got that far he heard the distant howls of Archie marooned in an outside kennel and he grinned at the sound. He was a very clever man and he would turn the wedding-night breakdown back into a honeymoon regardless of what sacrifices it demanded of him!

Archie broke off his cries mid-howl and pranced towards him on three little legs. Archie was not particularly attached to Cesare but he recognised him as a potential lead to his mistress...

# CHAPTER SEVEN

ARCHIE WHIMPERED OUTSIDE the bathroom door.

'You know you can do better than that,' Cesare told him, tossing him a fragment of chicken from one of the plates on the table by the bed.

For a three-legged dog, Archie could move fast and he caught the scrap in mid-air.

'Now…you have a mission,' Cesare reminded the scruffy little animal. 'You get her out of the bathroom.'

Archie hovered by the door, tried to push it but the balloon collar round his neck got in the way. Sitting back on his haunches, Archie loosed a sad howl that would not have shamed a banshee. Cesare threw him another piece of succulent chicken in reward. Archie gave a grand performance.

Lizzie woke up feeling cold, water sloshing noisily around her as she sat up wide-eyed. Archie was howling at the door…or had that just been a dream? Clambering hastily out of the bath, she snatched up a fleecy towel and wrapped herself in it, just as Archie howled again. Glancing at the watch on the vanity to see how long she had slept, she was taken aback to realise that a couple of hours had passed and that it was now almost one in the morning. Depressing the lock, she opened the door in haste.

'Oh, pet, I forgot about you! Have you been lonely?' Lizzie asked, squatting down to the little dog's level.

'Want some supper?' Cesare asked lazily from the bed on which he reclined.

Small bosom swelling at that insouciant tone, Lizzie was about to tell him in no short order what he could do with supper and then her tummy growled and she registered in surprise that she was actually very hungry. Of course, she hadn't eaten very much at dinner…

Straightening, she looped her damp hair back behind her ear and focused on Cesare's lean, darkly devastating face, clashing with the banked-down glitter of his stunning eyes. 'You still want answers, don't you?'

'I'd be a liar if I said otherwise,' he admitted, sprawling back with his hands linked behind his head, a position which only threw into prominence the muscular torso and flat ribbed stomach beneath his black T-shirt.

Lizzie breathed in slowly, belatedly registering the table of snacks by the bed and the candles that must have been relit while she slept. A surprising sense of calm after the storm enclosed her. The worst had already happened, hadn't it? What did she have to fear now? Not marriage, not sex, she decided, her chin coming up. Cesare had…*briefly*…scared her but that wasn't his fault. No, that fault could be laid at the door of her late mother's misjudgement of men and a stepfather who had given Lizzie nightmares long after he had passed out of her life.

'You know, when you got so angry, you scared me,' she told him baldly. 'My mother was married to a man who beat her up when he got angry.'

Cesare sprang off the bed, a frown pleating his ebony brows. 'I would never hurt you.'

'I think I know that already,' Lizzie said quietly. 'But running is still a reflex for me when men get angry. I can't help it. The two years Mum was married to that man were terrifying for Chrissie and me.'

'Did he hit you as well?' Cesare growled in disgust, appalled that he could have, however unwittingly, frightened her.

'He tried to a couple of times but he was drunk and clumsy and we were fast on our feet,' Lizzie confided. 'Let's not talk about it. It's in the past. But I should make one thing clear...' She hesitated. 'I'm only willing to talk about Andrew if you're willing to talk about Serafina.'

'And exactly who has been talking to you?' Cesare demanded, a muscle pulling taut at the corner of his stern, handsome mouth.

'Your grandmother mentioned her...and I'm curious too,' Lizzie confessed while she walked into the dressing room in search of a nightdress. Shedding the towel behind the door, she slipped it on, catching a glimpse of herself in a tall mirror. What remained of her fake glamour had evaporated in the long bath she had taken. The moist atmosphere had added frizz to her formerly smooth tresses and she suppressed a sigh. Cesare was getting the *real* Lizzie Whitaker on this particular night.

Emerging from the dressing room with Archie at her heels, she tried not to visibly shrink from Cesare's acute appraisal. The silk nightie was long and, to her, the very antithesis of sexy because it revealed neither leg nor cleavage. Her face coloured as she stilled for a split second, disturbingly aware of the intensity of that assessment from his smouldering dark golden eyes. A wave of heat shimmied over her, settling at the tips of her breasts and between her thighs in a tingling, throbbing awareness that mortified her. She knew he was thinking about sex. She also knew that he was making *her* think about sex. And she didn't know how he did it. Hormonal awareness was like an invisible electric current lacing the atmosphere.

Cesare watched the candlelight throw Lizzie's slender legs into view behind the thin silk and his mouth ran dry while the rest of him ran hot and heavy. Her pert breasts shimmying below the material in the most stimulating way, she curled up at the foot of the bed and reached for a plate of snacks. 'So, who goes first?'

'I will,' Cesare surprised himself by saying. Although he had initially been disconcerted by her demand he was now more amused that she should want to travel that far back into his past. It simply irritated him, though, that his grandmother was willing to credit that a youthful love affair gone wrong could still have any influence over him.

'Serafina…it's a beautiful name,' Lizzie remarked thoughtfully.

'She is very beautiful,' Cesare admitted, quietly contemplative as he sprawled back indolently against the headboard of the bed. 'We were students together. I was doing business, she was doing business law. It was first love, all very intense stuff.'

Lizzie watched him grimace at that admission. 'My first love was a poster of a boy-band member on the wall,' she confided in some embarrassment.

'A poster would've been a safer option for me. I fell hard and fast and I wanted to marry Serafina. She said we were too young and she was right,' he conceded wryly. 'She was always ambitious and I assumed that I'd have to start at the bottom of the business ladder. But then I made a stock-market killing and took over my first company and my prospects improved. Serafina started work at an upmarket legal practice with some very rich...and influential clients...'

'And at that point, you were still together?' Lizzie prompted when the silence dragged, his delivery becoming noticeably less smooth.

'Very much so. We were living together. Second week in her new job, Serafina met Matteo Ruffini and he invited her out to dinner with a view to offering her the opportunity to work on his substantial account.' His beautiful mouth took on a sardonic slant. 'Suddenly she became unavailable to me, working late in the evening, too busy to join me for lunch.'

His tension was unhidden. Lizzie registered that Serafina had hurt him and hurt him deep because he still couldn't talk about the woman with indifference. 'She was seeing Matteo?'

'*Sì*...and the moment *Prince* Matteo proposed, I was history. He had everything she had ever wanted. Social position, a title and immense wealth. The only flaw in his perfection was that she was twenty-five and he was seventy-five.'

'Good grief! That's a huge age gap!' Lizzie exclaimed. 'Did she tell you she'd fallen in love with him?'

'No. Possibly that would have been easier to accept, if not believe. No, she told me that he was just too good a catch to turn down and that if she contrived to give him a son and heir, she'd be rich and blessed for the rest of her life,' Cesare breathed with derision. 'I realised I'd never really known her. It crushed my faith in women.'

'Of course it did,' Lizzie agreed, the nails of one hand biting into her palm while odd disconnected emotions flailed her, particularly when she found herself thinking aggressive thoughts about the woman who had broken Cesare's heart. She had read him *so* wrong when they first met. He had been prepared to leap into the commitment and responsibility of marriage at a very young age. Clearly, he had genuinely loved Serafina and yet she had betrayed him in the worst possible way when she chose a life of rich privilege over love.

'Andrew?' Cesare pressed in turn.

'He was my best friend growing up. We had so much in common we should've been a perfect match and we stayed great friends although he never actually asked me out until I was in my twenties. I was already in love with him…at least I *thought* it was love,' she said ruefully. 'Everybody assumed we would be great together and when he asked me to marry him, Dad was ecstatic. I said yes but I wanted us to just date for a while.' Her face paling, she studied her tightly clasped hands. 'It was in private that Andrew and I didn't work out.'

'Obviously you didn't sleep with him,' Cesare murmured softly, watching the fragile bones of her face tighten, the vulnerable curve of her mouth tense, feeling his own chest tighten in response.

'No, I just didn't want to sleep with him,' she admitted in an awkward rush. 'I froze every time he got close and he said I was frigid but I didn't find him attractive that way. I thought I had a real problem with being touched. That's why I wouldn't date anyone after him and why I never blamed him for turning to Esther.'

'You don't have *any* kind of a problem,' Cesare asserted with quiet confidence. 'You were inexperienced; maybe he was as well—'

'No,' Lizzie broke in, running back through her memories while remembered feelings of inadequacy and regret engulfed her.

Yet even before she had fallen asleep in the bath she had realised that her enjoyment of Cesare's attentions had shed a comforting light on the past, which had always troubled her. Her only *real* problem with Andrew had been that he had always felt like the brother she had never had. She could see things as they had been now, not as she might have wished them to be: sadly, there had been zero sexual attraction on her side. She had sincerely cared for Andrew but he had always felt more like a good friend than a potential lover. When she compared how she had reacted from the first moment with Cesare, she could clearly see the difference and finally understand that what had happened with Andrew was not her fault.

'I liked and appreciated him but I never wanted him that way,' Lizzie admitted with regret. 'I still feel guilty about it because I was too inexperienced to realise that he was just the wrong man for me…and my rejections hurt him.'

'He seems happy enough now.' Cesare toyed with another piece of chicken.

Encouraged to think that further treats were in the pipeline, Archie got up on his haunches and begged.

'Oh, my goodness, look what he's doing!' Lizzie exclaimed, sitting forward with wide eyes to watch her pet. 'He can beg…I didn't even know he could *do* that.'

Cesare rewarded Archie with the chicken because he had made his mistress smile and laugh.

'Of course, I've never fed him like that. If he'd come to me for food when I was eating my father would have called that bad behaviour and he would have blamed Archie. I kept Archie outside most of the time.'

'I suspect Archie would've been clever enough to keep a low profile around your dad,' Cesare surmised.

'Did you ever have a pet?'

'I would have liked one when I was a kid,' Cesare confided. 'But I was constantly moving between my grandmother's home and Goffredo's apartment and a pet wasn't viable.'

'Did you organise all this food?' she asked, smothering a yawn.

'The staff are in bed. I don't expect service here late at night,' he told her quietly. 'I emptied the refrigerator.'

'And let Archie up to lure me out of the bathroom,' Lizzie guessed, settling their discarded plates on the low table and clambering in the far side of the bed to say apologetically, 'I'm tired.'

'Brides aren't supposed to get tired, particularly not when they've been lazing in the bath for hours,' Cesare informed her, amusement dancing in his dark golden eyes.

He could still steal her breath away at one glance, she acknowledged wearily as she closed her eyes. It was, as he had termed it, 'just sex' and she had to learn to see that side of their relationship in the same casual light. She wondered if that would be a challenge because she was already drifting dangerously close to liking him.

'Archie can sleep under the bed,' Cesare decreed. 'He's not sharing it with us.'

'We can't do anything, you know,' she muttered in a sudden embarrassed surge, her cheeks colouring. 'I'm…I'm sore…'

'It's not a problem.'

Relieved, she smiled and closed her eyes. As he stripped by the side of the bed Cesare studied her relaxed features and thought, *Mission accomplished, honeymoon back on track*. It was the same way he handled problems at work, mentally ticking off items on a to-do list while always seeking the most successful conclusion. But as he slid into bed beside Lizzie he reached for her and it wasn't a pre-programmed task. He reasoned that she was a very restless sleeper and if he left her free to move around she would annoy him.

Strangely enough, he acknowledged, in spite of the bathroom shenanigans, she hadn't annoyed him once. But then she wasn't the greedy, grasping type of woman he had deemed her to be. Why had he been so biased? After all, he had a stepmother, a grandmother and three sisters, none of whom were rich *or*

avaricious. Had he deliberately sought out lovers who
only cared about his wealth? And if he was guilty of
that, had it been because he genuinely only needed
carefree sex with a woman? Or because he preferred
to avoid the possibility of anything more serious developing? Almost ten years had passed since Serafina had waltzed down the aisle to her prince. He
refused to think that she had burned him so badly
that he had declined to risk getting deeply involved
with anyone else. Yet he hadn't even got an engagement or a live-in relationship under his belt during
those ten long years.

In the darkness, Cesare's wide, sensual mouth
framed a silent but vehemently felt swear word. He
did not appreciate the oddity of having such thoughts
about the sort of thing he had never ever felt the need
to think about before. It was that ring on his wedding finger that was getting to him, he brooded impatiently. It was feeling married and possibly just a
tiny bit trapped...with Archie snoring beside the bed
and Lizzie nestled up against him like a second skin.

Just like him, she was in this marriage for the end
game and the prize, he reminded himself squarely.
It wasn't a normal marriage but, if they planned to
conceive a child, the marriage had to work on a daily
basis and why should physical intimacy always lead
to a closer involvement than he wanted? The answer
was that sex didn't need to lead to anything more complex, he reminded himself stubbornly, certainly nothing that would break his rules of never getting more
closely involved with a woman. And it was no wonder
that he was feeling unsettled when he was in such unfamiliar territory. He hadn't tried to please a woman

since Serafina and he wasn't going to make a fool of himself trying to please Lizzie, was he?

Archie's snores filtered up in direct disagreement.

# CHAPTER EIGHT

CESARE GLANCED AT his wife and then at the party of
men watching her every move in a pantomime version
of dropped jaws as she alighted from his Ferrari. She
was a lissom figure in a turquoise sundress, her gorgeous silvery mane blowing back from her delicately
flushed face in the breeze, her shapely legs tapering
down to impossibly delicate ankles and high-heeled
sandals. He pushed up his sunglasses and gave the men
a warning look before closing his hand round Lizzie's
in a display of all-Italian male possessiveness that he
could not resist.

Lizzie sank down at the table in the *piazza* and
the waiter was at their side within seconds, doubtless
drawn by one glimpse of Cesare's sleek sophistication. He had an air of hauteur and command that got
them fast service everywhere they went and it was so
inbred in him to expect immediate attention that he
rarely even noticed the fact, although she was very
sure he would notice if he didn't receive it.

Now she feasted her attention on his lean bronzed
face. She was magnetised by his stunning dark golden
eyes as they rested on her and wondered what he was
thinking. She was *always* wondering what he was

thinking, had to bite her tongue not to ask, but it was hardly surprising that she was living in a state of constant befuddlement because their business-based marriage of convenience had become something else entirely…at least for *her*…

They had now been in Italy for a solid month. Cesare had made several business trips. He had flown his family *and* Chrissie in to visit for one weekend and the two days had passed in a whirlwind of chattering liveliness and warmth. Lizzie had never been so happy before and it scared her because she knew she was nourishing hopes that would ultimately lead to disappointment and the stark biting pain of rejection. *What? Only possibly?* jibed her more truthful self. Lizzie's emotions had got involved the very first night they'd slept together and she'd wakened in the morning to find herself secure in Cesare's arms.

For four whole weeks she had been living an idyllic life with an attentive husband, who was also a passionate lover, by her side. He had taken her out sightseeing, shopping, out to dinner in sun-baked *piazzas*, fashionable squares, and to wander through old churches lit by candles and the sunlight piercing the stained-glass windows. Today they had walked the seventeenth-century ramparts of Lucca. Her fingers toyed momentarily with the slender gold watch encircling her wrist, her most recent gift. If he went on a trip or even noticed that she lacked something he considered essential, he bought it for her. He was incredibly generous in bed and out of it. He was curious about her, knew everything there was to know about her childhood. His interest was intoxicating because she had never seen herself as being particularly interesting.

In fact, being the focus of attention of a very handsome, entertaining male had made her see herself in a kinder, warmer light.

In truth, when Cesare Sabatino was faking being a husband, he faked with the skill and panache of a professional, she conceded ruefully. He hadn't asked her to fall in love with him. It wouldn't occur to him that bringing an ordinary woman out to beautiful Tuscany and treating her like a much appreciated, highly desirable wife while keeping her in luxury might turn her head. But Lizzie knew her head had been thoroughly turned. She found him fascinating. He was a spellbinding mix of rapier-sharp intellect and disconcerting emotional depth and, of course, she had fallen head over heels for him. Archie now rejoiced in a collar with his name picked out in diamonds and a fourposter bed of his own. How could she *not* love the man who had given her adored pet those quite unnecessary, ridiculously expensive but deeply touching things?

And the result was that now she was terrified of falling pregnant, fearing that that announcement would ensure that their marriage cooled back down to a businesslike arrangement in which Cesare would expect her to be terribly civilised and behave as if she didn't give a damn about him. Within days of the wedding she had had the proof that she had not yet conceived and Cesare had just laughed and said that they had all the time in the world, as if it truly didn't matter to him if it took months to reach that goal.

'What if there's something wrong with one of us and it doesn't happen?' she had asked him anxiously.

He had shrugged and suggested that they give it a year before seeking medical advice. If for some reason having a child turned out not to be possible, they would deal with it when it happened, Cesare had told her fatalistically while urging her not to stress about getting pregnant.

'I hope you've got something special lined up to wear tonight,' Cesare mused over their wine. 'It's a real fashion parade.'

'I thought it was a charity do.'

'In Italy such events are always fashion parades.'

'I have at least four long dresses to choose from,' Lizzie reminded him. 'I won't let you down. Don't worry about it.'

'*Ma no*…certainly not,' Cesare cut in, stroking a long forefinger soothingly over her hand where it curled on the table top. 'You always look fantastic, *gioia mia*. Why would I be worried about you letting me down?'

'I'm not part of your world and I never will be. It's a challenge for me to put on fancy clothes and pretend I'm something I'm not,' Lizzie admitted in an undertone.

'You only need to be yourself. You have two, no, three…' he adjusted reflectively, amusement gleaming in his gilded gaze '…advantages.'

'Which are?'

'Beauty and class and my ring on your finger,' Cesare completed with cynical cool. 'I'm a powerful man. You will be treated with respect and courtesy.'

An involuntary grin lit up Lizzie's face and she laughed, biting back foolish words of love. What an embarrassment it would be if she were to lose control of her tongue around him now! After all, he was playing a very sophisticated game with her, utilising his

charm and a whole host of other extraordinary gifts
to make their marriage work as if it were a real marriage. If she were to suddenly confess how she felt
about him, he would be embarrassed and appalled to
learn that she didn't know how to play the same game.

'We should head back soon,' she commented unevenly.

'Would that leave us time for an hour or so in bed?'
Cesare sprang upright, dropping a large-denomination
note down on top of the bill, smouldering dark eyes
flashing over her with a sexual intensity that never
failed to thrill.

*'Again?'* There was a slight gasp in her low-pitched
response because she had yet to adapt to Cesare's high-
voltage libido. He seemed to want her all the time, no
matter where she was, no matter what she was wearing or what she was doing. She thought he was possibly a little oversexed but she didn't complain because
she always wanted him too and, in any case, the whole
point of their marriage was for her to conceive a child.

A light hand resting in the shallow indentation of
her spine, Cesare urged her back to the Ferrari. As she
clambered in beside him he turned his head and closed
a hard hand into the tumble of her hair to hold her fast
while he kissed her. His mouth was hungry and hot
and erotic on hers and every sense was on overdrive
by the time he freed her again and started up the car.

The air conditioning cooled her overheated skin
but the ache throbbing between her thighs was far less
controllable. Cesare skimmed up her skirt to bare her
thighs. 'I like looking at your legs, especially when I
know I'm about to part them,' he husked soft and low,
laughing when her cheeks flamed.

Early evening, Lizzie inspected her reflection in a black shimmering dress that delineated her slender figure with a spare elegance that appealed to her. She was learning what she liked and didn't like in her wardrobe and she didn't like fussy trims or frills or neon-bright colours that seemed to swallow her alive.

Warmth speckled her cheeks as she thought about the intimacy of the late-afternoon hours. She moved slowly in her heels, a touch of tenderness at the heart of her reminding her of Cesare's passionate energy between the sheets. In bed, sensual excitement ruled her entirely and she was enjoying every moment of exploring that brave new world.

Even so the image that lingered longest was of Cesare, lithe and bronzed and breathtakingly beautiful, relaxing back against the tumbled pillows and finally admitting how very relieved he was that Athene was now well on the road to recovery, having initially suffered a setback in the aftermath of her cardiac surgery. For days, he had tried to pretend he wasn't worried sick even though Lizzie had watched him freeze at every phone call, fearful of receiving bad news. That he had finally abandoned that macho pretence of unconcern to share his true feelings with Lizzie had meant a lot to her. She valued the little signs that revealed that Cesare was behaving more and more like one half of a couple rather than an independent, entirely separate entity. They had visited his grandmother in her convalescent clinic in Rome several times and Athene's sparkling personality even in a hospital bed and her strong affection for Cesare had touched Lizzie's heart.

In the morning they were flying out to Lionos and

one day after that Athene was coming out to join them.
Cesare had married Lizzie purely to gain that right to
bring his grandmother out for a stay on the island and
Lizzie regularly reminded herself of that unflattering
reality. But she was looking forward almost as much as
Athene was to seeing Lionos, which the older woman
had described in such charmed terms. She only hoped
that the enhancements engineered by the imperturbable Primo lived up to Cesare's expectations.

A limousine ferried Cesare and Lizzie to the venue
for the charity benefit in Florence. It was being held
in a vast mansion with every window lit and crowds
of paparazzi waiting on the pavement to take photographs of the guests arriving. Lizzie froze in surprise
when they were targeted, belatedly appreciating that
she was married to a male who, when in his home-
land, received the attention worthy of a celebrity for
his looks and spectacular business accomplishments.

'Did you enjoy having your photo taken?' Cesare
asked.

'No, not at all. I didn't feel glossy enough for the
occasion,' she confided.

'But you spent ages getting ready,' Cesare countered with all the incomprehension of a male who had
merely showered and shaved before donning a dinner jacket.

Her hazel gaze roving swiftly over the level of extreme grooming clearly practised by the other female
guests, Lizzie suppressed a rueful sigh. She didn't
look perfect and she knew it, reckoned she should
have foreseen that the attentions of a hairstylist and a
make-up artist would be necessary. But then how important was her image to Cesare? Did he really care?

Or would he soon be comparing her, to her detriment, to the women who had preceded her in his bed? Lizzie had done her homework on the Internet and she was uneasily aware that in recent years Cesare had spent a lot of time in the company of fashion and beauty models, invariably the very image of feminine perfection. Possibly she needed to make more of an effort, she conceded, uncomfortable with the comparisons she was making.

As they were surrounded by the leading lights in the charity committee of which Cesare was a director, the crowd parted and an exquisite brunette, wearing a very fitted pink dress overlaid with a see-through chiffon layer that simply accentuated her stupendous curves, approached them. Cesare performed the introduction. 'Our hostess, Princess Serafina Ruffini… Serafina, my wife, Lizzie.'

'Welcome to my home, Lizzie.' Serafina air kissed her on both cheeks and gave her a wide, seemingly sincere smile.

Shock winged through Lizzie and she was furious that Cesare hadn't warned her that the benefit was being held at his former girlfriend's home. Impervious to her mood and the manner in which her hand clenched tensely on his arm, Cesare talked about cancer research to an older man who seemed to be a doctor while Lizzie made awkward conversation with his wife, who spoke very little English. Italian lessons were going to be a must in the near future, Lizzie promised herself. Her attention crept back to Serafina, holding court on the other side of the room with a lively group who frequently broke into laughter.

Cesare had described his ex as *very* beautiful and

he had not been kidding. Serafina had almond-shaped dark eyes, skin like clotted cream, a wealth of dark tumbling curls and one of those enviable cupid's-bow scarlet mouths that men always seemed to go mad for. And, more worryingly, Serafina appeared to move in the same social milieu as Cesare, possibly to the extent that Cesare had not even felt it necessary to mention that Lizzie would be meeting her that very evening. For goodness' sake, he broke up with her almost ten years ago, Lizzie reminded herself impatiently. How likely was it that he was still hankering after what he had lost?

In conversation with one of the organisers, who spoke great English, Lizzie learned how indebted the charity felt to Serafina, not only for her recent decision to become their patroness but also for allowing her magnificent home to be used for a fundraising benefit. La Principessa, she learned, was worth a small fortune to the charity in terms of the PR and publicity she would bring their cause, which was raising sufficient funds to open a new hospice for terminally ill children.

It was very warm in the crowded room and perspiration began to bead on Lizzie's brow. She glanced longingly across the room to where several sets of doors stood open onto an outside terrace. As she stood there, a glass of water clasped in one hand, a sick sensation composed of both dizziness and nausea washed over her, leaving her pale.

'Excuse me, I'm warm and I think I'll step outside for a few minutes,' she told her companion and turned away, wondering if she should be taking refuge in the cloakroom instead, but praying that the cooler night air would revive her.

The terrace was furnished with tables and chairs, and lights and candles held the darkness at bay. Lizzie took a seat, gratefully feeling the clamminess of her skin and the faint sickness recede again and breathing the fresh air in deep while she wondered if she was simply tired or if, indeed, she could be in the very earliest stage of a pregnancy. Wonder at that faint suspicion curved her mouth into a ready smile but delight at the prospect was swiftly tempered by fear of what such a development might mean to her relationship with Cesare. Would he back off from their current intimacy? Would he stop treating her like a real wife?

'I saw you come outside,' a female voice said lightly. 'I thought we should get acquainted. I've known Cesare for so many years,' Serafina Ruffini told her with apparent warmth. 'You haven't been married long, have you?'

'No, only for a month,' Lizzie admitted, struggling to maintain her relaxed attitude in the face of Serafina's shrewdly assessing gaze.

'My husband, Matteo, passed away last year. I'm fortunate to have my seven-year-old son to comfort me,' Serafina confided.

'I'm sorry for your loss,' Lizzie murmured, guiltily dismayed at the news that the brunette was a widow. 'It must be hard for you and your son.'

'We're getting used to being a twosome.' Serafina signalled a waiter hovering by the door with an imperious gesture wholly in keeping with her rather royal air of command. 'Champagne?'

'No, thanks.' Lizzie smoothed a fingertip round the

rim of her glass of water while smiling valiantly as the brunette continued to watch her closely.

The champagne was served with a flourish. Serafina leant back in her upholstered seat. 'Of course, you'll know about my history with Cesare…'

Lizzie stiffened. 'Yes.'

'How honest can I be with you?'

'As honest as you like but I don't think Cesare would like us talking about him behind his back,' Lizzie opined quietly.

'He's an Italian male with a healthy ego.' Serafina laughed. 'Being wanted and appreciated by women is the bread of life for him.'

'Is that why you didn't marry him?' Lizzie heard herself ask helplessly. 'You believed he would be a womaniser?'

'No, not at all. I married for security. I didn't grow up like Cesare in a comfortable middle-class home,' Serafina confided, startling Lizzie with her frankness. 'I came from a poor background and worked very hard for everything I got and I had a great fear of being poor again. Matteo was a proven success while Cesare was only starting out in the business world. I loved Cesare but I'm afraid that the security which Matteo offered me was irresistible.'

Thoroughly disconcerted by that unembarrassed explanation, Lizzie murmured without expression, 'You made the right decision for you.'

Serafina saluted her with her glass in gratitude. 'I believe that I did but once I saw how well Cesare was doing in business, I naturally wished I had had more faith in him.'

'I expect you did,' Lizzie conceded tautly. 'But you

had a husband and a child by then and everything had changed.'

'But I still never stopped loving Cesare and, I warn you now, I intend to get him back.'

'You expect me to listen to this?' Lizzie asked, beginning to rise from her seat, having heard enough of Serafina's self-absorbed excuses.

'No, don't go,' Serafina urged impatiently. 'I'm sorry if I shocked you but I want you to understand that, right now, Cesare is set on punishing me for what I did to him almost ten years ago.'

Involuntarily, Lizzie settled back in her seat. '*Punishing* you?'

'What else could he have been doing when he married you? He married you to *hurt* me. Here I am, finally free and available and he marries you. What sense does that make?'

'Has it occurred to you that maybe he's over you and doesn't want you back?' Lizzie asked helplessly, provoked by the brunette's conviction that she would always be Cesare's most desirable option and reminding herself that she was supposed to be Cesare's real wife and should be reacting accordingly to Serafina's little spiel. 'Your affair ended a long time ago.'

'You *never* forget your first love,' Serafina argued with ringing conviction. 'He's even living in the house we planned together.'

'What house?'

'The farmhouse. We first saw it as students. It was a wet night and we made love in the barn,' Serafina admitted, a rapt look in her bright eyes as Lizzie hastily dropped her lashes to conceal her expression.

Too much information, Lizzie was thinking anxiously, an odd pain clenching her down deep inside. She could not bear to think of Cesare making love with Serafina and could have happily tossed Serafina's champagne into her sensually abstracted face. Serafina had married her older man for security and wealth while still loving and wanting Cesare. Lizzie did not think the brunette had any right to expect to turn the clock back or indeed any excuse to risk upsetting Cesare's new wife with intimate and threatening images from the past she had once shared with him.

'Even though I was already married to Matteo, Cesare still bought the farmhouse as soon as it came on the market,' Serafina told her smugly. 'Look across the valley in the evening from the pool terrace and you will see the Ruffini *palazzo* blazing with lights on the hillside. He wants me back, Lizzie, he's simply too proud to admit it yet.'

'I don't think he would've married me if that was his intention,' Lizzie commented in a deflated tone.

'Oh, I guessed that he married you to get that stupid island back into the family,' Serafina retorted with a wry little laugh and she shrugged. 'I don't care about that. Your marriage is temporary and I'll be waiting when he decides to forgive me.'

'Whatever,' Lizzie mumbled, thrusting her chair back and rising. 'You can hardly expect me to wish you luck with my husband and I really don't understand why you wanted to talk to me in the first place.'

'Because you can make things a lot easier for all three of us by quietly stepping back the minute Cesare admits that he wants his freedom back,' the princess pointed out smoothly. 'If it's a question of money.'

'No, I don't *need* money and I can't be bribed!'

Lizzie parried grittily, her cheeks reddening. 'I wish I could say it was nice meeting you…but it would be a lie.'

'You're a farmer's daughter with no education. Surely you don't believe you have what it takes to hold a man like Cesare's interest?' Serafina fired back with a raised brow. 'Cesare and I belong together.'

# CHAPTER NINE

LIZZIE COMPRESSED HER LIPS, said nothing and walked back indoors.

A pounding headache had developed at the base of her skull. How she got through what remained of the evening, she had no idea, but she smiled so much her mouth felt numb and she made polite conversation until she wanted to scream. She was angry with Cesare for ever loving a woman as selfish and grasping as Serafina. Serafina only wanted Cesare now because he had built up an empire worth billions. Nevertheless a few of her remarks stayed with Lizzie like a bruise that refused to heal.

*'You never forget your first love. He married you to hurt me. Cesare and I belong together.'*

And who was she to assume that that wasn't true? Cesare had never dreamt of regaining the island of Lionos in the way his father and grandmother had. Never having seen it, he had never learned to care for it and could probably well afford to buy his own island should that have been his wish. Was it possible that Cesare had been willing to go through with marrying Lizzie because he had a stronger motive? A desire to punish Serafina for her betrayal all those years ago? *Revenge?* Certainly that was how the princess had interpreted his behaviour of getting married just at the point when she was finally free again. Exasperated by the pointless thoughts going round and round in her sore head, Lizzie tried to blank them out by acknowledging that she knew no more about what Cesare felt for Serafina than she knew about what he felt for herself.

'You've scarcely spoken since we left the benefit,' Cesare commented as the limo drew up outside the farmhouse. He had noticed that she had seemed unusually animated throughout the evening. That had proved a surprise when he had assumed she might feel the need to cling to him in such exclusive and high-powered company. When she failed to demonstrate any desire to cling, instead of being relieved he had felt strangely irked and could not explain why. He had always felt stifled by women who clung to him. He had always valued independence and spirit in a woman more than feminine weakness and soft words of flattery.

Yet when the spirited and independent woman whom he had once loved had approached him at the benefit for a private word, he had been totally turned off by the experience, he acknowledged grimly.

'I'm very tired,' Lizzie said stiffly.

Cesare followed her into the bedroom, unzipping her dress without being asked. Lizzie let the dress glide down to her feet, stepped out of it and, regal as a queen in her underwear, walked into the bathroom without turning her head even to look at him.

He knew when he was getting the silent treatment. She was sulking and that was childish. He had never had any patience for sulks. He pulled a pair of jeans out of a drawer and stripped off his suit. Casually clad, he noted the beady little eyes watching him from below the canopy of the four-poster pet bed and surrendered. 'Come on, Archie...time for something to eat...'

Archie limped across the floor. The cast had been removed from his broken leg only the day before but Archie still thought he was a three-legged dog and had yet to trust the fourth leg to take his weight again. Cesare scooped the little dog up at the top of the stairs and carried him down to the kitchen where he maintained a one-way dialogue with Archie while feeding them both as he raided the fridge.

Teeth gritted, Lizzie emerged from the bathroom to a frustratingly empty bedroom. She had decided that it was beyond cowardly not to ask Cesare why he hadn't warned her that the benefit was being staged at his ex-girlfriend's home. She had not been prepared for that confrontation and was convinced she would have made a more serious effort to look her very best had she known she would be meeting the gorgeous brunette. The problem was that she was jealous, she acknowledged ruefully, green and raw and hurting with ferocious jealousy. She looked out of the landing window at the dark silhouette of the old stone barn and her heart clenched as if it had been squeezed dry. Cesare had made love to Serafina there, love, *not sex*. He had loved Serafina, cared about her, *wanted* to marry her. Yet Serafina had turned her back on his love in favour of wealth and social status. Having achieved those staples, she now wanted Cesare back.

Pulling a silky wrap on over a nightdress, Lizzie

headed downstairs. Cesare was sprawled on a sofa in the airy living room. In worn jeans and an unbuttoned blue shirt, he was a long sleek bronzed figure and heartbreakingly beautiful. Her heart hammered out a responsive and nervous tattoo as she paused in the doorway.

'Why didn't you tell me?' she asked abruptly.

Cesare always avoided dramatic scenes with women and walking out on the risk of one came as naturally as breathing to him. One glance at Lizzie's set, angry face and the eyes gleaming like green witch fire in her flushed face was sufficient to warn him of what was coming. Springing lithely upright, he strolled out past her and swiped the car keys off the cabinet in the hall. 'I'm going for a drive...don't wait up for me. I'll be late,' he spelled out flatly.

Taken aback, Lizzie moved fast to place herself in his path to the front door. 'Are you serious?'

'Perfectly. I don't want to argue with you, *cara*. I'm not in the mood. We're flying to Lionos tomorrow and Athene will be joining us. That is enough of a challenge for the present.'

It was a shock for Lizzie to register how cold the smooth, perfect planes of his lean dark face could look. His spectacular eyes were veiled by his thick lashes, his superb bone structure taut, his shapely mouth, defined by a dark shadow of stubble, a hard line of restraint. Alarm bells sounded in her head. 'You could've warned me that we were going to Serafina's house and that she would be our hostess.'

'I am not going to argue with you about Serafina,' Cesare asserted, his jawline clenching hard as granite.

'I'm *not* arguing with you,' Lizzie reasoned curtly. 'And why won't you discuss her with me?'

Velvet black lashes flew up on scorching golden eyes. 'She's none of your business, nothing to do with you.'

Lizzie flinched and leant back against the door to stay upright. She felt like someone trying to walk a tightrope in the dark and she was terrified of falling. 'She spent ten minutes talking to me outside on the terrace and made me feel very much as if she was my business.'

Feverish colour laced his incredible cheekbones. '*You*...discussed me with...*her*?' he framed wrathfully.

Lizzie found it interesting that, instead of being flattered as Serafina had suggested, Cesare was absolutely outraged by the idea. 'What do you think?' She hesitated, hovering between him and the door. 'I only wanted to know why you didn't mention that she would be entertaining us.'

Cesare ground his perfect white teeth together because he *had* thought of mentioning it, only to run aground on the recollection that theirs was not a normal marriage. They were not in a relationship where he was bound to make such personal explanations, were they? He focused on Lizzie's pale face on which colour stood out only on her cheeks. She looked hurt. He saw that hurt and instinctively recoiled from it, frustration rippling through him. He didn't want to share what had happened earlier that evening with Lizzie, not only because it would rouse her suspicions, but also because it was tacky and he *refused* to bring

that tacky element into what had proved to be a glorious honeymoon.

'Serafina is very much part of the local scenery.
Many of my friends are also hers. I have no reason
to avoid her. Seeing her is no big deal,' he delineated
stiffly, reluctantly, willing to throw that log on the fire
if it satisfied her and closed the subject.

'I don't believe you,' Lizzie whispered unhappily. 'If it had been no big deal, you would've mentioned it.'

'You know me so well?' he derided.

Lizzie paled even more. 'I thought I did.'

Cesare closed his hands firmly to her ribcage and
lifted her bodily away from the door.

'If you walk out, I'm not going to Lionos with you!'
Lizzie flung the worst threat she could think to make
in an effort to stop him in his tracks.

'In what fantasy world are you living that you think
you can threaten me?' Cesare breathed, freezing with
the door ajar so that cooler night air filtered in to cool
her now clammy skin.

'I only wanted you to explain.'

'I have nothing to explain,' Cesare parried drily.
'But you will definitely be telling me at some point
what Serafina said to you.'

'Honesty has to be a two-way thing to work. We've
been living like a married couple.'

'Because we *are* married.'

'You know what I mean…' Lizzie hesitated, reluctant to probe deeper but driven by turbulent emotional
forces she could not suppress. 'You've been treating
me as though I'm really your wife.'

There it was—the truth Cesare had hoped to evade

because he didn't know *how* that had happened, didn't know what to say to her, didn't even know how he felt about that development. Why did women always have to drag unmentionable issues out into the open and do them to death at a time of their choosing? How the hell had he got himself into such an untenable situation? He had started out fine, he acknowledged broodingly, laying down the rules, seeing what made sense, knowing what he should not do lest it lead to exactly this situation. And somehow it had all gone to hell in a hand basket in spite of *all* that careful pre-planning, *all* that practical knowhow and knowledge of the female sex. And here he was trapped as he had never wanted to be trapped…

'I want to know what Serafina said to you.'

'That she wants you back, that you married me to punish her, that I wasn't educated enough to hold you… Oh, yes,' Lizzie recounted and then, with a ghastly attempt at an amused smile, added, 'and that this was your mutual dream house, planned by you both on the wet night you made love in the barn…'

Cesare's eyes flashed flaming gold, his outrage unconcealed. He closed a hard hand to the edge of the door as if to emphasise the fact that he was still leaving. '*Madonna diavolo!* She shouldn't have involved you in this.'

At those words, at that suggestion that there was an involvement that she was unaware of, Lizzie swore her heart cracked right down the middle. 'No,' she agreed woodenly, because it was true.

Cesare steeled himself. He knew he had to speak, could not comprehend why ESP was suddenly warning him to shut up and say nothing. 'We don't have a genuine marriage. We are not a couple in the true sense of the word. We both know that…'

He paused as if he was hoping she would leap in and say something but Lizzie couldn't have found her voice had her life depended on it. At that moment she felt as if her life's blood were draining away in a pool on the floor and that dramatic image made her feel dizzy.

'I'm going to bed,' she mumbled, knowing that she was lying, knowing that sleep had never been further from her mind, but it seemed so incredibly important in that silence to act as if she were still able to function normally even if it was a complete lie to try and save face.

'This is all my fault,' Cesare breathed in a roughened undertone. 'Don't think I'm not aware of that. I shouldn't have brought something as volatile as sex into the equation.'

'And you were still doing it…only a few hours ago,' she framed unevenly.

Unusually indecisive, Cesare hovered in the rushing silence. Archie was looking at him from across the hall as if he had two heads, which absolutely had to be his imagination playing tricks on him, he reasoned wildly. He felt sick, he felt bad, he felt… No, he was being dangerously emotional and he knew what emotion did to him: it made him irrational and reckless and he wasn't going to go there again…*ever*! He was taking the right approach in correcting a serious mistake before it did any more damage. Aside of that aspect, they were both consenting adults.

'So, it's back to the business arrangement,' Lizzie assumed in a tight little voice.

'I think that would be wiser, don't you?'

Not recognising that cold, detached intonation, Lizzie finally dared to look at him again. He was poised by the door, devastatingly handsome, a long slice of bare brown torso showing between the parted edges of his shirt, tight jeans defining long, powerful thighs and lean hips. Slowly she raised her gaze, determined to be brave, determined to hold on to her pride even though he had rejected her in the worst possible and most hurtfully humiliating way. He had made it clear where he stood and she supposed that brutal honesty was for the best.

'Goodnight,' Lizzie said quietly and she turned on her heel.

In a split second the front door closed and he was gone. The Ferrari engine growled to life and she literally ran out to the terrace above the pool, frantically determined to see if she could pick out the Ruffini *palazzo* on the hillside. And there it was, a big white classical building lit up like a fairground. She had noticed it before but had never thought to ask about it. Now she watched the lights of Cesare's car heading down into the valley and she stood and she stood, arms wrapped defensively round herself while she waited to see if her very worst suspicions were correct.

At such a distance, she could not have been a hundred per cent certain but she was convinced that it was the Ferrari that she saw heading up the long, winding, steep drive to the *palazzo*. Cesare was going straight to see Serafina. Lizzie was in shock. Perhaps he had been seeing the other woman all along; Lizzie hadn't been keeping tabs on him everywhere he went. It seemed pretty obvious to her that Cesare had a dark

side and more secrets than she had ever had cause
to suspect and she had been ignorant and irrespon-
sible and very naive not to smell a rat sooner...but it
wasn't much good or any comfort to feel wise *after*
the event, was it?

# CHAPTER TEN

THE FOLLOWING MORNING, with her heart beating very fast, Lizzie studied a test wand, relieved that she had taken the opportunity to discreetly buy a pregnancy kit some weeks earlier.

And there it was straight away, the result she had both feared and craved: she was pregnant. It changed everything, she acknowledged in shock, and she walked out to the bedroom and unlocked the door she had locked the night before. Cesare would need access to his clothes but had she cared about that last night when her dream world had collapsed about her ears? No, she had not.

But now that she knew for sure that she was carrying Cesare's baby, she had to look to the future and beyond the business agreement they had originally made. She could not afford to be at odds with her child's father. That would only foster resentment between them and their child would suffer in that scenario. Unfortunately that meant that she had to be a bigger person than she felt like being just at that moment. She had to rise above what had happened, bury the personal aspect and stick to the rules from here on in.

He'd broken her heart. Well, she'd recovered from

Andrew; she would eventually recover from Cesare. Of course, she had never loved Andrew the way she loved Cesare; consequently getting over Cesare would be more of a challenge. Andrew had hurt her self-esteem and damaged her trust but Cesare had torn her heart out. To think of living even one day without Cesare somewhere nearby tore her apart, teaching her how weak and vulnerable her emotions had made her.

Yes, Lizzie acknowledged, tidying her hair, adding more concealer to hide the redness of her eyes, she had a long, long way to go in the recovery process. But now that she knew about the baby, it would have to start right now. She would have to put on the act of the century. She couldn't afford to show the smallest interest in what was going on between Serafina and him. He had made it clear that she had no right to ask such questions and she would have to respect that.

Had Cesare behaved badly? She thought he had. Scrapping the business-agreement-based marriage had been *his* idea, not hers. But honesty forced her to acknowledge that he had suggested at the time that they would have to see how well their marriage worked. In short, their marriage as such had been on a trial basis. And obviously, while it had worked incredibly well for Lizzie, it had not worked at all for Cesare. That hurt; that hurt her very much. It was a complete rejection of everything they had shared in and out of bed over the past month and it made her feel such an idiot for being so deliriously happy with him while failing utterly to notice that he did not feel the same way.

Lizzie went downstairs for breakfast, Archie at her heels. The instant the dog saw Cesare, who spoiled him shamelessly and taught him bad manners by feeding him titbits during meals, Archie hurried over to greet him. Cesare vaulted upright the minute she appeared. Unshaven, noticeably lacking his usual immaculate grooming, he still wore the same jeans and shirt. He raked a long-fingered brown hand through his tousled hair, looking effortlessly gorgeous but possibly less poised than he usually was.

'I won't lock the bedroom door again,' Lizzie promised, her heart-shaped face as still as a woodland pool. 'I'm sorry, I didn't think about what I was doing but the room's free now.'

'I'll get a shower before we leave for the airfield,' Cesare countered, his dark golden gaze scanning her expressionless face as if in search of something. 'Lizzie, we need to talk.'

Already having foreseen that he might feel that that was a necessity, Lizzie rushed to disabuse him of that dangerous notion. The very last thing she needed in her current shaky state of mind was a rehash of the breakdown of their relationship the night before. It wouldn't smooth over anything, wouldn't make her feel any better. How could it? Essentially he was dumping her and nothing he could say would ease that pain.

'That's the very last thing we need,' Lizzie told him briskly. 'All that needed to be said was said last night and we don't need to go over it again.'

'But—'

'What you said made sense to me when I thought it over,' Lizzie cut in, desperate to shut him up. 'This is business, nothing else. Let's stick to that from now on and I'll keep to my side of the bargain while your grandmother is staying with us on the island. I see no reason why we shouldn't bring this…er…project to a successful conclusion.'

Cesare blinked, disconcerted by the sound of such prosaic language falling from her lips. He was relieved that she was calm and grateful that she now intended to accompany him to Lionos for Athene's sake but he didn't agree with a single word she was saying. While, uniquely for him, he hesitated in a frantic inner search for the right approach to take with her, Lizzie took the wind out of his sails altogether.

'And that successful conclusion I mentioned?' Lizzie continued, a forced brightness of tone accompanying her wide fake smile. 'We're almost there because I'm pregnant.'

'*Pregnant?*' Cesare exclaimed in almost comical disbelief, springing back out of his seat again and yanking out the chair beside his own for her use. '*Madre di Dio*…sit down.'

Taken aback by his astonished reaction to her news, Lizzie sank down on the chair. 'It's not earth-shaking, Cesare. Women get pregnant every day.'

'You're my wife… It's a little more personal than that for me,' Cesare parried thickly, stepping behind her to rest his hands down on her slim, taut shoulders.

Alarmingly conscious of that physical contact, Lizzie froze in dismay. 'Could I ask you not to do that?'

'Do what?'

'Touch me,' she extended in an apologetic tone. 'I'll understand if you're forced to do it when your grandmother's around to make us look like a convincing couple but we're alone here and there's no need for it.'

Off-balanced by that blunt response, Cesare released her shoulders and backed away. He was thinking about the baby and he was fighting off an extraordinarily strong urge to touch her stomach, which he knew was weird, not to mention an urge destined to go unfulfilled.

'Forgive me,' he breathed abruptly. 'My immediate response was to touch you because I am full of joy about the baby.'

He had never looked *less* full of joy to Lizzie. In fact he looked a little pale and a lot tense, eyes shielded by his ridiculously long lashes, wide, sensual mouth compressed. She wanted to slap him so badly that her hands twitched on her lap. Like a magician pulling a white rabbit out of a hat, she had made her unexpected announcement, depending on it to wipe away the awkwardness lingering after their confrontation the night before. She had just let him know that he would never have a reason to touch her again *because* she had conceived. He should have been thrilled to be let off the hook when he didn't deserve it. Instead, however, a tense silence stretched like a rubber band threatening to snap.

'I didn't think it would happen so...*fast*,' Cesare admitted half under his breath.

'Well, it saves us a lot of hassle that it has,' Lizzie pronounced with as much positive emphasis as she could load into a single sentence. Hovering on the tip of her tongue was the highly inappropriate reminder that, after the amount of unprotected sex they had had, she thought it was more of a surprise that they hadn't hit the jackpot the first week.

'Hassle?'

'If we'd had to go for the artificial insemination, it

might have been a bit…*icky*,' she mumbled, momentarily losing her grip on her relentless falsely cheerful front.

*Icky,* Cesare repeated inwardly. It was a pretty good description of how he was feeling. *Icky.* He had suffered a Damascene moment of revelation while he was with Serafina the previous night. A blinding light that even he could not ignore or sensibly explain away had shone over the events and emotions of the past month and he had finally understood how everything had gone so very wrong. Unfortunately for him, since Lizzie had joined him for breakfast, he had realised that 'wrong' was an understatement. He had dug a great big hole for himself and she was showing every intention of being perfectly happy to bury him alive in it.

Cesare went upstairs, ostensibly for a shower but he wanted privacy to make a phone call. In all his life he had never ever turned to Goffredo for advice but his father was the only touchy-feely male relative he had, who could be trusted to keep a confidence. His sisters were too young and out of the question. Each would discuss it with the other and then they would approach Lizzie to tell all because she was one of the sisterhood now and closer to his siblings than he was. Goffredo had one word of advice and it was an unpalatable one. Heaving a sigh, he then suggested his son imagine his life without her and take it from there. That mental exercise only exacerbated Cesare's dark mood.

Lizzie wore a floaty white cotton sundress to travel out to the island and took great pains with her hair and make-up. She knew that in the greater scheme of things her appearance was unimportant but was convinced that no woman confronted by a beauty like Serafina could remain indifferent to the possibility of unkind comparisons.

Close to running late for their flight, Cesare strode down the steps, a cool and sophisticated figure in beige chinos and an ivory cotton sweater that truly enhanced his bronzed skin tone and stunning dark eyes. Climbing into the car, he barely glanced at Lizzie and she knew all her fussing had been a pathetic waste of time.

Archie sat right in the middle of the back seat, halfway between them like a dog trying to work out how he could split himself into two parts. To Lizzie's intense annoyance, her pet ended up nudged up against a hard masculine thigh because Cesare was absently massaging Archie's ear, which reduced her dog to a pushover.

By the time they reached the airfield and boarded the helicopter, Lizzie was becoming increasingly frustrated. Cesare's brooding silence was getting to her and she wanted to know what was behind it. How could he simply switch off everything they had seemed to have together? It hadn't ever just been sex between them. There had been laughter and lots of talking and an intense sense of rightness as well. At least on *her* side, she conceded wretchedly.

His long, powerful thigh stretched as he shifted position and a heated ache blossomed between her thighs. That surge of hormonal chemistry mortified her. She reminded herself that that side of their marriage was over, she reminded herself that she was pregnant and she *still* ended up glancing back at that masculine thigh. Suddenly she was remembering that only the day before she would have stretched out a hand and stroked that hard male flesh, taking the initiative in a way that always surprised and pleased him. How had they seemed to be so attuned to each other when they so patently could not have been? Had she deceived herself? Had she dreamt up a whole fairy tale and tried to live it by putting Cesare in a starring role? Was this mess all her own wretched fault?

With such ideas torturing her and with a companion, who was almost as silent, it was little wonder that Lizzie had been airborne for over an hour when she was jolted by Cesare simply and suddenly turning round from the front passenger seat of the helicopter and urging her to look down at what he called *'her'* island.

'And Chrissie's,' she said unheard above the engine noise, stretching to peer over his broad shoulder as the craft dipped. She saw a long teardrop-shaped piece of land covered with lush green trees. *'That's* Lionos?' She gasped in astonishment for it was much bigger than she had expected. In her head she had cherished a not very inviting image of a rocky piece of land stuck in the middle of nowhere, for her mother had not made it sound an attractive place. At the same time their inheritance had never seemed very real to either her or her sister when they could not afford even to visit it.

Within minutes the helicopter was descending steeply to land in a clearing in the trees and for the first time in twenty-four hours a feeling of excited anticipation gripped Lizzie. Ignoring Cesare's extended hand, she jumped down onto the ground and stared up at the white weatherboard house standing at the top of a slope. Like the island, it was bigger than she had expected.

'Athene told me that her father built it in the nineteen twenties and she had five siblings, so it had to be spacious,' Cesare supplied as he released Archie and the dog went scampering off to do what dogs did when they'd been confined for a long time. 'Primo says it really needs to be knocked down and rebuilt but he's done his best within the time frame he's had.'

'He's frighteningly efficient,' Lizzie remarked, mounting the slope, striving to ignore and avoid the supportive hand Cesare had planted to the base of her spine and a little breathless in her haste.

'Take it easy. It's hot and you're pregnant,' Cesare intoned.

'For goodness' sake!' Lizzie snapped. 'I'm only a tiny bit pregnant!'

In silence, Cesare rolled his eyes at that impossibility. He had all the consolation of knowing that he was reaping what he had sowed. Lizzie was not naturally either moody or short-tempered. In fact, in spite of her troubled childhood she had a remarkably cheerful nature, he conceded grimly. At least she had had a remarkably cheerful nature until he had contrived to destroy everything in what had to be an own goal of even more remarkable efficacy.

Primo greeted them at the front door and spread it wide. 'Workmen are still finishing off the utility area,' he admitted. 'But I believe the house is now presentable.'

Wide-eyed, Lizzie drifted through the tiled hall, which had been painted white, and moved on into a spacious reception room furnished with pieces that were an elegant mix of the traditional and the more contemporary. French windows draped with floral curtains opened out onto a terrace overlooking a secluded sandy cove. The view down the slope of a path through the trees to the beach was incredibly picturesque and unspoilt.

She walked through the house and as she peered into rooms some of her tension began to evaporate. In the wake of her mother's unappreciative descriptions, she was surprised to discover that it was actually a very attractive house and full of character. A room with a bathroom had been prepared for Athene's use on the ground floor. Lizzie mounted the stairs, which had wrought-iron ornamental balusters and a polished brass handrail. A bedroom had been sacrificed to provide en-suite bathrooms. Everywhere had been freshly decorated and kitted out, fabrics stirring softly in the breeze through open windows.

'What do you think?' Cesare asked from his stance on the landing.

'It's magical. I can understand why your grandmother never forgot this island. It must've been a wonderful house for kids,' she confided.

'Soon our child will follow that same tradition,' Cesare said gruffly.

'Well, possibly when he or she is visiting you. I won't be here as well,' Lizzie pointed out, quick to puncture that fantasy.

Cesare hovered in the strangest way, moving a step forward and then a step back, lashes suddenly lifting on strained dark golden eyes. 'And what if I wanted you to be here as well?'

'But you *wouldn't* want that,' Lizzie countered with

unwelcome practicality. 'You will either have remarried or you'll have a girlfriend in tow.'

'What if I don't want that? What if I want you?' Cesare shot at her without warning, unnerved by that veiled reference to the divorce that would be required for his remarriage.

Lizzie lost colour, wondering what he was playing at, wondering if this was some new game on his terms. 'But you *don't*...want me, that is. You made that quite clear last night.'

'I *do* want you. I want to stay married,' Cesare bit out almost aggressively. 'Last night, you took me by surprise and I was confused. I made a mistake.'

Lizzie shook her pale head slowly and studied him in angry wonderment, temper stirring from the depths of the emotional turmoil she had been enduring since he had blown all her hopes and dreams to dust. 'I can't believe I'm hearing this. First you ask me for a business-based marriage, *then* you ask me to give our marriage a try and then you tell me we don't have a *real* marriage. As I see it, that's pretty comprehensive and not open to any other interpretation!'

She swivelled on her heel and deliberately walked past him to enter the room on the other side of the landing.

'I'm trying to say I'm sorry and you're not even listening!' Cesare growled from behind her.

'You can't apologise for what you feel...neither of us can,' Lizzie parried curtly as she lodged by a window, hoping to look as though she were entranced by the view when in actuality all she could think about was escaping this agonising going-nowhere conversation with Cesare, who seemed not to have the first clue about how she might be feeling. 'I'm going to get changed and go off and explore.'

'Alone?' Cesare exclaimed.

'Yes. I like my own company. I had to—I worked alone for years,' she reminded him doggedly, walking past him on the landing, relieved when she saw the cases being carried upstairs into the master bedroom. 'I realise once Athene arrives tomorrow it'll be "game on" or whatever you want to call it…but could we… please not share a bedroom tonight?'

'Why are you not listening to anything I'm saying?' Cesare demanded in apparent disbelief. 'You won't even look at me!'

Lizzie had only felt free to look at him when he was *hers*. Now that he wasn't any more, she didn't want to fall victim to his essential gorgeousness all over again. Not looking was a form of self-defence, she reasoned wildly.

'Lizzie…' he breathed in a driven undertone.

Lizzie stiffened, tears prickling behind her wide eyes. 'I can't afford to listen to you. You upset me a lot last night and I really don't want to talk about that kind of stuff. It's pointless. I'm not really your wife. I may be living with you—'

'Expecting *my* child!' Cesare slotted in with greater force than seemed necessary.

'But you didn't choose to marry me because you cared about me, therefore it's not a proper marriage,' Lizzie replied as she reluctantly turned back to face him. 'And in your own immortal words everything else we've shared can be written off as "just sex".'

Cesare flinched at that reminder, his pallor below

his bronzed skin palpable. 'I care about you *now*. I want to *keep* you.'

'I'm not a pet, Cesare...' Lizzie stared at him and frowned. 'Are you feeling all right? You know, you're acting very oddly.'

Goffredo's one-word piece of advice returned to haunt Cesare. 'I'm fine,' he said brusquely, lying through his teeth.

All of a quiver after that pointless exchange, her nerves jangling, Lizzie vanished into the bedroom, closed the door and opened her case to extract a sun top and shorts. She needed to blow the cobwebs off with a good walk. Cesare was nowhere to be seen when she went downstairs again and she went into the kitchen where Primo reigned supreme and eventually emerged with Primo's luxury version of a picnic meal and a bottle of water. With a little luck she could stay out until dark, then dive into bed and wake up to a new day and the big show for his poor grandmother's benefit.

Cesare was furious when he discovered that Lizzie had left the house. He strode down to the beach but there was no sign of her and not even a footprint on the pristine strand to suggest that she had come that way.

Several hours later, sunburned, foot weary and very tired after her jaunt across Lionos, Lizzie returned to discover that Cesare had gone out. Thankful, she settled down to supper as only Primo could make it. Sliding into her comfortable bed, she slept like a log.

Athene arrived mid-afternoon the next day. Cesare decided to be grateful for that because it brought Lizzie out of hiding. It had not once crossed his mind that she could be so intractable that she wouldn't even give him a hearing and then he thought of all the years she had slaved for her unappreciative and critical father and realised that she would have needed a strong, stubborn backbone.

Relaxed and colourful in a red sundress, Lizzie ushered Athene into her former childhood home. Tears shone in the old lady's eyes as she stood in the hall, gazing down the slope at the beautiful view. 'I thought it would all be overgrown and unrecognisable.'

'You showed me a photo once. I had the trees cut back,' Cesare told his grandmother softly. 'Shall I show you around?'

'Yes, this is your home and Lizzie's now,' Athene said a little tearfully and fumbled for a tissue. 'I have so many memories of my brothers and sisters here and now that they're all gone...'

Lizzie watched Cesare mop up his grandmother's tears with a deft touch and the right words and, minutes later, Athene was laughing as she recounted a childhood adventure with her brothers. She accompanied them on the official tour and Primo served afternoon tea out on the terrace, apparently an old tradition that Athene loved.

'Primo is an absolute treasure,' Athene told Lizzie as Cesare murmured an apology and withdrew to answer his phone before walking back into the house.

'And even better he *cooks*, which I'm not very good at,' Lizzie admitted, topping up the older woman's tea.

'Have you and Cesare had a row?' her companion asked without warning. 'I'm not an interfering old woman but I can feel that something's wrong.'

Lizzie felt that even an award-winning actress would have been challenged to carry off a smile at that point. 'A hiccup,' she downplayed studiously, her cheeks burning tomato-red as if the lie might be emblazoned on her forehead.

'My grandson has a remarkable brain, which serves him well in business. He's not quite so good at relationships,' Athene remarked wryly, gentle amusement in her warm brown eyes. 'There's bound to be hiccups as you call them. He's set in his ways and you'll challenge him. That's good for him. After all, anyone with eyes can see how deeply attached you are to each other.'

Lizzie's opinion of Athene's shrewdness nosedived at that pronouncement but the awkward moment passed over and she managed to relax again. The old lady eventually nodded off in the shade and Lizzie went back indoors.

'I need to warn you,' Lizzie almost whispered round the corner of the door of the room Cesare had set up as an office. 'Athene thinks we've had a row but that that's normal, so not really anything to worry about…but we'll need to make a real effort to impress.'

'Wouldn't it be easier simply to talk to me?' Cesare suggested, rising from behind his desk, all sleek Italian designer style in his tailored oatmeal-coloured casuals.

Lizzie continued to hover defensively in the doorway. 'I just don't think we have anything to talk about.'

'Do you know what time I went to bed last night?'

Lizzie blinked in confusion. 'How would I?'

'I was out tramping round the island looking for *you*. Primo couldn't raise a signal on my cell phone until midnight and I only found out then that you had returned to the house hours earlier!'

Lizzie dealt him an astonished look. 'But why were you looking for me in the first place? I wasn't lost.'

Cesare studied her as if she were irretrievably dim. 'There are all kinds of hazards out there. Fast currents in the sea, steep drops, dangerous rocks...'

*Definitely behaving oddly,* Lizzie labelled as she breathed in deep. 'Cesare, I'm not some little fluffy woman who can't look after herself. I'm an outdoors woman, used to working in all weathers and accustomed to constantly considering safety aspects on the farm.'

'But I was *worried* about you!' Cesare shot back at her in furious frustration.

Lizzie tossed her head, platinum-blonde hair shimmering across her slight shoulders in the sunlight, green eyes wide and wary. 'Well, you didn't need to be. I should've thought you would've been more worried about how Serafina is managing while we're together here when you belong with her.'

'I do not *belong* with Serafina!' Cesare raked at her so loudly, she jumped.

'No?'

'Do I strike you as being an idiot? I was a boy when I fell in love with her and full of romantic idealism but I'm all grown-up now,' he completed grimly.

'Well, you went rushing over to that *palazzo* fast enough the other night,' Lizzie argued in a less aggressive prompt. 'That *was* where you went, wasn't it?'

His stunning gaze widened to smouldering gold eyes of challenge. 'You think I went over there to *be* with her?'

'What else was I supposed to think?' Lizzie asked tightly. 'You left me in anger...'

'I wasn't angry with you, I was angry with *her*!' Cesare exclaimed in full-volume contradiction and Lizzie hastily backed to the door to close it firmly shut. 'How dare she have the insolence to approach my wife with the tacky details of an affair that happened a decade ago? I'd never heard such rubbish in my life and I was determined to finally have it out with her.'

Tacky details scarcely dovetailed with Serafina's suggestion that the barn episode had been a very precious memory for them both. Furthermore Lizzie was transfixed by the idea that he had rushed out of the house in a rage because Serafina had dared to approach his wife. Lizzie went pink over her misreading of the situation. 'And did you have it out with her?'

'*Sì*...I said a lot that she will not forget in a hurry. If she wasn't so vain, she would have accepted a long time ago that I would sooner chew off my own arm than have anything to do with her again. How could you think *that* of me?' Cesare raked at her in apparent wonderment. 'A woman who walked out on me because I wasn't rich enough? A disloyal, deceitful woman with the morals of a whore... She first offered herself back to me three years after she married Matteo and she did it again last night, which outraged me.'

Lizzie was so astonished by what she was finding out that she was rooted to the floor where she stood. Not only did he no longer care about Serafina, he evidently despised her and her eagerness to get him back. There was nothing fake about the driving derision he exuded. 'And of course you said no?'

'I never thought about her again after that first incident,' Cesare admitted flatly. 'By that stage I was grateful that, by marrying her, Matteo had saved me from making a serious mistake. No sane man would want a treacherous woman but, unfortunately for him, Matteo was besotted with her.'

Lizzie nodded slowly.

'Serafina won't be bothering either of us again, I assure you,' Cesare spelled out. 'She told me that she's bored with the countryside and will be moving back to her home in Florence.'

Lizzie was thinking about him having spent hours searching for her the night before because he was concerned that she might have met with an accident. Even though she was a seasoned outdoorswoman, she could not help but be touched by his naive assumption that she required his protection. She had made so many silly assumptions about Serafina and suddenly it was obvious that she had been listening to an extremely vain and spoilt woman spouting her belief that she was both irresistible and unforgettable. Cesare, on the other hand, had recovered from Serafina's betrayal by appreciating what a narrow escape he had had. That, she recognised, was absolutely in line with his character while rushing off to be with Serafina while he was married would not have been.

'I'm glad she's moving...I didn't like her,' Lizzie confided in a case of severe understatement. A light-headed sensation engulfed her and she gripped the back of a chair. 'Sorry, I get a bit dizzy now and again.'

'Is that like being only a tiny bit pregnant?' Cesare enquired, scooping her up as she swayed and planting her carefully down into the armchair. 'You need to be taking more rest and eating more food.'

'And what would you know about it?' Lizzie mumbled, momentarily giving way to the heaviness of her body and slumping into the depths of the chair like a sagging cushion.

'Possibly as much as you,' Cesare dared. 'I contacted an obstetrician for advice.'

Her lower lip dropped. 'You did...what?'

'It's my baby too,' he countered defensively. 'I had no idea how to look after you properly. It made sense to consult someone with the relevant knowledge.'

Her eyes stung again. Against all the odds, he was making such an effort to put across the point that, although he didn't want a real marriage with her, he did care about her welfare and their child's. Her throat convulsed. The tears she had been holding back were gaining on her, no matter how hard she tried to hold them back.

As Cesare stared across the barrier of his desk he saw two tears rolling down Lizzie's cheeks and his last defences fell to basement level. *He* had caused this fiasco. *He* had made her unhappy.

'I'm sorry...I'm *so* sorry,' Cesare told her gruffly.

Lizzie opened her wet eyes to find Cesare on his knees at her feet, stunning dark golden eyes stricken. 'Sorry? What about?'

'I'm sorry I hurt you. For years I had this set of rules with women,' he breathed raggedly, grabbing both her hands and crushing them between his. 'I never got involved. I never got involved with anyone after Serafina. And then I met you and I...I thought it would be the same with you and I tried to stick to the same rules but you were too much for me, only I didn't see it...'

'Slow down...' Lizzie begged, struggling to work

out what he was telling her in such a rush. 'What are you saying?'

'That I'm mad about you, that I love you and I never want to lose you,' Cesare told her, crushing the life out of her poor fingers, his physical intensity as great as the emotional intensity now clear in his eyes.

Her lashes fluttered in bemusement. 'But you *said*—'

'Forget what I said. I was still trying to stick to my rules but it was idiocy,' he told her with a fierce fervour that was in itself impressive. 'I drove to Serafina's in a rage because she'd dared to try and upset you and I was driving back, thinking about what a vicious witch she is and thinking about you too...and that's when I realised.'

'That you love me?' Lizzie probed numbly, unsure what to believe, her thoughts spinning.

'I think I was scared to deal with what I was feeling for you, so I avoided thinking about it altogether...' Cesare hesitated. 'You know, I'm not much like Goffredo. I don't spend much time thinking about feelings and stuff.'

Lizzie was pleasantly surprised to learn that he had spent *any* time thinking about feelings but she couldn't smile when she was in shock. For the first time ever outside the bedroom she was seeing Cesare without the cool front he wore to the world and he wasn't half as smooth with words in the emotional category as he was with other things. Yet there was something hugely endearing about that inept surge of sentiment and confession because every syllable of it rang with raw honesty.

'So, you think you love me?' she pressed a little

shakily, scared to hope, scared to dream, scared he didn't yet know his own heart.

'I *know* I love you. I only had to think of how warm and happy everything has seemed since we got married. I only have to think of being without you to know that what I feel for you is so much more than I ever felt for Serafina,' he confessed huskily.

A huge smile suddenly lit up Lizzie's face as she finally dared to really look at him again, scanning the superb bone structure, the straight nose and the perfect mouth. This time around, she revelled unashamedly in his essential gorgeousness because for the first time ever he felt like *hers*.

'I didn't want to fall for you either. Mum made so many mistakes and she was never really happy. I was afraid of falling for you,' Lizzie admitted, freeing a hand to brush his thick black hair off his brow in a gesture that came very close to an adoring caress. 'I really did think we were going to go the business route and then...my goodness, I couldn't stop thinking about you, couldn't take my eyes off you, couldn't keep my hands off you. You're sort of addictive but I didn't want to get hurt.'

'I hope I will never hurt you again.'

'Why are you still on your knees?' Lizzie whispered, genuinely bewildered.

'I rang my father for advice. I didn't give him *details*,' Cesare stressed when she looked at him in dismay. 'I just admitted that I'd said some very stupid things and he had only one word of advice...'

Lizzie viewed him expectantly.

Cesare bit the bullet and confided, *'Grovel.'*

'Seriously?' Lizzie giggled, tickled pink.

'I'm only going to do it once because I'm never ever likely to screw up as badly with you again, *amata mia*,' Cesare delivered, springing back upright without any loss of presence to open the door before striding back to scoop his wife up out of her chair. 'I've learned a lot from this experience.'

'Have you?' Lizzie asked curiously, resting back against his broad chest, sublimely happy just to be in his arms again, breathing in the delicious scent of him and free to think about all the wicked bedroom skills he was undoubtedly about to unleash on her.

'For a whole month I took you for granted. I'll never make that mistake again. I love you. My family loves you.'

'Even my father said that you were a sensible man,' Lizzie inputted with amusement.

'Very sensible. You're a wonderful woman, *cara mia.*' Cesare lowered her the whole formidable length of his lean, hard body to the landing floor and kissed her with hungry, driving passion.

Lizzie was more than ready to drown now in his potent fervour to reconnect with her. Excitement laced her happiness with a heady sense of joy and quiet security. She simply knew that she had a glorious life ahead of her with her husband and her child.

On the ground floor, Athene was in a self-congratulating mood.

'I do hope I've sorted them out. Cesare's stubborn but his wife is soft. As if I would simply fall asleep in the middle of a conversation!' Athene chuckled as she took over Primo's kitchen to make her grandson's favourite cake. 'I think we'll have a rather late dinner tonight, Primo…'

\* \* \*

Three years later, Lizzie relaxed on the front veranda of the house on Lionos while she awaited Cesare's return from a business trip. Her children were with her. Max was two, a toddler with the unusual combination of his mother's pale hair and his father's dark eyes. He was industriously racing toy cars on the boards beneath her feet and making very noisy vroom-vroom sounds. In a travel cot in the shade a dark-haired six-month-old baby girl slumbered, sucking her thumb, while Archie dozed on the front doormat.

Gianna had not been planned, Lizzie reflected, her eyes tender as she bent down to try and extract her daughter's thumb from her rosebud mouth. She managed it but even in sleep within minutes the thumb crept back. She gave up when she heard the distant beat of the helicopter's approach, sliding upright to get a better view over the bay.

Max abandoned his cars and joined her. 'Papa… Papa!' he exclaimed, well aware of what that sound presaged in his secure little world.

Lizzie stroked her son's silky head and smiled dreamily. She always enjoyed the sunshine and the peace on Lionos but it would soon be disrupted by Cesare's forceful, exciting presence and she couldn't wait; she really couldn't wait. Three years had not dimmed the chemistry between them.

Athene spent spring to summer on the island, preferring her Rome apartment and its greater convenience in the winter. Lizzie had grown to love her husband's grandmother as much as she loved the rest of his family. He had been so blessed by all that love and warmth and to give him his due becoming a parent had made Cesare more sensitive towards his own relatives. He was much more relaxed with his large and convivial family than he had once been and his father and his sisters were frequent visitors to their homes in London, Tuscany and Lionos. Lizzie often teased her husband that she had stayed married to him because she couldn't bear the thought of losing his family.

Sadly, since her marriage she had seen much less of her own father and sister. Brian Whitaker came on occasional visits but he didn't like flying or foreign food or even people talking their own language in his vicinity. Lizzie had purchased a compact home for the older man in the village where he had grown up and he seemed as happy there as he would be anywhere. She had taken him to see a consultant for his Parkinson's disease and he was on a new drug regimen and showing considerable improvement.

Disconcertingly, although Chrissie regularly hitched a flight home with Cesare when he was in London on business, she had become fiercely independent and now had secrets she was reluctant to share. Lizzie had watched anxiously from the sidelines of her sister's life as things went badly wrong for the sibling she adored and troubled times rolled in. Cesare had advised her to let Chrissie stand on her own feet and not to interfere when Lizzie would more happily have rushed in and tried to wave a magic wand over Chrissie's difficulties to make them vanish. She had had to accept that Chrissie was an adult with the right to make her own decisions…and her own mistakes. That said, however, she was still very close to her sister and very protective of her.

The helicopter finally appeared in the bright blue

cloudless sky and descended out of sight behind the trees. Max was jumping up and down by that stage and clapping his hands. In a flash he was gone and running down the slope to greet his father with Archie chasing at his heels, shaggy ears flying, tongue hanging out.

'Go ahead,' a voice said softly from behind Lizzie. 'I'll sit with Gianna.'

Lizzie flashed a grateful smile at Athene and raced down the slope after her son like a teenager. Cesare took one look at his wife, pale hair flying, cheeks flushed below brilliant green eyes full of warmth and welcome, and set Max down again to open his arms.

'I really missed you!' Lizzie complained into his shoulder. 'You're far too missable.'

'I'll work on it,' Cesare promised, smoothing her hair back from her brow, wondering whether or not he should admit that he had worked night and day to get back to her within a week. He missed his family more every time he left them behind and planned complex travel schedules that minimised his absences.

'I shouldn't be whingeing,' Lizzie muttered guiltily, drinking in the familiar musky scent of his skin, her body quickening with the piercingly sweet pleasure-pain of desire that made her slim body quiver against his long, lean length.

'It's not whingeing. You missed me...I missed you, *amata mia*,' Cesare said huskily. 'We are so lucky to have found each other.'

They walked slowly back up the slope, Max swiftly overtaking them, Archie lagging behind. Cesare stilled to turn Lizzie round and curve loving hands to her cheeks to gaze down at the face he never tired of studying. 'I'm crazy about you, Signora Sabatino.'

'And me…about you.' Beaming in the sunshine, Lizzie linked her arms round his neck and tilted her head back invitingly.

She slid into that kiss like melting ice cream, honeyed languor assailing her in the safe circle of his arms. Cesare was home and a rainbow burst of happiness made her feel positively buoyant.

\* \* \* \* \*

# The Greek's Billion-Dollar Baby
## Clare Connelly

**Books by Clare Connelly**

**Harlequin Modern**

*Innocent in the Billionaire's Bed*
*Bought for the Billionaire's Revenge*
*Her Wedding Night Surrender*
*Bound by the Billionaire's Vows*
*Spaniard's Baby of Revenge*

**Secret Heirs of Billionaires**

*Shock Heir for the King*

**Christmas Seductions**

*Bound by Their Christmas Baby*
*The Season to Sin*

**Harlequin DARE**

**Guilty as Sin**

*Her Guilty Secret*
*His Innocent Seduction*

**Clare Connelly** was raised in small-town Australia among a family of avid readers. She spent much of her childhood up a tree, Harlequin romance book in hand. Clare is married to her own real-life hero and they live in a bungalow near the sea with their two children. She is frequently found staring into space—a surefire sign she is in the world of her characters. She has a penchant for French food and ice-cold champagne, and Harlequin novels continue to be her favorite-ever books. Writing for Harlequin Modern is a long-held dream. Clare can be contacted via clareconnelly.com or on her Facebook page.

## DEDICATION

For Emma Darcy, who wrote the first Harlequin
I ever read and thus gave me one of the greatest
gifts of my life—an enduring love of passionate,
escapist romance.

There is a piece of Emma Darcy in every book
I write.

# PROLOGUE

BEING EQUAL NUMBER TWO on the international rich list might have made Leonidas Stathakis the envy of the world, but Leonidas knew from personal experience that money was a poor substitute for having what you really wanted in life.

Billions in the bank didn't take away the empty throb of loss that dogged your steps when you'd had to bury your loved ones.

Being rich didn't take away the grief, nor the guilt, nor the pain and the sense of impotence at knowing you had put someone in harm's way—that you had failed to protect them.

This was his fourth New Year's Eve without his family. The fourth year he'd seen draw to a close with only memories of his wife, Amy, and their two-year-old son, Brax.

It felt like a lifetime.

When he closed his eyes, he saw her as clearly as if she were standing in front of him. He'd never forget the way she smiled, as though she'd struck a match inside and happiness was exploding out of her.

How could someone so full of life and vitality simply cease to exist? For all her strength, she'd been so weak at the end, so fragile. Ploughed into while walking Brax to the playground. What chance did either of their bodies stand against that hunk of metal, commanded by a madman?

Hair that had been a vibrant russet with eyes that were the same shade as the ocean beyond this hotel; he saw her as she'd been in life, and then, as she'd been in death.

He would never forget Amy Stathakis, nor the violent fate that had awaited her, murdered because of his father's criminal activities.

Dion Stathakis had destroyed their family, and, with Amy and Brax's death, had destroyed Leonidas's life.

Anger surged inside him and he curved his fingers more tightly about his Scotch glass, wondering how many of these he'd had. Not so many as to dull the pain yet, though in his experience it took more than a few quick drinks in a bar to get anywhere near the obliteration he sought. Especially at times like this, when his memories were at their clearest.

Happiness surrounded him. Loud, exuberant noises of celebration. People seemed to love marking the close of a year, celebrating the arrival of a new one, and he could understand that. At one time, he'd felt just the same—he had celebrated life with Amy.

Now, every day was something to be got through. Every year was simply something he survived—without them. His very existence was a betrayal. How many times had he thought he would give his life to return theirs? He was the son of the criminal bastard—he, Leonidas, should have paid for his father's crimes. Not his innocent wife and their beautiful son.

Bitterness threatened to scorch him alive.

He threw his Scotch back and, without his signalling for another, a hostess arrived at his table, replacing it with a substitute, just as he'd requested. There were some perks to being the owner of the place, and this was one of them.

He lifted his head towards her in acknowledgement, noting dispassionately how attractive she was. Blonde hair, brown eyes, a caramel tan and pale pink lips that were quick to turn into a smile. A nice figure, too. She had the kind of looks he had once found irresistible.

But not any more.

Yes, he could have opened himself to the hint of desire that stirred inside him. That started in his gut and, as his eyes dropped to her breasts, to the hint of lace he could see beneath the cotton shirt she wore, spread like flame, threatening to make him hard right there in the skyline view bar of his six-star hotel on Chrysá Vráchia.

But he refused the impulse. He turned his attention to his Scotch, taking pleasure in denying his body any hint of satisfaction on that score. It had been four years. Four years without Amy, four years without knowing the pleasure of a woman. It was a habit he had no intention of breaking...

# CHAPTER ONE

HANNAH HADN'T COME to Chrysá Vráchia to lose her virginity.

She hadn't come to this stunning Greek island for any reason other than she'd been in shock and needed to escape Australia. Her controlling aunt, uncle, and the cousin she'd thought of as a sister—who'd been sleeping with Hannah's fiancé.

She'd discovered them in bed together and been at the airport two hours later, booking the first available flight—which just happened to bring her here.

This stunning paradise she'd heard of all her life and wanted to visit. Golden cliffs, white sand beaches, turquoise waters, lush green forests—it was paradise on earth and the perfect place to chew through her honeymoon savings and rebuild her heart.

So apparently even the darkest storm clouds had silver linings.

No, Hannah hadn't come to Greece to lose her virginity but as her eyes kept straying to the man across the hotel bar, she felt the pull of desire deep in her chest, and something more.

Vengeance? Anger? No. It was less barbaric than that, less calculated.

Fascination.

She looked at the man across from her, cradling his Scotch with a brooding intensity that tied her tummy in knots, and she felt a surge of white-hot desire that was as unfamiliar as it was intriguing.

Waiting until they were married had been Angus's idea, but she'd gone along with it. She loved Angus, she liked the way he made her feel, the way he kissed her and held her tight. But she'd never really longed for him. She'd never trembled at his touch nor fallen asleep imagining his kisses.

And the idea of carelessly giving something away to a stranger, sleeping with a man she didn't know, felt like the perfect way to respond to her fiancé cheating on her with her cousin.

Hannah's chest tightened as flashbacks of that moment sliced through her. It was too raw. Too fresh.

Still…he looked like a man who wanted to be left alone. As she watched, a blonde waitress approached and said something *sotto voce*. He didn't even meet her eyes when he responded, instead looking towards the view beyond them, the dark night sky inky for now— though it would soon be illuminated with the fireworks that marked the conclusion of one year and the start of another.

Midnight ticked closer and Hannah sipped her champagne thoughtfully.

She'd never approached a man before. She had no

idea what to say. And it was a stupid idea. Hannah was twenty-three years old; there was a reason she was so woefully inexperienced with the opposite sex.

She was completely clueless.

No way could she click her fingers and change her personality, even if she wanted to.

Suppressing a sigh, she stood and moved towards the bar. If she wasn't going to do something *really* out of character and have a random one-night stand with a stranger, then she could do something *slightly* out of character and get a little bit tipsy.

She stood and looked about for a waiter, moving to the other side of her table, and deciding to go direct to the bar when she couldn't find one. But as she spun to the bar she connected with something impossibly hard and broad.

Something strong and firm, like concrete. Something that almost sent her flying across the room for the latent strength contained within its frame.

A hand snaked out to steady her and Hannah lifted her gaze, right into the obsidian eyes of the man she'd been unable to look away from for the past hour. He was rubbing his shoulder distractedly and a little pain radiated from her own, so she presumed they'd bumped into each other—hard.

'It's you,' she exhaled on a tremulous breath, trying to swallow even when her mouth was bone dry.

'It's me,' he agreed, his expression unchanging.

'You're like a brick wall,' she said before she could stop herself. The man's brows furrowed, and, if anything, he looked even hotter when he was all handsome and forbidding.

'Are you hurt?'

My pride is hurt. My heart is hurt. But this was not what he was asking. 'No, I'm fine.' And something like courage lashed at her spine, so she heard herself say, 'But I should at least buy you a drink. For getting in your way.'

A stern expression crossed his face and she felt the beginnings of embarrassment, certain he was going to say 'no', that she'd just made a complete fool of herself.

She bit down on her lower lip, wishing she could recall the words to her mouth. He stared at her for a long time, saying nothing, and with every second that passed her heart rate accelerated; she was drowning.

'That is not necessary,' he said, but made no effort to move. That alone was buoying. At least, Hannah hoped it was.

Her fingertips shook a little as she lifted them to her hair, straightening the auburn mane behind her ear. His eyes followed the gesture, a contemplative frown on his face.

'I wasn't watching where I was going,' she said.

'Nor was I. In which case, I should buy you a drink.'

Hannah's heart turned over in her chest, desire like a wave that had picked her up and was dragging her with it.

'How about I buy this round and you can get the next?' she said with a lift of one brow.

It was by the far the most forward she'd ever been in her life but seeing Angus in bed with Michelle had robbed Hannah of the ability to feel embarrassment.

His frown deepened. Then, he nodded a little, just a shift of his head. 'You have a deal, Miss…'

'Hannah,' she said, her own name emerging a little husky. She darted her tongue out and licked the outline of her lower lip, her eyes holding his so she saw the way the black shifted, morphing to inky and coal.

'Hannah,' he repeated, his European accent doing funny things to the simple two syllables, so her gut lurched.

'And you are?'

Surprise briefly flashed on his features. 'Leonidas.'

His name was just what she'd expect. Masculine, spicy and sexy, it suited him to a T.

'You have a table?' she asked, shifting her eyes to where he was sitting. A couple had already claimed it. She spun around and saw the same fate had befallen her own seat.

'I was just on my way to my room.' He said the words slowly, the frown not leaving his face, the statement almost spoken against his will.

But the question in the words didn't fail to reach Hannah's ears, nor her awakening libido. Desire throbbed low down in her abdomen, so heat flamed through her.

'Were you?'

Plan for seduction or not, Hannah knew she was moving dramatically out of her realm of experience.

'It has a view back towards Athens. Perhaps we could have our drink on my balcony?'

Hannah had no idea if he was seriously offering to show her the view, or if this invitation was for so much more—she hoped the latter, and had every intention of finding out.

It was stupid. So stupid, so completely out of character, but she wasn't acting from a rational place. Hannah had had her heart and trust broken and, wounded, she needed something. She needed to know she was desirable. She wanted to know what sex was all about. She had to push Angus way out of her mind.

And this man with his darkly quizzical gaze and mysterious, brooding face was everything she wanted—for one night only.

'I...' This was it. Her moment of truth. Could she do this?

The bar was busy and a woman passed behind Hannah, knocking her forward so Hannah's body was once again pushed against Leonidas's. This time, his hand reached out to steady her but it lingered, curving around her back and holding her there. Her eyes lifted to his, and doubts filled her. They were mirrored back to her, a look of confusion in his eyes, uncertainty on his face.

'I want you to come upstairs with me.' He said the words almost as though they were a revelation, as though he was completely surprised by the pull of this desire.

Hannah's pulse was like a torrent of lava, hot and demanding in her bloodstream. She wanted that too, more than anything.

'I just got out of a relationship,' she heard herself saying, her expression unknowingly shifting so her green eyes were laced with sadness. 'I was engaged, actually, until recently. I'm not looking for anything. You know, anything more than...' She looked away, shyness unwelcome, yet impossible to disguise.

'I don't do relationships,' the man said quietly. 'I don't generally do one-night stands, either.'

Generally.

The word was like an axe, preparing to fall. Hannah's eyes slid back to his and the hand that was at her back, holding her pressed to him, began to move up a little, running over her spine with a possessive inquiry that warmed her from the inside out.

'Nor do I.'

*'Theos...'* He said the word under his breath. 'I didn't come here for this.'

There was an undercurrent of emotion to his words, a sense of powerlessness that pulled at Hannah's heartstrings. And if she weren't completely drowning in this torrent of desire, she might have asked him about it. She might have insisted they find somewhere to talk. But desire was taking over Hannah's body, and she reached her hand around behind her back so her fingers could lace with his.

'Nor did I.'

His eyes glittered as they saw right through her, boring into her soul. 'A night out of time,' he said, pulling her with him, away from the bar, weaving with skill and ease towards the glass doors that led to the hotel foyer.

People seemed to move for him—he had a silent strength that conveyed itself with every step he took.

And with every inch they covered, Hannah's mind was yelling at her that this was stupid, that she was going to regret this, even as her heart and sex drive were applauding her impetuosity.

The hotel had been more than Hannah had expected,

despite its billing as one of the world's finest. It was true six-star luxury, from the white marble floor to the gold columns that extended to the triple-height ceilings, the glossy grand piano in one corner being expertly played by a renowned pianist, the enormous crystal chandeliers that hung overhead.

As they approached the lifts, a suited bellhop dipped his head in deferential welcome. 'Good evening, sir,' he murmured. 'Madam.'

His gloved hand pressed the button to call the lift and Hannah stood beside Leonidas, waiting in complete silence. The lift arrived seconds later and Leonidas stood back, allowing Hannah to enter before him.

She stepped into the plush interior, her breath held, her senses rioting with the madness of what she was about to do.

But the moment she felt regret or doubt, she closed her eyes and conjured the image of Angus's pale face brightened by his sensual exertions with Michelle and determination kicked inside her.

Not that she needed it—desire alone was propelling her through this, but anger was a good backup.

'You are no longer engaged?'

The lift pulled upwards, but that wasn't why her stomach swooped.

'No,' she said. 'I've left him—everyone—far behind.'

'You are angry?'

'No.' She was. And she wasn't. She was…hurt. Reeling. Confused. And if she *was* angry, it was mostly with herself, for having been so stupid as to believe him, to care for him, to get so hooked on the idea of the picture-perfect future that she'd stopped paying attention to the present, to whether or not Angus even made her happy.

The lift doors eased open silently, directly into a large living room. It took only a moment to realise they were on the top floor of the hotel and that this magnificent space must surely be the penthouse.

'Wow.' For a second, everything but admiration left her—this place was amazing. Every bit as decadent as the foyer but even more so because it was designed with a single occupant in mind. Everything was pale—cream, Scandinavian wood furniture, glass, mirrors, except for the artwork that was bold—a Picasso hung on one wall. There were plants, too, large fiddle-leaf figs that added a bold hint of architectural interest.

Sliding glass doors led to a balcony that showed a stunning view of Athens in the distance—glowing golden warm, an ancient city, so full of stories and interest.

'This is beautiful.'

He dipped his head in silent concession, moving towards the kitchen and pulling a bottle of champagne from the fridge. She recognised the label for its distinctive golden colour.

She watched as he unfurled the foil and popped the cork effortlessly, grabbing two flutes and half filling them.

'What brings you to Chrysá Vráchia, Hannah?'

There it was again, her name in his mouth, being kissed by his accent. Her knees felt shaky; she wasn't sure she trusted them to carry her across the room.

'A change,' she said cryptically. 'And you?'

His lips twisted and she felt something sharpen within him, something that sparked a thousand little questions inside her. 'It's routine. I come here every year.'

'What for?'

He didn't answer. Instead, he strode across the room, champagne flute in hand, passing Hannah's to her as though he were fighting himself, as though he were fighting this.

And she couldn't understand that.

If it weren't for the gale-force strength of her own needs, she might have paused to ask him why he was looking at her with such intensity, why he stared at her in a way that seemed to strip her soul bare.

But the incessant thrumming of her own desire was all Hannah was conscious of.

'Habit,' he said simply, swallowing so his Adam's apple bobbed in his throat.

She bit down on her lip, and his eyes dropped to her mouth, so her desire became louder, more urgent, desperation rolling through her. This was crazy. Madness. Necessary.

Outside, a spark of colour exploded through the sky—bright red, vibrant, its beauty an imperative they both resisted.

'Happy new year,' she said quietly, unable to take her eyes off his face.

*Happy new year?* He stared at the woman he'd brought up to his penthouse, completely at a loss for what the hell had come over him. For four years he'd come here to pay his respects to Amy, he'd undertaken this pilgrimage, he'd come here to remember her.

For four years he'd resisted any woman he found desirable, he'd ignored his body's hungers, he'd resisted anything except the debt he felt he owed Amy.

Then again, no other woman had ever slammed into his body. She had literally hit him out of nowhere, and the second his hand had curled around her arm, simply to steady her, his body had tightened with a whole raft of needs he no longer wanted to ignore.

He'd sworn he'd spend the rest of his life single, celibate.

Amy's.

But right here, with the starlit sky exploding beyond the glass wall of his penthouse apartment, something within him shifted. It was as though an ancient, unseen force was propelling him to act, was reminding him that grief could coexist with virility, that he could have sex with a woman without it being a betrayal to his wife.

He had loved Amy, even when their marriage had been fraught and neither of them particularly happy. She was his wife, he'd made a promise to her, and he had sworn he'd love only her for the rest of his life. So wasn't it loving another woman that was the true betrayal?

What did sex have to do with it?

No, denying his libido wasn't about what he owed Amy. It was punishment.

Punishment for being the son of a criminal mastermind. Punishment for being careless, for thinking he could turn his back on Dion Stathakis and live his life without the long, gnarled fingers of that man's sins reaching in and shredding what he, Leonidas, possessed.

He had been punishing himself because he deserved to feel that desperate pain of denial, that constant throbbing of need.

And he still should.

But there was something about Hannah that weakened his resolve to the point of breaking. He didn't believe in angels and ghosts, he didn't believe in fairy tales and myths, and yet, in that moment, it almost felt as if she'd been sent to him, a fragment of his soul, a promise that he could weaken, for one night, and go back to hating himself again tomorrow.

In the light of day, with the breaking of another year over this earth, he could resume his uneasy life.

But for tonight, or what was left of it, he could forget. With determination in his gaze, he put their champagne flutes down, knowing there was no turning back from this, no changing the immediate future.

'Happy new year.' And he dropped his head, surprising her completely if her husky little gasp was anything to go by, parting her lips so he could drive his tongue deep inside her and feel every reverberation of her body, he could taste her desire and welcome it with his own.

Just for this night, he would be a slave to this—and then, everything could go back to normal…

# CHAPTER TWO

PERHAPS SHE'D EXPECTED him to kiss her gently, to explore her slowly, but there was nothing gentle about this, nothing slow. It was a kiss of urgency and it detonated around them.

She made a groaning noise into his mouth, her desire roaring through her body, taking control of her.

This was not a warm, comfortable kiss. It was a kiss that redefined everything in her life, pushing new boundaries into place. She clung to his shirt for dear life and he kissed her deeper, his mouth moving over hers, demanding more of her, his tongue duelling with her own, his body cleaved to hers so not a breath of space remained between them.

It was a kiss of complete domination and she succumbed to it utterly.

'Just this one night.' He pushed the words into her mouth as he spun her body, tightening his arms around her waist and lifting her in his arms. He sat down on the sofa, pulling her onto his lap, pushing at her dress and making a guttural sound of frustration when he found the cotton of her underpants.

It was everything she wanted—the impermanence, the perfect treatment. She wanted to lose her virginity— it seemed ridiculous to be twenty-three and not know what sex was all about, yet the idea of a relationship made something inside her shrivel up and die.

She'd never trust another man, she'd never want love, or believe in love. She'd never be foolish enough to be- lieve *she* was lovable.

But sex?

This?

This was a balm to her soul.

She tilted her head back as he pushed her dress higher, over her arms and then from her body altogether, so she wore only her underwear, flimsy cotton, with no care whatsoever that this man she'd met less than an hour ago was seeing her like this.

If anything, she found her total abandon to this—to him—liberating.

There was no room for any such rational consider- ation, though, when he unhooked the bra and discarded it carelessly, then began to trace one of her nipples with his tongue, circling the peach areola lightly at first, so she was trembling on top of him, straddling his lap.

He moved his mouth closer to the tip of her nipple and, finally, surrounded it completely, sucking on her flesh in a way that burst starlight behind her eyes.

She swore, uncharacteristically, and he echoed it in his native tongue, reaching between her legs and push- ing at the trousers of his designer suit, unzipping them, unbuttoning them so that the arousal she could feel through the material was hard and naked.

He transferred his mouth to her other breast and the first, so sensitive from his ministrations, felt the sting of the cool, air-conditioned air and she arched her back in response.

It was completely overwhelming.

Or, she thought it was. But then, he moved his hand between her legs and through the waistband of her underwear, sliding a finger into her moist core, and she cried his name.

He stilled for a moment then moved his finger deeper, finding her sensitive cluster of nerves and tormenting it until she was panting, desperate, so desperate, before pulling his finger out, fixing her with a look of wonderment.

'You are so wet.'

She was, and shaking all over, desire like an electrical current and it was frying her completely.

'I know,' she groaned as his hands moved to the top of her underpants and began to push at them. She shifted her body, lifting herself up so he could undress her completely, needing to be naked, needing him.

She had no experience but she had instincts and they were driving her wild, needing her to act, to feel, to do. She groaned as she stood shakily, naked before him, wanting to experience everything. There was a type of madness overtaking her, building within her.

She reached a hand out for his and he stood, wrapping his arms around her, crushing her to his frame.

'Who are you?' he groaned into her mouth, the words making no sense.

'Hannah,' she said unevenly and he laughed, a husky sound.

'Yes. But what kind of mermaid or angel or fairy are you to come here and do this to me?'

She swallowed his words, kissing him right back, her tongue duelling with his, passion making their breath harsh and loud in the still night air.

'Leonidas,' she groaned his name and his hands curved around her naked rear, lifting her up, wrapping her legs around his body as he strode through the penthouse towards what turned out to be a bedroom. It was huge with the same view towards Athens. He eased her down without bothering to turn on the lights so every sparkle of fireworks was like a jolt into the room.

Her hands tugged at his shirt with such desperation a button popped off and flew through the room.

She cursed softly under her breath, her eyes apologetic when they latched to his.

He shook his head. 'Don't worry.'

She nodded, but he finished the job, stripping the shirt from his body to reveal a broadly muscled chest that had her pulse ratcheting up yet another gear so she was almost trembling with the force of her own body's demands.

'Wow.' She stared at the ridges of his torso, transfixed by the obvious strength there, and lifted her hands to trace his abdominals almost without realising it. 'Work out much?'

She didn't see the way his lips flickered into a smile, nor could she have any idea how rare that smile was. Her hands ran down his chest, finding the waist of his pants and pushing at them, her eyes lifting to his as she sucked her lower lip between her teeth.

She was completely inexperienced and yet Hannah felt no anxiety, no nervousness, nothing except desire bursting through her, jolting her body as though she'd picked up a bundle of live wires.

'I want you,' she said, in awe of how true that was. It went beyond needing revenge on Angus, it went beyond anything to do with Angus. There was nothing and no one in Hannah's mind as she lifted onto the tips of her toes so she could claim Leonidas's mouth with her own, her kiss curious, questioning and then desperate.

He kissed her back, their bodies moulded together, desire a flame that was growing bigger than either could control. 'I want to take this slow,' he groaned, his hands tangling in her russet hair, curling it up and holding it against her head. He took a step forward, pushing her backwards until Hannah collapsed onto the bed, his body following, the weight and strength of him an impossible pleasure.

'I want this,' she said again, more to herself than him. 'Don't take it slow.'

He lifted himself up to stare at her, his eyes showing emotions she couldn't comprehend, or perhaps her ability to comprehend was blunted by the sheer force of her own feelings, which were overwhelming her, robbing her of sense and logic and reason.

'You don't know...'

His words were engulfed by her kiss. Hannah was sick of being patient; she was sick of waiting. She'd never known desire like this but that didn't mean she wasn't prepared to answer its call. 'Please,' she groaned. 'Make love to me.'

The words were breathed into his being, sparkling like the light show beyond the window. Explosions of light, intense, glowing, hot. He separated her legs, nudging the tip of his arousal against her womanhood, and Hannah held her breath, she held everything.

For a split second, she contemplated telling him she was innocent, that she'd never done this before, but there was no time. He thrust into her and with her gasp he stilled, pushing up to stare down at her, his features harsh in the darkened room.

'*Theos*, Hannah, was that…were you?'

'Don't stop,' she said, shaking her head, but Leonidas was already pulling away from her, his body rock hard, his eyes pinning her with intensity. 'Please don't stop.' Her heart crumbled. She hadn't realised until that moment how desperately she wanted to know herself to be desirable. To know that someone wanted her enough to be unable to control their desire.

He swore under his breath and moved to the night stand, sliding open the drawer and pulling out a foil square. 'Not once have I forgotten protection,' he said thickly, the words coated in his own desires, which began to put Hannah's heart back together again.

She watched as he unfurled a condom over his length then came back to the bed, his body weight returning to hers, bliss fogging into her mind.

'You should have told me.' The words lacked recrimination. They were simple. Soft. Gentle. Enquiring. As if he was asking her to assure him she was okay.

'I didn't know how.'

*'I'm a virgin?'*

She laughed, despite the desire that was pulling at her gut. 'I was a virgin.'

'You are sure this is what you want?'

She nodded, lifting her hands up to cup his face. 'Please.'

But he didn't respond. Something tightened in his expression, his jaw moving as though he were grinding his teeth. 'I meant what I said, Hannah. One night. Nothing more.'

'I know that.' She nodded, thinking of the situation she'd left behind, the mess her private life was in. The last thing she wanted was the complication of more than one night.

And it was the freedom he needed, the reassurance he obviously craved, because he pushed back into her. Gently this time, slowly, giving her time to adjust and adapt, allowing her inexperienced body a chance to get used to this invasion, to feel his presence and relish in it before taking more of her, more of her, until finally she was crying his name over and over, the foreign syllables tripping off her tongue as rushed breaths filled her lungs.

His mouth moved from hers to her cheek then lower to the sensitive flesh at the base of her neck, his tongue flicking her pulse point while his hands roamed her body, feeling every inch of her, pausing where she responded loudest to his inquisition, teasing the sensitive flesh of her breasts, tormenting her nipples with the skill of his hands.

It was heaven.

Pleasure built inside Hannah like a coil winding tighter and tighter and she dug her nails into his back, moaning softly as the spring prepared to burst. She arched her back and rolled her head to the side, the fireworks gaining momentum as her own pleasure began to detonate. She lifted her hips in a silent, knowing invitation and he held her, his hands keeping her close to him, reassuring her as she lost herself utterly to the compelling, indescribable pleasure of a sexual orgasm.

It was intense and it was fast and it robbed her of breath and control. Her eyelids filled with light, her mouth tasted like steel. She pushed up on her elbows, staring into Leonidas's eyes, feeling quite mad and delirious with what she'd just experienced.

But it was nowhere near over.

He braced himself above her on his palms, watching the play of sensation on her features, and then he began to move again, his body stirring hers to new heights, his dominance something that made her want to weep.

She knew though, instinctively, that giving into the salty tang of tears would be a bad idea. Even while she was part mad with pleasure, she didn't want to show how completely he'd shifted something inside her, nor how much this meant to her.

Because Hannah felt a surge of feminine power and it was instantaneous and went beyond words. She didn't need to tell him how much this meant to her; she felt it and that was enough.

Angus had made her feel precious and valued, he'd made her feel like an *objet d'art* and that had been nice. It had been better than knowing herself to be an unwanted nuisance, which was how she'd spent a huge portion of her childhood since the loss of her parents. But he'd never looked at her as though he would die if he didn't kiss her.

He'd never looked at her as though the push and pull of their chemistry was robbing him of sense.

Leonidas was, though.

He moved his body and he stared into her eyes and she felt a cascade of emotions from him to her and none of them would be worth analysing, because this was just one night. A temporary, fleeting, brief night—a slice out of time.

Sitting on the edge of the bed, Leonidas cradled his head in his hands, staring at the floor between his feet. Early dawn light was peeking through the window. Hannah's rhythmic breathing filled the room, soft and somehow sweet. Sweet? How could breath be sweet? He turned to face her on autopilot, his expression grim.

He didn't know how, but it was.

She was sweet.

She'd been innocent.

He cursed silently, standing and pulling his pants on, watching her through a veil of disbelief. What the hell had come over him? Four years of celibacy and then he'd spontaneously combusted the second the beautiful redhead had literally bumped into him?

And it wasn't the red hair, nor the passing resemblance to Amy. If anything, that would have been a reason to keep his distance. No, this was something else. A kind of sexual starvation that he supposed was only natural, given he'd denied himself this pleasure and release for such a long time. But, *Theos*, a virgin?

He hadn't wanted that! He had wanted meaningless, empty sex. A quick roll in the hay to satisfy this part of him, to obliterate his grief, to remind him that he was a man, a breathing, living man with blood in his veins.

And instead, he'd taken a young woman's innocence. He'd been her first.

A sense of disbelief filled him as he watched her sleeping, her gentle inhalations, her lips that were tilted into a smile even in her sleep.

He'd always be her first. No matter what happened, no matter who she slept with, he was that to her.

It wasn't meaningless; it never could be. Thank God he'd remembered protection. He'd have put money on the fact she wasn't on birth control—why would she be? He could think of nothing worse than that kind of consequence from a night of unplanned pleasure.

And it had been a night of pleasure, he thought with a strong lurch of desire in his gut. Despite her inexperience, she had matched him perfectly, her body answering every call of his, her inquisitiveness driving him wild, the way she'd kissed and licked her way over his frame, tasting all of him, experimenting with what pleased him, asking him to tell her what he needed.

He groaned, a quiet noise but she stirred, shifting a little, so the sheet fell down and revealed her pert, rounded breasts to his gaze.

His erection throbbed against his pants. He took a step back from the bed.

One night, and dawn was breathing its way through the room, reminding him that this was not his life.

Hannah was an aberration. A mistake.

He had to leave. He had to forget this ever happened. He just hoped she would, too.

Hannah woke slowly, her body delightfully sore, muscles she hadn't felt before stretching inside her as she shifted, rolling onto her side.

A Cavalcanti masterpiece was on the wall opposite, the morning light bathing its modernist palette in gold, a gold she knew would be matched by the sheer cliffs of this spectacular island.

But none of these things were what she wanted to see most.

She flipped over, her eyes scanning the bed, looking for Leonidas. He wasn't there.

She reached out, feeling the sheets. They were cold. Her stomach grumbled and she pushed to sitting, smothering a yawn with the back of her hand. When had they finally fallen asleep? She couldn't remember.

A smile played about her lips as she stood, grabbing

the sheet and wrapping it toga style around her, padding through the penthouse.

'Leonidas?' She frowned, looking around. The glass doors to the balcony were open. She moved towards it, the view spectacular, momentarily robbing her of breath for a wholly new reason.

He wasn't out there.

She frowned, turning on her heel and heading back inside. It was then that she saw it.

A note.

And there was so much to comprehend in that one instant that she struggled to make sense of any of it.

First of all the letterhead. It was no standard issue hotel notepad. It bore the insignia of the hotel, but the embossed lettering at the bottom spelled 'Leonidas Stathakis.'

*Leonidas Stathakis?* Her heart began to race faster as she comprehended this. She didn't know much about the Stathakis brothers—she wasn't really *au fait* with people of their *milieu*, but no one could fail to have at least *heard* of the Stathakis brothers. To know that they were two of the richest men in the world. There were other facts, too, swirling just beneath the surface. Snatches she'd heard or read but not paid attention to because it had all seemed so far away. Crimes? The mob? Murder? Was that them? Or someone else?

She swallowed, running her finger over the embossing, closing her eyes and picturing Leonidas as he'd been the night before. As he'd stood so close to her and their eyes had seemed to pierce one another's souls.

Her pulse gushed and she blinked her green eyes

open, scanning the paper more thoroughly this time, expecting to see a few lines explaining that he'd gone to get breakfast, or for a workout—those muscles didn't just grow themselves—or something along those lines.

What she wasn't expecting was the formality and finality of what she read.

> *Hannah*
> *It shouldn't have happened. Please forget it did.*
> *The penthouse is yours for as long as you'd like it.*
> *Leonidas*

She read it and reread it at least a dozen times, her fingers shaking as she reached for the coffee machine and jabbed the button. Outrage warred with anger.

*It shouldn't have happened.*

Because she hadn't been what he'd expected? Because she hadn't been any good?

Oh, God.

Was it possible that the desire she'd felt had been one-sided? Angus had been engaged to her and been able to easily abstain from sex, yet he'd been fooling around behind her back.

Had she been a let-down?

Hurt flooded inside her, disbelief echoing in her heart.

She'd wanted to come to Chrysá Vráchia almost her whole life, but suddenly, she couldn't wait to leave.

# CHAPTER THREE

A WEEK AFTER leaving the island, Leonidas awoke in a cold sweat. He stared around the hotel room, his heart hammering in his chest.

Hannah.

He'd been dreaming of Hannah, the woman he'd met on Chrysá Vráchia. He'd been dreaming of her, of making love to her. His body was rock hard and he groaned, falling back onto the pillows, closing his eyes and forcing himself to breathe slowly, to calm down. To remember his wife.

And nausea skidded through him, because he knew he would never forget Amy. But for those few moments, when he'd lost himself inside Hannah, when he'd pierced her innocence, and possessed her so completely, he had felt…

He had felt like himself.

For the first time in many years he had felt like a man who was free of this curse, this guilt, this permanent ache.

He had lost himself in Hannah and, just for a moment, he had lost his grief.

He swore under his breath, and pushed the sheet back, his heart unable to be calmed. Leonidas walked to the plush kitchen of his Hong Kong penthouse, pressing a button on the coffee machine.

He watched it brew, an answering presentiment of disaster growing inside him.

'Do you need me to talk to him?'

Leonidas focussed on sounding normal. But in the month since leaving Chrysá Vráchia, he'd had a growing tension, balling in his gut, and nothing he did seemed to relieve it. It was guilt, he knew. Guilt at having betrayed his vows to Amy. At having broken the vow he made himself, that Amy would be the last woman he was intimate with.

The limousine slid through Rome, lights on either side.

'Yeah, sure, that's even better,' Thanos responded with sarcasm. Leonidas's younger brother shook his head. 'Kosta Carinedes will take one look at you and see Dad. Sorry.'

Leonidas winced—the physical similarities between himself and Dion were not news to him. 'So how are you going to convince him to sell?'

'He wants to sell,' Thanos murmured, tilting his head as the car slowed at a corner and paused near a group of beautiful women wearing skimpy shorts and singlet tops. 'He just doesn't want to sell to us.'

'Because of Dion?'

'Because of our name,' Thanos conceded with a nod. 'And because I am, quote, "a sex-mad bachelor".'

At this, Leonidas laughed, despite the bad mood that had been following him for weeks. 'He's got you bang to rights there.'

Thanos grinned. 'Hey, I don't think there's anything wrong with being sex-mad. We can't all live the life of a saint like you.'

Leonidas's expression shifted as though he'd been punched in the gut. He was far more sinner than saint, but he had no intention of sharing his slip-up with his brother.

'Offer him more money,' Leonidas suggested, cutting to the crux of the matter.

'It's not about money. This is his grandparents' legacy. They built the company out of "love",' he said the word with sardonic derision, 'and he won't sell it to someone who's constantly in the headlines for all the wrong reasons.'

Leonidas shrugged. 'Then let it go.'

'You're kidding, right? I told you what this means to me? And who else is interested in buying it?'

Leonidas regarded his brother thoughtfully. 'Yes. Luca Monato. And I know you two hate each other. But this is just a company. Let him have it, buy its competition and drive him into the ground. Far more satisfying.'

'It might come to that. But I'm not done yet.'

'What else can you do? I hate to point out the obvious, but Kosta's right. You're a man whore, Thanos.'

Thanos laughed. 'And proud. You could take a couple of pages out of my book. In fact, why don't you? I've got a heap of women you'd like. Why don't you call one of them? Take her for dinner and then back to your place…'

Leonidas turned away from his brother, looking out of the window of the limousine as Rome passed in a beautiful, dusk-filled blur. He thought of Hannah, his body tightening, his chest feeling as if it were filling with acid. 'No.'

'You cannot live the rest of your life like this,' Thanos insisted quietly, his tone serious now, their banter forgotten. There weren't many people on earth who could speak plainly to the great Leonidas Stathakis, but Thanos was one of them, and always had been. Side by side they'd dealt with their father's failings, his criminality, his convictions, the ruin he'd brought on their fortune and the Stathakis name.

Side by side, they'd rebuilt it all, better than before, returning their family's once-great wealth—many times over. They were half-brothers, only three months apart in age, and they'd been raised more as twins since Thanos was abandoned on their doorstep by his mother at the age of eight. Their insight into one another was unique.

Leonidas understood Thanos as nobody else did, and vice versa. Leonidas knew what it had done to Thanos, his mother abandoning him, choosing to desert him rather than find a way to manage his dominant character traits.

'What would you do?' Leonidas drawled, but there was tension in the question. Tension and despair.

Thanos expelled a sigh; the car stopped. Thousands of screaming fans were outside on the red carpet, here to catch a glimpse of the A-list Hollywood stars who'd featured in the film of the premiere they were attending.

'I can't say. I get it—you miss Amy. What happened to her and Brax—do you think I don't feel that? You think I don't want to reach into that prison cell and strangle our father with my bare hands for what he exposed you to? But, Leonidas, you cannot serve her by living half a life. Do you think Amy would have wanted this for you?'

Leonidas swept his dark eyes shut, the panic in his gut churning, the sense of self-disgust almost impossible to manage. 'Don't.' He shook his head. 'Do not speak to me of Amy's wishes.'

But Thanos wasn't to be deterred. 'She loved you. She would want you to live the rest of your life as you did before. Be happy. Be fulfilled.'

'You think I deserve that?'

'It was our father's crimes that killed her, not yours.'

'But if she hadn't met me...' Leonidas insisted, not finishing the statement—not needing to. Thanos knew; he understood.

'It's been four years,' Thanos repeated softly. 'You have mourned and grieved and honoured them both. It's time to move forward.'

But Leonidas shook his head, his time on Chrysá Vráchia teaching him one thing and one thing only: it would never be time. He had failed Amy during their marriage, in many ways; he wouldn't fail her now.

'Tuna salad, please,' Hannah said over the counter, scanning the lunch selections with a strange sense of distaste, despite the artful arrangements. In the four months since arriving in London and taking up a maternity-leave contract as legal secretary to a renowned litigator, Hannah had grabbed lunch from this same store almost every day.

Her boss liked the chicken sandwiches and she the tuna. She waited in the queue then grabbed their lunches and made her way back to the office as quickly as she could.

There was a wait for the lift and she stifled a yawn, sipping her coffee. Her stomach flipped. She frowned. The milk tasted funny.

'Great,' she said with a sigh, dropping it into a waste bin. Just what she needed—spoiled milk.

But when she got to her desk and unpeeled her sandwich, she had the strangest sense that she might vomit. She took one bite of the sandwich and then stood up, rushing to the facilities. She just made it.

It was as she hovered over the porcelain bowl, trying to work out whether she was sick or suffering from food poisoning, that dates began to hover in her mind. Months of dates, in fact, without her regular cycle.

Her skin was damp with perspiration as she straightened, staring at the tiled wall with a look of absolute shock.

No way.

No way could she be pregnant. Her hand curved over her stomach—it was still flat. Except her jeans had felt tight on the weekend, and she'd put it down to the sedentary job.

But what if it wasn't just a little weight gain? What if she was growing thick around the midsection because she was carrying Leonidas Stathakis's baby?

She gasped audibly, pushing out of the cubicle, and ran the taps, staring at herself in the mirror as the ice water ran over her fingertips.

Surely it wasn't true? It was just a heap of coincidences. She had a tummy bug and her weight gain *was* attributable to the fact she was chained to a desk for twelve-hour days. That could also account for her recent exhaustion.

That was all.

Nonetheless, when she left the office much later that day, still feeling unwell, Hannah ducked into a pharmacy around the corner from the Earl's Court flat she'd rented a room in.

She'd do a pregnancy test. There was no harm in that—it was a simple precaution.

In the privacy of her the bathroom, she unsealed the box, read the instructions, and did precisely what they said. She set an alarm on her phone, to tell her when two minutes was up.

She didn't need it, though.

It took fewer than twenty seconds for a second line to appear.

A strong, vibrant pink, showing that she was, indeed, pregnant.

With Leonidas Stathakis's baby.

'Oh, jeez.' She sat down on the toilet lid, and stared at the back of the door. Her hand curved over her stomach and she closed her eyes. His face appeared in her mind, unbidden, unwanted, and unflinchingly and just as he had been for months in her dreams, she saw him naked, his strong body and handsome face so close to her that she could breathe him in, except he was just a phantom, a ghost.

But not for long.

*It shouldn't have happened.* Despite the fact she'd torn his note into a thousand pieces and left it scattered over the marble bench-top of the luxurious penthouse kitchen, his words were indelibly imprinted into her mind.

Well, regardless of his regret, and the fact he hadn't respected her enough to say that to her face, she'd have to see him again.

There was nothing for it—she had to face this reality, to tell him the truth.

And she would—when she was ready.

Hannah checked the name against the piece of paper she clutched in her hand, looking around the marina with a frown on her face.

There was some event on, Capri Sailing Week or some such, and the whole marina was bursting with life. Enormous boats—or 'superyachts', as she'd been told they were called—lined up like swans, so graceful and imposing in the evening sun.

She knew from the search she'd done on the Internet that Stathakis Corp owned a boat that took part in the event. She also knew that Leonidas and his brother came to the event annually on their own 'superyacht'.

Photos had shown her a suntanned Leonidas relaxing on the deck, casting his eye over the race.

She'd closed out of the images as quickly as she could.

She didn't need to see him again. Not like that.

This was going to be quick, like ripping off a plaster. She'd tell him she was pregnant—not that she'd really need words. At more than five months along, she was quite visibly carrying a baby.

She'd been so tempted just to call him. To deliver the news over the phone and leave it at that, just as he'd written her a note instead of having the courage to face her the next morning.

But it was cowardly and she wasn't that. They were having a baby together—she couldn't ignore the ramifications of their night together and nor could he. At least she knew that, no matter what happened next, he'd regretted that night.

He'd regretted it, he wished that it hadn't happened, and he'd treated her with complete disdain and disrespect, skulking out in the middle of the night, leaving a note! It wasn't as if she'd have begged him for more—they'd both agreed to it being one night only. It was the salt in the wound of him vanishing, not even bothering to say goodbye.

That was the man she was having a child with.

She grabbed hold of that thought; she needed to remember that.

The Stathakis yacht was the biggest in the marina, and it was pumping with life and noise. Her eyes skimmed the yacht, running over the partygoers moving around with effortless grace, all scantily clad, from what she could see. Music with a heavy beat sounded loud and somehow seductive, so something began to beat low in her abdomen. There were staff, too, their crisp white shirts discernible even at a distance, the trays they carried overflowing with champagne flutes.

She narrowed her eyes, lifting a hand and wiping it over her forehead. She was warm—the sun was beating down, even now in the early evening, and she'd been travelling since that morning.

She was tired, too, the exhaustion of the first trimester not giving way in the second.

She moved closer to the yacht, mindful on her approach that security guards stood casually at the bridge that led to the deck.

As she approached, one of the men spoke to her in Italian. At her blank expression, he switched to Greek and then, finally, English. 'Can I help you, miss?'

'I need to see Leonidas Stathakis. It's important.'

The security guard flicked his gaze over Hannah, his expression unchanging. 'It's a private party.'

She had expected this resistance. 'If you tell him my name, I'm certain he'll want to see me.'

The guard's scepticism was obvious. 'And that is?'

'Hannah. Hannah May.' Her voice was soft, her Australian accent prominent.

The guard spoke into his walkie-talkie, the background noise of the party coming through louder when he clicked the button at its side. She discerned only her own name in the rapid delivery of information. Then, he clicked the walkie-talkie back to his hip.

'He says you can go up.'

'Thank you.'

Nerves were jangling inside her, doubts firing in her gut. Maybe she should turn around. Go back to London, or even Australia, far away. Call him with this information. Or not. She had no idea. She just knew suddenly the thought of coming face-to-face with Leonidas filled her with ice.

She was going to be sick.

'Miss? Are you okay?'

But she'd come all this way. She'd grappled with this for weeks now, she'd faced the reality of being pregnant with Leonidas's baby, trying to work out the best way to tell him. She had to tell him—there was nothing for it.

'I will be.'

Yes, she would be. She needed simply to get this over with. The faster the better. 'This way?' she prompted, gesturing towards the boat.

'And to the left.'

Hannah's smile was tight as she surveyed the crowd, not particularly relishing the idea of weaving her way through so many people. 'Thank you.'

She stepped onto a platform and then went up a set of polished timber and white stairs. At the top, another guard opened a section of the boat's balustrade, forming a gate. The noise was deafening up here. She braced herself for a moment, frozen to the spot as she recognised at least a dozen Hollywood celebrities walking around in a state of undress. Men, women, all in their bathers, suntanned, impossibly slender and toned with very white teeth and enormous eyes.

Hannah stared at them self-consciously, this world so foreign to her, so foreign to anything and anyone she knew. These people were his friends?

There was a loud noise, a laugh, and then the splashing of water. She turned, chasing the interruption, to see a handsome man standing above the pool, a grin on his chiselled face. It wasn't Leonidas, but she recognised him nonetheless from the few photos she'd pulled up while trying to find out how to contact Leonidas.

Thanos Stathakis, the playboy prince of Europe, all golden and carefree, and surrounded by a dozen women who were quite clearly vying for a place in his bed. She pulled a face, straightened her spine and began to cut through the party.

She didn't belong here. She didn't want to be here. She just needed to tell him and get out.

'Miss May?' A woman wearing a crew uniform approached Hannah, a professional smile on her pretty face. 'This way, please.'

Hannah nodded stiffly, falling into step beside the woman, almost losing her footing when she saw a Grammy award–winning singer breeze past, laughing, arm in arm with the undisputed queen of talk-show television.

Hannah stared after them, her heart pounding. She felt like a fish way, way out of water. The crew member pushed a door open and Hannah followed, grateful for the privacy and quiet the room afforded.

'Would you like anything to drink, miss?'

Hannah shook her head. 'No, thank you.'

She waited until she was alone and then scanned the room, her eyes taking in the obvious signs of wealth that were littered without care. The yacht was unlike anything she'd ever seen, the last word in luxury and money. Designer furniture filled out this room, a television the size of her bed on one wall, and through the glass partition a huge bedroom with a spa against the windows.

Leonidas's bedroom?

Her pulse picked up a notch and on autopilot she wandered towards it, her heart hammering against her chest as she pushed the door open.

Yes. She couldn't say how she knew, only there was something in the air, his masculine, alpine fragrance that instantly jolted her senses.

She backed out quickly, as though the very fires of hell were lining the floor in there.

She had to do this. She would tell him, and then leave, giving him a chance to digest it, and to consider her wishes. This would be over in minutes.

Minutes.

She waited, and with each moment that passed her nerves stretched tighter, thinner, finer and more tremulous, so, five minutes later, she honestly thought she might pass out.

She was on the brink of leaving the room and going

in search of Leonidas herself when the door burst inwards and he strode into the room, wearing only a pair of swimming shorts, and a look that—in the seconds before surprise contorted his expression—showed his impatience with her arrival.

He was partying.

He was probably the centre of attention, being just as fawned over and celebrated as his brother. Jealousy tore through her, but Hannah told herself it was outrage. Outrage that she'd been agonising over the baby they were going to have while he'd slipped out of bed and gone back to his normal life as though it had never happened.

If she'd held even a single shred of hope that he might be glad to see her, it disappeared immediately.

'Hannah.' His eyes roamed her face and then dropped lower, until he was staring at her stomach, and she felt the force of his shock, the reverberation of his confusion. It slammed into the room, slammed against her, and if she weren't so consumed with her own feelings she might almost have felt sympathy for him.

'Yes.' She answered the unspoken question, her voice slightly shaky. 'I'm pregnant. And you're the father.'

# CHAPTER FOUR

HIS EYES SWEPT SHUT, almost as if he could wipe this meeting from reality, as if he would open his gaze and she'd be gone. It wasn't until that moment Hannah realised that she'd been partly hoping he would react well to this news. While neither of them had planned this, nor wanted it particularly, a baby was still cause for celebration, wasn't it?

Apparently not.

When he opened his eyes and his gaze pierced her soul, it was with a look of rejection, and panic.

'No.' He glared at her. 'This cannot be happening.'

Hannah curved a hand around her stomach, trying to be generous, to remember he was shocked, that she'd had time to adjust to this news and he was being presented with it all now.

'Really?' She arched a brow, her obvious pregnant state contradicting that.

He swore in his native tongue and moved towards a bar in the corner, pulling out two bottles of mineral water. He stalked towards her and held one out and she took it without thinking, her fingers curving over the top.

But, oh, she was so close to him now, and the last five months disappeared, everything disappeared, except this wave of intense recognition and need, that same spark of hunger that had incinerated her on New Year's Eve.

Her breath escaped her on a hiss; she stood frozen to the spot, her eyes glued to his, her face tilted upwards, her body on alert for his nearness. It was an instant, visceral, physical reaction and it shook her to the core.

But even before her eyes, Leonidas's surprise was giving way to comprehension. His jaw tightened and he nodded slowly, releasing the water bottle into her grip and stepping away from her, turning to stare at the ocean.

'How do you feel?'

She was surprised by the question—she hadn't expected it, this rapid assimilation of information, acceptance and then a hint of civility.

'I'm mostly okay.' She nodded, opening the bottle and taking a sip gratefully. 'I'm quite tired but otherwise fine.'

He didn't react. 'Do you know what gender it is?'

Hannah nodded again, but he wasn't looking. 'Yes.' She reached into her handbag, her fingers fumbling a little as she lifted out an ultrasound picture. 'Here.'

At that word, he turned slowly, his expression grim, his gaze lowering to the flimsy black and white photograph. He made no effort to take it.

'It's a girl,' she said quietly.

He still didn't reach for the picture, but his eyes

swept shut as though he were steeling himself against this, as though it wasn't what he wanted. Hurt scored her being. But before she could fire that accusation at him, he was shooting another question at her.

'When did you find out?'

She swallowed in an attempt to bring moisture back to her dry throat. 'A while ago,' she admitted.

'When?'

A hint of guilt flared in her gut but she reminded herself she'd done nothing wrong.

'I've known for a few weeks.'

He stared at her, long and hard, for several moments. 'You didn't think I deserved to know when you did?'

She shook her head once, from one side to the other. 'You didn't think I deserved more than to wake up to a crummy note?'

He froze, completely still, and the sound of the glamorous party outside the room thumped and crashed. Hannah didn't move. She glared at him, waiting for his answer.

It came swiftly, his brow furrowing. 'So this was payback? Retaliation of some kind?'

She shook her head. 'What? No. It was nothing like that.' She sucked in a breath, not wanting to be dragged off topic. 'I just wanted a chance to get used to this before I had to deal with you.'

'And you are now used to it?' he demanded, heat in the question.

She let out a small laugh, but it was a sound completely without humour. 'I'm not sure I'll ever adjust.'

'I don't want anything from you, Leonidas,' she said firmly, not registering the way something like admiration sparked in his eyes. 'I had no idea who you were that night, nor that you're worth a squillion dollars. I have no interest in asking you for any kind of support payment or whatever.' She shuddered in rejection of the very idea.

'I mean it. This isn't my way of asking you to support me in any way. I don't want that.'

He spoke then, his voice low and husky. 'So what do you want?'

She bit down on her lip then immediately stopped when he took a step closer, his eyes on the gesture, his body seemingly pulled towards hers.

'I want...to know you'll be a part of her life,' she said quietly, her own childhood a black hole in her mind, swallowing her up. She would do whatever she could to make sure her own daughter never had to live with the grief she'd felt.

He was quiet, watching her, and nervousness fired in Hannah's gut. 'Don't misunderstand me,' she said thickly. 'I would happily never see you again. But our daughter deserves to know both her parents.' She lifted a hand, toying with the necklace she wore, running her finger over the chain distractedly. Hannah needed the security of knowing their child would have two people who loved her, two people in case something happened to one of them.

'I appreciate this news is probably an even bigger inconvenience to you than it was to me,' she said simply.

'I understand you didn't want this. You were very clear about that.' She cleared her throat, sidestepping him and moving towards the windows that framed a sensational view of the waters off the coast of Capri. 'But we are having a child together, and I don't want her to grow up thinking she's not wanted.' Hannah's voice cracked and she closed her eyes, sucking in breath, needing strength.

'You want me to be a part of our daughter's life?'

'Yes.' The word rushed out of her. She spun around, surprised to find Leonidas had come to stand right behind her, his eyes on hers, his expression impossible to comprehend.

'And what kind of part?'

She furrowed her brow, not understanding.

'Tell me, do you expect me to see her once a year? At Christmas, perhaps? Or for her birthdays, as well? Do you envisage I will spend time with my daughter according to a stopwatch?'

Hannah's eyes rounded in her face. 'I don't understand…'

'No,' he said succinctly and now she understood what was holding his face so completely still. He was angry!

'I will not be a figment of my child's life—the kind of father who exists like a tiny part of her.'

Hannah didn't get a chance to reassure him.

'My child will be raised by me.' His eyes were like flints of coal as he spoke. 'She will be raised with my name, and will have everything I can provide her with. She will be *mine*.'

At the completely possessive tone to his voice Hannah shuddered, because it was exactly how she felt, and they couldn't both raise their daughter.

'Don't make me regret coming here,' Hannah said quietly.

At this, his features grew taut, his jaw locked and his eyes showed a swirling comprehension that filled her with ice. 'Are you saying you contemplated not doing so?'

She paled, tilting her chin with a hint of rebellion. 'I've contemplated a great many things since I found out about her.'

'And was not telling me that I fathered a child one of those things you considered?'

Her cheeks glowed pink, revealing the truth of that statement. 'Briefly,' she conceded. 'Yes, of course. Wouldn't it be easier that way?'

Fury contorted his features and she rolled her eyes.

'I contemplated it for about three seconds before realising I could never do that. Obviously you deserve to know you're going to be a father. She's your child. I'm not saying you don't have a claim on her. But she's an innocent in this, she doesn't deserve to be pulled between us just because of that night.'

'I do not intend for her to be pulled between us.' He seized on this and, for a moment, she felt relief. Perhaps he was going to be reasonable after all, and not make this so difficult.

'You can be *very* involved,' she promised. 'I'm a reasonable person, Leonidas, and what I want most in this world is for our daughter to grow up secure in the love of her parents. But I want full custody. Full rights.' He didn't speak and she took strength from that. 'It's better this way, don't you see that?'

'Better for you,' he drawled, and then shook his head angrily. 'At least, you seem to think it is, but you do not have all the facts, Hannah.'

'No? What am I missing?'

He ground his teeth together. 'Does it not occur to you that there are risks to you, to her, in being connected to someone like me?'

She blinked, and something tapped the back of her mind, something she'd seen on an Internet search. Only she'd tried not to look too deeply at his life, his past—she'd felt dirty enough having to look him up on the internet to find the name of this boat.

'No one needs to know.'

His laugh was a mocking snort. 'That's simplistic and naïve. The tabloid press probably already has paparazzi on your trail. That's before you show up to this—one of the most hotly photographed events of the year—heavily pregnant and asking to see me.'

'I am not heavily pregnant,' she said, and then clamped her mouth shut in frustration and the sheer irrelevancy of that. 'And so what? Who cares? Lots of people have illegitimate children. There'll be a rumour. We'll say nothing, and then it will die down.'

'You are missing my point,' he insisted darkly. 'From the minute this news hits the public domain, you will become a part of my world, and so will she, whether you want to be or not. Thinking you can just hide away from that is unrealistic.'

'So?' she said, though she hadn't considered this, and didn't particularly like the way it made her feel. 'I'll cope.'

'As a bare minimum, you will find yourself and your every move open to speculation in the gossip papers, and our daughter will be photographed and written about even when doing the most mundane things. You will want my protection from this, Hannah, and she will certainly deserve it.'

'I'd rather find my own way to protect her,' Hannah said crisply. 'I can handle a few photographers, and as for the stories, I just won't read them.'

His smile was a grim flicker of his lips. 'Sure, give that a go.' It was pure sarcasm.

'In any event, it is not,' he continued, 'the photographers that I am concerned with.'

She waited, holding a hand protectively over her stomach without realising it.

'I was married once,' he said, finally, the words like steel.

She remembered. Oh, it had been buried deep inside her mind, but as soon as he said it she recalled reading that, somewhere, at some time.

'And my wife was murdered.'

Hannah sucked in a gasp, sympathy pushing every other emotion from her mind.

'As was my two-year-old son.'

Hannah was hot and cold, sorrow and pain shooting through her. She almost felt as though she might faint.

'They were murdered as a vendetta against my father.' The words were strained and urgent. 'They lost their lives to hurt him and punish him. They were killed because of who they were to Dion Stathakis, and to me. I will not let that happen again. I will not let that happen to our daughter.'

Hannah's chest hurt. She'd known she was pregnant for a few weeks and already she knew she would give her life for this baby. She couldn't imagine the desperate agony of losing a toddler, of knowing a toddler to have met such a violent end.

'I'm so sorry.' The words were thick with tears. 'That must have been unbearable.' She swallowed, but the tears she was so adept at fighting filled her eyes.

He didn't respond—what could he say?

'But isn't that even more reason for me to hide away? To let me move far away from you and your world?'

'You cannot hide her. Not from men like him.'

A shiver ran down Hannah's spine.

'Only I can protect you both.'

Fear made Hannah tactless. 'I beg to differ, given the past...'

His expression cracked with pain and she winced.

'I'm so sorry. That was an awful thing to say. It's just...'

'No, you're right.' He held up a hand to stall her. 'I did not appreciate the danger to Amy and Brax. I failed them.' His voice was deep and her heart ached. 'I had no idea they were being watched, nor that a madman would use them to seek revenge on my father. His conviction did much damage to our business, and my brother and

I worked tirelessly to make amends there, to return Stathakis Corp to its position of global prominence. That was my focus.

'I failed them, my wife and child, and I will never forget that, nor forgive myself.'

He straightened, his expression like iron. 'I will not make that mistake with her.'

He moved closer to Hannah, and she held her breath.

His hands curved over her stomach and she felt so much in that moment. It was as though a piece of string were wrapping from him to her, binding them, tying them together. If this had been a wedding ceremony it would have felt like a lesser commitment.

He focussed all his attention on Hannah. 'I will put everything I am into protecting you both, into ensuring men like that cannot get you. I cannot let you get on with your life as though this is simply an aberration when there may very well be a target over her head. Or yours, just because you happened to make the regrettable decision of sleeping with me one night.'

'You were the one who regretted it,' she pointed out and then shook her head, because that didn't matter any more. Panic was surging inside her; she felt as though she were falling back into a well only there was no light at the top of it.

She sucked in a breath but it burned through her lungs. 'Leonidas,' she groaned. 'I don't want anything to happen to her.'

'I won't let it,' he promised, lifting his hands to her

face, holding her steady for his inspection. 'I promise you that.'

'How can you stop it?'

His eyes roamed her face intently. 'I will protect you and our daughter with my dying breath, that is how.'

She shook her head, the madness of this incongruous with the sounds of revelry beyond the room. Fear had her forgetting everything they were to one another, the brevity of their affair, his quickness to leave her, the fact he'd intended for them never to see one another again—and she'd agreed to that. In that moment, he was her lifeline, and she lifted a hand to his chest to take hold of it.

'Do you really think we're in danger?'

His eyes held hers and she felt the battle raging within him—a desire to reassure and placate her and a need to be honest.

'I will make sure you are not. But you must do what I say, and trust me to know what is right for you, for her, for our family.'

*Family.*

The word seemed to tear through both of them in different ways, each reacting to the emotion of that word, the harsh implications of such a term.

He looked stricken and Hannah felt completely shocked. She hadn't had a family in a long time. And even though this had been foisted on both of them, the word felt warm and loaded with promise. She swallowed past a lump in her throat and shook her head, nothing making sense.

'How? What? Tell me, Leonidas. I need to know she'll be okay.'

'Marry me,' he said simply, the words like rocks dropping into the boat.

'What?'

'Marry me, as soon as is legally possible.'

She sucked in a breath, his words doing strange things to her. In a thousand years, she hadn't expected this, and she had no way of processing how she felt. Marriage? To Leonidas Stathakis?

'How the heck is that going to help?'

'You'll be my wife, under my protection, living in my home. We will be raising our child together.'

The picture he painted was so seductive. Hannah took a fortifying breath, trying to disentangle the irrational desire to make sure her daughter didn't suffer the same miserable upbringing as she had from what was actually the *right* decision. It was impossible to think clearly.

Hannah shook her head slowly. 'It would never work between us.'

'What is there to "work"?' he asked simply. 'You love our child, do you not?'

Hannah's eyes sparked with his. 'With all my heart.'

'And you want to do what is best for her?'

Hannah's chin tilted in silent agreement.

'So trust me. Trust me to protect you both, to ensure her safety. I will never let anything happen to either of you.'

She nodded, listening to his words, hearing the intent in them.

'I cannot have my daughter raised anywhere but

in my home,' he murmured, clearing his throat. She jerked her gaze to his and the depth of feeling in his eyes almost tore her in two. 'I need to *know* she is safe. That you are safe.' He turned away from her, stalking towards the table. He placed his palms on it, staring straight ahead, out into the water. The party raged outside their doors, but inside this room, it was deathly silent.

'We don't really even know each other,' she said quietly, even as her heart was shifting, and her mind was moving three steps ahead to her inevitable acceptance.

Two main points were working on her to accept. Whatever threat he perceived, there was enough of a basis in fact for Hannah to be seriously concerned. His wife and child had been murdered. His father was in the mob. These threats did not simply disappear—she was in danger, and so was their daughter.

And even if it weren't for that, there were other considerations. Hannah's parents had died unexpectedly and her whole world had imploded. She'd been moved to her aunt and uncle's—who she'd barely known—and been left to their dubious care. She'd been miserable and alone.

There were no guarantees in life, but weren't two parents better than one wherever possible? Wasn't it more of an insurance policy for their daughter to know both her mother and father? What if Hannah insisted on raising her alone, with Leonidas as a 'bit player' in their lives, and then something happened to Hannah? And what if by then he'd married someone else, and their child was an outsider?

As Hannah had been.

She expelled a soft breath, the reality of that like a punch in the gut. Because marrying Leonidas would mean she'd always be on the edge, that she'd never find that one thing she knew she really wanted, deep down: a true family of her own. A family to which she belonged. People who adored and wanted her.

But this wasn't about her; it wasn't about her wants and desires. All that mattered was their baby.

With resignation in her turbulent green eyes, she lifted her head a little, partway to nodding.

He saw it, and his eyes narrowed then he straightened, relief in his features. 'We will fly to the island today. My lawyer will take care of the paperwork.'

But it was all so rushed. Hannah spun away from him, lifting her water bottle from the table's edge and sipping it.

'I have a job, Leonidas.'

'Quit.'

There were only two weeks left of her maternity contract. It wasn't the worst thing to do, though she hated the idea of leaving her boss in the lurch. She dropped her hand to her stomach and thought of their baby and nothing else seemed to matter.

For her? She'd do anything.

'You will be safe on the island,' he insisted, as though he could read her thoughts and knew exactly which buttons to press to get her to agree.

'On Chrysá Vráchia?' she asked distractedly.

'No.' His expression took on a contemplative look. 'My island.'

'You have your own island?' Disbelief filled the tone of her words.

'Yes. Not far from Chrysá.' He moved closer, his eyes scanning her face. 'It is beautiful. You'll like it.'

She was sure she would, but it was all happening so fast. Even knowing she would agree—that she had agreed—she heard herself say softly, 'This is crazy.'

And perhaps he thought she was going to change her mind, because he crossed the room and caught her arms, holding her close to him, his gaze locked to hers.

'You have to see that I cannot let our child be raised away from me. And, following that logic, that it is best for us to be married, to at least try to present our child with a sense of family, even when we know it to be a lie.'

Her heart squeezed tight, her lungs expelled air in a rush. Because it was exactly what she wanted, exactly what she'd just been thinking. Still, cynicism was quick to follow relief. 'You really think we can fool our child into believing we're a normal couple?'

His lips were a grim slash and she had the strongest impression that he couldn't have been less impressed if she'd suggested he set fire to this beautiful, enormous yacht.

'I think we owe it to our child to try.'

# CHAPTER FIVE

His STATE-OF-THE-ART HELICOPTER flew them from the yacht to the airport, where his private jet was waiting.

It was the kind of plane Hannah had flown to Italy aboard, the kind that commercial airlines used, only it bore the name 'Leonidas Stathakis' in gold down the side. When she stepped on board it was exactly like walking into a plush hotel.

As with the yacht, everything was white or beige, and incredibly comfortable. Enormous seats, like armchairs, chandeliers made of crystal, and, deeper into the plane, a boardroom, a cinema and four bedrooms.

'Have a seat.' Leonidas indicated a bank of chairs, and as she did she couldn't shake the feeling that it was more like a job interview than anything else.

For the hundredth time since leaving his yacht, since lifting up into the sky and hovering over the picture-perfect Capri marina, Hannah questioned the wisdom of what she was doing.

But every time doubt reared its head and begged her to reconsider, she heard his words anew. *'My wife was murdered. As was my two-year-old son.'* And a frisson of terror sprinted down her spine and she knew she would do anything to avoid that same fate befalling their daughter.

Every primal, maternal instinct she possessed roared to life. She wouldn't allow their child to be harmed.

And nor would he.

She'd felt that promise from him and trusted him, had known he would lay down his own life if necessary to protect hers, to protect their child's.

And suddenly, the world seemed frightening and huge, and Hannah knew that if she walked away from Leonidas now, she would be alone, with unknown dangers lurking, with threats to their child she couldn't possibly appreciate, let alone avoid.

'The usual month-long notification period for weddings will be waived,' he explained, sitting opposite her, his long legs encroaching on her space so that if she wasn't very careful, they would be touching and the little fires still buzzing beneath her skin would arc into full-blown wildfires once more.

It took her a moment to collect her mind from the fears that were circulating and bring herself back to the present. 'Why?'

'What do you mean?'

Her sea-green eyes showed confusion. 'Well, isn't that the law? Why would that be changed for us?'

He lifted a brow and comprehension dawned.

'Because you asked for it to be, and you're Leonidas Stathakis.'

He shrugged. 'Yes.'

'And you get whatever you want?'

His eyes were like coal once more. 'No.'

Her heart twisted because of course he didn't. He'd just told her he'd lost his family—clearly his life wasn't that of a charmed man.

'Why rush, though, Leonidas?'

All of his attention was on her and she trembled for a different reason now, as the heat of his gaze touched something deep in her soul, stirring the remnants of their passion and desire anew. She swallowed, her throat dry, her cheeks blushing pink.

'Because there is no point in delay. Because I want you to be protected from this day, this moment. I will take no risks with our daughter's life,' he said firmly. 'Nor with yours. You should not have been brought into this.'

She opened her mouth to confront him, but he continued. 'Having sex with you was a moment of weakness, a stupid, selfish decision that I regretted instantly. Believe me, Hannah, if I could take that back, if I could have never met you...' He shook his head, looking away, as the plane began to move on the runway.

'I am sorry to have drawn you into my world. I am sorry that we must marry, sorry that we are having a child together. It is my fault, all of it. I cannot change that night, what happened between us, but I can do my damned best to ensure no further harm befalls you.'

'Harm?' she repeated, the word just a croak. 'You think of this pregnancy as harm?'

'I think it is a mistake,' he muttered. 'But one we must live with.'

Her temper spiked, disbelief at his callous words making her chest hurt. 'How can you talk about our baby like that?' she found herself whispering, even though that 'baby' was still very much inside her.

'You said as much yourself,' he pointed out logically. 'You didn't want this.'

'I didn't *plan* on it happening,' she corrected caustically. 'I'm twenty-three years old; I thought children would be way off in the future.'

He dipped his head in silent concession.

'But, Leonidas, almost as soon as I learned of this pregnancy, I have loved this baby, and I have wanted our daughter, and I have known I would put this child first. For ever and always.'

He digested her words, his expression giving little away, and then he nodded, as the plane hurtled faster down the runway before lifting into the sky.

'And in marrying me, I understand you are doing just that—putting our baby first. You do not wish for this marriage, and nor do I.' He ground his teeth together. 'And yet, for this child, here we are.' He reached into his pocket and pulled out his phone, not seeing the way her face paled at his harshly delivered words. 'I have some questions for you. My lawyer emailed them across.'

'Questions?' It was a rapid change of subject, one that made her head spin. 'What for?'

'The marriage licence. The prenuptial agreement. Setting up your bank accounts and the family trust.'

'Woah.' She was still reeling from his repeated insistence of how little he wanted this marriage, and, even though he was surely echoing her own thoughts, hearing them voiced made her head spin a little. It was all too much, too soon.

'Can't we just…take it one day at a time?'

'Let me make this clear,' he said, leaning forward, his expression that of a hard-nosed tycoon.

She swallowed, but refused to be cowed by his closeness, by his look of steel. 'Yes?'

'One week from today we will be married. You will be my wife: Mrs Hannah Stathakis. You will be marrying someone who is worth over a hundred billion American dollars. Your life, as you know it, is about to cease completely. There is no "taking it one day at a time". In what? Three months? Four? We will have a child. That is the deadline hanging over our heads. Within four months, we need to be able to find a way to relate, to exist as parents. We cannot delay. Surely you see that?'

It was all so shocking, so impossible to comprehend and also so reasonable. She heard his words and closed her eyes, because the final sentence was what really got through to her.

His net worth was awe-inspiring, his suggestion that she too might be worth a fortune, even his reminder that their daughter would inherit such a sum, were all details that caused her heart to pound, and not necessarily in a good way. But what he'd said that had really spoken to Hannah had been right at the end.

They had a deadline. A tiny little time bomb ticking away inside her belly.

They needed to find a way to make this work and he was showing himself to be cognisant of that.

'Your full name is Hannah May?'

'Hannah Grace May.' She nodded, tightening her seat belt and looking out of the window on autopilot. Capri was tiny beneath them, just a beautiful picture-book piece of land, looming from the sea, all verdant green against the deep blue of the Med, the superyachts tiny white shapes now, clean and crisp.

Was it really only that morning she'd flown in over Italy, and stared down at this exact same view? How certain she'd been then of being able to tell Leonidas she was pregnant and then depart, confident he'd accept her suggestion of being a small but vital part of their daughter's life.

'Birth date?'

She responded, thinking back to her last birthday, right before Christmas. Angus had thrown her a surprise dinner party and she'd pretended to be thrilled, but Hannah hated surprises, and she'd wondered how he couldn't know that about her. She'd wondered how he could think she'd like being the centre of attention like that, with everyone in the restaurant staring at her, waiting for her to smile and make a little speech thanking them for coming.

Hannah didn't like surprises but she'd chalked the party up to something they'd laugh about in ten years' time. Besides, he'd gone to a huge amount of effort, she wasn't about to be ungrateful in the face of that.

THE GREEK'S BILLION-DOLLAR BABY

She'd had no idea, though, that a way bigger surprise had been in store for her, nor that his 'effort' in arranging such an elaborate party was undoubtedly his way of compensating for the fact he was sleeping with Hannah's cousin behind her back.

Her jaw tightened, and unconsciously she gripped her hands tightly in her lap, the past rushing towards her, wrapping around her, forcing her to look at it, to be in it even when it was strangling her. To remember the sight of her cousin and her fiancé, their limbs entwined, the dark black sheets of Angus's bed in stark contrast to their flesh, Michelle's white-blonde hair glistening in the evening light.

It was a betrayal on two fronts. That her fiancé would cheat on her was bad enough, but with someone she'd been raised to think of as a sister?

Indignation and hurt made her breath burn a little.

Capri swam beneath her, ancient and striking, and it offered a hint of perspective. How many millions of people had walked those shores, swum in these seas, each of them with their own problems and concerns, none of those concerns mattering, really, in the huge scheme of life and this earth? One day, she'd forget the sting of this betrayal, the second loss of family she'd had to endure.

'Parents' names?'

She swept her eyes shut, thinking of her biological parents, seeing her mother's smile as she tucked Hannah into bed, stroking her hair, singing their goodnight song.

'Ellie—Eleanor—and Brad.'

There were more questions and she answered them

matter-of-factly—it was easier to simply provide the information than to launch into explanations with each point.

'Why did your engagement end?'

That question had her swivelling her head to him, and she was grateful that a flight attendant chose that exact moment to enter the cabin, offering drinks.

'Just water,' Hannah murmured.

'Coffee.' He focussed on Hannah. 'Are you hungry?'

She was. 'A little.'

'And some dinner.'

'Yes, sir.'

The attendant left, and Hannah thought—for a moment—Leonidas might have forgotten the question he'd posed. But of course he hadn't. This man probably never forgot a thing. 'Your fiancé?'

'Right.' She was surprised at how well she'd kept her voice neutral.

'He cheated on me.' She shrugged as though it didn't matter. 'It kind of killed my interest in marrying him.'

'I can imagine it would.' He was watching her as though she were a puzzle he could put back together if only he had enough time. 'You hadn't slept with him. His idea, or yours?'

'His.'

His expression showed surprise. 'Why?'

The flight attendant reappeared with drinks, placing them down on the armrest table each had in their seat and leaving again.

'Romance.'

Leonidas lifted a brow. 'You think sex isn't romantic?'

Heat exploded through her body and she clamped her knees close together to stop them from shaking. Sex with Leonidas had gone beyond romance. It had been passion and fire, everything she could imagine wanting from a lover.

'I wouldn't know.' She dipped her eyes lower, studying the carpet on the floor of the aeroplane as though it were a fascinating work of art.

'So how come you were a virgin?' he pushed.

Hannah lifted her gaze, forcing herself to meet his curious eyes. 'We decided we'd wait.'

'There was no one before him?'

She bit down on her lip, shaking her head from side to side. 'Is that so unusual?'

His expression showed cynicism and disbelief. 'In my experience, yes.'

She laughed then, shaking her head a little. 'Stop looking at me like that.'

'Like what?'

'As though I'm some kind of... I don't know. As though I'm an alien.'

'Your inexperience is rare, that's all,' he corrected. 'Particularly given the fact you were engaged.'

'Angus and I...' She swallowed, the bitterness impossible to completely suppress. 'We were friends for a long time. The dating thing came out of nowhere and I guess our relationship didn't completely transition. Sex wasn't a drawcard for me. I guess it wasn't for him, either.'

'You did not desire him?'

Ridiculously, Hannah felt a buzz of disloyalty at admitting as much. 'Not really. We weren't about that.'

'What were you "about"?'

'I loved him,' she responded, simply, 'and I thought he loved me. That was enough.'

Leonidas nodded thoughtfully. 'So that was also a pragmatic marriage.'

Hannah's eyes widened at his description. 'What do you mean?'

'You agreed to marry a man simply because it made sense, because you thought you loved each other, without having any idea if you were physically compatible. So this marriage—ours—already has more going for it.'

Hearing him refer to their marriage caused her heart to trip a little, banging against her sternum. 'How do you figure? Angus was one of my closest friends…'

'Which means very little given that he betrayed your trust and slept around behind your back.'

'Woah. Don't go easy on me, will you?'

'I don't think you want anyone to go easy on you, Hannah May.'

She startled a little at his unexpected perceptiveness. 'It was less than six months ago. It's still kind of raw.'

His expression barely shifted yet she had the feeling he was saving that little revelation, storing it away. 'He cheated on you. He doesn't deserve a second thought.'

She nodded, having said as much to herself.

'Is he still with her?'

Hannah reached for her water, sipping it, trying to tamp down on that little bundle of pain. 'No. Not according to my aunt.'

Leonidas nodded sharply, as if filing away that information. 'There is no love between you and me, Hannah, but there is desire enough to burn us alive if we are not careful. And there is a baby—which we both want to protect and cherish.'

'Yes. I do.'

'Neither of us wanted this, but we can make our marriage a success.' He said it with such fierce determination she almost laughed, as though she were simply a property he wanted to acquire, a piece of real estate he needed to buy.

Her own questions zipped through her. She sipped her water, balling her courage. 'Your wife and son... when did they...?'

His eyes were coal-like in his autocratic face. 'Almost five years ago.'

'I'm so sorry.' She spoke gently, softly. 'You said they were murdered?'

His eyes narrowed and his skin paled almost imperceptibly. 'Yes.'

'By whom?'

He held a hand up, silencing her with the gesture. 'I have no intention of discussing it, Hannah. My first marriage is off limits.'

The words smarted and she couldn't resist pointing

out his hypocrisy. 'But you were just asking me about my fiancé.'

'You were happy to talk about it.'

Hannah's brow furrowed. 'No, I wasn't. I answered your questions because we're getting married.' How strange those words felt in her mouth. 'And if you're going to be my husband, it seems like the kind of thing you have a right to know about.'

He tilted his head in concession but his gaze was steady. 'I will not discuss Amy and Brax.'

Hannah expelled an angry rush of breath. 'Well, that seems kind of dumb.'

He clearly hadn't been expecting that response. 'Oh, really?' There was danger in the silky drawl.

'Yeah, really.' The flight attendant returned, brandishing a platter loaded with Italian delicacies. Cheeses, ham, fruit, vegetable sticks and dips, breads, olive oil and vinegar. The aroma hit her in the gut and she realised she was actually starving.

But other feelings still took precedence. When they were alone again, she continued, 'You were married and had a son, and you lost them. You lost your family.'

Her voice caught because she knew more than enough about how that felt—to be safe in the bosom and security of your loved ones one day, then to be adrift at sea, cast out, alone, bereft, with none of the usual place markers to help you find your bearings.

'Thank you for the neat recitation of this fact.'

Her nostrils flared. 'I only mean that's a huge part of

you. Don't you think our child will want to learn about her half-brother one day? That's a part of *her* life.'

Despite the fact his expression remained the same, his breath grew louder, and she would have sworn she saw panic cross his eyes.

'No.' He said the word like a curse, harsh and compelling.

Hannah sat perfectly still.

'She will never know about Brax. *Never.*'

Hannah's heart thumped hard in her chest.

'I will not speak of them. Not to you, not to her, not to anyone.'

She truly didn't think he meant it as an insult—he was caught on the back foot and the sheer strength of his emotions made him speak without thinking. But the vitriol in the statement sliced through her, filling her organs with acid.

'You're seeing this marriage, and our daughter, as an abstract concept,' she said gently, even when her heart was hurting. 'You're thinking of her as a baby only. What about when she's ten? Fifteen? Twenty? When you and she are friends as well as family, when she's sitting here where I am, on a plane, opposite you, and she's asking her father about his life. Do you really think you can keep such a huge part of yourself shielded from her? And me, for that matter?'

He drank his coffee, before piercing her with his jet-black eyes. 'Yes.'

'You're being incredibly obtuse and naïve.' But the words lacked zing. They were said with sympathy. No one knew more about the toll grief took when it was kept locked deep inside a person.

'I am sorry you think so.' He pushed his untouched plate aside and pulled a newspaper from the armrest. He flicked it up, pointedly blanking her.

It was galling, and only the fact that his stance was obviously driven by a deep, painful sadness kept her silent.

He didn't want to talk about his family. Yet.

They barely knew each other, despite this bizarre agreement they'd entered into. They would marry—in a week—and the very idea stirred her pulse to life. But despite the marriage, they'd spent only a few hours in one another's company. They were virtually strangers. Of course he didn't want to crack his heart open and lay everything out before her.

He was guarding his privacy, as befitted the newness of all this. Over time, as they grew to know one another, he was bound to change, to open up to her more.

She lifted a strawberry, popping it in her mouth, tasting the sweetness, relishing its freshness. She wanted him to trust her, and she had to show him how. To keep opening up to him, even when it felt counterintuitive, even when the past had shown her to be more guarded with herself, to protect her feelings.

'I felt undesirable,' Hannah murmured, reaching for another strawberry.

Leonidas pushed the top of the paper down, so his eyes could meet hers. There was a trace of coldness there, from their earlier conversation. She pushed on regardless.

'With Angus. I didn't really feel anything for him, physically, and he suggested we wait until we were married, so I agreed. I heard about couples not being able to keep their hands off each other and, honestly, I thought there was something wrong with me.'

She bit down on her lower lip thoughtfully. 'I presumed I just wasn't really sexual. I thought he wasn't, either. Then I saw him in bed with someone else, and I found out they'd been sleeping together for over a month, and the penny dropped. He was sexual. He liked sex. He just didn't want me.'

Leonidas placed the paper on his knees, his steady gaze trained on her face.

'I never felt like I wanted to rip a guy's clothes off. It was as though hormones left me completely behind.' She shrugged and then homed her own gaze in, focussing on his lips. Lips that were strong in his face, powerful and compelling. Lips that had kissed her and tipped her world upside down.

'But you...'

He arched a brow, silently prompting her to continue.

'You left me breathless,' she admitted, even when a part of her wondered if she should say as much, if it didn't leave her exposed and vulnerable, weakened in some way. 'I can't explain it. I felt desire for the first time in my life and I...'

'Go on,' he prompted, the words a little throaty, and

she was so glad: glad that maybe he was affected by her confession in some way.

'I felt desirable for the first time in my life, too. I liked it. I liked the way you looked at me.' She turned away now, clearing her throat, looking towards the window.

Leonidas leaned forward, surprising her by placing his hand on hers. Sparks shot from her wrist and through her whole body. 'Your fiancé was an idiot for giving you a moment's doubt on this score.'

Her laugh was dismissive, but he leaned further forward, so their knees brushed. 'You are very, very sexy,' he said, simply, and heat began to burn in her veins.

'I don't mean that,' she said, shaking her head. 'You don't need to… I just meant to explain…'

'I know what you meant.' He sat back in his seat, regarding her once more. 'And I am telling you that you are a very sensual woman. You have no idea how I have been tormented by memories of that night, Hannah Grace May.'

# CHAPTER SIX

THE MEDITERRANEAN GLISTENED just beyond the window of his study. On the second floor of his mansion, and jutting out a little from the rest of the building, this workspace boasted panoramic views of the ocean. Leonidas braced his arms on the windowsill, staring out at it, his breath burning in his lungs, his head spinning as comprehension sledged into him from both sides.

In Capri, he'd acted purely on instinct.

His wife and child had died, but here was another woman, another child, and they weren't Amy and Brax—they'd never be to him what Amy and Brax were—but they were still his responsibility.

The fact he would never have chosen to become a father again was a moot point.

She was pregnant.

They were having a child—a daughter.

His chest clutched and he slammed his eyes closed, the taste of adrenalin filling his mouth. A thousand and one memories tormented him from the inside out, like acid rushing through his veins.

Amy, finding out she was pregnant. Amy, swelling

with his child. Amy, uncomfortable. Amy, in labour. Amy, nursing their infant. Amy, watching Brax learn to walk. Amy, patiently reading to Brax, loving him, laughing at him.

Amy.

His eyes opened, bleakness in the depths of their obsidian centres.

If sleeping with another woman was a betrayal of Amy, what then was this? Creating a whole new family, and bringing them to this island?

He grunted, shaking his head, knowing that wasn't fair. Amy would never have expected him to close himself off from life, from another relationship, another family.

But Leonidas had sworn he would do exactly that.

The idea of Hannah ever becoming anything to him besides this was anathema. Theirs was a marriage born of necessity, a marriage born of a need to protect his child, and the woman he'd made pregnant. It was a marriage of duty, that was all.

Flint formed in his eyes, his resolution hardening.

They would marry—there was no other option. Even if it weren't for the possible threat to Hannah's life, Leonidas acknowledged his ancient sense of honour would have forced him to propose, to insist upon marriage. Growing up in the shipwreck of his father's marriages hadn't undone the lessons his grandfather had taught him, nor the unity he'd seen in his grandparents' marriage.

Their child, their daughter, deserved to grow up with

that same example. Hannah deserved to have support and assistance.

And what else?

His body tightened as he flashed back to the way he'd responded to her that night, the way desire had engulfed him like a tidal wave, drowning him in his need for her. The way he'd kissed her, his mouth taking possession of hers, his whole body firing with a desperate need to possess her, even when he'd spent the past five months telling himself their night together had been a mistake.

It *had* been a mistake. It should never have happened, but it had, and, looking back, he didn't think he could have stopped it. Not for all the money in all the world. There had been a force pulling him to her; the moment their bodies had collided he'd felt as though he'd been jolted back to life. He'd looked at her and felt a surge of need that had gone beyond logic and sense. It had been an ancient, incessant beating of a drum and ignoring it had not been an option.

Perhaps it still wasn't...

Glass. Steel. Designer furniture. Servants. More glass. Famous art. Views of the ocean that just wouldn't quit. Hannah stared around Leonidas's mansion, the luxury of it almost impossible to grapple with, and wondered if she'd stepped into another dimension.

Did people really live like this?

He had his own airfield, for goodness' sake! His private jet had touched down on the island, a glistening ocean surrounding them as the sun dipped towards the horizon. She'd expected a limousine but there'd been several golf carts parked near the airstrip and he'd led her to one of them, opening the door for her in a way that made her impossibly aware of his breadth, strength and that musky, hyper-masculine fragrance of his.

When he'd sat beside her, their knees had brushed and she'd remembered what he'd said to her in the plane. *'You have no idea how I have been tormented by memories of that night.'*

Her belly stirred with anticipation and heat slicked between her legs.

At first, she hadn't seen the house. Mansion. She'd been too distracted by the beauty of this island. Rocky, primal in some way, just like Leonidas, with fruit groves to one side, grapevines running down towards the ocean and then, finally, a more formal, landscaped garden with huge olive and hibiscus trees providing large, dark patches of shade in the lead up to the house.

Leonidas had given her a brief tour, introducing Hannah to the housekeeper, Mrs Chrisohoidis, before excusing himself. 'I want to get some things organised.' He'd frowned, and she'd felt, for the first time, a hint of awkwardness at being here, in the house of a man she barely knew, whom she was destined to marry and raise a child with.

'Okay.' She'd smiled, to cover it, thinking that she had her own 'things' to organise. Like the room she was renting in Earl's Court and the job she was expected back at in a few days, and an aunt and uncle who deserved to know not only that she was pregnant but also that she was getting married.

None of these were obligations Hannah relished meeting and so she decided, instead, to explore. There was plenty of house to lose herself in, and with the approach of dusk, and only the occasional staff member to interrupt, she went from room to room, trying to get her bearings.

The property itself was spectacular. The initial impression that it was a virtual palace only grew as she saw more and more of it. But what she did realise, after almost an hour of wandering, was that there was a distinct lack of anything personal. Beyond the art, which must surely reflect something of Leonidas's taste, there was a complete lack of personal paraphernalia.

No pictures, no *stuff.* Nothing to show who lived here, nor the family he'd had and lost.

The sun finally kissed the sea and orange exploded across the sky, highlighted by dashes of pink. Hannah abandoned her tour, moving instead to the enormous terrace she'd seen when she'd first arrived. No sooner had she stepped onto it than the housekeeper appeared.

'Miss May, would you like anything to eat or drink?'

Hannah thought longingly of an ice-cold glass of wine and grimaced. 'A fruit juice?' she suggested.

'Very good. And a little snack?' The housekeeper was lined, her tanned skin marked with the lines of a life well-lived and filled with laughter. Her hair, once dark, had turned almost completely silver, except at her temples, where some inky colour stubbornly clung.

'I'm not very hungry.' Hannah wasn't sure why she said the words apologetically, only it felt a little as if the housekeeper was excited at the prospect of having someone else to feed.

'Ah, but you are eating for two, no?' And her eyes twinkled, crinkling at the corners with the force of her smile, and Hannah's chest squeezed because, for the first time since discovering her pregnancy, someone seemed completely overjoyed with the news.

Her flatmates had been shocked, her boss had been devastated at the possibility of losing someone he'd come to rely on so completely, and Leonidas had been... what? How had he felt? Hannah couldn't say with certainty, only it wasn't happiness. Shock. Fear. Worry. Guilt.

'My appetite hasn't really been affected,' she said.

'Ah, that will come,' the housekeeper murmured knowingly. 'May I?' She gestured to Hannah's stomach.

Mrs Chrisohoidis lifted her aged hands, with long, slender fingers and short nails, and pressed them to Hannah's belly and for a moment, out of nowhere, Hannah was hit with a sharp pang of regret—sadness that her own mother wouldn't get to enjoy this pregnancy with her.

'It's a girl?'

Hannah's expression showed surprise. 'Yes. How did you know?'

At this, Mrs Chrisohoidis laughed. 'A guess. I have a fifty per cent chance, no?'

Hannah laughed, too. 'Yes. Well, you guessed right.'

'A girl is good. Good for him.' She looked as though she wanted to say something more, but then shrugged. 'I bring you some bread.'

Hannah suppressed a smile and turned her attention back to the view, thinking once more of the beautiful coastline of Chrysá Vráchia, of how beautiful that island had been, how perfect everything about that night had seemed.

She'd longed to visit the island from the first time she'd seen footage of it in a movie and had been captivated by the cliffs that were cast of a stone that shimmered gold at sunrise and sunset. The fact she'd been able to book her flights so easily, the fact Leonidas had been there in the bar and she'd looked at him and felt an instant pull of attraction...the fact he'd reciprocated. It had all seemed preordained, right down to the conception of a child despite the fact they'd used protection.

When she heard the glass doors behind her slide open once more, she turned around with an easy smile on her face, expecting to see the housekeeper returning. Only it wasn't Mrs Chrisohoidis who emerged, carrying a champagne flute filled with orange juice.

'Leonidas.' Her smile faltered. Not because she wasn't happy to see him but because a simmering heat overtook any other thoughts and considerations.

'I am sorry I left you so long.'

'It's fine.' The last thing she wanted was for him to see her as an inconvenience—a house guest he had to care for. She knew the feeling well. Being foisted upon an unwilling aunt and uncle taught one to recognise those signs with ease. She ignored the prickle of disappointment and panic at finding herself in this situation, yet again.

This wasn't the same. She was an adult now, making her own decisions, choosing what was best for her child. 'You don't need to feel like you have to babysit me,' she said, a hint of defensiveness creeping into her statement.

His nod showed agreement with her words and, she thought, a little gratitude.

He didn't want to be saddled with a clinging housemate any more than she intended to be one.

'I will show you around, after dinner.'

'I've already had a look around,' she murmured, but her mind was zeroed in on his use of the word 'dinner'. It had all happened so fast she hadn't stopped to think about what their marriage would look like. Would it be this? Dinner together? Two people living in this huge house, pretending to be here by choice?

Or polite strangers, trapped in an elevator with one another, having to stay that way until the moment of escape? Except there was no escape here, no one coming to jimmy the doors open and cajole the lift into motion.

This was her life—his life.

'And I mean what I said. Please don't feel you have to keep me company, or have dinner with me or anything. I know what this is.'

'Ne?' he prompted curiously.

Mrs Chrisohoidis appeared then, carrying not only some bread, but a whole platter, similar to the one they'd shared on the flight, but larger and more elaborate, furnished with many dips, vegetables, fish, cheeses and breads.

'I make your favourite for dinner.' She smiled at Leonidas as she placed the platter on a table towards the edge of the terrace.

'Thank you, Marina.'

They both watched her retreat and then Leonidas gestured towards the table.

'She's worked for you a while?' Hannah eyed the delicious platter as she sat down and found that, to her surprise, she was in fact hungry after all. She reached for an olive, lifting it to her lips, delighting in its fleshy orb and salty flavour.

'Marina?' He nodded. 'For as long as I can remember.'

That intrigued her. 'Since you were young?'

He nodded.

'So she worked for your parents?'

'Yes.'

A closed door. Just like his wife and son.

Hannah leaned against the balcony, her back to the view, her eyes intent on the man she was going to marry. 'Did you grow up here?'

He regarded her thoughtfully. 'No.'

'Where, then?'

'Everywhere.' A laconic shrug.

'I see. So this is also "off limits"?'

Her directness clearly surprised him. He smiled, a tight gesture, and shook his head. 'No. I simply do not talk about my parents often. Perhaps I've forgotten how.'

She could relate to that. Aunt Cathy had hated Hannah talking about her own mother and her father. *'He was my brother! How do you think it makes me feel to hear you going on about them? Heartbroken, that's how.'* And nine-year-old Hannah had learned to keep her parents alive in her own mind, her own head, rather than by sharing her memories with anyone else who could mirror them back to her.

Angus had asked about them, but by then she'd been so used to cosseting her memories that it hadn't come easily to explain what they'd been like.

'They divorced when I was young.'

'That was hard on you?'

'Yes.'

Mrs Chrisohoidis appeared once more, this time with a little bowl of chocolates. 'For the baby,' she said, and winked as she placed them down on the table.

'But there was a silver lining, too, because part of the divorce was a new brother.'

'How does that work?'

'My father had an affair. Thanos was the by-product. It caused my parents' divorce, but they'd been catastrophically miserable, anyway. I was glad they were separating; glad there would at last be some peace. And Thanos arrived, only three months my junior.'

'That must have been strange. How old were you?'

'Eight.'

'And he lived here?'

At this, Leonidas's expression was thoughtful, darkly so. 'His mother gave my father full custody.'

'That must have been hard for her.'

Leonidas shook his head. 'Hardest of all for Thanos, I'm sure.'

'How so?'

'His mother gave him up quite willingly,' Leonidas said softly, his expression shifting to one of compassion so Hannah's heart turned over in her chest. 'Thanos was—and remains—an incredibly strong-willed, stubborn character. She could not cope with him.'

Hannah's jaw dropped open. 'But he was just a boy! Surely there were ways of making him listen to her?'

'Who knows? But one day, when he was eight, she showed up and left him with my father. She said she couldn't do it any more.'

Sympathy scored deep in Hannah's veins. 'That must have been so hard for him. And your mother!'

'My mother hated him,' Leonidas said grimly. 'She treated him like a street dog.'

Hannah felt as though she could cry! Having experienced exactly this treatment herself, she felt an odd link to Leonidas's brother, a desire to look at him and comfort him, to tell him he was worthy, just as she'd always wished someone would say to her.

'But your father took him in,' Hannah said quietly, hoping there was a happy ending for the little boy Thanos had been.

'My father was bullish about custody. He had money, resources, staff. He ensured he had the raising of us. We were *his*, you see. Not boys so much as heirs. Proof of his virility. As I got older, I came to realise that he enjoyed the story of Thanos and my closeness in age.

Far from finding it awkward, he relished the proof of his desirability. He boasted about it.'

Hannah ground her teeth together.

'You're not close to him?'

Leonidas took a sip of his wine; Hannah's gaze didn't falter. 'No.'

She had the feeling she was moving closer to ground he wished to remain private, topics he'd prefer not to discuss. Rather than approach it directly, she circled around it this time. 'Would you have preferred to stay with your mother?'

He frowned, thoughtfully. 'My mother was American. She moved to Las Vegas when they split. I didn't want to go.'

'It must have been hard for her. Leaving you, I mean.'

Leonidas's smile showed disagreement, but his response was a banal, 'Perhaps.'

'Do you see her much now?'

'Once a year, for an obligatory birthday visit.'

'Yours, or hers?'

'Hers.' He sipped his wine again, then turned to face Hannah. 'And you, Hannah?'

'What about me?'

His eyes swept over her face and then zeroed in on her lips, staying there for so long that they parted on a rushed breath and began to tingle; she was remembering his kiss and aching for it anew.

'What about your own parents?'

It was like being dragged into a well that was completely dark. She felt the blackness surround her and her expression closed off, her skin paling. She jerked her head, turning away from him and looking towards the horizon. The sun was gone but the sky remained tinged with colour.

Her breathing felt forced and unnatural and she struggled to find words.

'Hannah?'

She nodded. He had every right to ask—this street went both ways. She wanted to know about him, she had a strange, consuming curiosity to understand him. It made sense he would expect the same courtesy.

'My parents are dead.' How was it possible that those words still stung? It had been a long time, the reality of being orphaned was one she'd lived with for many years.

'I'm sorry.' She felt his proximity rather than saw him move closer. His body was behind hers, warm and strong, and instantly reassuring.

'It was years ago. I was only a child.'

He didn't say anything, but he was right there. If she spun around, they'd be touching.

'My mum used to love that movie—*The Secret Princess*. I watched it a little while after she'd died, and I wanted to go to Chrysá Vráchia ever since.'

He made a noise of comprehension and now she did turn, and, just as she'd expected, it brought their bodies together, his so strong and broad that she felt as if she could weather almost any storm if he was there.

'And then?' he prompted, shifting a little, so his legs were wider than her body, and he pressed his hands to the balcony balustrading behind her, so she was effectively trapped by him.

'Then?' Her voice was husky.

'You came to the island for New Year's Eve, to see the fireworks. What were you going to do then?'

'I hadn't really thought about it. But I guess in the back of my mind I always thought I'd end up in England. My mum was English so I have a passport and I've wanted to travel through Europe for ever.' Her expression was wistful. 'My honeymoon was going to be to Paris. I used to have a picture of the Eiffel Tower on my bedside table, and when you tapped a button on it the lights twinkled.' She shook her head wistfully. 'My parents gave it to me after a ballet recital and I've never been able to part with it.'

'You did ballet?'

'Only as a child,' she said, thinking of how her aunt had donated all Hannah's tutus and leotards to a community charity shop when Hannah had moved in. She pushed the memory aside, focussing on the present, on the circumstances that had brought her here. 'After I found Angus and Michelle in bed together, I just wanted to run away.'

'Naturally.'

'It seemed as good a time as any to pack up and see the world.' Her smile was wry. 'I left before I could change my mind.'

Leonidas nodded thoughtfully. 'Have you spoken to him since you left?'

'No. There's nothing more to say there.'

'You were friends before you became engaged?'

'Yes.'

'You don't miss his friendship?'

Hannah thought of Michelle and Angus and her life in Australia and dropped her gaze. 'I miss a lot of things. It's hard, having the rug pulled out from under you.' She lifted her eyes to his, sympathy softening her features as she remembered his own harrowing past. 'As you would know.'

A warning light glinted in his eyes. *Don't go there.*

'Who was the other woman?' His voice was gruff.

Hannah's heart constricted with now familiar pain. 'That was the really hard part.'

'Harder than your fiancé cheating on you?'

'Yeah.' She angled her face, so Leonidas had a perfect view of her profile, delicate and ethereal.

'Who was she?' he repeated, and Hannah sucked in a soft breath.

'My cousin, Michelle. More like a sister, really. After Mum and Dad died, I went to live with my aunt and uncle, and Michelle.'

He let out a soft whistle. *'Christós.'*

'Yeah.' Her laugh was a low rumble. 'You could say that, and I did—worse, in fact. I was devastated.'

Admitting that felt good. Saying the word aloud, Hannah recognised that she hadn't spoken to another soul about the affair.

'I lost everything that afternoon.'

'What did your aunt and uncle say?'

Hannah lifted her gaze to his, and a ridiculous sense

of shame made it difficult to maintain eye contact. Hannah shook her head, that awful afternoon burned into her brain like a cattle brand. 'Do you mind if we don't go down this particular memory lane?'

She flicked her gaze back to his face, catching surprise crossing his features. But it was banked down within a moment, and he stepped back, almost as though he hadn't realised how close they were, how he was touching her.

'Of course.' His smile didn't reach his eyes. 'Have a seat.' He gestured towards the table. 'There is much we have to discuss.'

# CHAPTER SEVEN

'WHAT WORK WERE you doing in London?'

Hannah sipped her fruit juice, a pang of guilt scrunching her chest when she thought of her boss, Fergus, and how she planned to leave him completely in the lurch.

'I'm a legal secretary.'

'Have you done this for long?'

She nodded thoughtfully. 'Since I left high school. My aunt and uncle lived in a small town. There weren't a lot of options for work. I would have loved to go away to university but it just wasn't practical.'

'For what reason?'

'Money, mainly.'

'I thought universities in Australia were subsidised?'

'They are,' she agreed, lifting a piece of fish from the platter. 'But I'd have had to move to the city, found a place to rent. Even with governmental assistance, I wouldn't have been able to afford to live out of home, to cover textbooks and rent.'

'Your parents left you nothing when they died?'

She felt censure in his voice and her back straight-

ened, defensiveness stirring inside her. 'They left a little. My aunt and uncle took a stipend each year, and
what's left I can't claim until I'm twenty-five.'

At this, Leonidas was completely still. 'Your aunt
and uncle took money from you?'

'It wasn't like that,' she said quietly. 'They took
money to cover the cost of raising me.'

His face showed pure contempt.

'You think that was wrong?'

A muscle jerked in his jaw and she felt he was weighing his words, choosing what to say with care. She
didn't know him well and yet she felt for herself how
uncharacteristic that care was.

'I do,' he said finally. 'Were they struggling finan-
cially?'

Hannah shifted her shoulders and repeated the line
she'd frequently been given. 'An extra person is an extra
expense.'

He studied her thoughtfully for several seconds, but
he evidently decided not to pursue this line of questioning, and she was glad.

Glad because she didn't like to talk about it, much
less think about it.

As a teenager, she'd been able to ignore her niggling
doubts, but as she'd grown older, and met more people,
she had come to see more and more at fault with the way
her aunt and uncle had treated her. A desire to defend
them didn't change reality, and the reality felt an awful
lot as if they simply resented her presence in their lives.

She felt it in her heart, but to confess that to Leonidas
was too difficult.

'What would you have studied?'

She relaxed visibly. 'That's easy.'

He waited, his eyes not shifting from her face, so that even when their conversation was smoother to navigate, her pulse was still racing.

He had beautiful eyes, but she doubted many women told him that. There were too many other things about him that required mention. His body, his lips, his clever, clever hands. But his eyes were breathtaking. Dark, rimmed with thick black lashes, and when the full force of their focus was given to one's face, concentration was almost impossible.

'Am I to guess?' he prompted, after several seconds.

Heat flooded her cheeks. 'I wanted to be a lawyer,' she said, curling her fingers around the stem of her orange juice–filled champagne flute, feeling its fine crystal. 'Law degrees take years and cost a bomb. The textbooks alone would have bankrupted my aunt and uncle.' She said it with a smile, as though it were a joke. 'Becoming a legal secretary was the next best thing. There was a conveyancing firm in another town, just a half-hour drive away. Angus worked there.' She cleared her throat, sipping her drink. 'That's how we met.'

'I see.' If it were possible, his expression darkened even further.

'I loved working at the firm, and I'm good at what I do.' Pride touched her voice. 'So maybe everything worked out for the best.'

'I can't say I agree with that,' he drawled, after several long moments. His eyes roamed her face. 'However, you no longer have any kind of financial impediment to you undertaking a law degree. You will obviously be based here, on the island, but there are many universities that offer degrees via distance. You could enrol in one to start next semester.'

Hannah's eyes were huge, and she was struck dumb, for many reasons.

'This island is beautiful,' she said thoughtfully, trying to imagine her future. 'But very remote.'

His expression glittered. 'Yes. By design.'

She nodded, the loss of his family naturally having made him security conscious. Nonetheless, the idea of being stuck here sat strangely in her chest. She liked a tropical paradise as much as the next person, but not without an easy escape route.

Not necessarily for ever. She shelved her thoughts, though. They'd only just arrived. There was time to find her groove as they adjusted to this new life.

'I love the idea of studying law as much as ever,' she said sincerely. 'But I'm kind of going to have my hands full for the next little while…'

'A baby is not an excuse to turn your back on your dreams,' he said simply. 'You will want for nothing, and help will be available whenever you need it. I will be available,' he added. 'This is *our* daughter, not your burden alone.'

Her heart turned over in her chest and his completely unexpected show of support and confidence had her opening a little of herself up to him.

'I'm nervous, Leonidas.' She lifted the fish to her

288 THE GREEK'S BILLION-DOLLAR BABY

mouth, chewing on it while she pulled her thoughts into order. 'The idea of becoming a mum scares me half to death.'

'Why?'

'How can it not? I have no idea what to do, or if I'll be any good at it. I mean, it's a *baby*. I've never even had a pet.'

His laugh was just a dry, throaty husk of a sound. 'A baby is not really anything like a pet, so I wouldn't let that bother you too much.'

'You know what I mean. I've never had the responsibility of keeping something alive, something totally dependent on me.'

She heard the words a second too late, before she could catch them, but as soon as they landed in the atmosphere she wished she could gobble them right back up. 'I'm sorry.' She leaned across the table and put a hand on his, sympathy softening her expression while his own features tightened to the point of breaking.

'Don't be. I know what you meant.'

She nodded, but the easy air of conversation had dissipated.

'Being nervous is normal. You just have to trust that you will know what to do when our baby is born.'

'And you have experience,' she said, watching him carefully.

'Yes.' He nodded, curtly, placing his napkin on his side plate and sipping his wine. Then, he stood, fixing her with a level stare. 'Marina will show you to your room when you are finished. In the morning, a stylist will arrive to take your clothes order, and then a jeweller will come to offer you some rings to choose from.'

She blinked up at him, his abrupt change of temperament giving her whiplash. He was obviously hesitant to discuss his first wife and son, but jeez!

'Leonidas…' Hannah frowned, not sure what she wanted to say, knowing only that she didn't want him to walk away from her like this. 'I can't ignore the fact you had a family before this. I get that you don't like talking about it, but I can't tiptoe around it for ever. You had a son, and I'm pregnant with your daughter. Don't you think it's natural that we'll talk about him, from time to time?'

'No.' He thrust his hands into his pockets and looked out to sea, the expression on his face so completely heartbroken that something inside Hannah iced over, because it was clear to her, in that moment, how hung up he still was on the family he'd lost.

And why wouldn't he be? They'd been wrenched from him by a cruel twist of fate, by the acts of a madman. Nothing about this—his situation—was by his choice.

Nor was it Hannah's, she reminded herself. She knew more than her fair share about cruel twists of fate.

The sky was darkening with every second, but pinpricks of light danced obstinately through, sparkling like diamonds against black sand. She followed his gaze, her own appetite disappearing.

'I don't want to force you,' she said gently, standing to move right in front of him. 'It's your grief, and your life. But I will say, as someone who's spent a very long time bottling things up, that it's not healthy.' She lifted a hand, touching the side of his cheek. He flinched, his eyes jerking to hers, showing animosity and frustration.

Showing the depths of his brokenness.

It called to Hannah; she understood it.

'You are an expert in grief, then?' he pushed, anger in the words.

'Sadly, yes,' she agreed quietly.

'Do not compare what we have experienced,' he said. 'To lose your parents is unbearable, I understand that, and I am sorry for you, what you went through. You were a child, robbed of the ability to be a child. But I caused my wife and son's death, As sure as if I had murdered them myself, I am the reason they died. Do not presume to have any idea what that knowledge feels like.'

That Hannah slept fitfully was hardly surprising. Leonidas's parting shot ran around and around her mind, the torment of his admission ripping her heart into pieces. To live with that guilt would have driven a lesser man crazy.

But it wasn't only sadness for the man she'd hastily agreed to marry.

It was worry.

Fear.

Panic.

Stress.

And something far, far more perplexing, something that made her nipples pucker against the shirt he'd given her to sleep in, that made her arch her back in her dreams, and meant she felt warm and wet between her legs when she finally gave up on trying to sleep, before dawn, and stood, pacing to the window that overlooked the ocean.

Memories.

Memories of their one night together and fantasies of future nights were all weaving through Hannah's being, bursting upon her soul and demanding attention.

The sun had just started to spread warmth over the beach. Darkness was reluctantly giving way to light, and the morning was fresh.

It was Hannah's favourite time of day, when the air itself seemed to be full of magic and promise.

She had only the clothes she'd worn the day before, and the shirt she'd slept in, which was ridiculously big even when accommodating her pregnant belly. Still, it was comfortable and covered her body. Besides, it was a private island. Who was going to see her?

Pausing only to take a quick drink of water in the kitchen, Hannah unlocked the front door of the mansion and stepped out, breathing in the tangy salt air.

Excitement and a sense of anticipation rushed her out of nowhere, like when she was a small girl, around six or seven, and her parents had taken her away on their first family vacation. They'd gone to the glitzy beachside resort of Noosa, in tropical Queensland, and Hannah had woken early and looked out on the rolling waves crashing onto the beach, the moon still shimmering in the sky, and her stomach had rolled, just like this.

There's something elemental and enlivening about

the sea, and this island was surrounded by a particularly pristine shoreline and ocean.

Without having any real intention of going to the beach, she found herself moving that way quickly, her bare feet grateful when they connected with cool, fine sand, clumps of long grass spiking up between it every now and again. Dunes gave way to the flatness of the shore. She walked all the way to the water's edge, standing flat-footed and staring out to the sea, her back to Leonidas's mansion, her eyes on the horizon.

This was not the tropical water off the coast of Queensland. Here, there were no waves, only the gentle sighing of the sea as the tide receded. With each little pause, each undulation back towards the shore, the water danced over Hannah's toes; the cool was delicious given the promise of the day's heat.

She could have stood there, staring out at the mesmerising water, all day, were it not for the sudden and loud thumping from directly to her left. She turned just in time to see Leonidas, earphones in and head down, eyes trained on the shore, galumphing towards her. There was barely enough time to sidestep out of his way.

He startled as he ran past, jerking his head up at the intrusion he'd sensed, then swore, pulling his earphones out and letting them dangle loose around his neck.

She wished he hadn't.

The simple act drew her eyes from his face to his body. There was nothing scandalous about what he was wearing. Shorts and a T-shirt—only the T-shirt was wet with perspiration and the firmness of his pecs was clearly visible.

She took a step backwards without realising it, not to put physical space between them but because she wanted to see him better. Her aunt would have told her to stop staring, but Hannah couldn't. As much as the tide couldn't cease its rhythmic motion, Hannah found it impossible to tear her eyes away.

She remembered everything about him and yet… seeing him again sparked a whole new range of wants and needs.

Thick, strong legs covered in dark, wiry hair looked capable of running marathons but she couldn't look at him without imagining him straddling her, pushing her to the sand and bringing his body over hers, his hard arousal insistent between her legs. Without remembering the feeling of his weight on her body, his strength, power and skill in driving her to orgasm again and again.

Her throat was dry and the humming of the ocean was nothing to the furious pounding of her own blood in her ears.

She dragged her eyes up his body, over dark shorts that showed nothing of his manhood, even when she was suddenly desperate to see it—to see all of him again, in real life, not her very vivid dreams.

She prepared to meet his gaze, knowing he must surely be regarding her with mocking cynicism, only he wasn't.

He wasn't looking at her face, wasn't looking at her eyes to see the way she'd been eating him alive. No, he was performing his own slow, sensual inspection and it was enough to make her blood burn.

His eyes were on her legs, desire burning in the depths of his gaze as he lifted his attention to the curve of her breasts and, finally, to her lips. They parted under his inspection as she silently willed him to kiss them. To pull her into his arms and remember how well that worked between them.

And when he didn't, she took a step forward herself, knowing it didn't matter who moved first, knowing it was imperative only that they touch once more.

It broke the spell. His gaze slammed into hers, surprise there, confusion and, yes, desire. So much desire that it almost drowned her. He made a deep, husky sound and stood completely still, his body hard like steel.

Hannah moved closer, her eyes holding a silent challenge. *Stop me if you dare.*

He didn't.

One more step and their bodies connected, just like that first night in the bar, when fate had thrown them together and passion had held them there.

The air around them cracked and sizzled as though a localised electrical storm had touched down. He was so much bigger than she was. Hannah stood on the tips of her toes, which brought her body flush to his, her womanhood so close to the strength of his arousal that she echoed his own guttural moan with a soft whimper.

'Hannah.' Her name on his lips wasn't a request, nor was it a surrender. He spoke her name as though he simply couldn't resist and she lifted higher onto her toes and kissed him, hungrily.

He was still. Completely still, so her mouth moved over his, her tongue tracing the outline of his lower lip, her breath warm against him, and then, after the briefest moment, he lifted his hands to the back of her head, holding her where she was, keeping her so close to him, and he opened his mouth, kissing her back. But not in the way she had kissed him.

This was a kiss driven as much by a need to possess as his kiss had been the first night they'd met. There was madness in his kiss, his desperation for her completely overwhelming.

The water rushed around them, chasing their ankles, its fervent pursuit matched by the coursing of blood in their veins.

Hannah couldn't have said if he pulled her to the sand or if she pulled him, but she was lying down then, her back against the cold ground, her legs bent, Leonidas's body on hers, just as she'd fantasised about, his weight sheer bliss.

His kiss didn't relent, even as his hands pushed her shirt up, revealing the scrap of her underwear.

He disposed of them and then his own shorts, lifting himself up to look at her, his eyes piercing her, confusion and something else moving through him.

'I told myself we wouldn't do this,' he groaned, his voice tormented.

She bit down on her lower lip, her own heart tripping in her chest as his arousal nudged at her sex.

'Why not?'

His answer was to nudge his arousal inside her, and she moaned low in her throat as she felt the power of his possession. It had been five months but her body welcomed him back as though he were her saviour. She arched her back instinctively, needing more, and he drove himself deeper, pushed up on his elbows so he could see her, watch her, as well as feel her reactions.

Her insides squeezed him tight, muscles convulsing around him as he stretched her body to accommodate his length.

'What are you doing to me?' he groaned, and then said something in his native tongue, the words, spiced and warm, flickering inside her blood.

'I don't know but you're doing it right back,' she whispered, digging her nails into his shoulders before running them lower, finding the edge of his shirt and lifting it, trailing her fingertips over his back, feeling his smooth, warm skin beneath her and revelling in the contact.

Higher the shirt went, until he pushed up off one arm, ripping it from his body and casting it aside, so that he was naked on top of her. She wanted to stare at him, but she was incapable of forming the words to demand that when he was moving inside her, his body calling to hers, demanding her response, invoking ancient, soul-deep rhythms and needs.

'Christós...' The word was dark, a curse and a plea. His expression was taut as he looked down at her, unable to fathom her, this, them. 'Who are you?'

There was no answer she could give; the question made little sense.

He didn't require an answer, in any event. He moved faster then, his hands cupping her breasts, his mouth possessing hers as he kissed her until she saw stars and his hard arousal thrust deep inside her and everything she was in the past and would be in the future seemed to be coalescing in that one single, fragile moment.

She dug her nails into the curve of his buttock as pleasure pounded against her, like one of those waves from her faraway childhood, incessant, demanding, ancient. She cried his name and he stilled, his body heavy on hers, but as she exploded with pleasure her muscles squeezed him tight and Leonidas dropped his arms to his side, holding himself steady above her, staring down at her, watching every last second of delirium take over her body.

He stared at her so that when she blinked her eyes open, her own disorientation at what had just happened filling her with uncertainty, he saw it and he dropped his head, kissing her again, as though he knew how much she needed it.

It was a brief reprieve, nothing more. She'd been drowned by their passion and then emerged for air, and now Leonidas was taking her back under with him, tangling her in his limbs, his hands roaming all of her body now, until he curved them behind her bottom and lifted her a little off the sand, so his arousal reached even deeper and she found insanity was once more in pursuit.

His name tripped off her tongue, pushing into his mouth. With every thrust of his arousal, his body tightened, his buttocks squeezing, his muscles firm. She felt him beneath her palms, all of him, and then he moved faster, deeper and she was lifting into the heavens again, her body weightless and powerless to resist.

He moved inside her and she called his name as she burst apart at the seams, *Leonidas*, over and over. She called to him—willing him to answer—and he did. He tangled his fingers through hers, lifting Hannah's arms up above her head, his eyes on hers intense as his own explosion wracked his body, his release simultaneous with hers.

Their breath was frantic, louder than the ocean and the flapping of birds overhead, their exhalations thick and raspy, drenched in urgency. Pleasure had made her lungs expire. He lay on top of her and she ran her fingers down his back, still mesmerised by the feeling of his skin, and this: the closeness, the weight, the intimacy.

It lasted only seconds, and then Leonidas was rolling off, beside Hannah, onto his back on the sand beside her, staring at the dawn sky.

'*Christós...*' He said the word low and thick. 'What are you?'

Again, a question that was almost impossible to answer. He turned his head to stare at her and there was confusion in his eyes, and a look of resignation.

'What do you mean?'

He reached out as though he couldn't help himself, his fingers catching a thick section of her hair and running through it, his eyes on the brassy tones.

'Are you real?'

The question made no sense.

She raised an eyebrow, propping up on one elbow, a smile tugging at her lips. 'I'm pretty sure I am.'

He didn't smile. 'I swore we wouldn't do this.'

Hannah expelled a sigh. 'You said that. I heard you. It doesn't make sense, though.'

His frown deepened. 'For four years I have been able to resist any woman in the world. For four years I have been single, and then you…'

Hannah was quiet as his words ran through her mind and their meaning became clear. 'You mean you hadn't been with anyone since Amy died?'

His expression was shuttered. He shook his head, his lips a grim line in his face. 'No.'

Hannah's chest hurt, as if it had been sliced in half and cut wide open. 'Why not?'

His nostrils flared. 'Many reasons.' His hand lifted to her hair again, toying with the ends. 'I enjoyed resisting temptation, choosing to be celibate, to be alone. And then I saw you and it was just like this. As though you are some kind of angel—or devil—sent to tempt me even when I know how wrong this is. I spent four years flexing my power here and you take it away from me completely.'

Hannah's voice was thick; she didn't know if she was flattered or insulted. She suspected a bit of both. 'Why is it wrong?'

He pushed up to standing then, just as he had the night before when she'd touched on areas he preferred not to discuss.

But she wasn't going to let him get away with it twice. 'I'm serious, Leonidas. *Why* is this wrong?'

# CHAPTER EIGHT

SHE WAITED AND WAITED and after a moment, she wondered if he wasn't going to answer her. He simply stood there, naked as the day he was born, staring out to sea, and she moved towards him, coming around in front of him so she could look up into his stubborn face.

'I don't know much about sex,' she said slowly, when he remained silent. 'But I do know that I want to feel more of this.' She gestured from him to her. 'I do know this is amazing and hot and incredibly addictive.'

He ground his teeth together, the action making his jaw tight, his expression grim. 'That night shouldn't have happened.'

Hannah shook her head, rejecting both the words and the sentiment. 'Neither of us planned that it would, just like we didn't plan for this to happen, but that doesn't mean it was wrong.'

He looked at her then, his expression impossible to interpret. 'You are so young.'

He said it as though it were a criticism.

'I'm twenty-three.'

'Yes, but you've been very sheltered.' He cupped her face then. 'You deserve better than this.'

'Than marriage to you?'

'Better than a lifetime with me.' His lips were grim. 'I'm not the man you want me to be.'

'And what do I want you to be?'

He expelled a soft breath then stepped back a little, just enough to put some distance between them. 'A clean slate.'

The words were strange. Discordant. At first, she couldn't make sense of them. But as he turned and pulled his shorts on, she saw the weight on his shoulders, the ghosts that chased him, and comprehension shifted through her.

'You're wrong.' She dropped the words like little, tiny bombs. He didn't turn around, but he froze completely still, so she knew he was listening. 'I know you have a past, just like I do. But I'm not going to marry you if you're telling me I'm going to be living with a brick wall. I'm not getting married if I think there's no hope of having a living, breathing, red-blooded man as my husband.'

He turned around then, his expression bleak at first, and then filling with frustration. 'And sex ticks that box for you?'

Hannah frowned. That hadn't been what she'd meant, but at the same time she knew it was a start. What they shared, physically, was a true form of intimacy. She didn't need to have loads of experience to recognise that. She could see it in his eyes when he held her. She could feel the uniqueness of what they shared. He was trying to fight it, and she knew why.

Intimacy like this must surely lead to more.

With Angus, she'd operated on the reverse assumption. She'd hoped their friendship would bridge the way to a satisfying physical relationship. And it might have, but it would never have been like this.

Nothing like it.

This kind of connection couldn't be learned.

It was raw and organic, primal, between two people.

She glared at him, challenging him from the depths of her soul. 'Yes,' she agreed. 'I'm not going to live here like a prisoner in a gilded cage, Leonidas.' Her voice cracked as she firmed up on that resolution. 'This island is stunning but it's no place to live if you're going to freeze me out.'

'Does it look like I am freezing you out?'

'But you want to,' she insisted. 'You want to fight this, not build on it.'

His features tensed, his lips just a gash in his face, and she knew she was right.

'And I won't stay here if that's the case.' She tilted her chin bravely, when outside this island was a world she wasn't sure she trusted any more. The reality of his wife and son's murder was still exploding inside her, and she didn't doubt there could be a risk to her.

But there was risk here, too. Risk in living with a man who was determined to ice her out. What if he acted the same with their daughter? What if she were born and Leonidas made no effort to get to know her?

His eyes narrowed. 'How? You forget my island is practically inaccessible to anyone but me…'

Hannah was breathless again, her pulse racing but for a wholly different reason. 'Are you seriously threatening to kidnap me?'

Frustration zipped through his body. 'No.' He raked a hand through his hair. '*Christós*, Hannah. You can't leave the island.'

'Ever?' she demanded, crossing her arms over her chest to still the frantic hammering of her heart.

'Not on your own,' he amended. 'I was careless once before, I cannot risk it again. I won't have more on my conscience.'

And her rapidly thumping heart softened, aching, breaking for Leonidas.

'I'm so sorry you lost them,' she said quietly. 'But I'm not going to be a prisoner to your fears.'

'They should be your fears, too.'

'I want to keep our daughter safe.' Her voice was level, careful. 'Somewhere between me living out there on my own and the luxurious prison you're proposing is a middle ground we need to find.'

His eyes held hers for several beats. 'I cannot agree to that.' The words were wrenched from him, gravelled and thick with emotion.

'Why not?' she demanded, her hands shifting to her hips.

'You cannot imagine what it was like,' he said, grimly. 'To get that call, to see their bodies.' He shook his head from side to side and stopped speaking, but his face was lined with grief.

Tears bit at the back of Hannah's throat; sympathy rushed through her. 'I can't even imagine that, you're right.' She lifted a hand to his chest, running it over his muscled flesh.

'I made a choice after they died. I planned to stay single for the rest of my life.'

Hannah's stomach clenched.

'I didn't want this. I have done everything I could to avoid it.' His words were heavy with despair. She felt it and wished she could take it away, but how? 'I knew we shouldn't have slept together. It was so selfish of me but I was careful, Hannah. I did everything I could to make sure this wouldn't happen. I didn't want this.'

She wasn't sure when she'd let herself care enough about him that his words would hold such a latent power to wound, but they cut her deep.

'You shouldn't have to live in this—what did you call it? Gilded prison? Because of me.'

She couldn't speak.

'But you do.' The words were grim. 'Surely you can see that? I can't risk anything happening to you, to her.' He lifted a hand to Hannah's stomach, curving it over the bump there. His eyes met Hannah's with a burning intensity.

'Let me protect you both. Please.'

'I am,' she said, quietly, stroking his chest, her eyes determined. 'But this is my life we're talking about.'

He gazed at her, his expression strangely uncertain. 'I know that.'

'I want to marry you.' The words felt right, completely perfect. 'I know it's the sensible decision.' And strength surged inside her. 'When my mum and dad died, I lost everything. Our home, my community, my school, my friends. I went to live somewhere new and different and I was miserable,' she said, frankly, so captivated by her past that she didn't see the way his expression changed with the force of his concentration.

'I don't want our daughter to ever know that kind of uncertainty. You're her dad, and by doing this together, she'll have two people who can love her and look after her. And as she grows older, we'll surround her with other people who'll love her and know her, so that if anything *ever* happened to us and she were left alone, she would eventually be okay. Don't you see that, Leonidas? I need her to be okay, just like you do, but, for me, one of the worst things we can do is isolate her. Keep her locked up from this world, so we're the only people she ever really knows. She deserves to live a full and normal life.'

'How come you were sent to live with your aunt and uncle?'

Hannah frowned. 'There wasn't anyone else.'

'And you didn't know them well?'

'No.' She shook her head. 'I'd only met them a few times. They weren't close to my parents.'

He frowned, lifting his hands to her face and cupping her cheeks. He stared down at her, his eyes ravaging her face. 'You were deeply unhappy there?'

Hannah didn't want to think of her life in those

terms; she hated feeling like a victim. And yet, what could she say? She'd been miserable. Only now that she was on the other side of the world and free from her aunt's catty remarks did she realise what an oppressive weight they'd been on her shoulders.

'I wasn't happy.' She softened the sentiment a little. 'I'm not sure my aunt ever really liked me, let alone loved me.'

He scanned her face but said nothing.

'I spent more than a decade living with people who cared for me out of a sense of obligation. People who resented my presence, who undoubtedly wished I wasn't in their life. I won't do it again.' Her eyes showed determination. 'We didn't plan this, we didn't intend for it to happen, but that doesn't mean we can't make this marriage work.'

Still, he was silent.

'Less than six months ago, I was engaged to another man. I had my whole life planned out, and it looked nothing like this. I'm not an idiot, Leonidas. If I ever believed in fairy tales, I've learned my lesson many times over. This isn't a perfect situation, but there's enough here to work with. Our marriage can be more than a business arrangement, a deal for shared custody. We can make something of this—we just have to be brave enough to try.'

His jaw was square as he turned to the water, looking at it, his face giving little away. 'I want you to be safe and, yes, I want you to be happy, Hannah. I want our daughter to have the best life she can. But beyond that, stop expecting things of me. You say you no longer believe in fairy tales? Then do not turn me into any kind of Prince Charming in your mind. We are a one-night stand we can't escape, that's all.'

# CHAPTER NINE

HANNAH STARED AT the black velvet box with a sense of disbelief. The jeweller was watching her, a smile on his face, and Hannah imagined how this must look from the outside. A tailor had arrived on the island earlier that day, armed with suitcases of couture, beautiful dresses, jeans, shirts, bathers, lingerie—everything the wife of Leonidas Stathakis might be expected to wear.

The dressmaker had stayed for hours, taking Hannah's measurements, and photographs of her for 'colour matching'—whatever that was—and to discuss wedding dress options, before disappearing again. All the while some servant or other had taken the suitcases and carefully unpacked them into the room Hannah was using.

'Her room,' though she had no idea when she'd ever think of it like that.

There had also been a doctor, who'd come to check her over and implement a new vitamin regimen, and promised fortnightly check-ups. Then there'd been a more detailed conference with Mrs Chrisohoidis regarding Hannah's favourite foods, flowers and any other thoughts she might have as regards the running of the house.

Hannah had changed into one of the simple white shift dresses—for comfort on a hot day—and pulled her red hair into a bun on top of her head. As she looked at the dozen engagement rings the jeweller presented, all set against signature turquoise velvet, she knew it must appear to be some kind of Cinderella fairy tale. Leonidas looked on, not exactly playing the part of Prince Charming, though what he lacked in warmth he more than made up for in physical appeal.

He was casually dressed, in shorts and a white shirt, but that did nothing to diminish his charisma and the sense of raw power that emanated from his pores. It burst into the room, making it almost impossible for Hannah to keep her mind focussed on this task.

'Just something simple,' she said with a shake of her head, thinking that each and every ring was way too sparkly and way, way too big. 'Maybe this one?' She chose the smallest in the box.

'Ah!' The jeweller nodded. 'It is very beautiful.' He lifted it out, holding it towards Hannah. 'Try it on.'

This was all wrong! She didn't want to choose her own engagement ring, and no matter how many pretty, sparkly, *enormous* diamonds twinkled at her, it didn't feel right. She closed her eyes for a moment and imagined Leonidas going down on one knee, proposing as though this were a real wedding, and a bolt of panic surged inside her. But this wasn't a fairy tale and he wasn't Prince Charming, just as he'd said.

*We are a one-night stand we can't escape.*

Her heart began to churn. With a sense of unease, as though she were about to commit massive tax fraud, she slid the ring onto her finger. It was a perfect fit. She stared down at it and, ridiculously, tears filled her eyes. Now! Here! After becoming so adept at blocking them, she felt their salty promise and quickly sought to disguise them in what should have been a happy moment.

'It's beautiful.'

Leonidas came to stand beside her, his presence a force, a magnetic energy, pulling her eyes upwards.

'Don't you think?' she asked him.

His eyes met hers and they were back on the beach, just the two of them, his body inside hers, his strength on top of her.

'It is.' He nodded, hesitation in his tone. 'But you do not have to decide now.'

'Of course not,' the jeweller agreed. 'I can leave the tray, if you would like to try each for a time?'

Hannah's head spun. Each ring had to feature a diamond of at least ten carats. What must the whole tray be worth?

She didn't want to spend a week prevaricating over which enormous diamond she'd drag around. She just wanted the jeweller to go. She wanted Leonidas to go. Her head was spinning; it was all too much.

*We are a one-night stand we can't escape.*

He was right, and yet she rejected that description, she recoiled from it with everything she was.

'That's fine.' She shook her head, the beginnings of a throb in her temples. 'This one will be fine.'

She wanted to be alone and perhaps it showed in her voice, because Leonidas was nodding his slow agreement. 'Very well. Thank you for coming, Mr Carter.'

The jeweller left and Hannah watched the helicopter lift off from the cool of the sitting room, taking him from the island and to the mainland of Greece, the sun setting in the background, casting the beautiful machinery in a golden glow.

The day had lived up to the morning's promise. Heat had sizzled and Hannah, having spent so much time preparing for what lay ahead, wanted to simply relax. She'd spied a pool in her explorations the day before and she thought of it longingly now.

'Greg Hassan is scheduled to sit with you today,' Leonidas said as he entered the room.

Hannah's temples throbbed harder. 'Who?' She failed to conceal her weariness.

'Head of security at Stathakis.'

Hannah's throat shifted as she swallowed. 'What do I need to see him for?'

'There are protocols you will need to learn.' He was tense, as if braced for an argument.

'I thought you said this island is far from the mainland, inaccessible to just about anyone...'

He tilted his head in agreement. 'This island is secure, *sigoura*. But there are still protocols to follow and there are always risks.'

His fear was chilling. But it was also very, very sad.

She saw the tension in his body, and she wished there were some way she could take it away for him, that she could tell him everything was going to be okay.

She didn't know that it was, but she knew you couldn't live looking over your shoulder.

'Can't you just go through the security stuff with me?'

'You will need to have a relationship with Greg,' he said firmly, his eyes roaming Hannah's face. 'He'll co-ordinate your movements, and our daughter's, arrange her security detail as she gets older.'

Panic flared inside Hannah. It was all too real and too much. To say she was overwhelmed was an under-statement. 'Do you mind if we don't talk about that right now?'

His expression shifted. 'Your safety is important.'

She nodded. 'I know. I'm just—well, I'm worn out, to be honest.'

Concern flashed in his expression. 'Of course. You must be, the day was full and in your condition...'

'It's just a lot to take in.' Her smile was more of a grimace. 'I thought I'd go for a swim and just let it all percolate in my mind.'

'Fine.' He nodded. 'I'll ask Marina to prepare a sim-ple dinner for you, for afterwards.'

Hannah nodded, unable to express why her stomach was swooping. 'Thank you.'

She didn't see Leonidas again that evening. She swam, gently pulling herself through the water, enjoy-ing the lapping of cool against her sun-warmed skin, and then she ate the dinner Mrs Chrisohoidis had prepared—a small pasta dish with some fruit and ice water.

She contemplated going in search of Leonidas afterwards, but the revelations of their conversation from that morning were still sharp inside her.

She slept heavily, which surprised her. When Hannah woke, the sun was up, the sky was bright, and everything felt calmer. Better. Just as her mother had always said it would.

She had a feeling she could handle anything.

She showered, luxuriating in the sensation of the water on her body, lathering herself in the luxury coconut-fragranced products before towelling dry and slipping on a pair of shorts and a loose shirt.

Her stomach rumbled and she put a hand on it unconsciously, smiling as she felt their baby inside her. She looked down, her eyes catching the glinting of her engagement ring and her heart twisted, because she'd worn another man's ring, once upon a time, and she'd become used to seeing that on her finger. Then she'd become used to her hand being empty and bare—she'd been grateful. Grateful she'd found out what Angus was really like before she'd married him.

And now, she was to marry Leonidas. It was a gamble, and she wasn't sure she had the nerves to gamble any more, but here she was, closing her eyes and hoping for the best—all for their daughter's sake. This was all for her.

She had a coffee and some pastries for breakfast and

was contemplating a walk on the beach when Leonidas appeared, wearing a similar outfit to the day before.

He wasn't alone.

'Hannah.' He nodded and she wondered if the man behind Leonidas thought the stiff formality of Leonidas's greeting unusual.

'This is Greg Hassan.'

The man in question didn't look anything like what Hannah had imagined. For some reason, 'head of security' conjured images of some kind of black belt muscleman in her mind, someone more like Leonidas, who looked as if they could snap someone with their little finger.

Greg Hassan was on the short side, and slim, with fair skin and bright blue eyes. Hair that had at one time been blond was now balding on top. Hannah was lost in her own thoughts so didn't notice the way he startled a little at the sight of Hannah. But then, he smiled, moving towards her with one hand extended. She met it, belatedly forcing a smile to her own face.

'Miss May, this won't take long.'

In fact, it took hours.

Greg Hassan left some time after noon, and Hannah's head was back to feeling as if it had been through a washing machine.

The island itself had state-of-the-art monitoring, there were panic buttons in each room, and alarms that were activated by unexpected air activity, including drones—the paparazzi had occasionally tried to send drones into the airspace to capture images but the new detection methods effectively made that impossible.

'As for when you travel,' Greg had continued, 'you'll

have a team of four bodyguards. One of them will be with you at all times, and another with your child.' He'd smiled reassuringly, as if this were *good* news, but Hannah had felt as if she were having her head held under water.

She was drowning and it hurt.

'As much as possible, we'll coordinate your movements in advance. If you wish to travel to Australia, for example, to see family, we'll send a team out ahead to set up and prepare for your arrival. When your daughter starts school, I presume you'll move to the mainland—' At which point Leonidas had interrupted and said that had not yet been decided. Greg had continued that in the event of their daughter attending a school in Athens, or a major city, the campus would be vetted, and their daughter would wear a watch with an inbuilt panic alarm.

Questions mushroomed inside Hannah's brain, but she hadn't wanted to ask them in front of the security chief.

Leonidas had escorted Greg Hassan from the building and then disappeared to work, leaving Hannah with a million uncertainties scrambling around her brain.

She kept busy, calling her boss, Fergus, and informing him of her decision, and sending a polite, carefully worded email to her aunt, advising her, as a courtesy, that she was pregnant and getting married. She didn't even want to think what the reaction would be. Hannah was careful to leave out any other details—particularly who the groom was.

She texted her flatmates and let them know she wouldn't be coming back, but saying she'd pay rent until they found someone else and she could get back to pack up her room.

It all felt so official, and officially terrifying, but also bizarrely right.

She didn't see Leonidas again until that evening. Hannah stood on the terrace, watching the sun set, her heart lifting as the golden orb dropped, already feeling some kind of soul-deep connection to this land.

She heard his approach, and then she felt his proximity, even though he didn't touch her. It was as simple as the air around her growing thick, sparking with an electrical charge that fired her blood.

She turned slowly to find him there, his eyes locked to her as though he couldn't help himself. But the minute Hannah looked at him, he blinked and looked away, turning his attention to the ocean.

They stood there in silence for a moment, Hannah trying not to react to the throb of awareness low in her abdomen, trying not to act on an impulse to throw herself at him.

As the stars began to shimmer, she found herself remembering the meeting of earlier that day, recalling all the questions that had flooded her. 'You don't travel with a bodyguard.'

'I always have security,' he contradicted.

'Not on New Year's Eve. I didn't see anyone else...'

'My hotel is a fortress when I am there.' He tilted his head towards her, his eyes scanning her face. In the evening light, his sharp features were all harsh angles

and planes. 'Additional guards would have been su-
perfluous.'

'Was it like this before the accident?'

'It was no accident,' he responded, whip-sharp.

'Before you lost them,' Hannah corrected.

'Euphemisms? Perhaps if we call it what it is—
murder—you will accept the security measures more
readily.'

Hannah wasn't sure she agreed.

'And no. Before they were killed, I was stupid and
lax with their safety. I was arrogant and thought myself, and everyone around me, invincible, despite my
father's connections.'

Hannah moved towards Leonidas, her heart sore for
him.

'Isn't that better than living with fear?'

'Living with fear might have kept them alive,' he
said, darkly.

'You don't know that.'

'I know they should never have been out wandering
the streets.' He ground his teeth. 'And that you and our
daughter will never be exposed to that kind of risk...'

Hannah tried not to feel as if she were drowning
again. She tried to breathe slowly, to feel the freedom
of this island, to understand why he felt as he did.

And she did. She could imagine what pain he must
be suffering, and the added layer of guilt. But the picture
he was painting was grim. Hannah couldn't imagine not
being free to simply wake up and decide to go to the

shops, or to visit a friend without having bodyguards do a preparatory security sweep.

'So she'll wear a panic button?' The idea turned Hannah's blood to ice, but then, so did the idea of anything happening to her.

His voice held a warning note. 'At least you'll both be safe.'

His feelings were completely understandable, but Hannah railed against them instinctively. She'd felt loss, she knew its pain well. Losing her parents, then losing her engagement to Angus, she understood what it was like to have everything shift on you.

And yet, being fearless in the face of that was a choice.

'How come there are no pictures of them?'

Leonidas shifted to face Hannah, complex emotions marring his handsome face. 'What?' The word was sucked from him.

'You were married, what, three years? How come there are no wedding photos? No baby pictures of Brax? If I didn't know about them, I would never have guessed they even existed.'

Leonidas shut his eyes, but not before she saw his grief, his heartache.

'It is not your concern.'

Hannah's insides flexed with acid. Another reminder. His wife and child were off limits. They weren't her concern. His life before her was not up for discussion.

More boundaries. Rules. Distance. It slammed against her and she ground her teeth, the limitations of this like nails under her feet.

'I understand it hurts.' She spoke quietly, lifting a hand to his chest. His heart was pounding. 'But not talking about it doesn't make sense.'

'Please, stop.' She felt his frustration like a whip at the base of her spine.

'Why?'

'Because it is my choice. Because she was my wife and he was my son.' His voice cracked with awful emotion and she swept her eyes shut for a moment, sucking in a breath.

'I know that. And they're a huge part of you, just like our daughter will be.' She carefully kept herself out of that summation.

'But I do not want to discuss them.'

'Why not? Don't you want to remember your son? Don't you want to talk to me—to someone—about his laugh, his smile, his first steps, his night terrors—all the things that made him the little boy he was?'

Leonidas's skin was paler than paper. 'I will never forget my son.'

'I know that,' she said quietly. 'But you can't honour someone by burying their memories.'

Her words hung between them, sharp like an insult, bony and knotty and troublesome and almost too much. She partially rejected the truths of that observation, but she knew from experience what this felt like—she'd been made to stay silent for years, to hold her grief inside, and she'd lost so much of her parents as a result. So many memories she should have been free to relish, to smile about, were gone for ever because of forced disuse.

'He was the light of my life!' he said suddenly. The

words were torn from him, animalistic for their pain. He held his ground, staring at her as though she were covering him in acid. 'He was the light of my damned life! Amy and I... I loved her but, God, she drove me crazy and we weren't...in many ways, we weren't well-suited.' He dragged a hand through his hair, his eyes pinpointing Hannah with his grief. 'We'd argued the week before they died. She'd gone to Athens and I was glad.' He groaned, his displeasure at reliving that time in his life evident in every line of his body. 'I was glad because I was sick of fighting with her, sick of disagreeing over unimportant matters. But Brax was my reason for living, my reason for breathing, the reason I would *never* have left Amy.'

Hannah's grief was like dynamite in her chest.

She waited, letting him speak, letting him finish. 'I loved her but Brax was my everything and then he was dead. Because of me.' He dug his fingers into his chest and her eyes dropped to the gesture, to the solid wall of tanned flesh that hid a thundering heart.

'You think I am at risk of forgetting a single thing about him? You think I need to speak to you about my son to remember the way balloons made him laugh riotously, or the way clowns terrified him, or the way he loved to swim and chase butterflies?' His expression softened with grief and love and Hannah held her breath, all of her catching fire with the beauty of that look—of the expression on Leonidas's face.

'Do you think I will ever forget how much he loved strawberries? Cheese? The way he called me Bampás, except he couldn't say it properly so he said Bappmas instead? These things are burned inside my brain, Hannah, whether I speak of them or not.'

It was too real, too raw. She needed to say something, but words failed her. She opened her mouth, searching, seeking, but Leonidas shook his head and then kissed her.

It was a kiss to silence Hannah, a kiss to suck away whatever she'd been going to say and swallow it up, because he'd made it obvious he didn't want her grief, her sympathy, her conversation.

He kissed her, and she resisted for a moment because he was finally opening up to her and she wanted to talk to him, to help him, to hear him. She stiffened in his arms, wanting to push at his chest, to tell him not to run away from this conversation but then he groaned, a guttural sound of such utter, devastating need, and any fight wavered, leaving only surrender.

Surrender and such deep, deep sympathy.

She *understood* the complexity of his emotions.

And the way he kissed her now, she understood what he needed. He wished he didn't want her like this; he'd said as much on the beach, but this flame was burning out of control no matter how they tried to manage it.

'Damn it,' he groaned, swooping down and lifting her up. Regardless of the fact she was five months pregnant, he carried her effortlessly, moving through the mansion with a determined gait.

He shouldered the door to his room open—Hannah hadn't been in here. She looked around, seeing the dark wood, the masculine touches, gathering a brief impression of a space that was huge and elegant before he laid her on the bed, his body coming over hers, his mouth seeking hers as his hands pushed at the waistband of her shorts, lowering them, his hands running over her body.

A gentle breeze rustled in off the Mediterranean, bringing with it salt and warmth. Hannah lifted herself up, kissing him as her hands pushed at his shirt, guiding it over his chest, up to his head. He broke the kiss so she could remove it and then she lay back, breathless, her eyes running over his chest.

The room was dark, but she could see enough. She drank in the sight of him as quickly as she could because he kissed her again, his tongue flicking hers, his hands worshipping her body.

He brought his mouth lower, pushing at her shirt, lifting it to her throat so he could take one of her breasts into his mouth, his tongue swirling over a nipple until she bucked beneath him, stars flashing in her eyelids.

'God,' she moaned, digging her heels into the bed, arching her back, begging him to take her, to thrust inside her.

His mouth moved to her other breast and his fingers took over, his palm feeling the weight of her breast, his thumb and forefinger teasing her nipple until she was a puddle of whimpering nerves.

'Please,' she husked, running her nails down his back.

His arousal was hard between her legs; his knee nudged her thighs further apart and then he thrust into her, the ache unmistakable, the same urge overrunning them both. She felt his need and mirrored the depth of it.

She lifted herself onto her elbows, finding his mouth, pulling his lower lip between her teeth and biting down on it, so he let out a sharp sound of shock and then a groan as he pushed her head back to the mattress, his kiss a complete domination and sublime pleasure.

Only she wanted more, she wanted to be in control of this. She kissed him back, just as hard, needing him to understand her—this. Needing to reassure him in some way.

She moved herself over his arousal, her breath pinched, her body screaming in relief.

Hannah's heart hammered against her ribs and pleasure burst, touching every single part of her, until she was all fire and flame, no room for thoughts and feelings, doubts and uncertainties.

Concerns of security, the future, their relationship, his grief, her loss, they all disappeared. What room was there for anything when there was this pleasure in life?

Her breathing was rhythmic and he couldn't take his eyes off her.

Her vibrant red hair spread over his crisp white pillows, glowing like copper, and his gut throbbed painfully.

Leonidas Stathakis had tormented himself for the four years after his wife's death, staying celibate even when his body had begged him to relent, even when he'd wanted to lose himself in a willing woman's arms.

He hadn't.

He hadn't given in, until he'd seen Hannah and something inside him had begun to beat, a drum he could no longer ignore.

And it was still beating, but harder and faster now. With Hannah under his roof, it was impossible to ignore this; just as she'd said.

Theirs wasn't a normal marriage, but they did have this, and suddenly, Leonidas didn't want to fight it any more.

He watched her sleep, her beautiful, pregnant body naked to his hungry gaze, and he gave up fighting altogether. Perhaps in the morning he'd feel differently, but, for now, Leonidas allowed himself to curve his body behind hers, to place an arm possessively over her stomach and to fall asleep for the first time in a long time with a woman in his bed.

## CHAPTER TEN

HANNAH WOKE, STRETCHING until her back connected with something hard and warm behind her. Her heart was racing, the meeting with Greg Hassan the day before having left a lingering sense of anxiety in her so that alarm was her first emotion, followed swiftly by something much warmer, much more tempting, when she corkscrewed in the bed and realised where she was, and who she was with.

Leonidas.

And he was awake.

Staring at her.

His naked body was not a mystery to her, and yet this was the first time she'd woken up beside him, or any man, and a hint of self-consciousness made her cheeks blush.

'I fell asleep,' she said quietly, her eyes dropping to his chest. 'I'm sorry.'

She didn't see the way his brows curved reflexively into a frown.

'Why are you apologising?'

Hannah lifted her gaze to his. 'I don't know. I guess

I would have thought you'd want your space. Or to not have me here.'

His frown deepened and there was silence for several beats. 'I would have thought so, too.'

More silence.

'You were right, on the beach, Hannah. There is something between us. This chemistry.' His eyes were hollow when they met hers. 'I don't want to fight it any more.'

Her blood hammered inside her, hope was rolling inside her but she stayed completely still, watching him, listening.

'I have been single a long time. Single by choice. I have no idea how to do this. And I don't want to hurt you.' His expression showed his doubts on that score.

'Why do you think you're going to?'

His face bore a mask of wariness.

'I don't want you to think that great sex is more meaningful than that.'

Hannah swallowed, her brain turning his words over, making sense of them. He was afraid—afraid to risk falling in love, afraid to risk getting close to anyone. She understood that. He'd loved and lost. He was gunshy now. But opening himself up to their intimacy was one thing—it was a definite step, and for now that was enough.

Hannah smiled slowly, her eyes sparkling in a way that made Leonidas draw in an audible breath.

'Don't worry, Leonidas Stathakis,' she said, pushing at his shoulder so he fell back on the mattress and straddling him at the same time, surprising him so his eyes flared. 'I'm very happy to just use you for sex for now.'

His laugh was throaty, his expression shifting into one of complete fascination.

'Is that right?' She took his erection in her hands, feeling his strength, running her fingertips over his length, her smile pure sensual heat.

'Oh, yes.' She pushed up on her haunches, then brought herself over his arousal, taking him deep inside her but so slowly that he dug his fingertips into her hips and pulled her the rest of the way, his eyes holding hers.

She bit down on her lip and arched her back and he pulled up then, sitting, wrapping his arms around her, sucking one of her nipples in his mouth, flicking it with his tongue. Her breasts were so sensitive that his touch was like an arrow firing right into her central nervous system. She cried out, his name heavy on her lips, her nails on his shoulders, and he held her tighter, thrusting into her. With her on top, he reached different places, and she felt a different kind of explosion building, more intense somehow, taking over her body.

'Leonidas.' She ran her fingers through his hair and then cupped his face, pulling him away from her chest so she could kiss his mouth, and he kissed her back, hard, their tongues duelling, even as he shifted their body weight, spinning her, rolling her onto her back so he could take even more of her, thrusting into her hungrily, deep, hard and fast, and Hannah pushed her hands up, wrapping her fingers around the bedhead and holding on for dear life, and pleasure threatened to explode her out of this world.

He leaned forward, catching her hands, peeling them off the bedhead, lacing his fingers through hers and, as on the beach, he pinned them above her head, so his hair-roughened torso was hard against hers and every single cell in her body reacted to this tactile contact, to his nearness.

Her orgasm splintered her apart and it was Leonidas who put her back together, each gentle murmur, his voice speaking in Greek, his kiss gentle now, soft, reassuring as she flew straight into the abyss.

'You don't think this is overkill?' Hannah murmured, surveying the island from the vantage point he'd driven her to. From here, she could see so much more than the house, including a full golf course, a helipad as well as the airstrip, and in the distance what looked to be a whole little village. There was a jetty, too, and another yacht was tied to it—not as large as the one in Capri, but still what Hannah had to imagine would be classed as a 'superyacht', beautiful and shimmering white.

'What is?'

'This island.' She couldn't help the smile that teased her lips. She'd woken that morning, in his bed, and something had felt easier between them. She knew there were demons driving him, controlling him, but they weren't the sum total of Leonidas Stathakis.

He shrugged nonchalantly. 'You don't like it?'

'Oh, I like it very much,' she contradicted, rolling

her eyes a little. 'But who wouldn't? I just don't think I'll ever get used to living like this.'

'It's just a bigger home than you're used to.'

Hannah laughed at that, lifting the takeaway coffee cup she'd brought with her, sipping on it, wondering if she'd ever con herself into enjoying decaf. 'By about three thousand times. And then there's the expansive private beach.'

He looked at her, a smile pulling at his lips, and her heart turned over because he was really, exceptionally handsome, and when he smiled, it was as if someone had turned the music up full volume.

Her eyes dropped to his lips and her pulse gushed through her body, stirring heat in her veins and antici- pation low down in her abdomen.

'I haven't thought about it in a long time,' he said simply. 'It's just the island, to me.'

'Naturally.' She was still smiling as she turned her eyes back to the view. 'Did you grow up here?'

'No.'

'Where, then?'

'Athens, mainly—Kifissia. My father's offices were in the city.' The words were flat, carefully blanked of any emotion.

But Hannah felt it. She felt it rolling off him in waves, crashing against her, just like the ocean to the shore. She swallowed, butterflies in her tummy mak- ing her hesitate a little.

'What happened with him?'

'You don't know?'

She shrugged, awkwardly. 'I had to look you up on the Internet, to work out how to contact you.'

His eyes roamed hers, probing thoughtfully.

'I mean, I saw a headline, but I didn't click into it.'

'Why not?' His expression showed genuine surprise.

'Because it kind of gives me the creeps. Doesn't it you?'

He arched a brow, clearly not comprehending.

'Well, it's not really any of my business. It seemed private to you and your family.' She wrinkled her nose, lost in thought. 'I guess there's a lot about you out there, and your brother, and your dad. But what kind of stalker would I be to read it?'

'Your stalkerishness is someone else's due diligence,' he said with a quirk of his lips. 'What if I'm some kind of pathological cheat?'

'Are you?' She turned her face to his, her eyes scanning his features.

'No.' The word was sombre.

Silence arced between them, electric and sharp. He seemed to be peeling her away, looking deep inside her, even though the question had been Hannah's.

'And see? I believe you.' Her own voice was a little husky.

'Why?'

Hannah replaced her coffee cup in the golf cart they'd been touring the island in, then spun around to face him, so their bodies were almost touching. 'Because you've never lied to me, Leonidas.'

His expression tightened imperceptibly, his jaw square.

'You told me on New Year's Eve that we'd only ever be one night. You didn't make big promises to get me into bed. You were honest. You were honest with me this morning. I don't think you know how to lie.'

Leonidas looked beyond her, to the horizon. 'Honesty is generally the best policy, is it not?'

'Yes.' Her smile was uneven.

'I would have thought, having learned of your fiancé's infidelity, you would be slow to trust anyone.'

'So would I.' Her voice was a little shaky. 'But you're nothing like Angus. You're nothing like anyone I've ever met.'

At this, Leonidas's expression tightened, and she understood that he was closing himself off, that she'd moved them into territory he couldn't yet traverse.

'What did he do, anyway?'

'Who?'

'Your father.'

'Ah.' He expelled a slow breath, as though fortifying himself for what would come next.

'I gather he's in prison?'

'Serving a twenty-year sentence.'

'I'm so sorry.'

'What for? Prison is where criminals should be.'

'Yes, but he's your dad…'

'Not any more.'

Hannah frowned. 'You hate him?'

'Yes.'

She nodded thoughtfully. 'Why?'

'My father turned his back on the Stathakis Corporation. He almost destroyed what my grandfather, great-grandfather, and his father had spent their lifetimes building. Ancient, proud shipping lines that funded investments in foreign hotels and then hedge funds—our operations were crippled because of him.'

'How? Surely your company's too big for any one man to destroy?'

'He began to fund the mob, Hannah.' His eyes were haunted now, furious too, zipping with tightly coiled emotions. 'My father—who was richer than Croesus—didn't just want money and the lifestyle it afforded. He wanted power. No, not power; he wanted people to be afraid of him. He wanted notoriety and reach.'

'I can't even imagine what drives a man to think like that,' she said with a gentle shake of her head. 'How could he have even met that element?'

'It's everywhere. Casinos, bars, commercial investments.' Leonidas expelled a harsh breath. 'He was always enamoured of that lifestyle. I'm only surprised it took so long for him to be arrested.'

'That must have been so hard for you.'

'I think of myself as a strong person but I have no idea how I would have coped without Thanos.' The confession surprised her, and softened her, all at once. 'Investigators from every country in which we do business went over our records with a fine-tooth comb. We lost anything that had been used to fund crime. Despite the fact Thanos and I had been groomed from a young age, at our grandfather's knee, to love our company like a member of this family, to work hard to better it, we had to watch it being pulled apart, piece by piece, to see it crumble and fail.'

Sadness clouded Hannah's eyes; the image he was painting was one that was loaded with grief.

'What did you do?'

His expression was laced with determination and she thought of a phoenix, rising from the ashes. 'We cut the failing businesses, sold them off piece by piece, got what we could for them and recouped by aggressively buying into emerging markets. It was a high-risk strategy, but what did we have to lose?'

Hannah felt the conversational ground shift a little beneath them. She knew there was danger ahead, but, again, something had changed, there was more clarity, as if a valve had given way and now there was a clear flow of comprehension, an understanding.

'You said Amy was murdered in a vendetta against your father?'

His features tightened, and his jet-black eyes glittered with hatred—not for her, but for the men responsible. 'Yes.'

It was like pulling fingernails, she knew. He didn't want to do this, and yet, he wasn't hiding from her, even when it was causing him pain.

'He cut a deal with a prosecutor. Multiple life sentences were reduced to a twenty-year term, all because he handed over the names of his associates.' Leonidas's contempt was apparent, his lips little more than a snarl.

'He didn't, for one second, think of how that would affect us—those of us out here, living in this world.'

'Perhaps he was just trying to do the right thing?'

Leonidas surprised Hannah then, because he smiled—a smile that was tinged with grief. 'You see the world through the veneer of your goodness,' he said after a moment. 'You think because your motivations are pure and good, everyone else's must always be?'

'No.' She frowned; it wasn't that at all.

'Yes,' he insisted. 'How else could you have become engaged to a man who was cheating on you? You trust and you forgive.'

'Is that a bad thing?'

He was quiet, staring at her for several beats. 'I hope not.'

Hannah expelled a soft breath. 'Maybe I do give people more than their fair chance. But I also see the truth—I know what people are capable of, Leonidas. I've seen it. I've felt it.'

She looked away from him then, her eyes gravitating to the yacht as it bobbed on the surface of the Mediterranean. Everything was clear and pristine, and so very beautiful, like stepping into a postcard.

Leonidas's fingers curled around her chin, gently pulling her back to face him.

'He hurt you?'

Hannah's eyes widened, and it took her a moment to think who he was referring to.

'He was my fiancé, and he had an affair... Of course that hurt. But it wasn't him alone; it was her, too. It was the fact that two of the people who were supposed to love me most in the world had been happy to betray me with one another.' She shuddered, the shock of that moment one she wasn't sure she'd ever get over. 'It wasn't losing Angus. It was the whole situation.'

His eyes devoured Hannah's face, tasting her expression, digesting its meaning. 'Have you spoken to her?'

Hannah shook her head. 'I couldn't. I can't. I don't know what I'd say. Growing up, our relationship wasn't always…easy.'

'Why not?' he pushed, and she had a glimpse of his formidable analytical skills. She felt his determination to comprehend her words, to seek out what was at the root of them.

'She was competitive, and frankly insecure. Her mother—Aunt Cathy—spurred her on, making comments about how we looked, or about grades.' Hannah sighed. 'I never bought into it. I mean, we're all our own person, right? Run your own race. That's what my mum used to say.' Her smile was nostalgic, and then, it slipped from her lips like the sun being consumed by a storm cloud. 'But my aunt…'

He waited, patiently, for her to continue. Hannah searched for the words.

'She measured us against each other non-stop.'

'And your cousin didn't measure up?'

Hannah's eyes shot to Leonidas's. 'I didn't say that.'

'No, you are being deliberately tactful on that score.'

There was enough praise in that observation to bring heat to Hannah's cheeks, but she denied it.

'I'm not being coy. I just don't think like that. Michelle struggled at school; I didn't. I suspect she has some kind of undiagnosed dyslexia—no matter how much time we spent going over things, she found the comprehension impossible. I think she wasn't able to read clearly, and covered it by acting uninterested.'

'You mentioned this to your aunt?'

Hannah nodded. 'Once. She was furious.' Hannah's expression was unconsciously pained, her features pinched tight as her gaze travelled back towards the ocean.

'And you, in comparison, excelled at your studies?'

Hannah nodded slowly. 'Some people respond well to the school system, others don't. I'm lucky in that I'm one of the former.'

'And a lifetime of feeling compared to has made you downplay your natural abilities even now, here, to me.'

She startled at that insight. 'It's the truth.'

'It is also the truth to say you are intelligent, and I would bet my fortune on the fact you worked hard at school, too.' He softened his tone a little, but didn't quit his line of questioning. 'Isn't it possible that your aunt resented how well you did, compared to Michelle? That she couldn't get help for her daughter because it would be admitting she was, in some way, inferior?'

'If I'm right and Michelle had a learning difficulty of sorts then she could have been helped, and achieved far better results than she did.'

He dipped his head in a silent concession. 'But your aunt didn't want to pursue that. And so, instead, she took away your dreams, condemning you to a life of mediocrity so her own daughter would look better in comparison?'

Hannah sucked in a sharp breath, his words like acid rain against her flesh. 'I don't think you could call my life mediocre...'

'You should have been studying law, poised to move into the career you really wanted. And your aunt should have been supporting you. This is what you meant, when you said you have felt what people are capable of?'

She opened her mouth to deny it, but he was too insightful. Too right. She shrugged instead, lifting her shoulders and turning away from him.

'Where was your uncle in all of this?'

'Gary?'

'You speak of your aunt and your cousin, but I have not heard you say his name once.'

'He worked a lot. We weren't close.'

'And yet he must have known how his wife was behaving. He did nothing?'

'It's not like that. Aunt Cathy isn't a monster. It's complicated.'

'How?'

Hannah shook her head thoughtfully. 'It was so long ago, and I don't really know anything for certain. It's more just things I've picked up from throwaway comments. I think she was very close to my dad— her brother. And when Mum entered the scene, Aunt Cathy was jealous. Hurt. My mum was...' Hannah's smile was melancholy and she closed her eyes, seeing

Eleanor May as she'd been in life—so vital, so beautiful. 'She was a pretty amazing woman. A diplomat for the United Nations, well travelled, passionate, funny, and so stunning.'

'So this is where you get it from,' he murmured, the compliment wrapping around her, filling her with gold dust.

Hannah smiled slowly, memories of her past pulling at her. 'I used to love watching her get ready for parties. She had this long, dark brown hair, like chocolate, that fell to her waist. She would coil it up into a bun, high on the top of her head, so that whatever dangly earrings she chose to wear would take your breath away.' Hannah felt him come closer, his body heat and proximity firing something in her blood.

'And she and Dad were so happy together. They used to laugh, all the time. I was just a kid when they died, but I'll never forget them, I'll never forget how lucky I was to have them as my example in life.'

He was quiet, but it didn't matter. Some part of Leonidas had slipped into Hannah, forming a part of her, so she understood—she understood his silence equated to disapproval of Aunt Cathy, and her inability to let Hannah properly grieve.

And long-held needs to defend Aunt Cathy were difficult to ignore. 'Cathy and Gary weren't like my parents. They married young, because she was pregnant. She lost the baby but they stayed together and it always felt a bit like they resented each other.'

She turned to face him then, her chest heavy with

the myriad sadnesses of the past. 'I don't want our marriage to be like that, Leonidas.'

Her eyes raked his face and she chewed her lower lip thoughtfully as he stared at her, his eyes unshifting from hers, his expression impossible to interpret.

'I was wrong about you.' Leonidas's words came out hoarse, thickened by regret.

'When?'

'I presumed you did not know enough of grief to counsel me, to offer me any thoughts on my own experiences. That was incredibly arrogant.' He lifted a hand, running it over her hair, his attention shifting higher, as if mesmerised by the auburn shades there, flecked with gold. 'I downplayed what you have been through because I couldn't believe anyone could feel loss like mine.'

'It's not like yours,' she said softly, gently, her heart breaking. 'No grief is the same. I can't imagine what it's like to lose your partner, nor your child.' She shook her head sadly from side to side. 'I'm five months pregnant and the idea of anything ever happening to our daughter fills me with a kind of rage I can't put into words.' Her lips twisted in a humourless smile. 'You must be a mix of anger and fury and pain and disbelief all the time.' She swallowed, rallying her thoughts. 'You don't need to apologise to me. I understood what you meant.'

'But I didn't understand you,' he insisted. 'I didn't realise that beyond the somewhat sanitised phrase of "orphan" are all the memories of parents you loved, parents who made you happy and secure, parents who were replaced by an inferior substitute—an insecure and competitive woman who spent her life trying to diminish you.'

Hannah's lips pulled downwards, as she tried to reconcile his vision of Aunt Cathy.

'You should have studied law,' he said, simply. 'And anyone who loved you would have pushed you to do that, supporting you, encouraging you, making it easier—not harder—to pursue your dreams.'

Hannah's heart turned over in her chest, because he was right. Even Angus hadn't said as much to her.

'Your parents left you money. That could have been used to fund your studies.'

'I couldn't access it yet, not for another two years.'

'But a bank would have loaned against that expectation, if your aunt and uncle couldn't cover your expenses in the interim. There were ways for you to live your dreams but she held you back because she didn't want you to succeed.'

Something sparked in Hannah's chest because he was right, and she'd made excuses for Cathy and Gary all her life and she didn't want to do it any more.

'I miss my mum and dad every day,' she said, simply, focussing on the only kernel of good she could grasp at. 'Especially now.' She ran a hand over her stomach, thinking of the daughter growing inside her, and love burst in her soul.

The air between them resonated with understanding, with compassion, and then Hannah blinked away, moving her focus to the vista before them.

Their conversation was serious, and yet she felt a

shifting lightness in her heart, a sense of newness. Perhaps it was simply the beauty of the day, or looking down over the horizon and seeing so much that fascinated her, so much to explore, but she found herself smiling.

'What's down there?' She nodded towards the village she could see in the distance. 'I thought this was a private island.'

'It is. That's the staff quarters.'

'Staff quarters?'

His smile was teasing. 'Where did you think all the people in the house went to at night?'

'I didn't think about it,' she said, and he smiled then, a smile that was natural and easy and that made her pulse feel as if it had hitched a ride on a roller coaster and were zipping and whooshing through her body.

'There are about fifteen gardeners, Mrs Chrisohoidis, her husband Andreo, who oversees the island, the domestic staff, chefs, and I have two personal assistants based out of the island for when I need to work.'

Hannah's eyes flew wide. 'Seriously?'

'And their families,' he said, still smiling, the words lightly mocking.

She shook her head from side to side, wondering at how anyone could have this kind of money.

'It takes a team to manage all this.' He gestured with his palm to the island.

She nodded. 'And then the yacht crew, too?'

He nodded. 'They stay on board, though there are dorms for when the boat is here over winter.'

'You must spend a fortune in salaries.'

'I suppose I do.' He wasn't smiling now, but he was looking at her with a heat that simmered her blood. He lifted a hand to her hair once more, tucking it behind her ear slowly, watchfully.

'There's the security team, as well,' he said, and she felt his past pulling him deep into a raging ocean.

'Greg Hassan lives here?'

'Greg lives in Athens. He oversees Stathakis Corp, including my brother Thanos's security arrangements, and our company procedures. He has a manager on the island, and there are thirteen guards permanently placed here.'

'Thirteen?' She exhaled. 'Security guards?'

'It used to be only four,' he said nonchalantly.

'But because of me it's thirteen?'

'Because of you, and because of her.' He dropped a hand to Hannah's stomach, and right at that moment one of the little popping sensations Hannah had become used to reared to life, and Leonidas's eyes widened in wonder.

'Did she just kick me?'

Hannah laughed, but there was a sting of happy tears against her eyelids. 'She's telling you we don't need anything like that kind of security.'

'I think she's giving me a high five of agreement.'

Hannah laughed and Leonidas did, too. She had no way of knowing how long it had been since he'd felt genuine amusement, or the occurrence might have taken her breath away even more than the sound did on its own.

\* \* \*

Hannah lay with her head on Leonidas's chest, in the small hours of the next day, listening to his heart. It beat slow and steady in sleep. She lay there, her naked body close to his, their limbs tangled with the crisp white sheets, their bodies spent, her body round with the baby they'd made, and she smiled.

Because there was such randomness in this, and yet such perfection, too.

How could she have known that one night of unplanned sensual heat would lead to this? She lay with her head on his chest, listening to the solid beating of his heart, and admitted to herself there was nowhere on earth she'd rather be.

# CHAPTER ELEVEN

'YOU'RE GETTING MARRIED?'

Thanos's voice came to Leonidas from a long way away.

'Where are you?' Leonidas stretched his long legs out in front of himself, crossing them at the ankles.

'Somewhere over the Atlantic.'

'You're going to New York?'

'It's model week.' Leonidas could hear his brother's grin, and experience told him that in approximately twenty-four hours there'd be tabloid headlines about Thanos's latest stunning conquest. 'Did you say you're getting married?'

Leonidas's eyes drifted to the window of his study, and beyond it, to where Hannah was lying beside the pool. The bathing costume was really just a couple of scraps of Lycra, and his fingers itched to remove it.

'Yes.'

'*You're* getting married?'

Leonidas grimaced. 'On Friday.'

'As in three days away *Friday*?'

'Yes.'

'*Christós.* I didn't realise you were seeing anyone.'

'I'm not. I wasn't.' He swept his eyes shut, his stomach clenching painfully. 'It's not like that.'

'So what is it like?'

Leonidas's chest felt as if it were being scooped out, replaced with acid. 'She's pregnant.'

Silence.

It stretched for so long that Leonidas thought they might have lost reception. The phones on their state-of-the-art jets were good, but not one hundred per cent reliable.

'Thanos?'

'I'm sorry, I'm just surprised. I thought you'd sworn off women for life.'

'So did I.'

'And yet?'

'And yet,' Leonidas agreed, his eyes roaming her body with a hunger that was not a part of him. He'd given up on fighting this, on fighting Hannah. She was breathing herself into his soul, and taking over small parts of him, forming his building blocks back into shape. Except for his heart, which would always be locked away, reserved for Amy and Brax.

The rest of him, he could share. Especially if it made her smile the way she had been.

'When? I mean to say, when will you have this baby?'

'She's due in four months.'

Thanos let out a low whistle. 'So you're marrying her for custody?'

The description turned Leonidas's stomach. 'I'm marrying her for security.'

A moment of silence and then, gently, 'Leonidas, the man who killed them is locked up for life. He'll never get out. There's no reason to think he wasn't acting alone.'

'It's organised crime. Do you really think he'd have operated without instruction?'

'Yes,' Thanos spoke swiftly. 'I think he was a lunatic, angry that our father had turned on his brother and so he took that out on you—an eye for an eye. There is no risk now.'

'Would you bet someone's life on that, Thanos? Would you bet the life of an innocent woman you were too weak to resist and that of her unborn child?'

More silence, and eventually, 'No.'

Leonidas didn't realise until that moment how badly he'd needed to hear that. 'Here with me, on the island, she is safe. Our child will be safe.'

'What's she like?'

'She's…' Leonidas tried to put into words a hint of Hannah, but it proved hard for some reason. 'She's nice. You'll like her.'

Thanos's disapproval came across in his silence. 'Nice?'

'Yes, nice. What's wrong with "nice"?'

Thanos was quiet. 'Does she know about Amy?'

Leonidas stiffened. 'Yes.'

'Leo.' Thanos rarely used the diminutive version of Leonidas's name. It slipped out, the boyhood moniker coming naturally to him now. 'You don't think it's a bit of an extreme way to keep someone safe? You couldn't just give her a security detail?'

Leonidas was surprised to realise he hadn't even considered that. Not for a moment. But he understood his reasoning. Having lost Amy and Brax, he couldn't risk anything else happening to the mother of his child, and the only way to be sure of that was to have her within eyesight. He and Amy had fought—often. They'd begun spending more and more time apart. He'd missed Brax like anything but he'd relished his space from Amy, even when he'd known he loved her—or that he had loved her once and needed to honour that love, for the sake of their child.

But he'd been careless, letting her go without taking an interest in how she was spending her time. He hadn't seen the danger and they'd paid the ultimate price.

No. Hannah would be by his side, 'til death do them part. And if they were separated and he couldn't protect her, then he'd make sure she had an army at her disposal.

'A detail wouldn't have been enough. It's my job to keep them safe.'

'I see.' It was clear Thanos didn't agree, though. 'And is this what she wants?'

Leonidas stood, moving to the window, and his legs felt a little like jelly when he thought about what Hannah might want. Perhaps she caught a hint of his movement in her peripheral vision, or perhaps she felt the tug of him in that strange way she had, but she lifted her gaze to the window of his study, lifting her sunglasses from her head so she could pierce him, through the glass, with the intensity of her emerald eyes.

His pulse slammed inside him.

'She agrees it's for the best.'

Thanos was quiet for a moment. 'It all sounds very sensible and safe, then.'

Leonidas nodded, but his insides were clenching in a way that wasn't even remotely sensible.

'Maybe you could take over negotiations with Kosta Carinedes now that you're about to be married with a kid. That's the kind of respectability he's looking for.'

Leonidas stiffened—the reality of that still difficult to contemplate. And though Thanos had obviously been joking, he was quick to retort, 'There is no way on earth I'm telling anyone who doesn't need to know about Hannah and our daughter. I plan on keeping this secret as long as I can.'

There was safety in secrecy.

Hannah smiled up at him, and lifted her hand, motioning for him to come to her, then pointing to the water.

He shook his head on autopilot, the last vestiges of restraint reminding him that there needed to be some boundaries, some restrictions.

She shrugged, standing up slowly, unfurling her petite frame and turning her back on him. She reached behind her as he watched, pulling on the string of her bikini top and lifting it over her head. Her hair, shimmering like a flame in the afternoon sunshine, ignited down her back.

He held his breath as she turned once more and blew him a kiss, her smile contagious, spreading over his lips, exploding out of her like diamond dust. And then she eased herself into the pool, her beautiful, pale breasts only half covered by the water.

He disconnected the call to Thanos, threw his phone on his desk and was already stripping his clothes as he made his way to the deck.

It was just a swim on a very hot day, nothing more.


Leonidas told himself he was simply doing what Hannah deserved. That it was easy for him to deliver on her dreams and that someone should do that for her, after everything she'd lost.

She was marrying one of the richest men in the world—she could have anything she wanted in life and Leonidas was going to make sure she knew that.

He couldn't give her his heart, he couldn't give her the version of happily ever after she wanted, but he could spoil her with every material possession so that she never noticed there was a gaping void inside her chest.

He told himself a thousand and one things but as he observed Hannah with undisguised interest, watched the way her face glowed with happiness and wonderment, he knew there was something more base in his reasons for bringing her here, to Paris.

The idea had come to him while they were swimming, earlier that day. They were marrying for some-what pragmatic reasons, but that didn't mean he couldn't make some of her dreams come true. And she had al-ways wanted to see Paris, had grown up staring at a tourist souvenir of the Eiffel Tower, and he could give her the real thing. He'd wanted her to have it.

Why?

Because it had mattered to him.

Because he could.

Because someone should spoil Hannah May.

'Leonidas.' She turned to face him, tears in her eyes. 'It's so much more beautiful than I'd imagined.'

Their penthouse hotel room looked over the glow-ing construction of the city's heart, the Eiffel Tower. He handed her a glass of non-alcoholic champagne, moving closer to her, still unable to tear his gaze from her face.

'Many locals would beg to differ.'

But even his cynicism couldn't dampen her mood. 'Then they're crazy.' She grinned. 'I've never seen any-thing more beautiful.'

'Haven't you?' His voice was thick and guilt rolled through him. He banked it down. This wasn't about him and Amy and Brax and the mess that was his life. This was about Hannah—she deserved to be happy, she deserved to feel joy, she deserved this. And he wasn't going to ruin it by brooding and regretting.

She lifted her eyes to his and heat seared him, as it had the first night they met, as it always did.

'I guess you come here all the time. You're prob-ably used to it.'

He skipped his gaze to the Eiffel Tower thoughtfully. 'Often enough.'

'I can't imagine seeing it as just another landmark. It's extraordinary.'

As she looked at it the hour struck and the tower went from glowing gold to glistening with silver and starlight. Hannah drew in a sharp breath and moved closer, through the billowing curtains and onto the small Juliet balcony with an unrivalled view of the tourist favourite.

'Tomorrow I want to go right to the top,' she said with a broad grin, turning back to face him.

'Why wait until tomorrow?' he prompted, holding a hand out to her.

'Because it's eight o'clock. Surely it's not open to visitors?'

'It's open until midnight,' he said with a smile.

'Then what are we waiting for?' she asked breathlessly, yet he didn't move. He stared at her, drinking in the sight of her like this, and something shifted in his gut—hope, lightness, release.

He ignored it, taking her hand and squeezing it tight in his own. 'Not a thing. Let's go, *agape mou*.'

Hannah slept with a smile on her face and woke with it still drifting over her lips. Her sleeping mind had been full of all the dreams that Leonidas had made a reality. The surprise trip to Paris—touching down in his private jet at Charles de Gaulle and being whisked through the ancient city in his sleek black limousine.

She hadn't been able to speak, she'd been too thrilled,

too fascinated, intent on catching every detail she possibly could. She'd craned forward in her seat, staring at the city as it passed and her heart had begun to throb and twist and race for how much the city lived up to her every dream.

And for how close she felt to her mother here. It had been Eleanor's favourite city—she'd spent a lot of time in Paris for the UN and had come home speaking about it, bringing the city to life in a young Hannah's imagination.

The Stathakis Hotel was in the heart of this thriving metropolis, poised on the edge of the Seine, showcasing views in one direction of the Eiffel Tower and in the other of the Arc de Triomphe, and in between all the winding streets and tiny little houses that made this city so singularly unique.

The penthouse was exquisite, just like the one on Chrysá Vráchia, only it was different—there was more of a flavour of France in its styling. The artwork was done by the hand of famous Impressionists, the furniture a little more elaborate and baroque; everything about it was sumptuous and romantic.

And it had been waiting for them when they arrived.

It had all been so perfect and Hannah had almost been able to ignore the presence of the security officers who'd accompanied them on the flight and through the streets of Paris. Constantly walking a discreet distance behind but always there, always watching and waiting.

And despite the joy of this city, a frisson of alarm travelled down her spine, a hint of worry at what had be-

fallen Amy and Brax and the threats Leonidas seemed
to imagine were still out there.

She turned over in bed, lifting a finger to his shoulder and tracing an invisible circle distractedly across
his tanned flesh.

His eyes lifted and he turned to face her, a look on
his face she couldn't interpret before he smiled.

Her heart turned over in her chest.

*'Bonjour.'*

His smile widened. *'Bonjour, mademoiselle.'*

'I like it here,' she said simply, dropping her head
to his chest but keeping her gaze trained squarely on
the picture-perfect Eiffel Tower beyond the window. It
was a perfect day—a bright blue sky called to her and
Hannah was already excited to explore this ancient city.

'I thought you might.'

And so he'd arranged this. Something pulled inside
her chest—pleasure—and she smiled softly. 'Is it possible, Leonidas, that you are a romantic at heart?'

His chest slowed, his body completely still. 'No.'
The word was like thunder in the midst of a sunny day.
She pushed up to look at him, not cowed by the stern
expression on his face. A week ago, she would have
bitten her tongue, but something had shifted between
them; she was different now. He'd made her different.

Hannah liked to think she wasn't the same girl who'd
agreed to marry Angus, who'd taken her aunt's decrees
as gospel. She bit down on her lower lip, watching him,
thinking, and then said, 'How did you meet her?'

His eyes dropped to hers, his expression unreadable.

She wondered if he was going to plead 'off limits', as he had at the start, but he didn't.

Though it clearly gave him no pleasure and considerable pain, he spoke slowly, quietly, the words dredged from deep within him. 'Through my brother.'

Silence. She didn't fill it.

'Thanos has a broad social circle.' Scepticism filled the words. 'Amy had just started modelling. She got pulled along to a party by some friends. I happened to be there.'

'She was a model?'

Leonidas nodded. 'She was beautiful and I was smitten.' His smile was dismissive but jealousy surged inside Hannah. She knew how petty that was. The poor woman had died and it was not for Hannah to envy her anything.

'Did you date for long before marrying?'

'No,' he laughed softly. 'I am not a patient man. When I see something I want I go after it.' His frown was another storm cloud on the horizon. 'We married quickly, privately, and before we really knew much about one another.'

Hannah tilted her head to the side, watching him. 'You say that as though it's a bad thing.'

'It can be,' he said thoughtfully.

Curiosity got the better of Hannah. 'Was she different from what you imagined?'

Leonidas flicked his gaze to Hannah's, his eyes showing torment. 'I loved her.' The words were defensive. 'But we weren't capable of making each other happy.'

Sympathy scored deep into Hannah's heart.

'I thought a baby might be the answer to that. I convinced her to fall pregnant, and by then she was so afraid of losing me I think she would have borne me a football team if I'd asked it of her.' He shook his head from side to side, anger in the tight lines of his lips.

'Why weren't you happy?' she asked curiously.

He expelled a soft sigh. 'Neither of us was happy.' He moved his gaze to the window, looking through it without seeing. 'Amy loved a certain lifestyle.'

'Money?'

He grimaced. 'Money was not the issue. Partying was. She loved to go out, to be seen, to be adored. She fell into my brother's crowd for a reason.'

Sympathy shifted inside Hannah's chest. 'And you're not like that?'

'I never have been. Thanos is the "playboy prince of Europe" and that suits him. He lives his life in the fast lane—life can never be loud enough, fast enough, drunk enough.' His smile showed affection. 'He's a tornado. And he attracts tornados.'

'Like Amy.'

'Yes. Like Amy. She was much more at home with his friends. I couldn't make her happy.'

'But you loved her.'

A heavy beat of silence throbbed between them. 'Yes.' He turned to face her. 'And I refused to let our marriage fail.'

Hannah expelled a soft sigh. 'You can't beat yourself up for things not having been perfect. I sometimes think life is a knot full of different threads. Some of them happy, some of them profoundly sad, but they all form a part of you.' She pressed a finger to his chest.

Leonidas lay back and gave his fiancée the full force of his attention. 'And you think you would have been happy with him?'

Hannah considered that for a moment. 'I think I would have been free with Angus. Free of my aunt and uncle and their low expectations, free of Michelle's jealousy. At least, I thought I would have been—clearly those jealousies were going to chase me into my marriage.'

'Do you still love him?'

'Angus?' She wrinkled her nose. 'The more time that passes, the more I think I didn't ever really love him. Not as anything more than a friend. But he was the first person in a long time to tell me he loved me.' Her lips twisted painfully. 'He was the first person who made me feel wanted—needed. And I loved that feeling.'

'I have something for you.'

Hannah stifled a yawn, the whirlwind, one-night trip to Paris having been both spectacular and exhausting. She placed her book down on her lap, lifting her gaze to Leonidas's face and feeling that now familiar rolling in her stomach as her nerves exploded. Desire lurched inside her, but it was more than just a physical need.

She longed for him in every way.

'Oh, yeah?'

'Yes.' He crossed the floor of the private jet, propping his hip against the broad armchair opposite her.

'Here.' He reached into the pocket of his shirt and pulled out a small black velvet pouch.

'What is it?' She took it without looking away from his face.

'Open it.'

She did just that, sliding the tip of her finger into the pouch's opening and reaching for the contents. It was tiny and sharp. She tipped it into her palm and smiled. Because there in her hand was the most delicate and beautiful replica of the Eiffel Tower she'd ever seen. A closer inspection showed it was made of diamonds and it was attached to a delicate chain.

'It's truly beautiful,' she said, her voice cracking with emotion.

'I thought you should always have something that brings you so much happiness right by your heart.'

Her heart! Oh, how it flipped and flopped at his thoughtful, kind words.

She felt as though she were soaring high into the heavens, right alongside the clouds outside the porthole windows of this designer jet.

She looked up at him, a smile on her face, holding the necklace out. 'Would you mind?'

He took it from her, arranging it around her neck and clipping it into place. It was a mid-length chain so the stunning charm dangled perfectly between her breasts.

'I love it,' she said sincerely, looking up at him. 'Thank you.'

His smile was the most beautiful thing she'd ever seen. Her pulse fired inside her, but then, his smile flattened and his face assumed a serious, distracted expression. 'You were right on the beach.'

She frowned, searching her memory.

'You said we could make something of this marriage and you were right.'

Her stomach clenched and her heart trembled.

'When Amy and Brax died, my heart died with them, and it's gone—for good. I cannot offer you what I think you deserve, but I can give you enough, I think, for you to want this. For you to be happy.' He crouched down at her feet, clutching her hands, staring into her eyes. 'Look at the life you can lead by my side. Look at how we can raise our child.' He lifted one of his hands to cup her cheek. 'There is enough here to build on, just like you said. We just have to be brave enough to try.'

She felt the once foreign but now familiar sting of tears in the back of her throat. He was speaking softly, as though he were offering a great gift, but all his words did was open up a hole in her heart and make her feel as though she were falling into it completely.

There was something so final and so *limiting* about what he was saying, and the timing of it filled her with despair. Their trip to Paris had been so full of magic and she'd felt so wanted and cosseted, but it had all been a sales pitch, him showing her what he could *give* her to make this marriage appealing. Because he wanted her to be safe, he didn't want the guilt of any harm befalling her, and because he wanted their child close. She'd seen the way he talked about Brax, the genuine love that had filled him—he'd be a great father to their daughter.

This trip hadn't really been about her—he hadn't brought her to Paris because he'd wanted her to see it, he'd done it because he'd wanted her to know what she could expect, being married to him. He'd thought showing her the enormous silver lining of being Mrs Leonidas Stathakis would compensate for the fact his heart 'had died' with his first wife and son.

She bit down on her lip, turning her face away from him without responding, not able to find any words that would express the enormous doubts that were harpooning her soul.

# CHAPTER TWELVE

HANNAH HAD BUTTERFLIES in her tummy and they wouldn't quit. She looked at the dress the couturier had brought earlier that day—it was the perfect wedding dress for this perfectly fake wedding.

'Keep it simple,' she had instructed, feeling as if the wedding was enough of a farce without a frou-frou white cupcake dress. And simple it was. A silk slip with spaghetti straps and cut on the bias so it emphasised the curves of her breasts, hips and the roundedness of her stomach. It was not a dress one would wear to a public wedding, in front of hundreds of people.

It was a dress to be worn for a lover. Beautiful, but so incredibly sensual. She ran her fingers over the silky fabric, and then dropped her gaze to the floor, where a pair of rose-gold sandals had been teamed with it. They were casual and comfortable and the perfect bit of whimsy to offset such a stunning piece.

She heard a noise and startled, quickly putting the simple gown back in the wardrobe and slamming the door, spinning around almost guiltily as Leonidas entered their bedroom. When had she started to think of it as theirs, rather than just his? It had been just under a week since she'd arrived on the island and she barely recognised the woman she'd been then.

'Marina has set dinner up on the terrace,' he said. He looked at her as he had on the plane, with a smile that was at ease, as though he'd made his peace with how this would work—he'd slotted her into a space in his mind and he was content with that.

She wasn't his wife by choice, but they could still 'make this work'.

Hadn't she said something along those lines to him, right at the beginning of all this? She'd been happy to take a pragmatic approach then. But something had changed and now the limitations of that sat strangely in her chest.

'Okay.' Hannah returned his smile, but it didn't light up her face as usual.

They walked in silence to the terrace, and when they reached it, Leonidas held a chair out for her.

Mrs Chrisohoidis had gone to a lot of trouble.

Candles flickered everywhere, and fresh flowers had been picked from around the island, filling the terrace with an even more delightful, heady fragrance than usual.

She breathed it in and told herself to relax.

She told herself nothing had changed. They were two people who were forging a relationship, who were getting married the very next day, and all the reasons for agreeing to this marriage were still there. Aside from the possible danger to her and their daughter, Hannah's desire to provide their child with a father was as strong as ever. To know that if anything ever happened to her, Leonidas would be there—that she would know and love him.

She was doing the right thing—these doubts would lessen once they were married and she could get on with building their marriage.

They would have a lifetime together. A lifetime to make sense of this madness.

But as Leonidas took the seat opposite Hannah, she realised with a terrifying bolt of comprehension that she didn't need a lifetime to make sense of this. He took the seat opposite her and she breathed out, relaxing.

Because he was there; he was near her.

She clutched the stem of her wine glass—filled with ice-cold apple juice—and stared at her groom, as a thousand memories exploded inside her.

Perhaps it was the starlit sky overhead, just like the night they met, but suddenly, Hannah seemed to be looking through binoculars, seeing everything larger and bigger and more true to life.

Why had she slept with him that night?

She'd never done anything like that, and yet one look from Leonidas had made her want to throw herself at his feet. That couldn't be anything other than desire, could it?

So why had she thought of him every day since? Why had he tormented her thoughts and dreams and filled her chest with a strange palpitation?

What was the underlying reason that had made accepting his proposal easy? Beyond the very sensible reasons of security and support, what had really made her agree to this?

Because marriage meant this.

Time with him. Sitting opposite him. Lying with him. Kissing him. Making love to him.

No, not making love.

It was sex. Just sex.

Except it wasn't.

She swept her eyes shut, remembering every kiss, every touch, the way he laced his fingers through hers and stared into her eyes when she exploded with pleasure.

'Hannah?' He leaned forward, curving a hand over hers, and she startled, piercing him with her ocean-green eyes. 'Are you okay? Is it the baby?'

She shook her head, and tried to smile, but her pulse was frantic and her stomach was lurching.

There was no way on earth she'd done something as stupid as fall in love with the man she'd agreed to marry.

Every step of the way he'd told her he didn't want that. Their marriage wasn't about love. It was convenient. Sensible. And yet a rising tide of panic made breathing difficult because they were due to say their vows in the morning, and Hannah knew hers wouldn't be a lie.

In one week…no. Not one week. This thread had begun to stitch its way into her heart that very first night, on Chrysá Vráchia.

She hadn't understood it then—how could she?

It was only now that she comprehended what she

THE GREEK'S BILLION-DOLLAR BABY

hadn't been able to with Angus. Love wasn't a choice, it wasn't a sensible, practical formula one could apply to the 'right' candidate to ensure a lifetime of happiness. It didn't work like that.

Love was as organic as breathing and laughing. Love was magic and, somehow, it had placed Hannah and Leonidas on the same island at the same time and the chemistry of their bodies had demanded something of them. It hadn't been about chemistry alone, though, she saw that now. He'd offered a one-night stand—and instead, she'd seen his heart and buried a piece of it in her own.

She gasped again, standing jerkily, moving to the balustrade and staring out at the inky black ocean. If it weren't for the sound of the waves, it would have been impossible to know what was beyond the balcony.

'Hannah? *Christós!* What is it?'

She shook her head, unable to speak, definitely unable to put any of this into words. She had to make sense of it herself first. 'I… It's nothing. I just wanted to look at the view.'

She felt his disbelief. 'There is no view. It's pitch black.'

She turned around to face him, surprised to find Leonidas standing right behind her. 'There are stars,' she said softly. 'Lights in the dark. See?'

Her huge green eyes shifted heavenwards, but Leonidas didn't look upwards. He stared at Hannah, worry communicating itself in every line of his body.

'There is also dinner, on the table,' he teased, the words only slightly strained. 'And I am hungry.'

Hannah nodded, even though she wasn't sure she could stomach any food.

'In a moment.' She gnawed on her lip, the realisation of a moment ago doing funny things to her, making her look at him in a wholly new way.

Was it possible to fall in love with someone so quickly? Was love at first sight something she even believed in? Could she be so impractical after everything she'd been through?

It didn't matter how she queried herself.

Her eyes only had to glance to Leonidas and she felt the pull from his heart to hers. She felt a soaring of something inside her that was new and different and refused to be grounded.

She was suffocating, this knowledge desperate to burst from her, but she held it back, keeping her mouth closed even when the words pressed against her lips.

They would marry the next day, and she would say her vows, knowing they were true and honest, and then she would gently show him how she felt. She would give him time to adjust. To feel his way into this.

She exhaled, the sensible approach filling her with relief.

Calmed, she moved back to the table, taking her seat and eating as much as she could—the butterflies in her tummy left little room for food, though.

'Where are you going?' he asked at the door to his room.

Hannah's smile was soft, and inside, she carried the knowledge that was continuing to unfurl inside her. She loved him. She loved him in an everlasting, for-the-rest-of-her-life kind of way. And tomorrow, they'd marry.

'It's the night before our wedding, Leonidas. Don't you know it's bad luck to spend it together?'

His brows arched heavenwards. 'A superstition?'

'Yep.' She nodded. 'And one I intend on obeying. Go to sleep. I'll see you in the morning.'

He groaned, pulling her closer, his eyes locked onto hers. 'I don't want you to go back there.'

He nodded down the corridor, and her heart turned over in her chest. 'Why not?'

She held her breath.

'Because.'

She laughed. 'That's not an answer.'

A frown pulled between his brows but before he could answer, she disentangled herself from his arms. 'It's one night, and then a lifetime.' Her smile almost reached her eyes. Leonidas stared at her, completely silent.

And Hannah stared back, unable to look away, three words whispering through her, begging to be spoken— a question to be asked.

'Goodnight,' she said instead, simply. And she turned away, walking towards the bedroom she'd slept in when she'd first arrived, opening the door and moving into it for what she believed to be the last time.

Of course it did rain in the Mediterranean on occasion. Summer storms weren't unheard of. But the rain that lashed the side of the mansion woke Hannah before dawn, the unfamiliar ruckus causing her to frown at first. She pushed her sheet back, moving towards the window and staring out of it, so fascinated by the sight of everything that had become familiar looking so foreign and unrecognisable now. It took her a moment to realise what day it was. The significance of the morning.

And then, to remember.

To remember who she was marrying and what he meant to her.

She gripped the wall behind her for support, turning and pressing her back to it as fear tightened inside her.

*'When Amy and Brax died, my heart died with them.'*

His words had been hammering away at her chest from the inside out since they'd come back from Paris.

She'd decided, the night before, that she would marry him and let things play out. She'd had a sense of confidence, a sureness, that one day he would feel the same as she did.

But what if he didn't? What if he was right, and his heart was gone for ever, any kind of love no longer in his power to give?

The rain fell harder and she turned to face it, pressing her forehead against the glass. The rain lashed the other side.

What if he didn't love her, and never would? What if he was no longer capable of love? What if she was about to tie herself to another man who was incapable of giving her what she needed?

Panic flared.

When Angus had proposed, she'd been grateful. She'd been grateful that someone loved her and *wanted* her. That someone was choosing her to be their wife and partner. Since her parents had died, she hadn't felt that, and so she'd agreed to marry him out of gratitude rather than love.

She'd known that, and it hadn't mattered. She'd valued feeling wanted above anything else.

But he hadn't really wanted her. Not enough. He'd betrayed her before they'd even said their vows—he hadn't deserved the trust she'd placed in him.

And Leonidas?

Hannah stepped away from the window, padding back to the bed, sitting down on the end of it and looking at her feet. She'd painted her toenails pale pink the day before, thinking how nice they'd look through the strappy sandals she planned to wear for her wedding.

Leonidas didn't want her. If she hadn't been pregnant, they'd never have seen each other again. The thought made her gasp into the bedroom and she held a hand over her stomach, because that very idea seemed impossible to contemplate.

Hannah could no longer disentangle her life from Leonidas's.

They were like roots from neighbouring trees, intertwined and interconnected, dependent on staying where they were for life.

But what if he didn't—wouldn't—couldn't love her?

She'd decided the night before that she would simply wait. Wait for him to realise what they were, what they shared. But could she really do that?

Hannah pushed up from the bed, knowing in her heart what she'd known even over dinner on the terrace.

She couldn't.

She couldn't do this if he didn't know how she felt. She had to be honest with him. She had to…she had to tell him.

And words she'd bit back the night before refused to be silenced now, so she closed the distance between their rooms quickly and pushed the door inwards without knocking, too distracted to wonder how she might find him, her thoughts churning through her.

He was standing with his back to her when she entered, wearing only a pair of grey boxer shorts, his body momentarily robbing her of the ability to think straight. He held a square piece of plastic paper in his hands and, at the intrusion, moved quickly to place it down on the windowsill behind him.

'Hannah.' He was surprised; then worried as he saw the pinched expression on her features. 'Are you okay?'

'No. Yes.' She shut the door behind her, moving deeper into his room, looking at this man and feeling as though everything and nothing made any kind of sense.

'What is it?' He stood perfectly still, staring at her as though he barely recognised her.

'I…need to talk to you.'

His expression didn't shift. 'Okay.'

She nodded, wringing her hands in front of her body,

knowing what she needed to say but not exactly sure how to express it.

'I've done something stupid,' she said, shaking her head.

'What is it?' He was quiet, patient, but there was something lurking just beneath his exterior. A darkness that she felt but couldn't navigate.

She expelled an uneven breath and padded across the carpet of his room until she was right in front of him. He stiffened a little.

'Leonidas, the night we met...' She tapered off into nothing, looking at him with eyes that were huge and awash with emotions.

'Yeς?'

'It came out of nowhere. I've never done anything like that in my life but I know that there's no way that wouldn't have happened between us. From the moment we literally bumped into each other, I felt this...magnetic pull to you. I know that sounds...ridiculous. But I looked at you and felt like I couldn't *not* go to your room with you. And, once I was with you, like I couldn't not be with you. I feel like, from the moment we met, there's been something bigger pushing us together.'

He was quiet, but she didn't let that discourage her. She'd expected this. She'd known he wouldn't necessarily welcome this confession.

'And then you disappeared and you were angry and I told myself it was for the best. That I was messed up after Angus and so none of this was making sense and I'd made a mistake with you.'

He didn't say it was a mistake, and she was so glad for that, because it would unstitch a part of her soul in a way she'd never recover from to hear those words now.

'But it wasn't a mistake. I never really believed that.' She shook her head slowly, an unconscious smile on her lips. 'I went to London but a part of me stayed on Chrysá Vráchia with you. A part of me stayed with you from that night, and I took some of you with me. I didn't stop thinking about you, Leonidas.'

He stiffened in front of her and there was wariness in his features, a look of panic that was the antithesis of what she wanted, but she pushed on, knowing she needed to do this.

She couldn't marry him and hope for the best—that was what she'd been planning to do with Angus and it had been stupid. Stupid, and a recipe for disaster.

'I don't know if I would have had the nerve to contact you if I hadn't been pregnant. But I do know I never would have forgotten you. I do know I never would have met anyone who made me feel like you did. I always laughed at the idea of love at first sight, but in one hour, you reached inside me and changed who I was. In one hour, you transformed me and I can't marry you today without telling you that I…that this…isn't just about our baby or security or anything so pragmatic and rational as that. This is me offering all of myself to you, for all our lives.' She reached down and laced her fingers through his, as he'd done so often with her.

He didn't speak, though. Her words filled the room, developing a beat of their own, throbbing with the strength of what she had offered him, and every moment that passed with utter silence was like a tendril wrapping around her throat, constricting her airways, making breathing almost impossible. She stood there, her breath raspy, and she waited.

'Why are you telling me this now?'

It wasn't exactly the answer she'd expected, but it didn't matter. Having said what she'd been thinking, she felt as if a weight had been lifted.

'Because I can't not,' she said simply, and his brow furrowed, his expression dark.

'Hannah.' It was a sigh and a plea. 'Don't do this.'

Hannah stood very still, regulating her breathing, trying to stay calm. Because this was important. This mattered. 'I got engaged to Angus for all the wrong reasons. I thought I loved him, I thought he made sense. But nothing about what I felt for him was love. Love isn't a tepid, calm, considered choice. Love isn't a choice at all. Love is a lightning bolt—'

'*Desire* is a lightning bolt,' he interrupted, shaking his head, his expression tense. He took a step backwards, raking a hand through his hair, staring at her with obvious frustration. His body was a taut line of impatience. 'Desire is what you felt for me that night, and it's what you feel for me still. It's clouding your judgment, and you have no experience to discern the difference between that and love.'

'I'm not an idiot,' she murmured. 'I get that there's desire here, too. I know I feel lust as well as love.' She swallowed, trying to order her thoughts. 'One of those things makes my mouth dry when you walk into the room, and the other makes me feel as though my feet are two inches off the ground when you smile at me.'

He wasn't smiling now.

'I was going to marry Angus, you know, even when I wasn't in with love him. I was going to marry him and hope that everything would just work out. I nearly made that mistake once and I can't do it again.'

Now Leonidas was completely still, his face like thunder. 'What are you saying?'

Hannah didn't know, but the words tripped out of her mouth before she could consider them. 'If you don't love me, Leonidas—not even a little bit—if that lightning bolt struck me and me alone, then we can't do this.' Her eyes filled with tears and she found herself powerless to halt their progress. 'If I didn't love you, maybe it would be different, but feeling like I do and marrying you…it would be hell. Every day would be a torment.'

His nostrils flared as he expelled an angry breath. 'We have discussed this. There is so much in our marriage that would be good, so much you would enjoy.' He forced a smile to his face but his eyes remained intent, disconnected. 'You will see the world, travel to places you cannot imagine, and all in five-star luxury…'

'With an army at my back?' she challenged.

'No matter what happens, the army is something you will have to adjust to.'

She shook her head, pushing that aside for the moment. 'That's not enough.'

'It has to be!' He spoke loudly, the words thick with

impatience. 'I have told you all along what I am offering. When you came to me in Capri I was clear, and I have been clear all along.'

'Are you saying you still feel that way? That nothing's changed for you since then?'

He regarded her through half-shuttered eyes, lifting his arms and crossing them over his broad, naked chest for good measure. 'Things have changed,' he conceded, finally.

Hannah relaxed, just a little.

'But I don't love you. I'm not free to love you, Hannah. I made a promise to someone and even though she's dead, it doesn't change that. I have told you this as well, and I cannot fathom why you can't just accept it.'

Misery exploded inside her. Hannah drew in a breath, her eyes firing to his, hurt unmistakable in their green depths. He looked away, his jaw rigid as he unfolded his arms and reached for the piece of plastic paper that was on the windowsill. It was a photo, she saw now, and he'd been looking at it right before she'd entered the room.

He handed it to her, his eyes holding a challenge when they met Hannah's.

She turned her attention to the picture slowly, scanning it and frowning as similarities leaped out at her. For the briefest second, she thought the photo was of her, but it wasn't. Close, though.

The woman in the picture was smiling, her lips painted a similar red to the colour Hannah favoured. Her eyes were wide-set and almond-shaped, like Hannah's, and an almost identical shade of green. Her skin was pale, like Hannah's, though Hannah had tiny freckles on her nose and it didn't look as if this woman had any.

Her hair was loose around her face, falling to beneath her shoulders, and it was the exact same auburn red of Hannah's own hair.

Hannah looked at the picture without comprehending, at first.

'Is this Amy?' she whispered, something in the region of her heart bursting, shattering his internal organs with the force.

'Yes. My wife.'

It was just three words, three tiny words, but they were wielded like a machete. Hannah lifted her face to Leonidas's, her skin completely blanked of colour, so that even in the midst of this conversation, he felt a blade of concern.

'Please sit down.' He gestured to the bed, putting a hand on her elbow, but she wrenched out of it, moving away from him, dropping her gaze to the picture. Her fingertips shook and her eyes were filled with tears, making it difficult to focus properly. But she'd seen enough.

Clarity—a different kind of clarity from what she'd experienced last night—settled about her.

'This is what you saw in me that night on Chrysá Vráchia, isn't it?'

Leonidas was quiet.

'If I didn't look like this—' Hannah lifted the photo in the air a little, at the same time she reached for her hair '—you wouldn't even have noticed me, would you?'

Still, he was silent. What could he say? How could he defend this? The evidence was staring back at her.

'Did you think of her when you slept with me?' Her eyes pierced him, the hurt and accusation in them like a physical weapon.

'No.' The word came out gravelled, and it was as if he were being roused from a long way away. 'You are similar, at first glance, but believe me, Hannah, I saw only you.'

She wanted to believe him, but pain was slashing her from all angles.

'But she was in my mind that night. She was a heaviness inside me.' He expelled a long, slow breath. 'That island is where I met her. On New Year's Eve, and it's where I proposed to her. I go there every New Year because I'm a sadist and it's my particular brand of torture. And this year, you walked in and for a moment, I felt like I'd slipped back in time…'

A sob filled Hannah's chest. She was such an idiot! She'd been falling in love with this man, and he'd been living with a ghost.

She groaned, spinning away from him blindly.

He moved after her, gripping her arm, holding her gently, turning her around to face him. 'But that's not why I slept with you.'

His eyes held hers. Even when she wanted to blink away, she couldn't. She was transfixed. Talk about sadism.

'No?' The word was just a whisper. She cleared her throat. 'So why did you?'

'I wanted *you*, Hannah. I've wanted you since that night. I've been tormented by how much I wanted you. And I've hated myself for that. When Amy was killed, I was furious. I swore I would never forget her, never move on with my life. I resisted any woman, any connection with anyone, until you. Even wanting you physically is a betrayal of what I promised myself, of what I owe Amy.'

His words were dragged from him.

'I had a family, Hannah, and they were murdered because of me. Do you think I have any right to close that book and pick up a new one? To simply move on because you're here and pregnant with my child?'

Hannah's heart broke a little more, but for Leonidas this time. He was trapped by his grief, and she couldn't fight that for him. He alone could forgive himself, could work out how to love Hannah and their daughter while still holding Amy and Brax in his heart.

Hannah looked down at the photograph of Amy, and felt a sense of kindredness with this woman, this poor woman. They had both loved the same man, and it bonded them in some way. Hannah handed the photo to Leonidas with an expression that was pure sympathy.

'What would she want?'

He shook his head slowly. 'Amy would want me to be happy.'

Hannah's heart chirruped a little. She stepped forward, so their legs brushed, and she lifted her hands to his chest. 'Then be happy, Leonidas. You'll never stop loving Amy and Brax, and I don't want you to. They're a part of you, and I want them to be a part of our lives.

I want to hear more about the little boy who made you laugh, I want to hear about him, I want you to keep him alive within me and one day his sister. You can't live in stasis for ever. I'm here, and I love you, and I'm asking you to open yourself up to this. To look inside your heart and see that I'm there, too.'

She dropped her hands to his, finding his wrists and lifting his palms to her belly. 'I'm asking you to marry me today because you love me, not because you're worried I'll be hurt, not because I'm pregnant. Marry me because you don't want to live your life without me in it.'

He stared at her as though he were drowning, but she was too far away to help him.

He stared at her as though nothing and no one could ever help him. As though he didn't want to be saved.

'I didn't suggest this because I wanted it,' he said, finally, his voice hoarse. 'I can't bear to be the reason someone else is in danger. I shouldn't have slept with you and I shouldn't have got you pregnant, but now that I have and you are, the least I can do is make sure you're safe and looked after.'

His words, so reasonable, so decent, were the polar opposite of what she wanted to hear.

Hannah stared at him for several moments, as the small seed of hope she'd let grow in her chest began to wilt.

'I don't want to be safe and looked after,' she said quietly. 'At least, that's not a reason to marry someone.'

His eyes narrowed. 'You don't think?'

'No.' She tilted her chin defiantly, even when she'd begun to shake. 'I can take care of myself, and our baby.'

'You have no idea what's out there.'

'And nor do you,' she interrupted forcefully. 'Neither of us has a crystal ball, but I know this: if I stay here and marry you, I'm going to regret it. I'm going to be miserable, and our child's going to be miserable. After my parents died, I went to live with my aunt and uncle and saw for myself how damaging this kind of relationship can be. I won't put our child through that.'

'Damn it, Hannah. You agreed to this…'

'Yeah,' she choked out the agreement. 'But that might as well have been a lifetime ago.'

'Not for me.'

She grimaced. 'No, not for you. And that's the problem. You can do this—you can marry me and sleep with me and hold me through the night and not feel a damned thing.' Tears burned her lashes but she dashed them away angrily. 'I'm not like that. This is real to me.'

'So stay for that. Stay because you love me. I'm not going to hurt you. Stay because you love me and I'll spend the rest of my life taking care of you, making sure you are happy in every way. Stay here, marry me. I promise you, Hannah, you will have everything you could ever want in life.'

'I'll have *nothing* I want,' she contradicted, but it was sad now, not angry. She blinked, as if she were waking up from a nightmare. 'I can't do this.'

His eyes didn't waver from hers. He stared at her, and

she felt a pull within him, a tug between two separate parts of him, and then he straightened, his expression shifting to one of calm control.

'You must.' He hesitated; she felt that pull once more, as if he were at war with himself. 'I cannot allow you to walk away.'

'Are you going to keep me here as your prisoner?'

He stared at her for several seconds. 'No.' His hesitation wasn't convincing. 'But I will fight you for our child. I need to know she's safe, Hannah, and only here, under my protection, will I believe that to be the case. I will sue for custody if I have to. I will do everything within my power to bring her to this island— I would prefer it if you were a part of that. For our daughter's sake.'

She drew in a breath, her eyes lifting to his as those words sliced through her. Words that made her body feel completely weak. The idea of someone as wealthy and powerful as Leonidas Stathakis suing her filled Hannah with a repugnant ache.

But then, she was shaking her head, and her heart thudded back to life.

'No, you won't. You're not going to drag me through the courts and make my life a living hell. You're not going to do anything that will garner the attention of the press, that will expose our daughter to harm. I don't mean physical harm. I mean the kind of harm that will befall her when she's twelve and goes on to the Internet and sees those stories. Do you think I don't know anything about the man I've fallen in love with?'

His jaw throbbed.

'You're not going to do that. You're not going to threaten me and you're not going to take her from me.' She swept her eyes shut, exhaling as she realised how right she was. 'You're a good person, Leonidas, and you're not capable of behaving like that. Whatever you might feel, you know our daughter belongs with me.'

'And not with me?' he prompted.

'Yes, with you, too,' she said simply. 'And we'll work that out. We'll work out a way to share her properly, to give her everything *she* deserves. For my daughter I would do almost anything—on Capri, I thought I'd even marry you for her. I thought needing her to have a "proper family" and to know her safety to be assured meant this marriage was essential.' She stared up at him, her eyes suspiciously moist, her voice unsteady. 'But I've got to know myself this week. I finally understand who I am and what I want—marrying a man who doesn't, and says he will never, love me would be a monumental mistake; one I have no intention of making.'

Only ten minutes earlier she'd been readying herself to tell him she loved him, and now Hannah was laying the groundwork for her departure.

'You told me this place is impossible to leave without your say-so. I'm asking you to let me go now. Today. This morning. To organise your plane or your helicopter or your yacht, something to take me away.'

His eyes narrowed; he regarded her sceptically for a moment, and when he spoke there was a bitterness in his words. 'And where will you go, Hannah? To Australia? To your horrible aunt and cousin? Or to London where you know barely anyone?'

Her chest pricked with blades of hurt. 'So you think I should stay here because there's nowhere better to be?'

'I think you should stay here because you want to and because it's best for everyone.'

'Not for me. I won't stay and be an instrument of your self-flagellation, another weapon for your sadism. You punished yourself every year by going to Chrysá Vráchia, and now you plan to punish yourself by having a wife you desire but won't ever love, because it would betray Amy. No, thanks. That's not for me.'

He let out a curse and crossed the room, but Hannah was done. She lifted a hand, stalling him.

'I'm sorry I couldn't disconnect my feelings as well as you did yours. I'm sorry I agreed to this only to change my mind, but I didn't have all the facts.' She reached for the enormous diamond engagement ring that had never really suited her anyway and dislodged it, sliding it over her knuckle and off her hand.

'I'll go back to London,' she said, thinking quickly. 'That makes sense for now. It's close enough that you can see her often.'

He made a noise of frustration. 'I don't want you to go.'

'I know that,' she whispered. 'But can you give me any reason that's good enough to stay?'

He didn't say anything, his eyes running over her face as if he could see inside her soul and find some way to induce her to remain. But there was none—not that he could give her.

'I have a house in London,' he said, his eyes dropping to her lips before he tore them away, looking over her shoulder. 'You should take it.'

'No, thanks.'

'Hannah,' he groaned. 'You're the mother of our child. I need you to be somewhere safe. Somewhere decent. Just…take the damned house for now. We'll sort out the paperwork later.'

'Once she's born,' Hannah compromised quietly. 'But my room is still available. All my stuff is still in it, in fact. I can go back and it'll be like nothing ever happened.' Her smile hurt, stretching across her face, filling her with grief.

'And what of your safety? Do you no longer care for that?'

She felt her stomach twist because he was doing everything he could to get her to stay—but for all the wrong reasons. 'I presume you fully intend to send guards to watch over me?'

He dipped his head in silent concession.

'I will cooperate with you on security, Leonidas.' Her eyes scanned his face. 'I'm not an idiot. If there's even a chance anything will happen to her because of who you are then I want all the help in the world to keep her safe. But that doesn't require marriage. It doesn't mean I have to stay here—with you.' She swallowed, a surreal sense of disbelief that this was happening taking over her.

He swore in Greek, bringing his body to hers, pressing their foreheads together, his eyes shut. 'We can make this work.'

But Hannah knew it was a lie. Not an intentional deceit, so much as a desire to give her what she needed without losing any part of himself. He didn't want to hurt her. He was a good person, and this hadn't been in his plan.

She swallowed past the lump in her throat, a throat that was raw and stinging. 'No, we can't.' She lifted up on her tiptoes then, because she couldn't resist, and pressed a kiss to his cheek. 'But at least we can say we tried.'

# CHAPTER THIRTEEN

THERE WERE NO photos of Amy and Brax in any of his homes for one very simple reason. Leonidas needed no photo in order to see them. They were burned into his retinas, his brain, his heart and soul. He saw them readily, and without any effort.

And now, Hannah was there too, and she was imprinted in a way that was impossible to scrub. He fell asleep with her smiling behind his eyelids and woke up with a start, seeing her visceral, deep pain on that last morning.

Her words were a whisper in his ears all day long. *'I'm here, and I love you.'*

Leonidas had become used to the torment of this— and it was a different torment, because, unlike Amy and Brax, Hannah was out there, within reach, a living, breathing person who loved him.

And he wanted her.

He needed her.

But he wasn't messed up enough to know he didn't deserve her. That he couldn't do that to her. Not when she'd fallen in love with him.

She deserved love. Hadn't he known that all along? Hadn't he wished she hadn't fallen pregnant to him purely because he knew she deserved to meet someone who would dedicate their life to loving her? Completely, unreservedly, in every way? She'd find that person, he was sure of it.

And what would happen then? Leonidas wondered. In fact, in the month since Hannah had left the island, Leonidas had thought about that a lot. When he wasn't drinking Scotch and glowering at the ocean, or snapping at the domestic staff and firing off ill-thought-out emails, he was imagining what Hannah's life post-Leonidas might look like.

Twice she'd agreed to marry the wrong man. Twice she'd let her kind, good heart lead her down the garden path.

Would third time be the charm for her? She was mesmerisingly beautiful, kind, funny, intelligent. She deserved someone who loved her. And their daughter?

Pain gripped his chest, because of course their daughter would be a part of that package. If Hannah met and married someone else, his daughter would have a stepfather. The idea filled him with sawdust, but even that wasn't enough. He couldn't go after her simply because he didn't want anyone else to have her.

He wasn't a spoiled three-year-old.

She'd fallen in love with him even though he didn't deserve that love, even though he could never give it back. She'd fallen in love with him and the kindest, fairest thing Leonidas could do for Hannah was accept her decision to leave.

He had to let her go.

'*Christós*, don't go easy on him, will you?' Thanos asked Leonidas.

Leonidas, sitting at the head of the table in one of the boardrooms of their London offices, threw his brother a quizzical expression.

'Did you see his hands shaking? He turned violet from rage.'

Leonidas shrugged. 'He wants to do business with us? Then he needs to lower his rate.'

Thanos laughed. 'I've never seen you quite like this.'

Leonidas compressed his lips. His personal life was a mess but that didn't mean his business life had to be. He'd become some kind of monster since Hannah had left the island—working eighteen-hour days seemed like the best way to put her out of his mind.

Every morning he'd woken to the security briefings, reporting on her whereabouts. Their only communication had been through his lawyers—him transferring a town house in London to her name, her not wishing to accept. He'd wanted to text her. To call her.

Hell, he'd wanted to see her. He'd wanted to see her so badly he'd felt as if he were running a marathon uphill, every single day that passed in which he didn't give into his impulses and get on a flight and go to London, knock on her door and demand she marry him after all.

He was a tyrannical CEO, so why not make it impossible for her to refuse marriage? Threaten harder, demand more.

But every time he imagined doing exactly that, he saw her as she'd been that last morning, her heartbreak evident in every line on her face, her softly spoken words when she'd told him he was a good person, that he would never hurt her.

And she was right about that—he couldn't hurt her. So he'd let her go, as he'd known he should. And every month that passed had filled him with an increasing ache, a desperation that was tearing him apart.

He needed her, but it was a selfish need, just as it had been all along.

He'd taken what he wanted from her, using Hannah to fill in the gaps of his soul without realising he was only adding to her own pains. He was becoming yet another thing she would need to get over.

He wanted to speak to her, but how could he? He took his cues from her and she was refusing to so much as acknowledge his gifts.

This week, however, had been by far the hardest. Three months after she'd left the island, a whole season later, he'd come to London. And he'd gone to bed every night looking out on this ancient city, knowing that she was only miles away. Imagining her, and the roundedness of her belly, the sweetness of her face in repose, the sound of her husky breathing.

He had tormented himself with her nearness—and the knowledge he had no right to see her. That he was here in London and not at her side.

'Leonidas.' He looked up as his brother's assistant entered the room. Belinda, somewhere in her fifties with pale hair and a permanently disapproving scowl, had worked for Thanos for almost a decade and it showed. She was tired and almost on the brink of a nervous breakdown—keeping Thanos's life on the rails could not be an easy occupation. At least they compensated her well for such a chore. 'Greg Hassan's on the phone for you.' She nodded sternly towards the receiver on a bench in the corner of the room.

'Thank you.'

Leonidas moved quickly across the room, telling himself not to panic even as the taste of adrenalin filled his mouth.

'What is it?' He had no time for pleasantries.

'Hannah's been rushed to hospital. Her waters broke.'

'What hospital?'

Hassan gave the name. Leonidas slammed the phone down and grabbed his coat without saying a word.

'Leo?' Thanos was right behind him. 'What's up?'

'The baby's coming.'

Thanos's smile was huge but Leonidas shook his head. 'It's too early. There's still a month to go.'

Panic wrapped around him. 'Stay here. I'll let you know.'

'Screw that.' Thanos's voice was firm. 'No way.'

Leonidas didn't want company, but he knew better than to argue with Thanos. Besides, he didn't have the energy and he didn't much care. He just needed to get to Hannah, to know everything was okay.

It was peak hour and the hospital was across London. 'Helicopter,' he muttered, shouldering out of the office with an impatience that was overtaking his soul.

Thanos didn't say a thing, simply nodded and took out his phone, giving orders for the helicopter to be readied. On the roof, they climbed into the sleek black chopper and it fired to life.

'Which hospital?' their pilot asked.

Leonidas repeated the name and the pilot lifted off. Thanos turned to Leonidas, his own features taut. 'Try not to worry, Leo. You'll be there soon.'

It didn't feel like soon enough to Leonidas. Despite the fact the helicopter cut through the sky like butter, he couldn't believe he'd ever let her leave him, leave the island. He couldn't believe she'd gone into labour on her own—that he hadn't been there to help her.

Finally, the chopper touched down on a neighbouring roof to the hospital. The engine wasn't even cut before Leonidas was jumping down, keeping bent low as he ran across the roof.

Thanos caught up to him as the elevator doors opened and neither spoke as the lift careened to the floor. Thanos ran the rest of the way, his heart pounding with every step he took.

'Hannah May,' he said as he arrived, the reception desk mercifully quiet.

'What ward?'

'I don't know.' Leonidas raked a hand through his hair.

'Obstetrics.' Thanos, right behind him, spoke more calmly.

'Let me see.' The nurse moved slowly, pressing her finger to a clipboard, a frown on her face. 'I don't see her.'

'She was brought in earlier. She must be here,' Leonidas demanded.

'Could you check again?' Thanos suggested, putting a hand on Leonidas's chest and pushing him a little away from the counter. His eyes held a warning—a suggestion: *I'll handle this.*

Leonidas paced from one side of the reception to the other, cursing in his head, adrenalin coursing through his veins.

'This way,' Thanos interrupted him, nodding towards the lifts. They went as fast as they could but everything in this old building was slow. When they reached the obstetrics ward and found the corridor they needed to walk down was closed because of mopping, Leonidas almost shouted the hospital down.

'Calm down,' Thanos insisted.

Yeah, right. When they arrived at the desk for the obstetrics ward, Thanos joined the back of a long queue to find out where Hannah was but Leonidas moved through the doors, and he stood stock-still. Because he heard her. He heard her cries and his heart jerked out of his chest.

A scream, pain; he was running down the corridor towards her voice, so close, his hand reaching for the door.

'You can't go in there, sir.' A man was running behind him, an older man, frail. Despite his security guard uniform, Leonidas didn't think he'd have much chance of stopping a terrified six-and-a-half-foot man in the prime of physical fitness.

'Try and stop me.'

'Sir, stop.' A woman now—a nurse. 'This corridor is off limits to visitors.'

'I'm not a damned visitor. My...' *Christós*, what could he call her? Not his wife. Not his fiancée. She was nothing to him now, just as she'd wanted. His chest rolled. 'My daughter is being born in here.' He hiked his thumb towards the door.

Thanos appeared behind the frail security guard.

'And if you wait in the reception, we'll let you know as soon as your baby arrives.'

He swore angrily. 'No. I want to be in there. Hannah needs me.'

For a moment, the nurse's face flashed with sympathy, but then she was all business again. 'Miss May was very clear on this point. There was no one she wanted called, no one she wanted notified. She told me she is alone.'

Leonidas couldn't meet his brother's eyes. Pain and raw disbelief filled him as he digested this, feeling the rejection of that statement, the line she'd drawn in the sand excluding him from this moment—knowing he deserved no better.

'Tell her I'm here. Please.' The words were hoarse, his stomach rolling, his expression full of desperation.

The nurse relented. 'I will. Please go and wait in reception for now.'

'But I—'

'This is not your call,' the nurse insisted with a quiet firmness in her voice. 'If she wants to do this on her own, you have to accept it.'

Leonidas stared at the nurse, then at the doors, then back at the nurse. Hannah's scream tore through the air and Leonidas felt an agonising need to go to her, to hold her, to do *something...anything* to help her.

'Please.'

'It's not my call.' She lifted a hand to his chest. 'I'll tell her you're here. Go and wait for me out there.'

Every bone in his body railed against this; every fibre of his being demanded he stay, that he fight her, that he fight to be with Hannah. But she didn't want him. She was doing exactly what she'd said she would—making her own life.

Despair swallowed him up. He stalked out of the corridor and into the reception room, which was full of happy, waiting family members. Leonidas was the only one who looked as if he could murder someone with his bare hands.

Thanos sat on one of the chairs, his calmness infuriating to Leonidas.

Leonidas was not calm.

Every time he heard her cry out his body was a tangle of pain, of outrage and impotence. How could he let her go through this—without him?

What could he do to help?

Nothing.

But that didn't change the fact that he was living a moment of sheer terror, that he'd spent the last three months in a state of agony and now it had come to this. Her pain filled him and worry—irrational, desperate anger at his own stupidity—drove through him like a blade.

He'd wasted time. He'd gambled. And now he could lose everything.

When a team of two nurses ran through the waiting room and disappeared into the corridor, he followed. When they pushed into Hannah's room, his heart dropped. A doctor followed.

Leonidas couldn't bear it.

He pushed into the room, and almost wished he hadn't when he saw the pain on Hannah's face, the look of sheer terror.

'Sir, I told you, you can't be here.' The nurse who was at Hannah's legs shot him a fierce look but Leonidas ignored her.

He strode to Hannah's side and took her hand in his, his eyes burning into Hannah's.

'I belong here.'

She looked up at him, her expression showing him only pain, only hurt, and he swallowed, fear tearing through him. 'I belong here.'

She didn't say anything, so he stayed; he kept her hand in his and she squeezed it so hard he wondered if circulation might completely stop, half hoping it would so he could feel something like the pain she was enduring.

He stroked her hair at times, and she said nothing to him—nothing to anyone—there were only the indiscernible, guttural sounds of her cries.

She dug her nails into his flesh and gave one last, agonising cry, the nurse lifting a pink and red baby with a shock of dark hair into the air, wiping her quickly with a towel and hitting her on the back until a robust cry emerged into the room.

Tears filled Leonidas's eyes, emotions swirling through him. He looked down at Hannah and she was sobbing, but a smile was on her lips as she held her hands out for their daughter, pulling her to her chest. Leonidas had never seen anything more beautiful, more perfect.

They were his family—they were his.

'You didn't have to come.' Hannah had recovered enough from the delivery to be trying to make sense of what Leonidas was doing at the hospital—and how he'd got there so quickly. Seeing Leonidas again was going to take a lot more recovery time. It had been three months. Twelve weeks. So many nights wondering if she'd done completely the wrong thing, wanting to crumble and beg him to take her back, needing him on every level, loving him enough to take whatever crumbs he would give her.

And in this moment, when her hormones were rioting and she was looking at their beautiful daughter, it took all her wherewithal to remember why she'd left him.

To remember that he didn't love her, didn't want her, that his heart belonged to someone else and always would.

He'd mercifully left the room again after the delivery under threat of the police being called, so Hannah could be cleaned up in privacy and transferred to a different room—one that was smaller and less medical in its design.

She was exhausted, but her heart was bursting—their daughter was asleep in a tiny crib across the room.

'Did you think I wouldn't?'

She shook her head.

'Did you really want to keep me from this?'

She swallowed, looking at him and seeing him almost for the first time. He was so handsome but there was a torment in his face that robbed her of breath.

'I was going to let you know once she was born.'

That her statement had hurt him was obvious, but when he spoke it was quietly, gently, and that somehow hurt even more.

'No doubt.'

He paced across the room and Hannah's eyes followed him hungrily before she realised what she was doing and looked away. A nurse had brought a tea in a few moments earlier, before Leonidas had returned. Hannah reached for it now, cupping the mug in her hands gratefully.

'You were in so much pain,' he said slowly, turning to face her, his eyes roaming over her in the same hungry way she'd been looking at him a moment earlier. 'I thought you were dying.'

'So did I, believe me,' she quipped, but without humour. She sipped her tea then held it in her lap.

Leonidas moved to the crib, staring down at their daughter, and Hannah had to look away—so powerful was the image of the father of her daughter, the man she loved, the pride on his face, the love she saw there… it tore her apart.

Tears filled her eyes and she blinked, sipping her tea again, jerking her head away so she was looking at a shining white wall.

'Three months.' He said the words as though they were being dragged from deep within him. 'You've been gone for three months.'

The tone of his voice had her pulling her face back to him, and she saw pain there, disbelief. Hurt.

'Three months and it has felt like a decade.' He swallowed, his Adam's apple jerking in his throat.

Her own grief was washing over her. 'I had to leave.'

His eyes narrowed. 'Because you love me.'

She swept her eyes shut. 'Yes.' There was no sense denying it. True love didn't disappear on a whim. It was love. Simple, desperate, all-consuming love.

'*Theos*, Hannah.' He moved towards the bed and she stiffened, bracing for his nearness. She'd come on in leaps and bounds, was learning how to live without him, but she wasn't ready to be touched by him. She couldn't.

'You don't have to be here,' she said urgently, arresting his progress across the room. 'You really don't.'

'I want to be,' he said simply, walking once more. He stood at her side, staring down at her, and her heart flipped in her chest, heavy with love, pain, rejection, fear, need.

'No,' she whispered. 'You don't understand. You can't be here. It's too hard. I don't want you here.'

'Hannah,' he sighed, looking at her, perhaps innately understanding she couldn't bear to be touched by him, not now, not after how he'd rejected her love. 'I've spent the last three months telling myself I was doing the right thing. I knew you were safe, I made sure of that, and I told myself I had to give you what you wanted. I had to let you live your life away from me because I couldn't return your love.'

Hannah made a small, strangled noise of panic.

'And then Greg Hassan called and told me you were on your way to the hospital and—*Theos, agape mou*—I have never felt anything like this fear and panic.'

He pressed his hand to his chest, staring down at her. 'I was so terrified that something had happened to you and all I could think was how I'd wasted all this time. *Christós*, Hannah.' He dropped his head forward for a moment, catching his breath.

'I've been so focussed on what I lost, so angry at what happened to Amy and Brax, at the fact it was my fault, because of who I am, that I didn't stop to realise how lucky I am to have had that time with them. If I could do it all again, knowing how it would end, I would still choose this life.'

His eyes showed such strong emotions then, and her heart cracked. 'I had a son.' His voice was wrenched with grief. 'A beautiful, perfect boy.'

Hannah sobbed; how could she not? And her eyes

shifted to their sleeping daughter, her heart twisting inside her.

'I lost them, and it nearly killed me. I spent four years afterwards living some kind of angry half life. Until I met you, and something shifted inside me, something elemental and important, and it terrified me because I thought the only way I could atone for what happened to Amy and Brax was to keep myself walled off from anyone for the rest of my life.'

Another sob escaped Hannah.

'I avoided human contact, I was rude and arrogant, an impossible bastard. And then I saw you...'

His eyes held hers and Hannah was back on Chrysá Vráchia, the power of that moment, of their connection, searing her blood.

'Greg Hassan called and told me you'd been rushed to hospital and I thought something had happened to you, and I realised I've been shutting myself off to what I have no doubt would be an incredible life with the woman I love because I'm afraid of what *might* happen.'

Hannah's eyes flared wide, her expression showing disbelief and confusion.

'That lightning bolt got me too, Hannah. It struck me and I have been trying to pretend it didn't, fighting you this whole way.'

She shook her head but now he bent down so their faces were level, and so close she could feel his warm breath fanning her cheek.

'You are so brave—do you know that? To have been

hurt like you were by Angus and still put yourself out on a limb, telling me you've fallen in love with me—'

She shook her head urgently, and, despite the emotions rioting inside her, she was clear on this point, because she'd had months to think it over, to see it as it was. 'Loving you freed me up to realise I felt nothing like love for Angus. How I feel for you is so different.'

'I know.' He leaned forward a little. 'You love me, and you love me even though I have pushed you away, even though I have been stubbornly clinging to a kind of anger that is ruining my life. You love me even when I took your love and refused to acknowledge I returned it. You have loved me when I was so far from being the man you deserved.'

Hannah bit down on her lip, her eyes holding his. 'Love isn't a choice.' She frowned, lifting a hand to his cheek, because the words had come out all wrong. 'And even if it were, I would choose to love you. You deserve happiness, Leonidas. You deserve it.'

'I wanted to give you everything,' he said quietly. 'When you spoke about your aunt and uncle, your cousin, Angus, all the people who had you in their life and didn't appreciate you, I wanted to scream. You should have the world at your feet; I wanted to give it to you. But you don't really want private jets to Paris, do you?'

She shook her head. 'I mean, that's all well and good, but it's not what really matters.'

'No, it's not,' he agreed, dropping his head to hers, pressing his lips lightly to her forehead. 'All that matters is here, in this room, with you and me. Please tell me I haven't permanently ruined things between us.'

She swept her eyes shut, fear shifting inside her because she didn't want to be hurt again; she didn't want to feel pain.

But nor did she want to live a life without Leonidas in it.

'I'm completely in love with you,' he said. 'Madly, utterly, in every way. I was transfixed by you at Chrysá Vráchia but presumed it was just…that. Infatuation. I couldn't stop thinking about you. I don't know when I fell in love with you, but I do know that from the beginning you have been under my skin and a part of my being. I do know that I want to spend every day we have together showing you that you are the meaning to my life.'

She bit down on her lower lip to stop another sob—a happy one—escaping.

'Life is a gift, and I was wasting it. I don't want to do that any more.'

She expelled a shaky breath, inhaling his masculine fragrance, her stomach swooping and dropping, happiness beginning to flow into her body for the first time in a long time.

'That day on the island—our wedding day—'

She turned to face him, waiting silently for him to finish his thought.

'It was hard. Nothing about marrying you quickly, in secret, away from loved ones, felt like what I wanted. Making you my wife, yes. But like that?' He shook his head, and then reached into his pocket, pulling out a black velvet box. Hannah's eyes dropped to it, her smile transforming her face.

'So I would like to ask you again, Hannah, if you would do me the honour of becoming my wife. I love you with every single part of me. My heart and soul are, and always will be, yours.' He took her hand and lifted it to his lips, pressing a kiss to her inner wrist. 'You brought me back to life and made me myself again. But better, because you've taught me so much about compassion and love, respect and patience. You are so much more than I deserve.'

At that, she shook her head silently, because her throat was filled with tears and she wasn't sure she'd be able to get any sensible words out.

'But I will spend the rest of our lives, however long that may be, striving to be good enough for you, *agape mou*.'

Hannah sobbed then, as he handed the ring box to her.

She hadn't loved her engagement ring—it had been so enormous and flashy. But she'd come to love it because it had promised a future with Leonidas. She cracked open the box and smiled, because it wasn't even the same ring.

Instead there was a single diamond, still large but not break-your-finger huge, surrounded by a circlet of emeralds.

'It's beautiful,' she whispered, her eyes filling with tears.

'Two weeks after you left the island, I was in Athens.

I saw it in a window and bought it without even realising what I was doing. I have been carrying it around ever since, as though it made you close to me in some way.' His smile was rueful. 'I told myself I could give it to you as an "I'm sorry" gift, if nothing else. But in my heart, I imagined you wearing it on this finger.' He ran his hand over hers. 'And wearing it as a promise to become my wife, to live this life by my side.'

She sobbed then, and held her hand out, so he could slide the ring onto her finger; it fitted perfectly.

'And this is my promise to you,' he said gently, fixing her with a look that seared her soul. 'I will love you and cherish you, be faithful to you, care for you, protect you, adore you and worship you for as long as we both shall live.'

Hannah nodded, still too choked up to respond with words. And really, what words were needed? They'd said all that was necessary and, more importantly, each felt the truth of their declaration, deep inside their beings—and always would.

The only thing left was to marry, and to live happily ever after.

# EPILOGUE

'I KNOW YOU said you wanted me to see the world, but this is more than I ever imagined.'

'Do you like them?'

Hannah gave her husband a droll look before turning back to the golden vista beneath her, her green eyes taking in the flat expanse of the Egyptian desert before focussing on the familiar peaks of the ancient Pyramids. The helicopter hovered at a distance, giving a perfect vantage point over them.

'They're stunning,' she said simply. Because they were. It was hard for Hannah to say which of the countries they'd visited in the past eighteen months was her favourite. They all had a special place in her heart, and for different reasons. Going to a special opera performance at the Coliseum had been incredible, a private tour of the Pantheon had taken her breath away, exploring New York with Leonidas by her side, coming to know his Greek island as though she were a local, snorkelling off the shore, swimming in the pool, learning to speak his language and enjoy his food—it had all been remarkable: but all the more so for having Leonidas by her side.

And though she'd planned to wait to tell him her news, with the ancient Pyramids glistening beneath them, a testament to humanity's strength, intelligence, and determination, Hannah felt the words burst out of her.

'I got an email two days ago.'

'Yes?'

She nodded, pride making her eyes sparkle. 'My application was accepted.'

'Your application…?'

She nodded, excitement a thousand arrows darting beneath her skin. 'Law school.'

Leonidas's smile transformed his face and Hannah's heart clutched at the sight. Love was a lightning bolt, yes, but it was also this—a genuine, complete desire to see your loved one succeed in life. Leonidas had been Hannah's champion, he had supported her, overcome her doubts when she'd worried she wouldn't have what it took to apply for her degree, and then when she'd doubted she'd be able to meet the study schedule.

He'd moved all the pieces effortlessly so she could apply, and still be hands-on with their daughter, Isabella.

Her dreams had become his dreams.

'I never doubted for one second that you would be accepted.'

'Because you're Leonidas Stathakis and I'm your wife?' she teased.

'Because you're *you*,' he corrected, leaning forward and kissing her. 'Brilliant, intelligent, motivated, fiercely strong.'

Hannah's heart was flying higher than the Pyramids, way up in the sky.

She was going to achieve her dreams, and even though she liked to think she could have done this on her own, she was so glad it was happening this way— she was so glad she got to share it all with Leonidas.

Hours later, back on the yacht in the Red Sea, with Isabella fast asleep, Hannah reading in the armchair, Leonidas looked at his wife and felt a quick surge of panic, familiar to him now, whenever he contemplated how close he'd come to losing all this.

He had almost shut the door on love and happiness in life because of fear.

He would never make that mistake again.

\* \* \* \* \*

# Defying Her Billionaire Protector
## Angela Bissell

**Books by Angela Bissell**

**Harlequin Modern**

*Irresistible Mediterranean Tycoons*
*Surrendering to the Vengeful Italian*

**Angela Bissell** lives with her husband and one crazy Ragdoll cat in the vibrant harborside city of Wellington, New Zealand. In her twenties, with a wad of savings and a few meager possessions, she took off for Europe, backpacking through Egypt, Israel, Turkey and the Greek islands before finding her way to London, where she settled and worked in a glamorous hotel for several years. Clearly the perfect grounding for her love of Harlequin Modern! Visit her at angelabissell.com.

# DEDICATION

For my friend Lisa, a brave, beautiful and inspiring
woman. Thank you for your valuable insights—
and for letting me have a spin in your wheels.
Here's to many more Princess Days in the sun!

# CHAPTER ONE

'*MAMMA MIA!* HERE they come.'

Marietta's hands stilled over the keys of her computer, her assistant's warning—low-voiced yet laced with an unmistakable thread of anticipation—shattering her train of thought like crystal under a hammer. She looked up in time to see the courier pushing open the glass doors of the gallery she managed in the heart of Rome's affluent Parioli district. In his arms he cradled a huge, hand-tied bouquet of roses.

*'Bellissimo.'* Lina moved from the storeroom doorway and stood by Marietta's desk at the rear of the gallery. 'They are the best yet!'

Marietta would have liked to disagree with that assessment, but Lina was right. The long-stemmed roses *were* beautiful, each head—at least two dozen of them—exquisite, the velvety petals a vivid red that in the whiteness of the gallery made Marietta think, perversely, of blood.

Her thoughts snapped to the elegant spray of white

orchids that had been delivered earlier in the week—
surprisingly, because until then the flowers had always arrived on a Friday. Pretty and delicate, the
orchids, like the roses, had been lovely to look at,
but their sweet, cloying scent had lingered in her
nostrils and left her feeling faintly ill long after she
had disposed of them.

Even the note that had come with them had been
heavily perfumed, and she'd wanted to destroy that
too. Had wanted to rip the card and its intimate typewritten message into tiny, indecipherable pieces and
flush them down the toilet.

But she'd been told to keep the notes in case they
held any clues, so she'd shoved the card into a drawer,
along with all the others, and vowed that when this
was over—when her secret-admirer-turned-stalker
was caught or simply grew tired of his antics—she
would set a match to those cards and enjoy watching them burn.

The courier strode over the polished concrete towards them, and Marietta felt her stomach doing
a little surge and roll. She didn't want to touch the
roses. She definitely didn't want them near enough
for her to smell.

'Ciao.'

The young courier's broad smile did nothing to
quell her dread. His gaze shifted sideways—drawn,
unsurprisingly, to Lina's tall, willowy form—and
Marietta saw the predictable flare of male appre-

ciation on his face give way to surprise—or maybe *shock* was a better word—the moment the man sitting behind her stood.

He strode around her desk, straight into the courier's path, and she imagined she heard the young man's jaw crack, his mouth dropped open so fast. His face lost its colour, paling several shades as he took in the large, imposing man before him. She felt a twinge of sympathy for the guy; Nicolas César, ex-legionnaire, head of the widely revered global conglomerate César Security and her brother's good friend, could scare the wits out of most people—and that was on the days he *didn't* look hell-bent on throttling someone.

He stared down at the courier from his massive height and extended a large, capable-looking hand. A hand that appeared elegant and bone-crushingly strong all at the same time. 'Give them to me.'

Nico's deep voice rumbled with the kind of natural authority only a fool with no thought for self-preservation would dare to challenge. Wisely, the younger man didn't hesitate. He handed over the roses with a haste that might have amused Marietta had anything about this situation been remotely funny. His eyes darted back to Lina, but her attention was firmly fixed on the other man, and, as if understanding he couldn't possibly compete with all that eye-popping masculinity, the courier shot Marietta a bemused look and hurried out of the gallery.

She gripped the titanium hand rims on the wheels of her custom-made chair and reversed a few feet from her desk. Although Nico stood on the other side, with a great slab of horizontal glass between them, she needed the comfort of the extra distance before she looked at him.

Not, she told herself, because she wasn't used to looking up at people. Thirteen years in a wheelchair had accustomed her to seeing the world from a diminished height, and she'd long ago reconciled herself to that aspect of her disability. And although able-bodied people often thought of her as being *confined* to a wheelchair—as though the chair and not her paralysed legs were the prison—for Marietta the use of her modern, ultralight chair for mobility was a choice. One that gave her the freedom to work and travel. To live her life with a level of independence any single, career-focused woman of thirty would wish to enjoy.

But Nicolas César wasn't anything like the people Marietta encountered on an ordinary day, and it wasn't only his unique physicality that set him apart—wasn't only the impressive breadth of his shoulders, the fact that he stood taller than most. On par with her six-foot-four brother—or the fact that his dark trousers and close-fitting black shirt moulded the kind of lean, hard-muscled physique that spoke of discipline and sweat and the good fortune of strong, resilient genes. Rather, it was the raw power he exuded from every inch of that undeniably masculine frame—the overriding impression that here was a man few others dared trifle with—that made Marietta's hormones sit up and take notice.

Which irritated her enormously.

Sexual attraction was a complication she didn't need in her life right now—or *ever*, for that matter. Especially to a man so far out of her physical league her pride smarted just to look at him.

'Are you not going to interrogate him?' she asked, and her annoyance with herself—with that hot, inescapable lick of feminine awareness—lent her words a much pithier edge than she'd intended.

Dark blue eyes thinned and settled on her, making her aware that her sarcasm wasn't lost on Nico, and guilt instantly pricked her. He was here to help because her brother had asked him to. That Leo had done so without consulting her first was no fault of Nico's. Unleashing her frustration on him was childish. Unfair.

He held her gaze, his silent, prolonged eye contact causing her skin to flush and her insides to squirm with something far more unsettling than guilt. She didn't look away and wasn't sure she could even if she wanted to. His eyes were such a dark, mesmerising blue. Staring into them made her feel as if she'd been dragged beneath the surface of a vast, bottomless sea and could no longer breathe.

She opened her mouth to offer an apology—and

418 DEFYING HER BILLIONAIRE PROTECTOR

drag some much-needed air into her lungs—but Nico spoke first.

'Bruno has cleared the staff at the florist's shop and vetted the couriers they use. There is no need for me to...' he paused for a fraction of a beat '...*interrogate* him.'

That slight yet deliberate emphasis on the word *interrogate* elevated Marietta's discomfort. Looking at him, it wasn't at all difficult for her to visualise Nicolas César in the role of interrogator—nor did she have any trouble imagining that anyone on the wrong side of that arrangement would quickly find themselves either pleading for mercy or spilling their deepest, darkest secrets to him. Or both.

At the same time, she imagined any man who possessed that degree of dark, potent magnetism would rarely, if ever, want for female companionship. Women flocked to him wherever he went, no doubt, drawn like hummingbirds to nectar by his hard-edged looks and his big, powerful body.

And that would be *before* he opened his mouth.

Before that deep-timbre voice, with its French accent and slight North American inflection, poured over them like heated syrup and turned their insides all gooey.

Marietta suppressed a little shiver.

*Did Nico make his lovers plead?*

*Did he make them scream?*

The shiver turned into a hot flush that cascaded

through Marietta's body and scalded her from the inside out. *Madre di Dio.* What was wrong with her? She had no business allowing her thoughts to veer in that direction. No business entertaining hot, lurid fantasies about her brother's friend. Life had taught her some harsh lessons—lessons that had moulded her into a realist—and realists like her did not waste their time fantasising about things they would never have.

And yet she wasn't without aspirations. Cementing her place in the art world, achieving success and recognition as an artist in her own right, supporting herself independently of her brother's wealth and generosity—*those* were her goals, the dreams that got her out of bed in the mornings.

Plus she had a wish list tucked away—a 'bucket list', some people called it. Everyone had one, didn't they? Everyone wanted to see things and do things that breathed some excitement, some *magic* into their ordinary lives.

Marietta was no different. As an incomplete paraplegic she could no longer walk, but living with a spinal cord injury didn't mean she couldn't push her own boundaries, do things that were a little adventurous or wild.

Paraplegics around the world skydived and flew planes and competed in rigorous sports.

Every item on Marietta's wish list was doable. Some more challenging than others, given her physical limitations, but all of them realistic. She certainly didn't have her head in the clouds. She knew what was possible and what wasn't. And there was no reason whatsoever that she couldn't tandem skydive. Or float in a hot air balloon. Or travel to Egypt to see the pyramids.

But what were the chances of a man who could crook his finger and have any woman in the world—any *able-bodied* woman in the world—he wanted desiring her?

Now *that* was pure fantasy—a pointless, fanciful daydream she needn't waste her time indulging.

What she did need to do was stay focused, remember what was important: her job, her independence, her art.

Especially her art.

But now all of that was under threat. In danger of being disrupted by some anonymous admirer who *must* be mentally unstable, or, if she were being less kind, completely deranged.

*Six weeks*. That was how long she'd been receiving the bunches of flowers and the notes she'd thought quaint and amusing—even flattering—at first. But over the weeks the messages had gone from sweet to intense, their content growing more personal, more intimate. More possessive.

It was the note that had come with a bouquet of thirteen crimson tulips on a Friday two weeks ago, however, that had for the first time left her truly spooked.

*Such a beautiful dress you wore yesterday, amore mio. Red is perfect on you—and my favourite colour. You see? We were made for each other! S.*

Those words had clamped a cold fist around her throat and squeezed hard as their import had slowly sunk in. And she had realised something she hadn't considered before then—that he, whoever *he* was, was following her, watching her, *stalking* her.

Gooseflesh rose on Marietta's forearms and she resisted the urge to rub them, to scrub away the sensation of something unpleasant crawling over her skin.

She'd been so shaken she'd confided in her sister-in-law, Helena—which in hindsight had been a mistake. Helena, in spite of Marietta's pleas for her not to, had told her husband—Marietta's brother—who had, of course, flipped. Within minutes Leo had been on the phone, severely chastising her for not going directly to him and urging her to involve the police.

Advice she'd promptly ignored. She hadn't wanted to create a fuss and her big brother was, as always, being over-protective. The fact he'd waited an entire forty-eight hours before calling on his friend Nico for assistance was, she reflected now, nothing short of astonishing.

That Nico, whom she'd last seen at Leo and Helena's wedding two years before, had, in the first instance, sent his man Bruno rather than handle the matter himself, was something Marietta had *not*, she'd assured herself, been a little disappointed about.

Nicolas César was, after all, a busy man—CEO of a renowned global network that provided security and protection services to some of the world's most powerful corporations and influential figureheads. Dealing with an overzealous admirer was never going to figure high on his priority list, no matter how solid his friendship with her brother.

And yet…here he stood. Or perhaps *towered* was the better word, she thought, conscious of a crick in her neck. Of the warm pulse of blood beneath her skin. Her heartbeat had not quite settled back into its normal rhythm since he'd walked, unannounced, into the gallery some forty minutes earlier.

After a brief, polite greeting he'd asked to see the cards Bruno had told her to keep, and then, despite the fact they were written in Italian, had proceeded to read every intimate word until Marietta's face had burned with mortified heat. Then—since it was mid-afternoon on a Friday, and that meant another bouquet was likely on its way—he'd commandeered one of the soft chairs reserved for the gallery's clientele and artists and waited for the flowers she had silently prayed wouldn't come.

'Where's Bruno?' she asked now. Not because she missed the rigid presence of the dark-suited man, but rather because she could see the small white envelope attached to the roses and wanted to delay, if only for a minute longer, having to open it.

'Following up a lead.'

*A lead.* That sounded vague. 'What sort of lead?'

He didn't answer her. Instead he turned to Lina, as if he'd not heard the question or had simply chosen to ignore it.

Marietta tamped down her annoyance—only to feel it flare again when she glanced at her assistant. *Santo cielo!* Had the girl no pride? No sense of dignity? Marietta wanted to snap her fingers at her. Tell her to wipe that silly doe-eyed look off her face. To straighten up and pull her hip back in, instead of jutting it sideways in a come-hither pose she probably wasn't even aware she'd adopted.

Nico detached the envelope from the roses, his strong fingers snapping the straw ribbon like a strand of cotton, and handed the bouquet to Lina. 'Get rid of them.'

Lina—foolish girl—beamed at him as if he'd paid her a compliment rather than barked an order at her. Marietta bristled on her assistant's behalf. Lina, however, was oblivious. Without so much as glancing at Marietta for confirmation, she took the roses and disappeared out to the back—heading, presumably, for the outdoor dumpster behind the building.

Marietta couldn't help herself. 'That was rude.'

Nico's eyes narrowed on her again…so blue. So disconcerting. 'Pardon?'

'Lina,' she clarified. 'You could have asked nicely. Barking commands at people is rude.'

One heavy eyebrow arced, ever so slightly, towards his dark brown hairline. 'She did not look upset.'

Of course she hadn't looked upset. She'd looked smitten and flushed and…*ravenous*. As if she'd wanted to drag Nico into the storeroom, bolt the door shut and tear his clothes off—with her teeth.

Marietta was sure Nico knew it, too.

And yet, to his credit, he hadn't encouraged her attentions. Hadn't seemed to give out any inappropriate cues. In fact he'd seemed barely to notice her—unlike some of the male visitors to the gallery, who appeared more entranced by Lina's legs than by the sculptures and paintings on display.

And the girl had good legs—long and shapely—and a good body that she dressed, or on occasion *under*dressed, to showcase. Why shouldn't she? She was tall and graceful. Feminine, yet lithe.

*Unbroken.*

Everything Marietta might have been and wasn't, thanks to one fateful split-second decision. One irreversible moment of teenage stupidity. A moment that had altered the course of her life and shattered what little had remained of her childhood innocence.

Still—as a few well-intentioned if slightly insensitive people had pointed out during the long, excruciating months of her rehabilitation—she'd been lucky.

She had survived.

The three teens in the car with her—including the alcohol-impaired driver—had not. Two had died on impact with the concrete median barrier, the third on a gurney surrounded by the trauma team trying desperately to save her.

For Marietta, the sole survivor of that tragic car crash, a long string of dark, torturous days had followed. Days when she'd lain unable or sometimes unwilling to move, staring at the ceiling of the hated rehab unit. Reliving those final moments with her friends and wishing, in her darkest moments, that she had died alongside them.

But she had not died.

She had fought her way back.

For the brother whom she knew had taken the burden of responsibility—and blame—upon himself. For the second chance at life she'd been given that her friends had not. For her mother—God rest her soul—who would have wanted Marietta to fight with the same courage and determination with which she'd battled the cancer that had, in the end, cruelly won. And—even though she'd stayed angry with him for a long time after he'd died—for her father, who'd fought his own grief-fuelled demons after his wife's death and tragically lost.

Her chin went up a notch.

She had faced down every brutal obstacle the universe had thrown at her and she was still here. She would *not* let some stranger, some clearly unhinged individual, disrupt the life she'd worked so long and hard to rebuild. And she certainly wasn't afraid of some pathetic words on a little white card.

She held out her hand for the envelope. Nico hesitated, then handed it over. Willing her hands not to shake, she tore open the flap and pulled out the card. She sucked in a deep breath and started to read—and felt the cold pasta salad she'd had for lunch threaten to vacate her stomach.

Marietta's hands had started to shake.

She glanced up, her espresso-coloured eyes so dark Nico couldn't differentiate between iris and pupil. They were glassy, enormous—larger than usual—and, he noted, unblinking. Combined with her sudden pallor, the tremor in her slim hands, they conveyed an emotion Nico had more than once in his life been intimately acquainted with.

*Fear.*

He cursed under his breath, reached over the glass-topped desk and whipped the card out of her hands.

His Italian wasn't impeccable, like his native

French or his English, but he had no trouble reading the typewritten words. His fingers tightened on the card but he took care to keep his face expressionless. Marietta was a strong woman—something he'd intuited the first time they'd met in passing at her brother's office, and again at Leo's wedding—but right now she was shaken and he needed her to be calm. Reassured. *Safe.*

Anything less would be a disservice to her brother, and Leo was a good friend—had been ever since their paths had crossed via a mutual client eight years ago. Nico had recognised in the Italian the qualities of a man he could like and respect. Leo's company specialised in cyber security, and his people occasionally lent their technical expertise to Nico's own. Outside of business the two men had become firm friends—and Nico did not intend to let his friend down.

He slipped the card into a plastic folder along with the others. Aside from an insight into their composer's mind, the notes offered nothing of real value and no means by which they could track the original sender. The flowers were always ordered online, the cards printed by the florist, the words simply copied from the order's electronic message field.

Bruno had been confident at first. Online orders meant a traceable digital trail to IP addresses and credit cards. But whoever Marietta's stalker was he was careful—and clever. Their tech guys had chased

428   DEFYING HER BILLIONAIRE PROTECTOR

their tails through a series of redirected addresses and discovered the account with the florist had been opened using bogus details. The invoices were sent to a rented mailbox and payments were received in cash via mail.

It all indicated a level of premeditation and intent neither Nico nor Bruno had anticipated. And Nico didn't like it. Didn't like it that he'd underestimated the threat—assuming, at first, that they'd be dealing with nothing more troublesome than a jilted boyfriend. It galled him now to accept that he'd been wrong because he knew better than to assume.

But he was here now, in Rome, with the meetings he'd had scheduled for today in New York cancelled after Bruno's call twenty-four hours earlier.

And they *would* find this guy. They'd break some rules, sidestep some local bureaucracy, and they would find him.

He strode around the desk and dropped to his haunches in front of Marietta's chair, bringing his eyes level with hers. She jerked back a little, as if she wasn't used to such an action, and he wondered briefly if it were not the accepted thing to do. But he'd have done the same with any woman he sought to reassure, conscious that his height, his sheer size, might intimidate.

'We *will* stop him, Marietta.'

Her eyes remained huge in her face, her olive

complexion stripped of colour. 'He's been in my home...'

Nico ground his jaw. 'Perhaps.'

'But the note—'

'Could be nothing more than a scare tactic,' he cut in. Yet the tension in his gut, the premonitory prickle at his nape, told him the truth was something far less palatable. More sinister.

*I have left you a gift,* tesoro. *On your bed. Think of me when you unwrap it. Sleep well,* amore mio. *S.*

On impulse he took her hand—small compared to his, and yet strong rather than dainty or delicate. Her fingers were slender and long, her nails short and neat, manicured at home, he guessed, rather than by a professional.

Incredibly, Nico could still remember clasping her hand on their very first introduction—four, maybe five years ago at her brother's office. Their handshake had been brief but he'd noted that her skin felt cool, pleasant to the touch, her palm soft and smooth in places, callused in others. He remembered, too, seeing her at Leo's wedding a couple of years later. Remembered watching her, intrigued and impressed with the way she handled her wheelchair—as if it were a natural extension of her body.

In the church she'd glided down the aisle be-

fore the bride, composed and confident, unselfcon-
scious—or at least that was the impression she'd
given. Her sister-in-law, a beautiful English woman,
had looked stunning in a simple white gown, but it
was Marietta to whom Nico's attention had been repeatedly drawn throughout the ceremony.

In his thirty-six years he'd attended two other
weddings—his own, which he preferred not to dwell
upon, and an equally lavish affair in the Bahamas to
which he had, regrettably, allowed a former lover to
drag him—but he could not recall a bridesmaid at
either who might have outshone Marietta in looks
or elegance.

With her thick mahogany hair piled high on her
head, the golden skin of her shoulders and décolle-
tage bare above the turquoise silk of her long bridesmaid's sheath, the fact she was in a wheelchair had
not diminished the impact of her beauty.

And then there were the shoes.

Nico could not forget the shoes.

*Stilettos.*

Sexy, feminine, four-inch stilettos in a bright turquoise to match the gown.

That Marietta could not walk in those shoes had
made him admire her all the more for wearing them.
It was a statement—a bold one—as though she were
flipping the bird to her disability...or rather to anyone who thought a woman who couldn't walk was

wasting her time wearing sexy shoes, and it had made him want to smile.

Hell, it had made him want to grin.

And that was an urge he rarely experienced.

'Nico?'

Marietta's hand twitched in his, jerking his thoughts back to the present. He refocused, realised his thumb was stroking small circles over her skin. Abruptly he broke contact and stood. 'Stay here. Keep Lina with you.'

She wheeled back and looked up at him. 'Where are you going?'

'Your apartment.'

She frowned, a smudge of colour returning to her face. 'Not without me, you're not.'

'It is better that you stay here,' he said evenly.

'Why?'

When he hesitated a fraction too long, her fine-boned features twisted into a look of horror.

'*Mio Dio.* You think he might be there, don't you?' She stared at him accusingly. 'But you said the note was just a scare tactic.'

'*Could* be,' he corrected. 'I won't know for certain until I've checked it out.'

'Then I'll come with you.'

'I'd prefer you didn't.'

Her shoulders snapped back, her eyes, wide with shock and fear only seconds before, now narrowing. 'It's my apartment. I'm coming whether you *prefer* it or not.' Her delicate chin lifted. 'Besides, you need me. You won't get in without my security code and key.'

'Both of which you are about to give to me,' he told her, keeping his voice reasonable even as he felt his patience slipping. He was unaccustomed to people arguing with him—especially women.

Marietta folded her hands in her lap. The gesture combined with her conservative attire—a sleeveless high-necked lilac silk blouse, long black pants and, perhaps less conservative, a pair of purple high-heeled suede boots—made her look almost demure. Yet there was nothing demure in the set of her shoulders or the bright glint of defiance in her eyes.

'Do people always jump when you bark?'

He crossed his arms over his chest. Outwardly he was calm. Inside, impatience heated his blood dangerously close to tipping point. *'Oui,'* he said, injecting a low note of warning into his voice he hoped she had the wisdom to heed. 'If they know what is good for them.'

Her eyebrows rose at that, but the shrug that rolled off her shoulders was careless. 'Well, I'm sorry to disappoint you—' she looked pointedly at her legs and then back at him '—but you might have noticed I can't jump very high these days.'

Nico flattened his mouth, returned her stare. Channelled his trademark control—or tried to. 'You are wasting time, Marietta.'

'Me?' Somehow she managed to look utterly innocent. 'You're the one holding us up, Nico. We could
have been halfway there by now.'

He sucked in a breath and exhaled sharply. Leo
had warned him that Marietta could be stubborn.
Resolute. Headstrong. No doubt those qualities had
served her well through some difficult times, helped
her overcome the kind of obstacles most people, if
they were fortunate, would never have to face in their
lifetime. He respected those qualities, admired them,
but right now he'd settle for a lot less lip and a great
deal more acquiescence.

The determined glitter in those liquid brown
eyes told him he had zero chance of getting it. Nico
couldn't decide if that surprised him, impressed him,
or angered him.

People did not defy Nicolas César.

They *obeyed* him.

Fortunately for Marietta he had neither the time
nor the patience to stand there and argue. He un-
crossed his arms. Muttered an oath. 'Wait here,' he
growled. 'I'll bring my car to the front of the gallery
and collect you.'

A smile broke on her face that almost made the
pain of his capitulation worth it. He blinked. *Mon
Dieu.* Did she give that smile freely to everyone she
met? If so, he wouldn't be surprised to find a thousand infatuated admirers lurking in the wings.

'No need,' she said, and rolled her chair forward

to a small cabinet beside her desk. She pulled out an enormous leather handbag. 'I have my car in the lane out back. I'll drive myself and meet you there.'

Lina reappeared at that moment, minus the roses. She tossed her blonde hair over one too bony shoulder and gave him a smile that lacked even a fraction of the impact of Marietta's.

'Can you please close up tonight, Lina?' Marietta said to the girl. 'I doubt I'll be back. Call me if you need anything. I'll see you in the morning.' She lifted her gaze to Nico's. 'I suppose you already know my address?'

'*Oui,*' he said, and noted with a small punch of satisfaction how her pretty mouth tightened at that.

'Okay. Well, I'll see you there, then.' She wheeled past him, towards the rear of the gallery.

'Marietta.'

She stopped, glanced over her shoulder at him. '*Si?*'

'If you get there first, wait for me. Do not go in.'

Her mouth pursed. 'Is that an order?'

'You may consider it one.'

Only the flare of her fine nostrils betrayed her annoyance. 'Very well,' she said, then continued on her way.

For a moment Nico watched her go, her long dark hair swinging behind her, her olive-skinned arms, defined by muscle yet still slender and feminine, propelling the wheels of her chair forward with strong, confident movements.

She disappeared through a rear door and Nico spun away, making his own exit through the front of the gallery and down a short flight of stone steps. He strode along the wide tree-lined street to where he'd parked the silver sports car Bruno had had waiting at the airport for him this morning when his jet had landed.

He wrenched open the driver's door and scowled.

He would very much enjoy giving Marietta a lesson in obedience, but he had no doubt her brother would kill him—slowly and painfully—if he knew the methods Nico had in mind.

# CHAPTER TWO

MARIETTA DROVE HER bright yellow sedan into the basement of her apartment building and swung into her reserved space near the elevator. She cut the engine, pushed the door open and used her arms to shift herself around until her legs dangled out of the car.

She loved her modified car. In addition to its customised hand controls, the rear passenger door on the driver's side had been altered to open in the reverse direction, so she could reach around from the driver's seat, open the door and pull her wheelchair out of the back. She did so now, and with a little shuffling, some careful hand placements and a couple of well-executed manoeuvres she transferred herself out of the car and into her chair.

It was a routine refined and perfected through years of practice, and one she could probably perform in her sleep.

She put her handbag in her lap and took the elevator to the lobby, confident Nico couldn't have beaten her there despite the extra minutes she'd needed to get in and out of her car. He probably had a faster, flashier set of wheels, but she knew the roads between here and the gallery like the back of her hand—not to mention half a dozen shortcuts only a local would know to use.

And yet when she rolled out of the elevator onto the lobby's shiny sand-coloured marble, there he stood. She frowned, confused as much as miffed. The building, she knew, was secure, the double doors from the street controlled by keypad access day and night. 'How did you get inside?'

'One of your neighbours was on his way out and let me in.' His voice was dark. His expression, too. *'Imbécile.'*

His deep scowl deterred her from jumping to the defence of whichever neighbour had earned his disapproval. The man had no doubt thought nothing of it, but even Marietta had to admit that giving entry to a stranger off the street showed a dreadful disregard for security.

'I'm on the ground floor,' she said, deciding to leave that subject well enough alone, and wheeled her chair around.

Silent, his big body radiating tension like ripples of heat from a furnace, Nico followed her through the lobby, across the quiet interior courtyard with its great pots of manicured topiaries and into a small vestibule housing the front doors of her apartment and one other. As soon as they stopped his hand appeared, palm up, in front of her face.

'Key.'

For a second—just a second—Marietta contemplated ignoring his curt command, but this, she acknowledged, was not the time for bravado. Her stalker might have been in her home.

Her stalker might *still* be in her home.

Her stomach gave a sharp, sickening twist and she promptly handed over the key and watched, heart thumping, as Nico unlocked the door.

'Stay here,' he ordered, and she nodded, her mouth suddenly far too dry to protest. He went in, leaving the door an inch ajar behind him.

Marietta clutched her handbag in her lap and waited. Endless minutes ticked by, followed by more endless minutes. When Nico still hadn't reappeared and she could no longer stand the suspense, she nudged the door open, inched forward and hovered on the threshold.

'Nico?' she called out, her voice echoing off the parquet wood flooring in the entry hall.

Nothing.

'Nico!' she tried again, louder this time.

Still nothing.

This was ridiculous. She wheeled down the hallway, a hot mix of impatience and adrenaline spurring her on.

'I told you to stay put.'

Nico's deep voice slammed into her from behind. She turned her chair around and blinked, her brain instantly grappling to interpret what her eyes were seeing. The sight of Nico standing in her bedroom doorway—which, in her haste, she'd sailed straight by—was easy enough to compute. The rest—the blue latex gloves sheathing his large hands, something red and lacy dangling from his fingers—was enough to send her senses into a floor-tilting spin.

She stared at the bizarre image before her a moment longer, until her breathing resumed some kind of normal rhythm, then gripped the hand rims of her chair and started forward—only to have Nico plant his feet firmly in the doorway and block her path.

She hiked up her chin, wishing there was a way to plough through that imposing wall of muscle. 'Let me in,' she demanded, and reached for the scrap of red lace.

He jerked it out of reach. 'Marietta—'

'No. This is *my* home, Nico. Whatever he's done, whatever he's left for me, I want to see.'

It took every shred of determination she possessed not to back down under the full force of Nico's reprimanding stare. Finally, just as she began to think he wouldn't budge, his rigid stance loosened.

He pointed a latex-clad finger at her. 'Do not touch anything. There could be DNA and prints to lift.' Then he stepped aside, allowing her to enter.

Marietta's gaze went straight to the bed. To the

crimson box lying open on her cream cotton coverlet and the items of luxury lingerie spilling haphazardly from between layers of soft white tissue. Scattered around the box and all across her bed were dozens upon dozens of red and white rose petals.

She moved closer, made out a red satin and black lace chemise, a sheer negligee and a pair of skimpy scarlet knickers. She closed her eyes, turned away, fighting a sudden stab of nausea. When she opened them again, her gaze landed on the item in Nico's hand. A bra, she registered now. A lacy, see-through concoction designed to be sexy and revealing as opposed to any kind of practical.

Her gaze jerked up, collided with Nico's, and for a fleeting moment it seemed as though something arced in the air between them. Something hot and bright and electric.

Which just went to prove how easily stress could affect the mind—because surely she had imagined that strange ripple of energy in the room that had felt almost like... What? Sexual awareness?

Heat flooded her face. *Si*, she was definitely stressed—not to mention embarrassed and *horrified*.

She yanked her gaze away from Nico's and took one last look at her bed. Did her stalker think he would one day share it with her? Thick bile coated her throat and the heat drained from her face, leaving her cold and clammy.

'Was there a card?' she managed to ask.

Nico turned away from her to lay the bra on the bed. 'No,' he said, snapping the gloves off his hands. He turned back to look at her, his blue eyes dark and unreadable. 'You're pale, Marietta. Do you have anything to drink?'

She nodded. *Si*, a drink…something to wash the bile out of her throat, shave the edge off her nerves. She wheeled out of the room. She wouldn't be able to sleep here tonight. Perhaps she could stay at Leo's penthouse for the weekend? He'd be travelling to Tuscany this evening, back to Helena and their adorable baby boy Riccardo. Leo's apartment building—a stunning renovated historic structure in the heart of the old city—wasn't as wheelchair-friendly as this one, but there was an elevator at least. Or perhaps she could telephone a girlfriend?

Her mind spun in jerky circles until she reached her lounge and paused. She looked around the cosy, light-filled room. Had her stalker been in here, too? Had he snooped through every inch of her beloved home? Had he *touched* her things?

Angry and sickened, she dumped her handbag on her plum-coloured sofa and headed for the solid oak sideboard. The cabinet housed a small selection of spirits—brandy, *limoncello*, and a bottle of whisky for her brother when he visited.

She grabbed two cut-glass tumblers and, hearing footsteps on the hardwood floor behind her, twisted her chin round to look at Nico. 'What will you have?'

He shrugged, the movement accentuating the breadth of his shoulders under his black open-necked shirt. 'Whatever you're having.'

She chose the brandy, unscrewed the cap and started to pour. But her hands shook and the liquid sloshed out too fast, hit the rim of the glass and splashed onto the sideboard. She cursed, the mishap pushing her to the verge of ridiculous tears, and then Nico's hand was closing over hers. Without a word, he removed the bottle from her grip and poured a generous measure into each tumbler.

Feeling foolish, she took the glass he handed her and tried to ignore the lingering effect of his touch. It was the same hot, static-like sensation she'd experienced at the gallery, when he'd crouched in front of her and taken her hand in his. Except his touch then had lasted longer, she recalled, and his thumb had rubbed gentle, delicious circles on the back of her hand, setting off a chain reaction of tiny sparks under her skin.

She took a gulp of brandy and welcomed its distracting burn. 'I don't understand,' she blurted when the heat had abated. 'Why me?' It was a question with no logical answer, she knew. She threw up a hand in helpless frustration. 'Your company provides protection services to public figures,' she said. 'You must know something about this sort of thing. Why would he go to such lengths to get my attention and yet keep his identity a secret?'

Nico stood with one hand wrapped around his glass, the other shoved in his trouser pocket. He paused, as if carefully weighing his response. 'In his mind, he's courting you, and he wants total control over this stage of his fantasy,' he said finally. 'The longer he remains anonymous, the more time he has to build the perfect relationship with you in his head and avoid the risk of real-life rejection.'

Marietta grimaced. 'That is totally twisted.'

Nico knocked back his brandy in a single swallow that made the muscles in his strong throat visibly work. 'I agree,' he said, then put the glass down and pulled his mobile phone from his pocket.

'Who are you calling?'

'Bruno, the police—' he tapped the screen and pressed the phone to his ear '—and your brother.'

Marietta sighed. *Eccellente.* An army of men was about to invade her beloved home. She chafed at the intrusion—at the very knowledge that she could no longer handle this situation by herself—but, loath as she was to admit it, she had no choice. She'd have to accept help.

Her brother arrived first, and he must have driven like a madman to complete the journey from his office in less than twenty minutes. He looked like a madman, too, with his tie skewed, his hair on end, his handsome face creased with worry—an expression that grew considerably darker the moment he looked in her bedroom.

'I'm fine,' she told him as he tipped up her chin and searched her face with dark, probing eyes. His jaw clenched, as if he didn't trust himself to speak, then he simply dropped a kiss on her head and stalked across the room to Nico.

Shortly afterwards, Bruno turned up, with a thin middle-aged man he introduced as a private forensic specialist, and, surreal though it all seemed, her lovely peaceful home began to resemble an official crime scene.

Marietta reached again for the brandy bottle and refilled her glass. She'd suffered through countless indignities during the painstaking months of rehabilitation and therapy after her accident, but this was a violation beyond her experience—beyond anything she'd equipped herself to deal with.

And it was so unfair—even though she knew life *was* unfair. Life didn't owe her anything. Which was why she had worked so hard for everything she had: her job at the gallery, which provided a steady income, the loft she'd bought and turned into a nice little earner by converting it into an art studio and hiring out the space to working artists, and her own art career—which, with a few exhibitions of her paintings and some lucrative commissions under her belt, was finally taking off.

Admittedly she'd accepted some help from Leo in the early days, but she'd repaid him every euro she'd borrowed—despite his vociferous protests. While her dear brother had never understood his little sister's need to assert her independence, he had finally accepted it.

She looked around at her apartment, filled with strangers. For years she'd prided herself on her strength and resilience, but she didn't feel at all strong and resilient today. She felt helpless and afraid and she hated it. Her gaze travelled across the room to where her brother and Nico stood by the window, deep in conversation, their dark heads bowed. Leo had already swooped in like a man possessed, bent on taking control. How long before he tried to smother her in a suffocating blanket of protectiveness?

And then there was Nico. A man so commanding, so authoritative, she imagined the world would stop on its axis if he so ordered it.

As though sensing her scrutiny, the men stopped talking and looked up, two sets of eyes—one midnight-dark, the other a startling blue—settling on her. At once unease bubbled up inside her. She didn't like the looks on their faces. Didn't like the determined set of Nico's jaw or the hint of something too much like apology in Leo's eyes.

Marietta lifted the brandy she'd poured without spilling a drop this time and took a large, fortifying gulp.

Those expressions told her the men had decided something—and she wasn't going to like it.

\* \* \*

Nico had lied. First to Marietta and then, by omission, to her brother. Her stalker *had* left a note, and it was now in the hands of the forensic technician who was under strict orders to keep it out of sight. Leo already looked white-lipped and murderous. If he saw the sexually explicit language in the card he would undoubtedly lose the tight rein he held on his temper.

And Marietta—well, she'd already seen more than Nico had intended her to, thanks to a stubborn streak as wide as the Atlantic. Why she couldn't have simply obeyed him and stayed put, he couldn't fathom. Most of the time women were eager to please him, not defy him, and yet Marietta seemed to have a unique talent for the latter.

He handed his friend a double shot of whisky and Leo tossed the liquid down his throat, then glared at the empty glass as if he'd like nothing more than to smash it against a wall.

'How the hell did he get in?'

Guilt sliced through Nico's gut like a jagged knife. He'd failed to anticipate this turn of events. Failed to predict accurately the threat to Marietta's safety. Not least of all, he'd failed his friend.

And Nico didn't *do* failure—not on any scale. He had tasted that bitter elixir ten years ago and his failure then had cost him his wife's life.

He jammed his fists in his pockets. Focused his

thoughts with the same ruthless discipline that had seen him survive that brutal plunge into darkness and come out the other side—eventually.

'The windows don't appear to have been tampered with.' He gestured with his chin to the secured latch on the window by which they stood. 'My guess is he took an old-fashioned approach and picked the lock on the front door.'

'And the building?' Leo's scowl darkened. 'It should be secure twenty-four-seven.'

'He could have talked his way in.' Tension bit deep into Nico's shoulders. *He* had gained access the same way; it had been appallingly easy. 'Or waited and slipped in behind someone.'

*'Dio.'* Anger billowed from Leo in palpable waves. 'This is insane. What did the *polizia* say?'

Nico balled his hands more tightly in his pockets. The attitude of the two plain-clothes officers who had turned up at the apartment had reeked of apathy. 'They'll file a report, but don't expect too much action from that quarter,' he warned. 'They're viewing it as a romantic prank, at worst.'

Nico hadn't missed their exchange of lascivious grins over the lingerie and he'd wanted to knock the officers' heads together, plant his boot firmly in the seats of their pants. Just as he'd wanted to kick *himself* earlier, when he and Marietta had been in her bedroom and his thoughts had gone to a dark, carnal place they'd had no right to go. Not with Marietta. She was a victim, he'd had to remind himself, a woman who needed his help—and wondering how her ample breasts would look encased in that barely there bra had been wrong on too many levels to count.

Leo swore now—a vicious expletive that drew not so much as a blink from Nico. Five years in the French Foreign Legion as a young man, followed by several stints as a private military contractor, working alongside war-hardened ex-soldiers, had broadened his vocabulary to include every filthy word and crude expression known to man in half a dozen languages.

'Find him, Nico,' Leo grated, his expression fierce. 'Do whatever you have to to keep her safe.'

*Do whatever you have to.*

Those five words seemed to strike Nico in the gut one by one, like the consecutive blows of a steel mallet, and they left him savagely winded. He'd heard those same words before, ten years ago, from his former father-in-law's mouth.

*Do whatever you have to.*

And Nico had.

He'd utilised every resource within his power. Called in every favour owed him. Employed every conceivable tactic within the law—and beyond—to get Senator Jack Lewisham's daughter back.

But it wasn't enough. It all went belly up. And

Nico committed one critical, unforgivable sin: he underestimated the men who had taken her.

He failed. Failed to bring the senator's daughter home. Failed to save his wife's life.

Her father, who'd only grudgingly accepted Nico as a son-in-law in the first place, was inconsolable— a man irreparably broken by the loss of his only daughter.

He had not spoken to Nico since.

*Do whatever you have to.*

He glanced over at Marietta, nursing her brandy in her hand, quietly studying them. She was pale, but beautiful, those dark, intelligent eyes sizing him up. No doubt she was a little annoyed that she was not privy to his and Leo's conversation. She was a woman of undeniable strength, yet the pallor of her skin, the obvious tension around her eyes and mouth, belied her show of composure. He could see it in the rigid set of her shoulders, her too-tight grip on the glass, the unblinking wideness of her eyes.

Marietta wasn't afraid.

She was petrified.

Nico turned back to Leo, an idea seeding, taking shape in his mind. An extreme idea, perhaps, for it would mean sacrificing the sanctity of his personal space for a time, but extreme circumstances called for extreme measures. He clamped a hand over his friend's shoulder. 'Do you trust me, *mon ami*?'

Leo looked him in the eye. 'Of course,' he said

at once, his voice gruff. 'You do not need to ask me that, Nicolas.'

Nico nodded. It was the answer he'd hoped for. *'Très bien,'* he said. 'I have a suggestion.'

# CHAPTER THREE

'ABSOLUTELY NOT!'

Marietta looked from her brother to Nico and back to Leo. *They had to be joking.* Yet neither man wore an expression she could describe as anything other than deadly serious. They both looked stern, formidable, standing side by side with their feet planted apart, their arms folded over their broad chests. Looking at them was akin to seeing double, and she wanted to slap them both.

*'Pazzo!'* she cried, gesturing with one hand in the air to emphasise just how crazy she found their proposal.

They had the gall to stare at her then, as if *she* were crazy. As if the idea of disappearing to some island off the coast of France until her stalker had been caught was the perfect solution and they couldn't understand why she didn't agree.

And not just *any* island.

Oh, no.

*Nico's* island.

Nico's *home.*

*With Nico.*

Heat that had nothing to do with anger and everything to do with the idea of being holed up on a remote island with Nicolas César scalded her insides.

Torture. That was what it would be. Exquisite torture of a kind she didn't dare contemplate.

She swigged down her brandy, set the glass on the sideboard and wheeled towards her kitchen. Enough alcohol. *Coffee.* That was what she needed. An injection of caffeine to hone her senses—and her tongue—for the showdown she was about to have with her brother.

He followed, his dark mood like a gathering thundercloud at her back.

'Marietta, just stop for a minute and think about this.'

'I don't need to stop in order to think.' She yanked the lid off a tin of coffee beans, unleashing a rich, nutty aroma that failed to please her the way it normally did. 'I'm a woman, so I can multitask, and I *am* thinking about it. I'm thinking what a stupid, *stupid* idea it is.'

She ignored his heavy sigh.

'You can't do this,' she ploughed on, pouring a handful of dark beans into her cherished *caffè* machine—her first port of call in the mornings, when strong coffee was a prerequisite for coherent speech.

'You can't just sweep in here and go all Big Brother on me. I'm not a rebellious, out-of-control teenager any more. I'm thirty years old. You're not responsible for me.'

An abrupt silence fell.

Marietta spun her chair around, regret, hot and instant, welling in her throat. 'Leo, I… I'm sorry.'

His jaw tightened. 'I will always feel responsible for you.'

'I know.'

Instantly she hated herself for hitting that sensitive nerve—the one that had been flayed raw by her accident thirteen years ago and had never completely healed. Leo blamed himself. Believed he should have tried harder to keep her at home that night.

The truth was no one could have saved Marietta except herself. *She* was the one who had sneaked out of the tiny flat she and Leo had shared. *She* was the one who'd gone to the party he'd expressly forbidden her to attend. *She* was the one who'd climbed into the back seat of a car with an inebriated driver.

Her decisions that night had borne consequences she had no choice but to live with, but the hell she had put her brother through was a heavy cross she would always bear.

The last of her temper dissolved. Leo loved her… wanted to keep her safe. How could she stay angry with him over that?

'I can't just drop everything and disappear.' She

tried for a softer, more reasonable tone. 'I have a job. Responsibilities. And Ricci's party is a week from tomorrow. Helena's had it planned for months. What if this guy hasn't been caught by then?' She shook her head. 'I can't stay away indefinitely—and I won't miss my nephew's first birthday.'

Leo crossed his arms, perched his lean frame on the edge of her low granite bench. 'Your life could be in danger, Marietta. Have you considered that?'

Now she wanted to roll her eyes, accuse him of being melodramatic—but *was* he? What had happened today felt serious, even if the *polizia* were inclined to view it as a prank. And after today's performance who could predict what kind of sick encore her stalker had planned?

A dull throb started up behind her eyes and she pressed her thumb and forefinger against her lids.

'When you cannot eliminate the source of danger your best defence is to remove yourself from its path.'

Nico's deep voice rumbled into the room and she jerked her hand down from her face. He loomed in her kitchen doorway, his sheer presence so commanding, his physique so powerful, that for a moment she couldn't help but feel a sense of reassurance—of safety—steal over her.

Still. That didn't change anything.

She couldn't put her life on hold indefinitely.

'A week, Marietta,' Leo urged. 'Give Nico a week.'

She looked at Nico. 'And how exactly are you going to catch my stalker if you're on an island with me?'

'I have faith in my people. He's upped the ante and so will we.'

'And if I insist on staying in Rome?'

'Then I'll appoint a bodyguard who'll shadow you day and night, wherever you go.'

'And I will stay,' Leo said. 'For as long as necessary.'

*No.* She gave an adamant shake of her head. 'You can't, Leo. It wouldn't be fair to Helena—or Ricci. You should be in Tuscany with them this weekend, not babysitting me.'

He shrugged. 'They'll come to Rome.'

Marietta pressed her fingertips to her temples. She knew her sister-in-law well. Helena was a kind, capable woman who wouldn't hesitate to uproot her domestic idyll for Marietta's sake. But Marietta's conscience wouldn't allow it. This was *her* problem to handle. How could she justify disrupting their lives when she had an alternative?

*A week.* Could she forego her independence, abandon her life, for a week? She looked at her brother and saw the deep lines of worry etched into his face. Her safety would give him peace of mind and didn't she owe him that much? He'd made so many sacrifices when they were younger, worked himself ragged to give them both a chance at a better life.

Doing what he asked of her now seemed a small thing in return.

She pushed her hands through her hair. Released her breath on a long sigh. '*Si*. Okay,' she said. 'One week.'

Marietta sat in the front passenger seat of her brother's car the next morning and chewed the inside of her cheek, fighting the powerful urge to blurt out that she'd changed her mind and all this was too sudden, too unexpected, and she couldn't possibly travel at short notice like this. Travel—for her—required careful planning, special considerations, and they hadn't given her a chance to plan a damned thing.

'Quit fretting, *carina*.' Leo glanced over, then returned his attention to negotiating the chaotic morning traffic. Even on a Saturday Rome's roads were flat-out crazy. 'Nico has everything under control.'

She cast him a sideways look. 'Will you stop doing that?'

'What?'

'Reading my mind.'

He grinned. 'If I knew the secret to reading women's minds, I would be a very rich man indeed.'

Had Marietta been in the mood for banter she would have reminded her brother that he *was* a rich man. Instead she turned her gaze out through the side window and watched the blur of busy streets and *piazze* and sidewalk cafés go by. She believed

Leo when he said his friend had everything under control—and that was the problem. Nico had all the control and she had none. It made her feel adrift, somehow. Alienated from her life. She didn't even know where exactly in the Mediterranean they were going. Until yesterday she'd never heard of Île de Lavande.

She rested her head against the soft leather seat.

Island of Lavender.

At least the name was pretty.

Perhaps she'd find some inspiration there for her next series of paintings? The European summer was in its twilight, but Nico had said the island was still warm, so she'd gone light on clothes and made room for packing her brushes and a set of fast-drying acrylic paints, a sketchpad and a small canvas. She'd even squeezed in a collapsible easel.

She supposed a few quiet, uninterrupted days of sketching and painting wouldn't be so bad—but only a few. She'd agreed to a week, no longer, and she still planned to be back in time for little Ricci's party. Nico's men would just have to pull out all the stops to find her stalker, because she wasn't compromising on that.

As for the gallery—she'd made two phone calls from Leo's apartment last night: one to her boss, the owner of the gallery, who'd expressed her support and understanding once apprised of the circumstances, and the other to Lina, who'd assured

Marietta that everything would run smoothly in her absence.

Too soon, the powerful car decelerated and the runway of the Aeroporto dell'Urbe came into sight. They drove through a security checkpoint and then they were on the Tarmac, headed for a sleek silver and black jet with the circular logo of César Security emblazoned on its tail.

Nico appeared in the open hatchway and Marietta leaned forward in her seat for a better view of the aircraft—and him.

And, *mamma mia*, he looked good. Faded jeans clung to long, muscular legs, he wore an untucked, open-necked white shirt, and a pair of dark shades obscured those deep blue eyes. His dark brown hair was stylishly mussed and his angular jaw sported a layer of stubble that only exaggerated his masculine appeal. He looked less formidable than yesterday. More relaxed, despite the ever-serious expression he wore.

*Edible*, an inner voice whispered, and she felt her face flame. *Santo cielo!* Her mind was *not* going there.

He jogged down the steps with an easy masculine grace, and he was pulling open the car door before her cheeks had even had time to cool. He hunkered down beside her.

'*Bonjour*, Marietta.' He removed his sunglasses

and the impact of that blue gaze arrowed all the way to her stomach. 'Are you ready for our journey?'

The morning breeze ruffled his hair and carried into the car the scent of soap and lemons, along with something more earthy and rich. Marietta tried not to breathe in, but the need for air prevailed. She frowned, growing more irritable by the second. No man should smell that enticing. That delectable.

'Do you have half-decent coffee on board?'

A muscle quirked at the side of his mouth—a mere flicker of movement that might have turned into a smile if he'd allowed it.

Had she ever seen Nico smile? It occurred to her that she hadn't—not properly.

'The coffee is *exceptionnel*,' he said, and she wished he wouldn't speak French.

It did squishy things to her insides and there was nothing good about squishy. *Nothing.*

He slid his shades back on. 'There's a lift on standby if you want it.'

She shook her head. '*Grazie*, but Leo will carry me on,' she said, preferring that simple, no-fuss solution over the mechanical platform that could raise her, wheelchair and all, to the door of the plane. Besides the ground crew there were few people around, but all the same she hated anything that created a spectacle or shone a spotlight on her disability. People often stared without meaning to, and though she'd grown inured to the curiosity of others, occasionally the attention still bothered her.

Minutes later her luggage was stowed and she was settled in a large, soft leather seat, her wheelchair reassembled and within reach should she wish to move about the plane's roomy interior once they were airborne. Out on the Tarmac, Nico and Leo exchanged final words. A moment before, when Leo had kissed her goodbye, silly tears had pricked the backs of her eyes, and she blinked now to clear her vision, annoyed because she rarely allowed herself to cry. She'd taught herself to be strong, to handle whatever challenges life threw at her, and all *this*—this was just another obstacle to overcome.

'I hear you're after some good, strong coffee, honey.'

Evelyn, the flight attendant who'd earlier introduced herself and then disappeared to give Marietta and Leo privacy, stood now by Marietta's seat, her cherry-red lips stretched into a friendly smile.

Marietta pulled herself together and looked up at the slender uniformed blonde. '*Si. Grazie.* Black and very strong, please.'

Not how she'd have ordered coffee in a bar in Rome—requesting a *caffè* in Italy automatically got you what the rest of the world labelled espresso—but Evelyn wasn't Italian, and Marietta wasn't in the mood for weak, watery coffee.

Evelyn tilted her head. *'Un caffè ristretto?'*

Marietta felt her brows climb and the other woman laughed. It was a pleasant laugh. Bubbly and bright.

'I know.' Evelyn winked. 'Who'd have thought a gal from Mississippi would know how to make proper Italian coffee.'

Marietta couldn't hold back a smile. 'You just improved my morning.'

Another long-lashed wink. 'My pleasure, honey. One coffee coming up,' she said, and Marietta decided right then that she liked Evelyn. Very, very much.

A short while later they were airborne. An hour after that they were cruising at forty-one thousand feet above sea level, halfway between Rome and their destination of Toulon, on the southern coast of France. Marietta knew this because Evelyn was a veritable fount of information. Unlike Nico who, aside from enquiring about her comfort prior to take-off, had uttered scarcely a word in the time since.

He sat in one of the cushioned club-style seats on the other side of the cabin, facing in her direction, so that if he looked up from his laptop they could easily converse. He hadn't. Not once in the last sixty minutes. Which made the challenge of snagging his attention almost impossible to resist.

'Here you go, honey.'

Evelyn placed a glass and the bottle of mineral water Marietta had asked for on the shiny walnut table in front of her. Marietta smiled her thanks. The *honey* might have sounded patronising from anyone else. From the tall, statuesque American it was just part of her charm.

Marietta watched her return to the other end of the cabin. It had to be an exciting life, jetting around the globe. Evelyn wore no rings, so presumably she was single, free of ties. Marietta didn't doubt she worked hard, but the perks had to be rewarding.

She waited until Evelyn was out of earshot before speaking. 'I like her.'

Nico's head came up and in her mind Marietta did a little self-congratulatory air-punch. Finally she had his attention.

'Pardon?'

'Evelyn,' she said, and watched to see his reaction. Because he had to know how beautiful his flight attendant was. No man could fail to notice a pair of legs as long and toned as Evelyn's, never mind that everything else about her was flawless and elegant.

Though Marietta felt sordid even thinking it, she couldn't help but wonder what level of 'personal service' Evelyn gave her boss. They were two beautiful people in the prime of their lives; they *had* to be aware of each other. Evelyn embodied the kind of physical perfection a man like Nico would no doubt look for in a sexual partner.

And yet he was frowning at her as if he hadn't a clue what—or whom—she was talking about.

'Your flight attendant,' she said, and stared at

him, astonished. 'You don't *know* the names of your flight crew?'

He shrugged. 'I have many hundreds of employees,' he said, his tone implying that he considered that a perfectly adequate excuse—and then he returned his attention to his computer.

*End of conversation.*

Marietta sniffed. 'Well, I like her,' she said to the top of his head. 'She's very good at her job. And she has spectacular legs.'

*That* got his attention back.

He looked at her and she shrugged. 'I'm an artist,' she said. 'I appreciate beauty in all its forms. And you have to admit Evelyn has great legs.'

'I hadn't noticed.'

'Really?' Her voice rang with disbelief.

*'Oui,'* he said, holding her gaze for a drawn-out beat. 'Really.'

And then something happened that she wasn't prepared for. His gaze dropped. First to her mouth, where it lingered for several seconds—long enough to make her self-consciously moisten her lips—and then down to her chest, where it rested only briefly. And yet the effect of that very deliberate scrutiny was so shocking, so profound, he might as well have touched her.

Heat prickled over her skin, from her neck to her breasts, and her heart pounded so hard, her pulse beat like the wings of a moth trapped in her throat.

Then his gaze came back to her face and she knew he must see the heightened colour there. One side of his mouth did that flickering thing again. That quirk that wasn't quite a smile.

'I'm a breast man myself,' he said, as casually as if he'd said he preferred beans over peas, or his steak medium rare, and then he went back to his work as if the air all around them *wasn't* sizzling and popping in the wake of that brief, electrifying exchange.

Marietta pressed her lips together. *Touché*, she conceded silently. Because shocking her into silence had no doubt been his intent. She uncapped her mineral water, filled her glass and took a long swig. But the cool liquid didn't douse the heat in her cheeks. Or the embarrassment washing through her. She had pushed him—deliberately provoked a reaction. Because... *Why?* Because she was bored? Because she felt ignored? Because Nico was the most beautiful, aloof man she'd ever met and some needy, feminine part of her craved his attention?

Oh, now, *that* did not sit well.

Marietta did not need a man's attention. She did not need a man, full stop. Her body might be broken beyond repair, but she had rebuilt her life regardless and it was everything she wanted. Everything she needed. Her job, her success as an artist...it was enough. It had to be enough.

Because she was done with wanting things she

would never have. Things that couldn't be. Things that were simply not written in her destiny.

*You are a realist.*

And Nico… Nico was just a fantasy.

# CHAPTER FOUR

THE WEATHER IN Toulon was clear when they circled in for landing, the bright blue of the sky stretching as far as the eye could see along the Côte d'Azur, enhancing the beauty of a coastline that was coveted by holidaymakers and frequented year-round by the world's famous and rich.

Nico had no interest in the glamorous beaches and glittering nightlife that gave the French Riviera its reputation as a decadent playground. Toulon featured on his itinerary several times a year only because it was the nearest mainland airport to Île de Lavande, the quiet, secluded home he retreated to when he wasn't residing in Paris or New York or travelling across continents for business.

On occasion, however, when his mind grew restless and his body demanded a certain kind of release, he'd linger on the mainland for a night and venture into a glitzy casino or high-end bar. He'd order a shot or two of something—whatever he fancied on the night—and wait for them to come. And they always did. Those women with no hidden agendas who, like him, were simply looking for a good time. He would choose one—only ever one…gluttony wasn't his thing—and take her to a luxury hotel suite, order champagne and anything else she desired from the menu and let her flirt and tease for a while if that was her wont.

But not for too long.

He could be a gentleman when he chose, but he was no saint. Not when his thoughts were dark and his body primed and the only way to obliterate his memories was by losing himself in the pleasure of soft flesh and tight, wet heat.

Sometimes, if the sex was outstanding, he'd take a number, hook up with the same woman again, even indulge in the occasional dinner or outing. But only if she understood that pleasure was the only offer on the table. He had nothing more to give. Nothing beyond the physical certainly.

Julia had been his one love.

His one chance at a normal, happy life.

He didn't deserve another. Didn't want another only to have it brutally torn from him.

The jet touched down and he channelled his thoughts back to the present as they taxied to a stop on a private strip of Tarmac, close to where his helicopter awaited. He released his seat belt and stood, glancing over to where Marietta sat, as silent now as she'd been for the last hour of the flight.

DEFYING HER BILLIONAIRE PROTECTOR

He still didn't really know what their conversation in the air had been about. He'd wasted no time shutting it down, sensing it was going nowhere good, nowhere *safe*, but in so doing he'd spiked his awareness of her, and that awareness was still humming in his body like an electric current he couldn't switch off.

Was she upset with him? Hard to tell. Her gaze was focused out of the large oval window so that all he could see was her proud, elegant profile. *Dieu*, but she was lovely. High cheekbones. Straight nose. Flawless skin. Hair like burnished mahogany. And her lips were soft and full—ripe for tasting.

He clenched his jaw *Not helpful.*

'Marietta?'

He half hoped she *was* annoyed. A little reserve, a touch of coolness between them, might be a good thing. He had one objective and that was to keep her safe. This spark of attraction he felt—there was no room for it.

She turned her head then and his hopes met a swift end. She didn't look angry. Didn't even look mildly irritated. Hell, she was *smiling* at him.

'Are we flying to the island in that?'

For a moment he didn't register the question, blindsided as he was by that smile. The pretty flush on her cheekbones. The breathless quality to her voice that seemed to stroke right into him.

She looked out through the window again and he leaned down, followed the line of her gaze to where his chopper sat on the Tarmac, its long rotor blades and black paintwork gleaming in the sunshine. A man in blue overalls and a fluorescent orange vest moved around the craft, completing a thorough safety check that Nico himself would repeat prior to take-off.

'*Oui,*' he said. 'The island is accessible by boat, but the chopper is faster.'

'I've never been in a helicopter.' Her gaze swung to his. 'Will you pilot it?'

'Of course.'

She fired another look out of the window and then undid her seatbelt and smoothed the creases from her grey linen pants. 'Okay. I'll wait here while the luggage and my wheelchair are transferred,' she said, her voice turning brisk. 'Take me last.'

'There's a lift—'

'No,' she cut across him. 'No fuss. Please.' Her gaze didn't quite meet his. 'It will be quicker and easier if you carry me.'

*Easier*, Nico reflected ten minutes later as he settled Marietta into the cockpit of the chopper, was a relative term. Because the effort of willing his groin not to harden in response to holding a soft, warm woman in his arms—a woman who smelled enticingly of strawberries and vanilla and something faintly exotic—had not come anywhere close to being easy.

He strapped her into the harness, made a couple of adjustments that brought his fingers dangerously, agonisingly close to her breasts, then hastily withdrew his hands.

'Comfortable?' She nodded and he handed her a black helmet. 'This has a built-in headset so we can communicate. I need to do a final weather check and then we're set.'

Her gaze turned skyward. 'The weather looks perfect.'

'*Oui*. But we're flying twenty miles south over open sea. The marine winds can be unpredictable.'

Rather like his body, he thought grimly.

Marietta's heart raced and she gripped the edges of her seat. She looked down at the deep, surging swells of the Mediterranean Sea, then up again to the lone mass of land looming in the distance. Silhouetted against a bright blue sky, the island's long, uneven shape teased her imagination and made her think of a great serpent slumbering on the horizon.

She'd always wanted to fly in a helicopter and now she was hurtling over the ocean in one and struggling to hold back a grin. Which was crazy. What reason did she have to smile or feel breathless and giddy?

Yesterday her life had been turned upside down, her home invaded by a man who at worst was a predator and at best was a disturbed individual in dire need of a shrink. Yet somehow, right at this moment, all of that seemed very distant and she really was fighting an insane urge to grin.

She let her gaze roam the cockpit's interior, fascinated by the dials and buttons and levers. Beside her, Nico looked at home in the pilot's seat, his large hands working the controls of the powerful machine with dexterity and ease.

*Strong* hands, she thought, recalling how he'd carried her from the jet to the helicopter as if she weighed next to nothing. As if carrying a woman was something he did every day and the experience left him unaffected. While *she* had been hyper-aware of *everything*. From the hardness of his body and the citrusy scent of his cologne to the tanned triangle of chest in the opening of his shirt and the glimpse of dark hair at the base of that V.

She'd wondered whether the texture of that hair was soft or coarse. If it thickened and spread across his chest or was merely a dusting. If it arrowed into a fine line that bisected his stomach and travelled into the waistband of his pants and lower.

Inappropriate thoughts she should not have had then and should not be having now. Not about the man she was going to spend the next few days cooped up with on an island.

She dragged her attention off his hands and back to the mass of land ahead of them that was appearing more substantial by the second. Running her gaze along the nearest stretch of coastline, she made out three separate white sand beaches and, nestled into the lee of a lush hill range, a large village and a port, where rows of colourful boats were moored to long wooden wharves jutting into clear turquoise waters.

'You own a whole *village*?'

A short burst of static came over the headset before the rich timbre of Nico's voice filled her helmet. It was an odd sensation—as if he was inside her head and all around her at the same time.

'No. I own sixty percent of the island, including the southern and western coasts. The rest—including the northern beaches, the olive groves to the east and a small commercial vineyard—is now owned by various locals whose families have lived on Île de Lavande for hundreds of years.'

'*Now* owned?' she said. 'Did they not always own it?'

'*Non*. For several centuries the island was owned by a single aristocratic French family. They employed caretakers and servants who settled on the land with their families. It wasn't until a wealthy American industrialist bought the island in the early nineteen-hundreds and decided to sell off some parcels of land that the locals finally had the opportunity to become landowners instead of leaseholders.'

Fascinated, she took a moment to absorb it all. 'How do the islanders make their living? Fishing?'

'*Oui*. And from olives and wine. Most of which they sell to the mainland. Plus a controlled level of tourism.'

'Controlled?'

'Limited numbers of tourists, and only at certain times of the year. During those months a passenger and car ferry visits twice a week—no more. The villagers rely on the revenue, but they also want to protect the environment—and their privacy.'

'Are most of them descended from the original settlers?'

'Many of them, *oui*.'

'That must be amazing—to know the history of generations of your family.' Silence crackled in her headset. 'Do you have any familial links to the island?' she asked.

*'Non,'* he said.

'So…you have family living in France?'

*'Non.'*

The message in that second abrupt no was clear. *Subject off-limits*. Marietta bit down on her tongue—and her curiosity—and focused on the scenery.

Ahead, an old sturdy fishing vessel rode the ocean swells as it chugged slowly into the calmer waters of the harbour. Nico flew the chopper directly over the boat, low enough to see the broad smiles on the fishermen's upturned faces. They raised their arms and waved and Nico waved back—and Marietta's surprise lasted only a second. Mr Security Conscious *would* know his neighbours, she realised. Even a whole village of them.

They neared land and he banked the helicopter to the right, angling them over the port and the outskirts of the village. She glimpsed red-tiled roofs and open shutters on whitewashed houses, an old stone church and the crumbling remains of a sprawling derelict structure on the crest of a hill.

'Where's your home?'

'Further around the coast,' he said. 'Twenty-five minutes by road from the port.'

The village fell behind them and she looked down, saw rows upon rows of pine trees extending into the island's interior. It was lush and dense—much more fertile and beautiful than she'd expected.

'Will you show me some of the island while we're here?'

'Perhaps. If time allows. We have work to do first.'

She turned her head to look at him. 'What kind of work?'

'Questions and answers.'

Her brows knitted. 'I don't understand…'

'We are going to dissect your life, Marietta. Day by day. Hour by hour. Minute by minute. You are going to break down every routine for me—everything you do, everywhere you go, everyone you meet—until we have ruled out the possibility that your stalker is someone you know or have met.'

A groan rose in her throat. 'But I've answered all of Bruno's questions. *And* yours.'

'And you will answer them again,' he said. 'As many times as I need you to. Until I am satisfied.'

His tone was uncompromising and a shiver rippled through her. *How ironic.* Yesterday she'd spared a thought for anyone unfortunate enough to find themselves interrogated by Nicolas César—soon she would experience for herself that very ordeal.

Her mood well and truly dampened, she stayed silent for the rest of the flight, even stifling her exclamation of *wow* when she spotted the house perched on a high plateau above a steep limestone cliff.

Sleek, white, and über-modern, the expansive single-level dwelling might have dominated its surroundings. Instead, its simple understated design complemented the landscape, with acres of glass reflecting the sky and the rich, fertile land all around it. On the ocean side a flat terrace featured a large swimming pool, which sparkled like a sheet of cobalt glass in the sunshine. On the inland flank, a circular courtyard sat at the head of a long winding driveway which descended into a thick forest of towering pines.

Marietta surveyed the property as Nico set them down on a dedicated helipad a short distance from the courtyard.

It was, she decided after a moment, just like its owner.

Stark. Remote. And beautiful.

# CHAPTER FIVE

'ENOUGH!'

The shrill note in Marietta's voice brought Nico's head up. He laid his pen on the legal pad he used for old-fashioned note-taking and leaned back in his chair. 'Take a breath, Marietta.'

'Don't patronise me,' she snapped, a flash of Italian temper darkening her eyes to the colour of hot, bitter espresso. She squeezed them shut and pinched the delicate bridge of her nose.

Nico stretched out his denim-clad legs, crossed his bare feet at the ankles and waited for her to calm down.

'I'm sorry.' She dropped her hand, opened her eyes. 'I didn't mean to snap. I just don't see how where I choose to buy my fruit and vegetables on a Saturday morning can possibly be relevant.'

A warm, gentle Mediterranean breeze rippled the surface of the pool and swayed the enormous umbrella which shaded the outdoor table where they sat. Sighing, Marietta scraped her long hair back from her face and secured the lustrous swathe into a high ponytail which she fastened with an elastic band from her wrist.

Toying with his pen, Nico studied her. He couldn't detect a scrap of make-up on her this morning and still she was beautiful. 'More coffee?'

She nodded. 'Please.'

He refilled her cup from the heavy silver coffee pot his part-time housekeeper Josephine had set out for them, along with a selection of fruits, thick yoghurt, freshly baked croissants and homemade jams.

It had been good of Josephine to drive up from the village on a Sunday morning. She and her son Luc had already been at the house in the hours prior to Nico and Marietta's arrival, cleaning, stocking the kitchen and installing special handrails in the guest en-suite bathroom at Nico's request. He appreciated their commitment; he'd given them only a day's notice and yet they hadn't complained at a time when their family-run bistro had to be busy with the final late-summer run of tourists.

Josephine had said she'd returned this morning to check that everything was satisfactory, but Nico figured it was curiosity as much as solicitude that had brought her back. In the four years since he'd built his home on Île de Lavande, he'd never invited a guest there—had never allowed anyone inside his sanctuary aside from the select few he employed for its upkeep. In that respect Marietta was something of a novelty, and she had—not surprisingly—charmed his housekeeper.

It was a charm she had not extended to *him* for the last hour and a half, he noted dryly. He sat forward, picked up his pen. 'Tell me more about Davide,' he said, and watched her expression instantly shutter.

'There isn't much to tell. We had a relationship and then we broke up. End of story.'

'You were together for two years.' The same length of time he and Julia had been married. 'It must have been serious,' he said, ignoring the sudden sharp clench in his chest.

Her shoulders, bare aside from the straps of her pale blue tank top, hitched up. 'For a while, *si*.'

'Who broke it off?'

'I did.'

'Why?'

'That's personal.' She picked up her sunglasses from the table and pushed them onto her face. 'And if you think Davide could be my stalker, you're wrong. He's moved on. Married. Started a family. What is it the English say? You are barking into the wrong bush.'

His mouth twitched despite himself. 'Up the wrong tree.'

She flicked a hand in the air. 'Whatever. Anyway, it can't be Davide. The cards are always signed off with an *S*.'

He put down his pen again. Worked to keep the

impatience out of his voice. 'First, the *S* could stand for anything,' he said. 'Second, I know this is difficult, but any previous romantic partners must be considered as potential suspects until they've been definitively ruled out.'

Her graceful chin took on that stubborn tilt he was learning to recognise. 'How do you know my stalker isn't a complete stranger?'

'I don't. And I haven't discounted the possibility. But the majority of stalking victims are stalked by someone they know—two-thirds of female victims by a former or current partner.' He paused before driving home his point. 'It is extremely likely that you have met or know your stalker in some capacity. He could be your neighbour. Someone you've met through work. Maybe the guy who sells you fruit at the market on a Saturday morning.'

She shuddered visibly. '*Santo cielo*. It could be anyone.'

'*Exactement*. And the sooner we narrow the field of potential suspects, the closer we get to identifying the real perpetrator.'

She sat a little straighter in her wheelchair, pulled in a deep breath and slowly expelled it. 'Okay.' She folded her hands in her lap. 'What do you want to know about Davide?'

'How did he react when you ended the relationship?'

She hesitated. 'He was upset.'

'Angry?'

'A little,' she said, quietly. 'Mostly hurt, I think.'

'He didn't want it to end?'

She reached for her coffee, took a careful sip, then replaced the cup before answering. 'He'd asked me to marry him.'

Nico blinked.

'I know,' she said, before he'd fully processed that potentially critical piece of information. 'A perfectly normal, eligible, good-looking guy asks a crippled girl to marry him and she says no.' She laughed, but the sound wasn't at all pretty. 'You're thinking a girl like me can hardly afford to be choosy, right?'

A flash of anger—and perhaps indignation—snapped his brows down. 'That is not what I was thinking.'

'But you were thinking *something*,' she challenged.

He felt a pulse leap in his jaw. 'I was thinking you should have told me this sooner.'

'Is that all?'

'*Non,*' he said tersely. 'I was also thinking the poor bastard must have been crushed when you turned him down.'

Marietta's chin jerked back—with surprise or scepticism? He couldn't tell.

'Why did you reject his proposal?'

She picked up her coffee again, took another sip, as if buying time to compose herself. When she put the cup down her hand wasn't quite steady. 'Davide wanted to *fix* me.'

'What do you mean?'

'He was obsessed with the idea of curing me.'

'Your paralysis?'

'*Sì.*'

He frowned. 'And that was a bad thing?'

'For me it was. It made our relationship untenable.'

'Why?'

Her slim shoulders lifted, dropped. 'Because I didn't share his obsession.'

Nico rubbed his jaw, assimilating that. 'So you don't believe in the possibility of a cure?'

A small groove appeared on her forehead. 'I believe there's hope for a cure. Technology and medicine will always advance, and people who are passionate about finding a way to reverse spinal cord damage will always be looking for the next major breakthrough. But at some point you have to stop chasing the miracle and get on with the business of living. And that means learning to accept the hand you've been dealt. Davide couldn't do that. He couldn't accept that I wouldn't one day get out of this chair and walk. Instead he spent every spare minute researching medical journals and the latest treatments he thought I should try.'

Marietta paused. She was glad suddenly that she'd put her sunglasses on, because if eyes truly were the windows to the soul she didn't want Nico seeing into hers. Didn't want him seeing the hidden part of her that still hurt whenever she thought about Davide and his obsession with 'fixing' her.

She might have shared his enthusiasm if she hadn't already travelled that same road with her brother in the early years after the accident, when Leo convinced himself—and her—that there was a real chance she would walk again. His tenacity and determination were contagious and she let herself get swept up in the possibilities—agreed, once Leo convinced her he could afford it, to travel to Germany and undergo the experimental treatments he'd researched.

But in the end it all turned into nothing more than a wild rollercoaster of shattered hopes and dreams. An enormous, heartbreaking reality check that devastated her for a time—until she picked herself up and fiercely told herself that from then on she was going to be a *realist*, not a dreamer.

And then, scarcely a year later, she met Davide and became that naive, hopeful fool all over again. The one who was stupid enough to think she could have something as ordinary as a husband and a family. The doctors had told her years before that she was physically capable of bearing children but she'd firmly quashed that dream—because what man would want to have a family with *her*?

But then Davide had come along, and at some point during their relationship she'd forgotten that *ordinary* didn't exist for her. That *ordinary* was a fantasy. That *ordinary* was something she had forfeited the night she'd climbed into the back seat of that car with her young, ill-fated friends.

'He said he loved me, but the woman he loved was the version of me in his head,' she said now, unable to stop a hint of bitterness creeping into her voice. 'The one he wanted to turn me into. The one who could walk.'

Nico shifted in his chair. 'Were you not tempted to consider any of the treatments?'

And now he was delving deeper than he needed to go. Deeper than he knew he should go. Finding Marietta's stalker and keeping her safe until then were his only concerns. He needn't care about anything else. Caring, he reminded himself, made people vulnerable, weak—and in his line of work, there was no room for weakness.

'I've been down that road,' she said. 'I had several surgeries and experimental stem cell procedures at a specialised clinic in Berlin. The results were negligible. A tiny bit of muscle movement, some increased sensation—that's all.'

'And Davide knew this?'

'*Si.* He said I gave up too easily.'

Nico's mouth settled into a grim line. She'd made the right decision to ditch the *imbécile*. Any man fool enough to label this woman a quitter didn't deserve her.

He closed the pad, pushed his chair back from the table. He would call Bruno, relay the information he deemed useful and tell him to take a closer look at the ex. Bruno had already compiled a superficial dossier on Davide, but now Nico would give the green light to dig deeper. Pay the guy a visit.

'We're done?' She sounded surprised. Or relieved. Maybe both.

He stood. 'For now,' he said, aware of something like relief coursing through his own veins.

These last two hours had been intense—for both of them—and he suddenly wanted some distance from this woman. Wanted her out of his sight so that he could concentrate on work and stop noticing things about her he had no legitimate need to notice.

Like the way those full lips of hers pursed when she was thinking and one cheek hollowed slightly, as if she were biting the inside of it. Or the way she sometimes used her hands to emphasise a point and at other times clasped them in her lap to give the impression of composure. Or the way she occasionally rubbed her shoulders or the back of her neck, as if the muscles there were cramped and needed loosening. Or—and this was by far the most disturbing of all his observations—how pink and delectable her tongue looked when it darted out to rescue a flake of croissant from her bottom lip.

Nico picked up the pen and pad and stepped back. *Oui.* Distance. A lot of it—and for the rest of the day, preferably. 'You did well, Marietta. Relax now. Enjoy the sunshine.'

She looked up and he saw his reflection in duplicate in her oversized sunglasses. 'What are you going to do?'

'Work.'

'All day?'

'Probably.' He turned towards the house. Pretended not to see the sudden slight pout on those voluptuous lips.

'What about sightseeing?'

He pulled up. 'Pardon?'

'Sightseeing,' she repeated. 'You said you would show me the island.'

He frowned. 'If time permitted.'

Her chin rose in that tenacious way of hers that stirred irritation and something much hotter, more dangerous, inside him.

'I've answered your questions,' she said.

He curled his fingers around the pen. 'My priority is to keep you safe until your stalker is caught, Marietta, not babysit you or play tour guide.' Her head drew back as if he'd spat in her face, but he ruthlessly fought the urge to soften his tone. 'Now, if you'll excuse me, I have work to do.'

He turned and strode into the house. Into his study. Where he tossed the pen and pad onto his desk with such force the pen pinwheeled across the glass surface and onto the floor.

Grunting, he leaned down to pick it up and told himself the burn he could feel deep in his gut was irritation.

Not an attack of conscience.

And *not* desire.


Marietta dropped her sketchpad and pencil onto the solid wooden table where she'd sat earlier with Nico and pulled out her earbuds, trading the orchestral tones of her classical playlist for the natural summer chorus of cicadas and the distant cries of gulls circling over the ocean.

She closed her eyes, breathed in the briny scent of the sea and the distinctive floral notes of the wild lavender that stained the island's clifftops a vibrant purple and gave Île de Lavande its name.

It was beautiful here, peaceful—a world away from the crazy pace and relentless noise of Rome—but the creative inspiration she'd hoped for had proved elusive and her efforts this afternoon had been disappointing, to say the least.

She was in the wrong headspace. Upset with Nico and more so with herself for letting him affect her like this. Allowing him to make her feel guilty and ungrateful simply because she wanted to see more of his beautiful island. She understood that he was busy. Understood that he must have had to rearrange his schedule to bring her here. But this outlandish idea had been *his*, not hers.

And she had tried to co-operate. Had tried to prevent her temper from flaring as she'd answered every personal, invasive question he'd fired at her.

He should not look so gorgeous. Should not have sat there in his worn jeans and his white T-shirt, with his feet bare and that film of dark stubble on his jaw that gave him a deliciously rough, disreputable edge. How could she concentrate with all that flagrant male energy swirling around her like a hot mist, drenching the very air she needed to breathe?

She opened her eyes and let her gaze drift beyond the terrace towards the clifftop and the blue expanse of sea that was so vast Marietta felt very insignificant all of a sudden, and for some reason very lonely.

Her brows tugged together.

*Santo cielo.*

What was wrong with her?

She didn't wallow like this.

She was strong—a battler like her *mamma* had been—not a dreamer given to fits of melancholy like her father, a man who had become so lost in his grief, so consumed by addiction, that he'd neglected his children and forced his son to assume the role of provider before he'd even reached his teens.

Looking back on those years always reminded her how lucky she had been to have Leo. She'd been only seven when their mother died, so Marietta's memories of her were limited, but she knew in her heart that Estelle Vincenti would have been proud of her son for stepping up.

*And would she have been proud of you?*

Marietta's frown sharpened as the question popped into her head. She liked to think her mother would have forgiven the fractious, rebellious teenager she'd been—the girl who'd acted out in the absence of a mother's love and influence—and regarded the woman she'd become with pride and affection.

Yet she would never know for certain the answer to that question, would she?

Her eyes prickled and she cursed.

*Enough.*

It was being stuck here on this remote estate with a man who clearly didn't wish to spend more time with her than was necessary that was plunging her into this funk. A friendly voice and distraction—that was what she needed. She turned her wheelchair and headed for the house. She'd call her sister-in-law, Helena, and see how the plans for Ricci's birthday party were coming along.

Except when Marietta reached the beautiful blue and white guest bedroom she'd been given and fished her mobile out of her bag, she discovered the phone was dead and realised she'd forgotten her charger.

She swore again, and wheeled out of the room. Had she seen a landline phone anywhere in this sprawling modern abode? She rolled along the wide

hallway and paused outside the open door to the
study where Nico had spent most of the afternoon.
He'd emerged half an hour ago and declared that he
was going for a short run. She'd pasted on a smile
and waved him off as if she couldn't care less what
he did.

She looked into the room. It was neat and masculine, with lots of sharp edges and straight lines, glass
surfaces and sleek, pale wood. A textured black rug,
a tan leather sofa and a matching desk chair were the
only soft furnishings.

And on the glass-topped desk sat a phone.

More eager by the second to hear a familiar voice,
she glided over to the desk and dialled her sister-in-
law's mobile number.

'Helena,' she said a moment later. 'It's me.'

'Marietta!' Helena's posh English voice rushed
down the line. 'I've been thinking about you all
weekend. This whole business is just dreadful. Is
everything all right over there? Is Nicolas treating
you well?' A fleeting pause. 'He'd *better* be treating you well.'

Marietta smiled to herself. 'Everything's fine. A
little quiet, that's all.'

She stared out of the large window which faced
the terrace, her gaze trailing over the pool and the
table where she'd sat drawing for much of the afternoon. Her brows pinched. Had Nico watched her
from his desk while he'd worked?

'Tell me about Ricci's party,' she said, pushing aside that thought. 'How's the planning going?'

'Great. Except Leo is such a proud *papà* he's invited half of Tuscany—and Rome...'

Marietta was still smiling as she wound up the call, some ten minutes later. 'Give Ricci and Leo my love. I'll see you in six days.'

'Are you sure?'

'Of course. I'll be there,' she said firmly. 'I'm not missing Ricci's first birthday for anything.'

She hung up feeling lighter, less maudlin and more like herself. This ugly business of her stalker would be over soon and she'd have her life back. She reversed away from the desk, turned towards the door—and saw something against the wall on the far side of the doorway she hadn't noticed upon entering. It was a piece of antique furniture totally at odds with the rest of the decor and yet so lovely it commanded her attention for a long moment. She inched closer and recognised it was a vintage rolltop desk, crafted from a rich golden oak which gleamed as if someone had polished it only yesterday.

And, oh, it was *magnifico*. A stunning piece of craftsmanship her artist's eye couldn't fail to admire. Lured by its beauty, she brushed her hand over the intricate gold leaf designs on the drawer-fronts and fingered the little gold lock and key at the bottom of the tambour lid. She'd always adored the idea of these old-fashioned desks, with their hidden nooks and crannies, and before the left side of her brain could issue a caution she had turned the key and pushed up the slatted tambour to reveal the interior.

Immediately Marietta knew she had gone too far—gone somewhere she shouldn't have—because everything inside the desk…every item sitting in its neat, allotted space…was too pretty and feminine to belong to a man.

Unease flared, even as curiosity kept her gaze fixated. One of the central nooks accommodated a pretty peach-coloured writing compendium, with an elegant silver pen lying on top and a bright orange reading glasses case alongside it. In the next cubbyhole sat a large trinket box, fashioned from dark wood with mother-of-pearl inlay, and a smaller silver box with an ornamental lid. A neat stack of hardcover books filled another space, and below them a solid silver photo frame lay face-down on the desk's polished surface.

*Don't look.*

But the strident command in her head couldn't stay her hand. Her fingers stroked the velvet backing of the frame and then tilted it up. She stared at a photo of a much younger Nico, in profile, gazing adoringly at a striking golden-haired woman in a long white veil and wedding dress.

A door opening and closing, followed by the sound of footsteps and fast, rough breathing, catapulted Marietta's heart into her throat. The footsteps travelled down the hall, then retreated, and seconds later, through the window, she saw Nico emerge onto the terrace.

His back was to her but she could see he was breathing hard, his impressive shoulders lifting with each deep, controlled breath. His T-shirt stuck to his broad back and his running shorts emphasised narrow hips, a taut backside and long, muscular legs. He was hard and honed, every sweaty, musclebound inch of him, and for a few seconds Marietta lost all sense of her surroundings as some visceral response to all that hardcore virility short-circuited her brain and triggered a burst of heat in her belly and breasts.

He turned and strode into the house. 'Marietta?'

She jolted back to herself and looked at the photo, still in her hand. Gently, her fingers shaking a little, she replaced the frame. She'd wasted precious seconds and now it was too late to avoid discovery. She couldn't close up the desk with the necessary care—she'd never risk damaging this beautiful antique—and get out of the study undetected.

She clasped her hands in her lap and swallowed hard. She had trespassed, but not with any malicious intent. This was a minor transgression, she assured herself. She would own it.

'I'm in your office,' she called out.

He was there within seconds, and she saw on his face the exact moment he registered the raised lid of the desk. Saw his nostrils pinch and flare, his mouth flatten into a hard line, and knew with a sharp mix of certainty and regret that he wouldn't simply shrug off the intrusion.

His large body went still—so still it frightened her.

Her heart thundered in her ears. 'Nico, I'm sorry.' The apology spilled out in a breathless rush. 'I came in to use the phone and saw the desk and it was so beautiful... I... I didn't think.'

If possible his features grew tighter, his eyes harder. He said nothing, and the silence, broken only by his harsh breathing, was awful.

'I'm so sorry,' she said again, and her voice cracked. Because this time she wasn't only apologising for opening the desk. This time she was telling him she was sorry about his wife. She knew nothing about his marriage, of course, but the photograph, the desk so lovingly preserved—almost like a shrine— told her two things.

Nico had loved his wife.

And his wife was no longer alive.

Marietta's throat constricted. 'Please say something,' she whispered.

He moved to the desk, carefully lowered the lid and laid his palms on the tambour. He didn't look at her, and somehow that was ten times worse than his hard, silent stare.

'Go,' he said at last, and the command was all the more terrible for its quietness.

'Nico—'

'Get out, Marietta.'

Still he didn't look at her, and the rebuff needled deep, even though she knew she'd earned it. Smothering the impulse to apologise yet again, Marietta turned her chair and wheeled out of the room.

# CHAPTER SIX

Nico walked out to the terrace with two crystal tumblers balanced in one hand and an unopened bottle of vintage cognac from the back of his liquor cabinet cradled in the other.

He paused. Marietta sat in her wheelchair at the table by the pool with her back to him, her slender form silhouetted by the dying light of the sun, which was now no more than a sliver of fiery orange on the horizon. Her long mahogany hair spilled in loose waves down her back, and before he could censor his thoughts he found himself wondering how it would feel to slide his fingers through those thick tresses, wind them around his hands...

He tightened his jaw. Shook off the thought as swiftly as it had surfaced. Marietta was his friend's sister and right now her safety was his responsibility. This incessant awareness of her was an unwelcome distraction and he needed to shut it down. At the very minimum he needed to control his thoughts and reactions around her—especially after today, when he had not reacted well to finding her at Julia's desk…had not known how to handle the unexpected gut-punch of emotion or the glitter of sympathy in Marietta's eyes.

Seeing the woman who'd lit a slow-burning fire in his blood these past forty-eight hours alongside the only mementoes he had of his dead wife had unbalanced him, had fired a shock wave through his brain that had stolen his ability to do more than clip out a few terse words.

And that look he'd seen on Marietta's face .. Apology mixed with *pity*, of all things. His gut had hardened, everything within him rejecting that look. Rejecting the idea of Marietta feeling sorry for him. Of *anyone* feeling sorry for him. Nico elicited a range of reactions from people—respect, obedience, trust, fear—but rarely sympathy or pity. If ever. Witnessing both in Marietta's eyes had left him feeling sideswiped. Exposed. Something he had worked hard for the last decade *not* to feel. And yet even now, years later, he didn't always succeed in burying his feelings—did he? Occasionally the darkness would try to claim him. The guilt and the burning sense of failure that had dogged him ever since Julia's death would rise up and torment him.

He strode to the table and set down the bottle and glasses. He'd come out here to make peace, he reminded himself. Not to examine his inner workings.

Marietta looked up, her liquid dark eyes startled at first, then veiled and wary. One graceful eyebrow rose. 'Are we celebrating something?' She looked from the bottle to him. 'Perhaps you've caught my stalker and you're gracing me with your presence to tell me I can return to civilisation tomorrow?'

Nico let the sarcasm slide. He'd avoided her for much of the day and she was upset with him. Women didn't like to be ignored—he remembered that much from his too brief time as a married man. He took in her pale cotton pants, the soft green halterneck top which clung to her generous curves and left her golden shoulders exposed. Had she changed especially for dinner? A needle of guilt pricked him. She'd knocked on his study door an hour ago, offered to fix a meal for them, and he'd grunted a response through the closed door, telling her to eat without him.

He opened the bottle and poured a double shot of cognac into each tumbler, put one in front of Marietta and settled in a cushioned seat beside her. 'You do not consider Île de Lavande to be civilised?' He swirled the cognac in his glass. 'Or perhaps you are referring to the company?'

Colour crept into her cheeks but her chin stayed elevated. 'I'm sure parts of Île de Lavande are very civilised—I'm simply yet to see most of the island. As for the company—so far it's been…' She shrugged minutely. 'Satisfactory.'

Despite the tension in the air Nico felt his facial

muscles twitch, and then his lips were stretching into a rare smile. Had a woman ever described him as 'satisfactory' before? No. He didn't think so. On the infrequent occasions when he indulged in female company, he made damn sure the woman was a great deal more than *satisfied* when he was done with her.

He raised his glass. '*Touché*, Marietta.' He swallowed a mouthful of the expensive cognac and noted she hadn't touched hers. 'You are angry,' he observed.

'No…' she began, and then stopped, shook her head and puffed out a quiet sigh. '*Si*. A little,' she confessed. 'I made a mistake and you won't accept my apology. I'm angry with myself *and* with you.'

He lifted his eyebrows. 'That's a candid statement,' he said, which maybe shouldn't have surprised him. Marietta had never struck him as a smoke-and-mirrors kind of woman. She was headstrong and honest. Unafraid to speak her mind.

She reached out suddenly, and curled her hand around his wrist. 'I didn't mean to intrude, Nico,' she said softly. 'And I truly am sorry—about your wife.'

Heat radiated from her touch—a sharp, unsettling contrast to the inevitable icy chill that swept through him whenever he thought about his wife—and then she was sliding her hand away, sitting back.

'How long were you married?'

His chest grew uncomfortably tight. 'Two years.'

'She was very beautiful.'

So she *had* taken a good look at the photograph. He

didn't know how he felt about that. He took another generous sip of cognac, held the liquid in his mouth for a moment before letting it burn down his throat. He *did* know he wasn't going to have this conversation.

'Who did you call?' he asked, and the abrupt change of subject elicited an immediate frown.

'*Scusi?*'

'You said you went into my study to use the phone,' he reminded her. 'Who did you call?'

'My sister-in-law.'

'Because…?'

Her shoulders stiffened. 'Because I wanted to hear a friendly voice,' she said, her tone turning defensive, faintly accusing.

Nico cursed himself silently. He'd come out here to make peace, to defuse the tension between them before it sprouted claws—not to pick a fight. He had no wish to speak of his late wife, no desire to dredge up the darkness that lurked too close to the surface, but he could have deflected Marietta's curiosity in a less antagonistic manner.

'Forgive me,' he said, his voice gruff, the words alien on his tongue.

Rarely did he apologise or seek forgiveness. The last time had been ten years ago, the day of Julia's funeral, and on that day his father-in-law had been disinclined to forgive.

'You may call whomever you wish, whenever you wish,' he said. 'The house and its facilities are yours to use as you desire. However, I will ask one thing of you.' He held her gaze, kept his voice low. Measured. 'Please do not ever again speak of my wife.'

For a long moment Marietta's gaze didn't falter from his, then her lashes lowered, shielding her expressive eyes from him. She backed her chair away from the table.

'Understood,' she said, glancing up, her gaze reconnecting with his briefly. '*Buona notte*, Nico.'

And then she turned her chair around and wheeled into the house, leaving her drink sitting untouched on the table.

Nico watched her go and something pierced him. Something, he thought darkly, like regret. He reached for her glass, downed the double shot of cognac and scowled into the empty tumbler. That had *not* gone at all how he'd planned.


'It's not the ex-boyfriend, boss.'

Nico leaned back in his chair, his phone pressed to his ear. 'Are you positive?'

'Yes,' Bruno said. 'The guy was in Vienna on business all day Friday. And my gut says it's not him. He's settled, content. Devoted to his wife and kid. The wife's a looker, too.'

Nico ignored that last comment. He ran his hand through his hair, across the back of his neck. A long, restless night had left him edgy. Irritable. 'Forensics?'

'Waiting on a DNA profile from the hair strand found in the bedroom.'

'Chase it up. Today. Then contact those fools from the *polizia* and check their records for a match.' He drummed his fingers on his desk, cast a brooding look out of the window. 'And the neighbours?'

'One left to interview. Female. In her fifties.'

'Okay. *Bien*. Review that list of artists I emailed to you yesterday and get—' Nico broke off, sat forward, then surged up out of his chair. *What the hell?* 'Bruno, I'll call you back.'

He slammed down the phone, strode through the house and out onto the limestone terrace. Raising a hand to shield his eyes against the midmorning sun, he stared beyond the pool to the cliff's edge—and felt his heart punch into his throat.

He paused, drew a deep breath and loosed his voice on a furious bellow. *'Marietta!'*

She didn't hear him—or chose to ignore him. The latter, most likely. Anger spiked and he spat out a curse.

He veered onto a little-used dirt path that meandered through tall grasses and clusters of wild lavender and rosemary. The wheels of her chair had left tracks in the dirt. Tracks that led directly to the edge of the plunging forty-foot cliff.

'Marietta!' he shouted again, and knew she'd heard him this time because her shoulders flinched. And yet she didn't so much as turn her head.

Another few strides and the pump of adrenaline through his veins gave way to relief. She was sitting farther back from the edge than he'd thought. He reached her side, balled his hands lest he curl them over her slender shoulders and shake her.

'What the *hell* are you doing?'

She looked up, her expression faintly astonished. 'Enjoying the scenery,' she said, her air of calm making his jaw clench.

He jammed his fists in his jeans pockets. 'Is there something wrong with the view from the terrace?'

'Of course not. But I sat on your terrace all day yesterday. I need a change or I'll go mad. Besides...'

She rolled forward and he pulled his hands out of his jeans so fast he heard one of the pockets rip.

'I've been dying to look at the beach down there.'

He stepped in front of her. 'That's far enough.'

She huffed out a breath. 'Seriously, Nico. You're as bad as my brother. What do you think I'm going to do? Push myself over the edge?' She craned her neck to peek around him. 'Are those steps cut into the cliff?'

He ground his molars together. '*Oui.* But they're extremely old. Probably eroded. Unsafe.'

'Probably? You mean...you don't *know*?' Her eyebrows arched. 'As in...you've never been down there before?'

He folded his arms over his chest. 'It's just a beach.'

'But it's *your* beach...and it's a beautiful beach. Why would you not go down there?'

A vein throbbed in his temple. *Mon Dieu*. Had he ever met a woman so infuriating? So unpredictable?

He let his gaze rake over her, from her high glossy ponytail to her sun-kissed shoulders, all the way down to the pink-painted toenails poking out of her strappy white sandals. Her white knee-length shorts left her pale, delicate shins visible and her stretchy pink spaghetti-strap top made her breasts look nothing short of magnificent.

*How could a woman look so alluring and be so annoying all at the same time?*

He brought his gaze back to her face. Colour flared over those high cheekbones and a pulse flickered at the base of her throat. Their eyes met and hers widened a fraction—and he wondered if she felt it too. That pulse of heat in the air. That pull of attraction.

Belatedly he realised she'd spoken again. 'Pardon?'

'A prisoner,' she repeated, frowning at him. 'I feel like a prisoner, Nico.'

*A prisoner.*

His gut twisted hard, turning in on itself, and his mind descended instantly to a dark, savage place.

Julia's final, terror-filled days on this earth had been as a prisoner, held captive by the kidnappers who'd extracted a hefty ransom from her father—then left her in a ditch to die.

'Nico?'

Marietta's voice penetrated the sudden thick haze in his head.

'Are you all right?'

He gave himself a mental shake, shoved a lid over that dark, bottomless hole before it sucked him into its destructive vortex. 'I'm trying to keep you safe, Marietta. That's all.'

'I know. But my stalker's in Rome—there's no threat to me here.'

She edged her chair forward until her toes nearly touched his shins. When she tilted her head back the appeal in her huge brown eyes had a profound effect on him.

'Nico... I spent six months of my life in a rehabilitation unit—two of those months flat on my back, staring at the same ceiling and walls, day in, day out. I had no control…no choice… I felt angry and scared and trapped—I guess that's why I get a little stir-crazy when I'm cooped up in one place for too long.'

Guilt coiled inside him. He hadn't considered that the isolation in which he found solace would, for Marietta, feel like captivity.

Silently cursing his thoughtlessness, he dropped to his haunches in front of her. 'Tell me what you'd like to do today.'

Her face broke into a smile and for a second—just a second—Nico felt as if he'd stepped out of the darkness into the light.

# CHAPTER SEVEN

'COFFEE TO FINISH?'

Nico's question drew Marietta's attention from the young couple sitting several tables away in the bistro's outdoor courtyard. She looked across the table she and Nico shared, its surface crowded with empty platters and dishes from their delicious seafood lunch. '*Si*. Please.'

A moment later Josephine's son, Luc, came to clear their table and take their coffee order. He was pleasant, relaxed and friendly—like the rest of his family, all of whom Marietta had met upon their arrival at the quaint seaside restaurant.

Nico's presence had drawn the entire Bouchard clan out to greet them—Josephine and her husband Philippe from the kitchen, and her father, Henri, from the cool, shaded interior of the family-run bistro. The old man had smiled broadly and the two men had greeted each other with obvious warmth—surprising Marietta, until she'd reminded herself that people were multi-faceted and Nico was no different.

Until yesterday she would never have guessed he was a widower—a fact that stirred a pang of emotion every time she thought of it.

A burst of laughter from the young couple drew her gaze back to them. Tourists from the mainland, she guessed. The guy was good-looking, his girlfriend pretty—blonde and suntanned, her slender legs long and bare below a short summer skirt. Their faces were flushed, from the sun or maybe from the wine they were drinking, and they looked happy. Carefree. In love.

'I spoke with Bruno this morning.'

She looked at Nico, so big and handsome here in the open-air courtyard, with its colourful potted flowers and its miniature citrus trees in terracotta planters dotted around the tables. Overhead an umbrella shaded them from the sun's brilliance and beyond the broad span of his shoulders the water sparkled in the harbour. She couldn't imagine him looking carefree—not with that constant air of alertness about him—but he did look more at ease than she'd ever seen him before. That rare smile—the one she'd caught her first glimpse of last night—had made a couple of stunning reappearances, and each time it had stopped the breath in her lungs.

'Is there any news?' she asked, wondering why he hadn't mentioned it before now, and yet grateful that he hadn't. For a while over lunch she'd felt like just another tourist, enjoying the island.

'Your ex is in the clear.'

Relief surged, even though she hadn't for a moment suspected Davide. 'So...what now? Are there other leads?'

'A couple.'

She waited for him to elaborate. When he didn't, she suppressed a flutter of annoyance. 'I *am* going back in five days,' she reminded him—because staying on the island beyond Friday and missing Ricci's birthday was still a compromise too far.

Nico remained silent, evoking a frisson of disquiet. But then Luc arrived with their coffee and Josephine came out to ask if they'd enjoyed their meal.

'*Bellissimo!*' Marietta exclaimed.

Josephine beamed. 'You will come and join us for dinner one evening before you leave, *oui*?'

'Of course,' she said, then, fearing she'd spoken out of turn, cast a quick glance at Nico.

But he simply murmured an assent that had Josephine looking pleased before she bustled back to the kitchen.

Marietta sipped her coffee and noticed the young couple get up to leave. The girl giggled and swayed, and her boyfriend caught her but he too was staggering. Grinning, he tossed some euros on the table and then guided the girl out onto the street towards a parked car—and Marietta's belly clenched with alarm.

She dropped her cup into its saucer, reached across the table and grabbed Nico's arm. 'Stop them,' she said urgently, and pointed with her other hand. 'That couple—about to get into the red car. He's drunk.'

Frowning, Nico glanced over his shoulder and then back at her. 'Are you sure?'

'*Si*. I was watching them.' Panic tightened her grip on his arm. 'Nico, please…'

He stood abruptly and strode out onto the street, calling something to the young man, who already had the driver's door open. An exchange in French followed and the younger man's demeanour morphed from jovial to belligerent—and then outright combative when Nico snatched his key away from him.

Nico, looking remarkably cool for a man who had just dodged a wildly thrown punch, pinned the tourist against the car, and then all of a sudden Luc and his father Philippe were there, helping to defuse the situation.

The tension eased from Marietta's shoulders but an icy chill had gripped her and her hands shook. She curled them tight, closed her eyes for a minute.

'Marietta?'

She looked up. Nico was crouched beside her chair, and she searched over his shoulder for the couple.

'They're inside,' he told her. 'Josephine's encouraging them to stay, to drink some water and coffee, have something to eat.'

She nodded, grateful, and yet still the iciness inside her wouldn't abate. She had been that girl once—young and beautiful, with her whole life ahead of her. If only someone had stopped her and her friends from getting into that car...

She shook her head. Dispelled the thought. She knew better than to dwell on *if only*. She picked up her cup, took a fortifying gulp of coffee, felt relieved when Nico stood. He returned to his chair but then studied her, and her skin heated and prickled despite the chill in her veins.

'You did a good thing.'

'*We* did a good thing,' she corrected.

He shrugged. 'You were the one who noticed them—and you were right. The kid's way over the limit.'

Marietta wrapped her hands around her cup. Stared into the dark brew. 'I couldn't watch them get into that car.'

Nico was silent a moment. 'Your accident?'

She looked up. 'You know about that?'

'Only what your brother told me—that your paralysis resulted from a car crash.'

Her stomach gave a hard, vicious twist. It always did when she recalled her fragmented memories of that night. The mangled wreckage and broken glass. The whimpers of the girl dying beside her. Her own pain and then—worse—no pain at all. Nothing but numbness and fear.

Her grip on her cup tightened. 'I was young and stupid…drinking at a party Leo hadn't wanted me to attend. I knew my friend had had too much to drink when he offered me a ride.' She grimaced. It was never easy to admit your own stupidity. 'I still got into that car.'

'And your friend…?' Nico asked quietly.

'He and the two girls in the car with us died.' She pushed her cup aside, her mouth too bitter suddenly for coffee. 'I was the only survivor.'

'I'm sorry, Marietta.'

Nico's voice was deep and sincere, but she told herself the warmth spreading through her belly was from the coffee, not the effect of that rich, soothing baritone. 'I made a mistake and I live with the consequences of that mistake every day,' she said. 'If I can stop someone else from suffering a similar fate, I will.'

Because no one deserved to suffer what she had. To have their life so drastically altered by one foolish, split-second decision. To have to face up to the bitter realisation that their future was going to be vastly different from the one they'd envisaged. She'd always wanted a career in art, and she'd achieved that, but as a girl she had dreamed of other things, too—love, marriage, children—things she'd eventually had to accept were no longer in her future.

Nico's blue eyes were unfathomable, as always, and suddenly she regretted opening up to him. This man knew so much about her already, and she knew next to nothing about him—especially his past. She'd known he'd served in the French Foreign Legion—that alone was fascinating—but knowing he was a widower... It touched something inside her. Made her want to see beneath that tough, formidable exterior. And yet she couldn't imagine she ever would. Nico guarded his privacy like a fortress—and he'd made it clear two-way sharing wasn't on the agenda.

'Anyway,' she said, 'the accident was a long time ago. I try not to dwell on the past.' She brightened her voice. 'Lunch was lovely. Thank you. Can we go and see the old ruins now?'

His thick brows drew together. 'You really want to see a crumbling pile of ancient stones?'

'I thought we were doing what *I* want to do today?'

His eyes narrowed. 'You are a stubborn woman, Marietta Vincenti.'

She raised her chin. 'So I've been told.'

Nico stepped onto the terrace with a bottle and two glasses in his hands and a strong sense of *déjà vu*.

Tonight, however, the bottle was an expensive Burgundy rather than cognac, and the mood in the air—if not entirely tension-free—was an improvement on yesterday.

He couldn't remember the last time he'd spent almost an entire day with one woman. Marietta was beautiful and he couldn't deny she made his blood heat, but she also fascinated him on a level most women didn't. She was strong. A woman who'd fought her way back from a major life-altering trauma—*a survivor*.

She was different from the women whose company he normally sought and that was the attraction, he assured himself. Nothing more.

And he couldn't deny that today had been...pleasurable.

She had charmed the entire Bouchard clan, including old Henri, and though the incident with the young couple had seemed to shake her she'd bounced back—enough to demand he take her to see the old fortress.

Her fascination with the ruins had bemused Nico. The ancient stronghold that had once defended the island against marauding pirates was, to his eye, no more than a dull, crumbling edifice, and yet Marietta had taken the time to snap photos from every vantage point her wheelchair had allowed her to reach.

Then she had asked him to piggyback her up the spiral staircase of the stone tower to see the view.

It had been torture. Sweet, exquisite torture.

Those soft, lush breasts pressed into his back. Her slender arms looped around his neck. Her warm breath misting over his nape.

He had thought that lifting her into and out of his Jeep throughout the day had tested his control. Carrying her on his back, all that feminine warmth and vanilla and strawberry scent enveloping him, had been a hundred times more challenging.

She was wheeling out of the house now, a platter of cheeses, olives and cured meats expertly balanced on her lap. A bread basket filled with the fresh mini-baguettes Josephine had given them this afternoon already sat on the table.

A minute later she was piling thick slices of cheese into a baguette. 'I shouldn't be hungry after our enormous lunch,' she said. 'It must be all the sea air.'

Nico watched her bite into the baguette. He liked it that she wasn't overly dainty in the way she ate. She tackled her food with enthusiasm. Appreciation. A sign of her Italian heritage, perhaps?

'The air quality here is pristine,' he said. 'I crave it when I've been in Paris or New York or any major city for too long.'

She swallowed. 'Do you have homes in Paris and New York?'

'Apartments.'

She nodded—as if that didn't surprise her. Her head tilted to one side. 'So, what does a man who runs a multi-billion-dollar global security company do with his time off?'

He fingered the stem of his glass. Tried not to notice how her mouth wrapped around the end of her baguette. 'That depends,' he said finally.

'On what?'

'On what kind of recreation I'm in the mood for.'

He enjoyed the sudden bloom of pink in her cheeks more than he should have.

Her gaze thinned. 'Holidays,' she said. 'Where do you go on holiday?'

'I don't.'

She frowned. 'You don't take holidays?'

'This is where I come to unwind.'

'Alone?'

'*Oui,*' he said. 'Alone.'

Her eyes widened. 'So you don't bring your... friends here?'

He lifted an eyebrow. 'Do you mean to ask me if I bring my lovers here, Marietta?'

The colour in her cheeks brightened. She picked up her wine glass, took a large sip and sat back. 'Do you not get lonely here on your own?'

He shrugged. 'I like the quiet.' Which wasn't strictly true. He craved the isolation more than the quiet itself. The disconnection from the world and the people in it.

Marietta looked towards the ocean and the setting sun. Half a dozen shades of orange and gold—colours she would no doubt give fancy names to—streaked the sky. 'It *is* peaceful here. And beautiful.' Her gaze returned to his. 'Are there no other places you'd like to visit, though? Things you'd like to see?'

He shifted in his chair. 'I've seen more things in

this world than you can imagine,' he said. 'And most of them I never wish to see again.'

He heard something dark and bleak in his own voice then. Marietta studied him, and he shrugged off the notion that she could somehow see the darkness inside him…the *emptiness* he'd never been able to fill since losing his wife.

'Well,' she said, 'I haven't seen enough of the world. There's plenty of places I'd like to see…things I'd like to do.'

'Such as…?'

'The pyramids in Egypt.'

His brows dropped. *Was she kidding?* 'Do you have any idea how volatile that region is?'

She lifted her shoulders. 'Isn't the whole world "volatile" these days?'

'*Oui.* Which is why travellers need to be more selective about the destinations they choose. More safety conscious.'

'I agree. But no one can live in a protective bubble, can they? If people did they'd never go anywhere, never do anything. Living involves risk, whether we like it or not.'

'Risk can be minimised through sensible choices.'

Marietta sighed. 'You sound like my brother.'

'That's because Leo is a smart man,' he clipped out.

She flicked her hair over one shoulder. She wore another halterneck top tonight, this one red and floaty and partially see-through. Nico kept his gaze above her collarbone.

'None of that diminishes my desire to see the pyramids,' she said. 'In fact it doesn't change anything on my wish list.'

His brows sank lower. 'You have a *list*?'

'*Si*.'

'Tell me about it.'

Her chin notched up a fraction. 'I'm not sure I want to.'

'Tell me,' he commanded.

Something flashed across her face. Annoyance, he guessed. She took a slow sip of her wine, fuelling his impatience.

'Okay—I want to do a tandem skydive.'

*Mon Dieu.*

'No.'

The word shot from his mouth of its own volition.

Her eyebrows rose. 'I don't need anyone's *permission*, Nico.'

His jaw tightened. 'It's dangerous.'

'So is getting into a car and driving on the *autostrada*,' she said, and the significance of that statement didn't escape him. 'Besides...' She flung a hand in his direction. 'I bet *you've* jumped out of a plane plenty of times. Don't elite soldiers do that sort of thing?'

The reference to his soldiering days gave Nico only brief pause. His service in the French Foreign

Legion was no secret. The Legion's flame-like emblem and motto—*Honneur et Fidélité*—were inked on his upper left arm and had been for eighteen years. He had knocked on the Legion's door—literally, because that was the only way to gain entry—on the day of his eighteenth birthday, gone on to serve his five contracted years, and then got the hell out.

No doubt he'd mentioned his service to her brother at some point, though Nico never spoke of those years in any detail. Trekking through humid, insect-ridden jungles and dry, shelterless deserts, defending himself and his unit against lethal attacks from rebel forces and random insurgents, policing war zones where their allies had been indistinguishable from their enemies and they hadn't known who to trust—none of it made for idle conversation.

Still, those five years had put into perspective the many childhood injustices he'd suffered as a ward of the French state—had made them seem almost trivial. Insignificant. And, yes, during his time as a legionnaire—and as a military contractor—he'd jumped out of a few planes.

'Irrelevant, Marietta. What else is on your list?'

She sipped her wine, took her time again. 'A hot air balloon ride. Let me guess,' she added. 'That's dangerous, too.'

'You think floating two thousand feet above the ground in an oversized picnic basket is *safe*?'

She rolled her eyes. 'This from the man who flies a helicopter?'

He scowled. No comparison. His chopper was a solid machine, designed and built by aeronautical specialists to exacting safety standards. A hot air balloon was nothing but yards of silk filled with...*hot air*. It would be a frosty day in hell when he climbed into one of those things.

'Is there anything remotely sensible on your list?'

Her lips curved, as if she were actually enjoying this conversation. 'Sensible isn't any fun, is it? But, yes—there are things you'd probably consider low-risk.'

'Like?'

'Swimming in the ocean...' That little smile continued to play about her mouth. 'Naked.'

And just like that, the steady, persistent hum of awareness in his blood intensified—until he felt as if a high-voltage current arced through his veins.

'Somewhere private, of course,' she said, and then her eyes widened as if she'd had an enlightening thought. 'Your beach would be perfect!'

All at once an image of Marietta floating naked in the clear seawater at the foot of his cliff flashed into his head. Heat and lust ignited in his belly, along with the certain knowledge that she *did* feel the same pull of attraction he did. He could see it—in the sudden hectic colour in her cheeks. In the way her eyes glittered and held his in silent challenge.

She was provoking him.

*Playing with fire.*

He lunged up out of his chair, strode to her side and seized her chin. The dark look he gave her should have subdued and intimidated. Instead her lips parted, soft and inviting, as though she were anticipating…a *kiss*.

*Dieu.*

He *wanted* to kiss her. Wanted to crush his mouth onto hers and let her feel the full, unleashed power of the lust she was deliberately inciting. Wanted to punish her for dangling temptation in front of him like an enticing treat he didn't deserve.

He held himself rigid. Controlled. 'Be *very* careful what you wish for, Marietta.'

And then he released her and stalked into the house, back to his study—where he should have stayed in the first place.

Nico stood near the edge of the vertiginous cliff and stared down at the small crescent-shaped beach he had never set foot upon.

On this side of the island the coastline was rocky, precipitous in places, but here and there the cliffs formed inlets with sandy sheltered beaches and calm channels of crystal blue water ideal for swimming.

Yesterday he had told Marietta the steps carved into the ancient rock face might be eroded, but in truth they appeared sturdy—probably as safe now as they had been a century ago. Until this morning he'd never thought about using them. Had never given the beach more than a passing thought.

Had he been in a war zone, he'd have cast his trained soldier's eye over the isolated cove and deemed it a death trap—the perfect location to fall prey to ambush—but he wasn't a soldier any longer and the island wasn't a war zone.

And he wasn't standing here right now thinking about danger hotspots and military manoeuvres.

He was thinking about the woman he had wanted to kiss last night and her damned wish list. About the sand down there on his beach and whether it was coarse or soft. About the temperature of the water— and Marietta's skin... How she would feel pressed against him if they swam together naked.

Ridiculous, *insane* thoughts.

Thoughts he would not normally entertain.

But, by God, she'd got under his skin. Ignited a hunger that hadn't relinquished its grip but rather had burned hotter, fiercer, during the night.

Did she understand what kind of man she was toying with? What sex with him would mean and— more importantly—what it *wouldn't* mean?

He jammed his hands into his jeans pockets.

He was not a tender, romantic man. He was an ex-soldier with a grisly past. A man who had loved and lost and vowed he would never again tumble into that soul-destroying abyss. His liaisons with women served one rudimentary purpose, and for that reason he chose experienced women. Never innocents.

And yet Marietta was no ingénue. She was smart and confident. Strong and resilient. A woman who didn't fear the world, who understood what it meant to accept the consequences of her actions. *A woman who knew what she wanted.*

Did she want *him*?

He closed his eyes, searched the dark, twisted labyrinth of his conscience. Which would make him the better man? Indulging her? Or keeping his distance?

He opened his eyes and studied the ancient steps.

Were they as solid as they appeared?

He pulled his hands from his pockets and moved closer to the cliff's edge. *Only one way to find out.*

# CHAPTER EIGHT

MARIETTA CLUNG TO Nico's back as he paused at the top of the cliff, her belly a cauldron of excitement and nerves. She couldn't believe they were doing this.

She peered over his shoulder, all the way down to the crescent-shaped strip of white sand at the foot of the cliff. It was a very, *very* long way down, and the steps hewn into the rock face were much steeper than she'd imagined. Her arms tightened reflexively around his neck.

'I've got you, *chérie*.'

His deep voice seemed to resonate through her chest, and the unexpected endearment made her pulse hitch.

'Ready?' he said.

'Yes.'

*As ready as I'll ever be.*

And then he started down the steps and the buzz of anticipation turned into a wild flutter. They *were* doing this. And she really couldn't believe it. Not after last night, when he'd stormed off and she'd been certain she had pushed him too far.

She'd sat by the pool, watching the rich golds and ambers and deep purples of the sunset bleed into one another, and tried to attribute her uncharacteristic behaviour to having had too much sun during the day. Too much wine with her supper.

But neither of those excuses was valid.

The truth was she had wanted to provoke him— because a reckless yearning had been building in her all day. A yearning to find out if a man like Nico could be attracted to a woman like her—a woman whom society largely viewed as *disabled*.

She knew the wheelchair frightened most men. Some wrongly assumed she couldn't have sex or wouldn't enjoy it. Others, she guessed, were re- pelled by her useless legs. Davide had been differ- ent in that regard, and their sex-life had been healthy, satisfying—though not the kind of passionate, all- consuming sex she'd fantasised about as a teenager.

She had a feeling deep in her belly, where the but- terflies had gathered *en masse* now, that sex with Nico would be the kind of wild, passionate sex she'd long ago resigned herself to never experiencing.

And Nico *was* attracted to her. She had seen the evidence as soon as she'd made that provocative sug- gestion about swimming naked at his beach. Had seen it stamped on his face—a raw hunger her body had instinctively responded to with its own power-ful throb of need.

He had almost kissed her. Standing there grasp-ing her chin and glaring down at her, anger and de-sire pulsing off him in waves, he had looked like a man fighting for control.

And, oh, she had *wanted* him to kiss her. Even knowing that if he did it wouldn't be gentle. That there would be fire and fury behind his kiss. When he hadn't—when he'd walked away from her in-stead—her disappointment had been so intense it had felt like a physical blow against her ribs.

He'd negotiated the last few steps now, and Mari-etta's eyes widened as he carried her across the sand to where a blue-and-white-striped awning stood in a sheltered lee off the cliff. Beneath the awning lay a picnic rug and a bunch of big, comfy-looking cush-ions, and on a corner of the rug, shaded from the di-rect heat of the midday sun, sat a large wicker basket.

'Nico!' Her voice came out breathless. 'How many trips did this take you?'

'A few.'

He knelt on the rug and she slid off his back, the friction between their bodies teasing her already over-sensitised nipples into hard, aching nubs. She plucked her tee shirt away from her breasts before he turned, glad that she'd put the loose-fitting white tee on over her yellow bikini top. She slipped her hands under her legs and straightened them out in front of her.

Nico propped two cushions behind her back. 'Comfortable?'

She nodded, looked around her. 'It's beautiful, Nico.'

She ran her hand through the warm sand. The pearly-white granules felt luxuriously soft as they sifted through her fingers. She looked towards the calm water in the inlet. It was a clear, stunning turquoise—the kind seen on postcards of exotic locales that most people only ever dreamed of visiting. Best of all, the cove was utterly, totally private.

'I can't believe you've never been down here before.'

Nico shrugged and kicked off his sneakers. He wore khaki shorts and a black polo shirt and he looked big and vital and masculine. He lifted the lid off the hamper. 'I didn't know what you'd want to eat…' He started pulling out items. 'So I brought a bit of everything.'

He wasn't joking. There were fruits, olives, crackers, breads, pickles and a variety of meats and cheeses in a small cooler, plus water, soda and two bottles of wine—a red Cabernet and a chilled white. Cutlery, plastic plates and glasses emerged as well, along with condiments and a packet of paper serviettes.

Marietta couldn't help but laugh. 'I bet you never go anywhere unprepared.'

Nico opened a water bottle and handed it to her. 'Who's the guy you want to be with when disaster strikes?'

She rolled her eyes. 'You,' she conceded.

A smug look crossed his face. He planted his hands on his thighs and surveyed the enormous spread of food. 'I hope you're hungry.'

'Not *this* hungry.' She reached for a bunch of green grapes and smiled. 'But I'll give it my best shot.'

In the end, however, Marietta found she could eat very little. Thoughts of what they might do together after lunch made her stomach too jittery. She did manage a small glass of white wine, hoping it would lend her some much needed Dutch courage.

Now she lay on her back under the awning, her eyes closed, wondering if she needn't have bothered with the wine. If perhaps she'd been a fool to think anything was going to happen beyond a picnic lunch on the beach. Because Nico hadn't suggested they swim, nor made a move to touch her, nor even so much as uttered a word in the last fifteen minutes.

Yet a definite tension permeated the air. Her sixth sense could intuit it—just as her other senses could detect *him*. The scent of soap and the faint tang of clean, male sweat. The sound of his breathing, deep and even. And his *heat*. She could feel the heat that seemed always to radiate from him, as if his body were a non-stop furnace. Whenever he was close that heat enveloped her, penetrating her skin, sinking into her bones and making her feel as if she were melting.

She opened her eyes and turned her head to look at him. He lay beside her, his eyes closed, but she knew he wasn't sleeping. Nico didn't strike her as the kind of man who indulged in daytime naps. In fact she half suspected that even at night he slept with one eye open. She let her gaze drift down, away from his strong profile, and mentally braced herself for the heart-stopping impact of his bare torso.

He was utter perfection. Hard muscle, smooth skin, dark, crisp hair in all the places a man should have hair—including a liberal sprinkling over his sculpted pecs and a narrow line bisecting his washboard abs. A black ink tattoo adorned his upper left arm and a long rough-edged scar curled over the same shoulder.

*I've seen more things in this world than you can imagine—and most of them I never wish to see again.*

His words from the previous evening came back to her, sending a shiver through her now as they had then. Nico had sounded so grim in that moment, so haunted, and she'd wanted to ask him what he'd seen that had been so terrible he never wanted to see it again. That had made him into a man who guarded his privacy and kept himself aloof from the world. But she had reined in her curiosity, knowing it wouldn't be welcome. Knowing instinctively that if she probed, their conversation would be over before it started.

Her gaze trailed the jagged line of the scar, and she recognised the tattoo on his arm as the emblem of the French Foreign Legion. Had the awful things he'd seen been the horrors of war? Of course. They must have been. Soldiers who served in conflict zones witnessed first-hand the worst of mankind's atrocities.

'Why did you join the Legion?'

She grimaced as soon as the words were out of her mouth. She hadn't meant to speak them aloud. She opened her mouth to retract the question—but he spoke first.

'Because I was eighteen and full of testosterone and didn't know what else to do with my life.'

Nico kept his eyes closed as he spoke. He'd surprised himself by answering her question. Normally he shut down conversations that ventured too far into personal territory, but right then he figured talking was the lesser of two evils. The greater evil—the dark, sexual desire prowling through him—couldn't be unleashed. Not on Marietta.

He realised that now.

Belatedly.

*Hell.* What had he been thinking? She wasn't one of the easy, vacuous, forgettable women with whom he occasionally hooked up for the sole purpose of satisfying his physical needs. She was Marietta, his friend's sister—a woman he respected. A woman who was *un*forgettable.

He had told himself she was no ingénue, and she wasn't. No innocent would have goaded him last night without understanding where such provocation could lead. What she was *inviting*. And yet as they'd sat there on the sand, sharing food and idle small talk—the kind of simple pleasure his late wife would have loved—he'd looked at Marietta and thought about the incident at the bistro, her concern for the young couple. And he'd realised that after everything this woman had been through, she was still pure. She still had compassion in her heart. Still cared about others.

How could he touch her and not taint her with his darkness? He had nothing to give her. Nothing to offer beyond the pleasures of the flesh.

'Did your parents not object?'

He slid his right hand under the back of his head and continued to keep his eyes closed. She'd taken her tee shirt off after they'd eaten, and seeing her in that yellow bikini top only inflamed his libido.

'I didn't have parents,' he said.

'Oh… I… I'm sorry, Nico.' She fell silent a moment. 'Did you lose them when you were young?'

'My mother died of a stroke when I was six,' he said, surprising himself yet again. He couldn't remember the last time he'd spoken of his childhood. Couldn't remember the last time someone had shown

an interest, aside from Julia. 'She was a solo parent—
I never knew my father.'

He heard Marietta shift, felt the weight of her
gaze on him.

'Did you live with relatives after your mother
passed away?'

'My mother didn't have any relatives. I became
a ward of the state and spent the remainder of my
childhood in children's homes and foster care.'

'Oh, Nico… That must have been difficult.'

It hadn't been a walk in the park. His mother
had been a good woman, a loving *maman*, and he'd
missed her. But he'd survived. Years of being shuf-
fled around in an indifferent welfare system had
thickened his skin.

'Don't go all sympathetic on me, Marietta. Every
second person out there has had a difficult childhood.' He opened his eyes, turned his head to look
at her. 'I understand you and Leo lost your mother
young—and your father a few years later?'

'*Si.* And I missed my mother desperately—which
is probably why I acted out as a teenager. But Leo
and I had each other. You…' Her voice grew husky.
'You had no one.'

And he hadn't needed anyone. Certainly hadn't
wanted to get close to anyone. *Why bother?* he'd
thought as a boy. *Why attach yourself to someone
just so they could leave you or die.*

It was a pity he hadn't remembered that lesson

before he'd married Julia. Instead he'd let life teach it to him all over again—only much more brutally the second time around.

He shrugged, looked up at the awning shielding them from the sun. 'There are worse things in life than being alone.'

'Like going to war?' She touched him then, trailing the tip of one finger over his scar. 'Did you get this when you were in the Legion?'

He sat up, forcing her hand to fall away. *'Oui.'*

'How?'

*Mon Dieu.* Did her curiosity know no limits?

'It's a shrapnel wound,' he told her, because maybe if he shared something ugly with her she'd see the damaged man he was and realise she didn't want him. Not the way she thought she did.

'From an explosion?'

'A suicide bomber.' He twisted his head around to see her face. 'A twelve-year-old boy.'

*'Mio Dio…'* she breathed, her expression horrified. 'That's awful.'

'That's the modern face of war.' He kept his voice hard, unaffected, *emotionless*. Because that was what he'd learned to do as a soldier. Control his emotions, follow orders, focus on the job and divide those he encountered into one of two camps—ally or enemy. Except that last part hadn't always been easy.

Marietta pressed her palm against his bare back, the contact so unexpected he nearly flinched.

'I'm so sorry for all the terrible things you must have seen, Nico,' she said, in that soft, sympathetic voice that seemed to curl around him, *through* him.

Her hand moved, stroking over his skin, setting fire to a host of nerve-endings which all led like a series of lit fuses to one place. *His groin.*

'Marietta,' he growled, 'what are you doing?'

Marietta wasn't sure she knew the answer to that question. She only knew that she'd felt compelled to reach out in some way, and that once she'd touched him—once she'd made contact with all that smooth, hot skin and sculpted muscle—she hadn't been able to draw her hand away. Hadn't *wanted* to.

He moved with lightning speed. Before she understood his intent he was leaning over her, one hand clamped around her wrist, imprisoning her hand above her head. His expression was dark. Almost angry.

Her heart thumped in her chest.

'You don't want this, Marietta.'

'Want what?' she whispered—but she knew what he meant. Of course she did. She wasn't naive. He hadn't carried her all the way down here just to have lunch on the beach.

But something had changed since they'd got here. Something had caused him to withdraw, have second thoughts.

It felt like a rejection—and it stung.

'Not what—*who*,' he said harshly. 'You don't want *me*, Marietta.'

She pushed up her chin, feeling reckless and bold. Angry even. How *dared* he tell her what she didn't want? 'Why?'

He breathed hard, his nostrils flaring. 'I'm not the kind of man you want to get close to.'

'Why?' she challenged again, her blood thundering in her ears now. 'Because you've seen some terrible things? *Experienced* some terrible things? Things you don't think I could possibly understand?' She struggled to free her wrist. 'Let me go, Nico,' she demanded.

He did, and she levered herself upright, forcing him back from her. 'Do you think you're the only one with scars?' She leaned forward over her legs, exposing her back. 'The one under my left shoulder blade is from the accident,' she told him. 'The rest are from surgeries—*failed* surgeries—and every one of them represents a shattered hope. A shattered dream.'

She dropped back to her elbows, locked her gaze with his.

'I lay in the wreckage of that car for thirty minutes, with two dead friends and another friend dying beside me, before the emergency services arrived.' She hiked up her chin, swallowed down hard on the lump in her throat. 'I haven't been to war, Nico. I haven't seen or done the things you have. But I *do* know something about death and survival.'

Her blood continued to pound, flushing her skin, making the pulse in her throat leap. The after-effects of the wine combined with her anger and the sight of all that potent, half-naked masculinity before her spurred her on to more recklessness.

She reached out and laid her palm against his chest, her fingers nestling in the fine covering of crisp hairs. 'Maybe I *don't* know what kind of man is hidden away in here. But whoever he is—whoever you *think* he is—he doesn't scare me.'

Deliberately she glided the tip of her little finger over his nipple and heard the sudden sharp hiss of his indrawn breath. But his big body remained taut and rigid, unmoving except for the powerful rise and fall of his chest beneath her hand. She searched his face, looking for signs of desire—for the flash of hunger she'd seen there last night—but the seconds stretched and nothing happened.

The flush receded from her skin and her insides turned cold and then hot again with a horrible, humiliating thought.

She snatched her hand back.

*Dio.* Had she read this all wrong? Had she imagined something that wasn't really there?

The moment seemed to click into slow motion. Nico's eyes narrowed, his mouth opening as if he was about to speak. But she gave her head a violent shake and fell back onto the cushions, squeezing her eyes closed. She couldn't look at him. He was too perfect. A man like him could have any woman in the world. Why would he take *her*? Unless…

Her face burned. *Stupid, stupid…*

'I think you're right.' She forced the words out between stiff lips. 'I *don't* want this.' Pride made her voice brittle. Defensive. 'I don't need pity sex.'

A sound came from above her—a harsh, ferocious growl of a sound—and she snapped her eyes open.

Nico grasped her wrist, not gently, and pulled her hand to his groin.

'You think *this* is pity?'

A gasp caught in her throat. Nico's eyes blazed into hers, but it wasn't the glittering anger and raw desire she saw that stripped her lungs of air—it was the irrefutable evidence of his arousal, big and thick and rock-hard against her hand. Heat coiled in her belly, and she curled her fingers around his impressive length. *Santo cielo*. He was enormous—and hard. For *her*.

A low, guttural curse shot from his mouth. 'Marietta—' The way he rasped her name was half-warning, half-groan. 'I want you,' he said roughly, tightening his fingers around her wrist, thrusting his groin harder into her hand to encourage her grip. 'Make no mistake about that. But you need to be certain this is what you want—because believe me when I say *this* is the point of no return.'

The fierce heat in his gaze, the solid, rigid length of him in her hand, extinguished her doubts. She squeezed him, giving her answer, and he pulled her hand away from him and loomed above her. Anticipation shivered through her and then his mouth covered hers, and that sudden, shocking clash of lips was ten times more electrifying than she could ever have imagined.

The world spun and she reached blindly for an anchor, until her hands latched on to the hot, hard flesh of his shoulders. He moved and she tightened her grip on him, terrified he was going to end the kiss, but he simply angled his head so he could take it deeper. His tongue stroked over her lips, then thrust between them —and the explosion of heat and earthiness in her mouth was unlike anything she'd ever experienced.

When he raised his head colour slashed his cheekbones, emphasising their prominence, and his eyes had darkened to an inky blue. His gaze raked over her face and lower, down to her breasts in the revealing yellow bikini. He fingered the gold clasp holding the triangles of fabric together and then, with a single flick, unfastened the top. The fabric fell away, exposing her to his scrutiny.

'Spectaculaire...' he murmured, and cupped his hand around her right breast.

Her shoulder blades arched off the cushion, her body straining instinctively into his touch. When his thumb stroked over her extended nipple the sensation was exquisite, but nowhere close to being enough. She needed *more*…

She moaned. 'Nico…'

A dark, anticipatory gleam lit his eyes. He lowered his head and sucked her nipple into his mouth, gently at first and then, when she gasped and drove her hands into his hair, harder, using his tongue and his teeth to tease and torment, until she cried out some incoherent words, which he obviously took as encouragement, because he popped her nipple out of his mouth and lavished the same attention on her left one.

Her nails scraped over his scalp. '*Dio*… Nico…'

Something broke loose inside her. Something wild. Demanding. She thrust her chest upwards, urging him on until she was conscious of nothing else besides the heat of his mouth and his tongue and the tight, coiling sensation inside her. Time stopped, ceased to exist, and she didn't know if seconds or minutes had passed when she registered the faint metallic slide of a zipper—realised Nico's hand was at the front of her shorts.

She froze. Only for a moment, but he felt it. His mouth slipped off her nipple, and she wanted to groan.

'I'm not changing my mind,' she said hurriedly, cursing the insecurity that had struck her out of the blue.

She tried pulling his head back down, but he resisted.

He cupped her jaw. 'You froze. Why?'

Inexplicably, her hands trembled. She let go of him and curled them against her stomach, closed her eyes.

'Marietta—'

'My legs,' she whispered. 'They're not...' *Not beautiful.* Her face heated.

'Open your eyes.'

She did, and they prickled dangerously. *Madre di Dio.* What was wrong with her? She *wanted* this. He wanted *her.* Why was she suddenly afraid of revealing her body to him?

'You are beautiful, Marietta,' he said. 'And I want *all* of you.' His hand tightened on her jaw when she would have looked away. 'Do you understand me?'

She stared at him, and then she swallowed and nodded. He dropped a scorching kiss on her mouth. Then he pushed to his feet, removed his shorts and briefs and stood before her fully naked.

The moisture evaporated inside her mouth. Her imagination had not done him justice. He was glorious, every part of him lean and muscled. Her gaze trailed from his broad chest down over the ridges of his abdomen and lower, to where his arousal jutted proudly from the nest of dark hair at the juncture of his thighs. Her belly turned molten. He was so hard. So *big.*

He dropped to his knees, slid the zipper the rest of the way down and removed her shorts and bikini bottoms. Heart pounding, she shrugged off the straps of her bikini top. And then he scooped her into his arms, stood, and carried her across the hot sand into the water.

Kissing, touching, exploring Marietta while immersed in the tepid sea water was the most erotic build-up to sex Nico had ever experienced.

He'd fooled around in water before—taken a woman against the side of a pool more than once—but this...

This was different.

Or maybe it was simply that he was wound so impossibly tight with need for her that he felt as if he might explode at any moment?

*God help him.*

He hadn't even buried himself inside her yet.

He gave a low, tortured groan, reached between their bodies and pried her fingers from his hard, engorged length before he embarrassed himself and came in the water.

The action earned him a small, petulant frown, but when she reached under the surface, he again seized her wrist.

'*Chérie,*' he growled, 'it will be over before it starts if you keep doing that.'

Her smile was playful, naughty, dialling up the heat in his blood and at the same time reinforcing his sense of relief.

This was the Marietta he knew.

Confident. Spirited. *Pushy.*

The way she'd challenged him on the beach—her boldness, the things she'd said, even her scars—had made him want her even more, until resisting his desire, resisting *hers*, had been impossible. And yet the woman who had frozen beneath him had been vulnerable, insecure—a version of Marietta he hadn't seen before—and his chest had ached with a fierce need to reassure her. To chase the uncertainty from her eyes and bring *this* woman—the one who fired his blood, who challenged him at every turn—back to him.

She wound her arms around his neck now, clinging to him like a silken-skinned mermaid, pressing her lush, caramel-tipped breasts against his chest. He had sucked on those responsive nipples at every opportunity, enjoying her gasps of pleasure as he'd coaxed them into tight, sensitive nubs.

They were ten metres or so from the shore, the water chest-deep, and his feet on the seabed prevented them from drifting.

He kissed her, savouring the warm, salty taste of her mouth and the erotic playfulness of her tongue as it dived between his lips and then retreated, duelling with his.

After a minute he pulled back. Despite his previous claim about the point of no return, he needed to make certain she understood what this was—and *wasn't.* To offer her one last chance to change her mind. Even though it would kill him if she did.

'This is all I can give you,' he said. 'These few days—'

Her fingers landed across his lips. 'I'm not looking for anything more,' she said. 'Here and now—this is all I want...'

And with that the final barrier fell. He dropped an open-mouthed kiss onto the wet, satiny skin between her neck and shoulder and slid his hand under the water, seeking out the silky curls and the velvety V of flesh he'd briefly explored once already—and planned to do so more thoroughly now.

'Tell me where it feels good,' he urged, eager to learn her pleasure points. To understand where she had sensation and where she didn't. He slid his fingers along the seam of delicate flesh, parting, probing, locating the precise spot that made her throw her head back and arch those magnificent breasts against him.

'Oh, *Dio...* There, Nico... *There...*'

He hoisted her higher in the water and clamped his mouth over her nipple, sucking hard while increasing the pressure and movement of his fingers. Her nails sank into his back and the sound she made as she came—something between a purr and a little feminine roar—was the sexiest damn thing he'd ever heard. His body throbbed urgently, almost painfully in response. She dropped her head onto his shoulder, her body going limp in his arms, and cursed in Italian.

Satisfaction rocked through him. 'Was that on your wish list, *chérie*?'

'No...' she mumbled into his neck. 'But I think I'll add it, just so that we can do it again and cross it off.'

'I have some other ideas for your list.'

She lifted her head, her dark eyes slumberous. 'Tell me.'

Nico shook his head, shifted her onto his back and started towards the shore. 'I'm going to show you instead.'

# CHAPTER NINE

MARIETTA HAD EXPECTED Nico to lay her down on the cushions beneath the awning and take her right there on the beach—and she'd have been lying if she'd said a part of her hadn't wanted him to. But he had muttered something about sandy blankets and comfort and now they were in his bedroom—a huge room characterised by clean lines and simple masculine decor—lying naked on soft cotton sheets in a bed so enormous it could have slept an entire family.

Her insides were still molten from the orgasm she'd had in the ocean. She had never climaxed like that before—so easily, so *quickly*. With Davide—and on the occasions when she'd experimented by herself—she'd needed a lot more stimulation. But Nico had brought her to her peak with such little effort it had been almost embarrassing.

She stared at him now, unashamedly, her gaze trailing the length of his powerful body as he lay on his side, stretched out beside her. His arousal was just as proud and fierce as it had been in the water, when she'd wanted so desperately to touch him, and it nudged her hip now, so thick and long she wondered a little nervously if she'd be able to accommodate him.

He drew a fingertip over her belly. 'Comfortable?'

Frustration spiralled. She *was* comfortable, lying on her back, one arm thrown above her head, soft pillows plumped under her shoulders for support. But she didn't *want* to feel comfortable. She didn't want Nico to be solicitous—to treat her like a china doll that might break in two if he was too rough with her. She wanted to feel hot and sweaty and breathless. Wanted to feel his weight on top of her, crushing her into the bed as he drove into the hollow place inside her begging to be filled.

His fingertip traced around her belly button and then her nipples, trailing circles of fire over her skin.

'Is there anything I should know?' he said, his voice rough—as though he wasn't quite as in control of himself as he appeared. 'Anything I can do to make it better for you?'

Her thoughts veered towards the tiny niggle of nervous concern at the back of her mind. Heat surged into her face, and his eyes narrowed.

He gripped her chin. 'What?'.

She swallowed. 'I used to sometimes have issues with—' she closed her eyes, her cheeks burning like hotplates '—with lubrication.'

Silence followed. She cracked her eyes open, expecting to see an awkward look—maybe even disappointment—on Nico's face. Instead his blue eyes glittered with something like…*determination*. As if she had tossed down a gauntlet and he was accepting the challenge. Slowly he rose to his hands and knees.

'Are you worried I won't be able to make you wet for me, *chérie*?'

Her eyes widened. 'No! It's not that… It's just—'

Her eyes grew rounder still as he straddled her, placed his large hands on her skinny thighs and spread them apart.

When he dropped to his stomach, his intent obvious, she babbled again. 'It's not you… It's just that… My body—*oh!*'

Suddenly his mouth was on her—*there*—and the powerful jolt of sensation forced her head back onto the pillow. She caught her breath, clawed her fingers into the sheet beneath her. His mouth was so hot, and his tongue…

*Santo cielo!*

His tongue was running over and over the spot where her nerve-endings were still very much intact. And then his finger was gently seeking entry, stroking, massaging, sliding deep into…*wetness*. She felt the sweet burn within, the build-up of tension that teased with the promise of a shattering release. Moments later the pressure reached its zenith and she cried out, silence impossible as she split into shards of white light that beamed her skywards and kept her suspended there for a weightless, timeless moment before casting her back to earth.

The bed moved, and she forced open heavy eyelids. Nico was braced above her, his gaze hot. *Satisfied.*

'It's wet down there, *ma petite sirène.*' He kissed her, thrusting his tongue into her mouth, letting her taste herself. '*Very* wet,' he added, and reached over to the nightstand for a condom.

Soon he was sheathed, poised between her legs. He slid his mouth over hers, kissing her long and deep. He lifted his head, his expression as he stared down at her stark. Intense.

'I can't hold back,' he warned, his voice ragged. 'I can't be gentle with you.'

She thrilled to those words. She didn't want gentle—she wanted wild. *Passionate.* She scraped her fingernails down his back and dug them into his firm buttocks.

'Don't be,' she said boldly.

And then he pushed inside her and her mouth slackened on a gasp of pleasure. In one long, powerful thrust he filled her up, and when he started to move, sliding out and thrusting in, again and again, she had no trouble feeling him.

She knew a moment's regret because she couldn't wrap her legs around him, couldn't flex her hips to meet his powerful thrusts. But Nico didn't seem to care; when she looked at him she saw only lust and fierce pleasure carved into his stark features.

He went taut above her, and a second later he shuddered and groaned, signalling his release, and then he was collapsing onto her, pressing his face into her neck.

Marietta wrapped her arms around him and smiled to herself. The weight of his body crushing her into the mattress was, she decided, the most delicious feeling in the world.

Nico awoke from an unusually dreamless sleep, and as he hovered in that place between oblivion and wakefulness he was aware of an unfamiliar sense of…contentment.

He turned onto his side and blinked.

Sunlight streamed through the massive bedroom window and he guessed from the angle that it was late morning—long past the time he would normally rise. He wouldn't normally leave the blinds up either, but last night Marietta had wanted to lie in bed and watch the sunset and he'd indulged her, spooning against her as he'd listened to her *ooh* and *aah* over the fiery sky until his body had stirred and he'd given her something much more impressive to *ooh* and *aah* about.

When the sky had finally turned a deep navy blue and the stars had begun to wink he had turned her onto her back and taken her again, watching her moonlit face as she climaxed before giving in to his own mind-shattering release.

He watched her now, asleep beside him, the sheet rumpled around her waist and her breasts bare. Her ebony eyelashes were dark against her skin, her long mahogany hair fanned out in thick waves across his pillow. The night had been warm and humid, but she'd tucked the sheet around her lower half, conscious of her legs even after everything they'd done together—all the ways he'd explored her—over the last twenty hours.

He didn't understand her insecurity. Marietta was a beautiful, sensual woman and he didn't give a damn about her legs.

He curled a thick strand of dark lustrous hair around his fingers. He'd known his attraction to her was strong, but he hadn't predicted just how fiercely and completely his hunger for her would consume him. He had the feeling she had been seared into his memory for life—and yet he knew the danger of collecting memories. Knew how treacherous they could be. How they could lurk in your soul, lying in wait for the moment when you finally thought you were strong and then raising their insidious heads just so they could remind you of what you'd once had—what you'd lost.

Marietta's eyelids fluttered open and she turned her head, blinked sleepy, liquid brown eyes at him.

Nico shook off his maudlin thoughts, curved his mouth into a smile. 'Morning, *ma petite sirène*.'

She stretched her arms above her head. 'What does that mean?'

'My little mermaid.'

She blinked, took a moment to process that, then turned her face towards the window. An adorable scowl formed on her face. 'It can't be morning.'

'It is,' he assured her. 'Late morning, in fact.' He circled a fingertip around her left nipple and the nub of caramel flesh puckered and hardened. 'Time to wake up.'

She stretched again, shamelessly thrusting those perfect breasts towards him. 'Coffee…' she mumbled. 'Mermaids need coffee to wake up.'

He took her hand and guided it to his groin. 'I have something better than coffee to wake you up.'

Her eyes flared, her lips parted—and suddenly his little mermaid didn't look sleepy any more.

Over the next forty-eight hours time slowed and blurred and the outside world ceased to exist—or at least that was how it felt to Marietta. They made love at regular intervals and in between they ate and swam, either at the beach or in the pool. When Nico disappeared to his study every so often to work she would paint, parking herself in front of her canvas and the easel which he'd erected for her in a sunlit corner of the living room.

In no time at all she started feeling as though she were living in one of those protective bubbles, the thought of which she'd scoffed at only nights before. Which was dangerous, she knew. Bubbles were pretty, but they were temporary. Sooner or later they burst—and hers was about to burst very soon. Because it was Thursday afternoon, and that meant that tomorrow she would return to Rome.

*A good thing too*, she told herself, slotting tubes of paint into their storage container. This thing with Nico couldn't last. A few days of indulgence—that was all it was meant to be. He'd been up-front about that, and so had she.

She had a life to return to. An excellent, satisfying life where there was no room, no need, for unrealistic expectations.

Plus she had little Ricci's party in two days' time. That would cheer her up. Help her get rid of this silly ache which had settled in her chest this morning and so far had refused to budge.

Nico appeared in the doorway of the living room. He'd been working in his study for no more than an hour and still her breath hitched as if she were seeing him for the first time in days.

She smiled, forced herself to sound brighter than she felt. 'I thought I'd get a head start on packing up my things. I assume we'll leave early in the morning?'

'We're not,' he said.

She paused in the process of wrapping her brushes in a cloth. 'Oh…? What time *will* we leave, then?'

'We're not leaving.'

She blinked at him, and for a fraction of a second her heart soared. Because if they weren't leaving then she wouldn't have to say goodbye to him just yet. She wouldn't sleep with him tonight knowing it was the last time they would ever make love. The last time she would ever feel him inside her, filling her. Making her feel beautiful and desirable and wanton and *whole*.

And then her brain reasserted itself. 'What do you mean, we're not leaving?'

'Exactly that.' He came into the room. 'You're not going back to Rome tomorrow.'

His tone left no room for misinterpretation. He wasn't giving her a choice. He was *telling* her.

For the first time in days, her temper flared. She put her brushes down. 'One week, Nico. I agreed to come here for *one week*.'

He crossed his arms over his chest. The gesture reminded her of the way he and Leo had confronted her six days ago. How they had bulldozed her into coming here. She'd been angry, hating the loss of her independence, the sense of having control of her life stripped away. Which was why she'd laid down her own rules—rules Nico was now completely ignoring.

'Until your stalker is caught, this is the safest place for you to be.'

She folded her arms, mirroring his pose with an equally resolute one of her own. 'And *when* will you catch him?' she demanded to know. 'Next week? Next *month*?'

Something glittered in his eyes. 'Is that an appalling idea, *chérie*? Spending an entire month with me?'

She pressed her lips together before she could blurt out the word *no*. The idea didn't appal her. Not in the slightest. In fact it made her feel light-headed. Euphoric. And that was wrong.

Wrong, wrong, *wrong*.

She wasn't *meant* to want more of him.

'This is hardly a joking matter,' she said. 'I have a job to get back to. A *life*. And it's my nephew's first birthday party on Saturday—I told Leo and Helena I wouldn't miss it.'

'I've spoken with Leo and he agrees you should stay.'

Her anger bloomed, swift and bright and vivid like a bloodstain on cotton. *How dared they?* 'That's not Leo's decision to make—nor, might I add, is it yours!'

She seized the wheels of her chair and propelled herself towards the doorway.

'Where are you going?'

'To call my sister-in-law,' she snapped.

'Why?'

'Because she's got more sense than you and my brother put together!'

And maybe Helena could change her husband's

mind. If Marietta had Leo on her side Nico would have to let her go—a thought that only sharpened the ache in her chest.

And that made her angrier still.

Sisterhood, it turned out, was overrated.

Helena had sided with the men. Marietta had wanted to express her anger over the phone but found she couldn't. Her sister-in-law's stance came from a place of caring and concern, and Marietta wasn't angry with Helena. She was angry at the situation—and with Nico for his high-handedness. He hadn't even consulted her first. He'd simply made the decision.

She managed a smile for the young waitress who had arrived at the table with her dessert and then realised the courtesy was a wasted effort. The girl was more interested in casting pretty smiles at Nico, even though she looked as if she was barely out of her teens and he was surely too old for her.

He had that powerful effect on women. She imagined he always would. He'd carry those rugged good looks and that dark sex appeal into his later years and become one of those sexy, distinguished-looking older men to whom women of all ages flocked.

The thought didn't improve Marietta's mood.

And if Nico had hoped a nice meal and the buoyant atmosphere of the Bouchards' seaside restaurant would, he was in for disappointment. She picked up her spoon and cracked the hard caramelised top of her *crème brûlée* with a sharp jab.

'You're still angry.'

She glanced across the table at him. He was clean-shaven for the first time in two days and the skin over his hard jaw looked bronzed and taut in the golden candlelight which flickered from the glass holder on the table.

'Of course,' she said, opting for honesty, because no matter how hard she strove for the kind of composure she'd often admired in her sister-in-law she'd never been very good at hiding her emotions. 'I'm missing an important family event by staying here, Nico.'

His long fingers toyed with his espresso cup. 'You would put a child's birthday party above your own safety?'

'It's not just any child's party,' she retorted. 'It's my *nephew's* very first birthday and a milestone I won't get to share with him now.'

Nico regarded her. 'It means that much to you?'

'*Si.*'

She laid down the spoon. *Crème brûlée* was her favourite dessert, but she didn't really have the stomach for its rich creaminess right now. The only reason she'd ordered it was to delay the end of their meal and their return to the house. If their post-dinner entertainment followed the trend of the last two evenings they would very quickly end up naked—and

she didn't want that to happen. Not yet. She wanted
to nurse her anger awhile longer and she knew that
as soon as he touched her, the second he was deep
inside her, she'd forget she was supposed to be angry
with him.

'They're my family,' she added, sitting back in her
wheelchair. 'The only family I'll ever have.'

His eyes narrowed. 'What do you mean?'

She shrugged, but inwardly she cringed. That
statement had been too honest. Too revealing. 'Exactly that,' she said, tossing his words from that afternoon back at him.

He looked at her for a long moment. 'Can you
not have children, Marietta?' he asked quietly, and
the intimacy of the question—from a man who rou-
tinely avoided conversations of a personal nature—
threw her.

She hesitated. 'There's no medical reason I can't
have children,' she admitted, pushing her dessert
plate away. 'It's possible...physically.'

His gaze narrowed further. 'So there's nothing
stopping you from having a family of your own?'

Her chest tightened. He made it sound so natural.
So easy. As if having a broken back didn't make her
different. 'It's not that simple,' she said, her voice
stilted.

'Why?'

She frowned at him. Around them the restaurant
was busy, with the clink of tableware, the buzz of

conversation and frequent bouts of laughter lending the place a lively air. Josephine had seated them at a private table, however, set in a quiet corner by a large window overlooking the harbour.

Marietta glanced around, assuring herself that their conversation wasn't being overheard. 'Generally speaking, a woman needs a husband before she has children,' she said.

He lifted an eyebrow. 'And you object to marriage?'

Her frown deepened. Why was he asking her these questions? Why was he interested?

Why should he *care*?

Her breath caught in her throat.

*Did* he care?

Hastily she crushed the thought. He was making conversation, showing a polite interest in the woman he was temporarily sleeping with.

She cleared her throat. 'Marriage is fine,' she said. 'It's just not for me.'

'Because of Davide?'

'Partly.' She lifted her shoulder. 'When push comes to shove, few men want to tie themselves to a cripple for life.'

Nico's brows slammed down, his face darkening. 'Don't call yourself that,' he said tersely.

'What? A cripple?' She affected an air of indifference. 'Why not? That's how most people see me.'

Which wasn't strictly true. She was fortunate; she

had people in her life who saw the woman first and foremost and not the disability. But equally there were those who *never* saw beyond the wheelchair. Never saw *her*.

Blue eyes blazed at her from across the table. 'That's not how *I* see you.'

Her heart lurched. She believed him, but how *did* he see her? As a woman who needed protecting? A perk of the job? She'd already guessed she was one of a long string of short-term lovers he'd taken in the years since his wife's death. She'd told herself it didn't matter to her, ignored the taunting voice that had cried *liar*.

'I know,' she said quietly.

Nico's gaze stayed pinned on her. 'Davide was an idiot,' he said. 'But he's one man. Why write off your dreams because of one bad experience?'

Her shoulders stiffened. 'Because I'm a realist—and some things simply aren't destined to be.' She sniffed. 'Anyway, you have no idea *what* my dreams are. Not every woman longs for the white picket fence, you know.'

He raised his eyebrows. 'So you don't *want* children?'

'No.' But that was a lie. A lie she had repeated in her head so often she'd almost believed it. Her stomach knotted.

'But family is important to you?'

'So are other things,' she said, hating the defensive note in her voice. 'My job—my career as an artist...'

She trailed off. Her words had sounded hollow and they shouldn't have. She was utterly passionate about her art. Determined to make a full-time living from it eventually. In the meantime she had a job she loved, her apartment, her studio for hire... It was enough. Of *course* it was enough.

So why had Nico's questions got her all tied up in knots?

She took the white napkin off her lap, folded it carefully and placed it on the table. 'Thank you for dinner,' she said, avoiding his eye. 'I'm ready to go when you are.'

The Bouchards came out to farewell them, dropping kisses onto Marietta's cheeks, and she wondered what assumptions they'd made about her and Nico's relationship.

Not that it mattered. Sooner or later she'd be gone from Île de Lavande and she'd have no reason to return—a thought she found inordinately depressing as Nico drove them home on the winding mountain road. When they arrived, he parked in the courtyard by the house, went to open the front door, then returned and lifted her out of the Jeep. He carried her towards the house.

'Nico!' she cried. 'My chair!'

He kicked the front door closed, barely breaking stride. 'You won't be needing it for a while.'

Outrage and something else she didn't want to acknowledge sent a lick of heat through her veins.

Her voice rose on a high note of fury. 'I'm *not* sleeping with you tonight!'

He reached his bedroom and dropped her unceremoniously onto his bed, so that she sprawled inelegantly on the grey silk coverlet.

He shot her a dark, blistering look and started unbuttoning his shirt. 'I don't plan on doing much sleeping.'

She pushed onto her elbows, glared up at him. 'I'm still angry with you!' she flung at him.

He shrugged off his shirt and threw it to the floor. The moonlight illuminating the room washed over his powerful torso, making him look like a statue of some demigod cast in pewter.

Marietta's mouth dried.

*'Bien,'* he said in a low, rough voice, simultaneously toeing off his shoes and unbuckling his belt. 'I like that fiery temper.'

He shoved the rest of his clothes off and when he straightened the full extent of his arousal was plain to see. He curled his hand around himself and the sight of him doing so was deeply erotic. Utterly mesmerising.

'It turns me on,' he said, quite unnecessarily, and then he was climbing onto the bed.

She shook herself, shot her arm out and slapped her palm against his chest. 'Stop!'

'You don't mean that,' he said, and his lips curved into a smile of such utter carnality that her belly flooded with hot, liquid need. Then he pushed up her top, freed her left breast from its lacy confines and sucked her nipple into his mouth.

Marietta gasped, her traitorous body arching in response to the exquisite sensations he inflicted so effortlessly. She lifted her hands, intending to beat them down upon his bare shoulders, but somehow her fingers ended up buried in his thick hair.

His head lifted, his blue eyes glittering with triumph. 'Do you still want me to stop?'

She gave him a mutinous glare, then dragged his head down and kissed him, sinking her teeth into his lower lip for a second before pushing his head back up.

'This won't make me forget that I'm angry with you,' she warned him.

That wicked smile returned, making her insides quiver.

*'Chérie,'* he said, lowering himself on top of her, his hard body crushing her into the mattress, 'by the time I'm done with you, you won't remember your *name.'*

# CHAPTER TEN

'DID I DRAG you out of bed, my friend?'

Leo Vincenti's voice carried over the video feed with a distinct note of dryness.

Nico thrust his hand through his dishevelled hair and peered at his friend's image on his computer screen. Leo sat in his office in Rome, looking immaculate in a crisp shirt and tie, making Nico even more aware of his unshaved jaw and the rumpled tee shirt he'd hurriedly pulled on after realising he was late for the video call he and Leo had scheduled for this morning.

'Long night working,' he said as he ruthlessly smothered the image of his friend's sister naked and spread-eagled on his bed.

*Dieu.* He hadn't considered how truly awkward it would be to look his friend in the eye after all the things he had done with Marietta last night.

Never had he known sex to be so… so *combustible.* So all-consuming. And still he wanted more. Still his groin twitched at the mere thought of sliding between her thighs and burying himself inside her wet, welcoming heat.

He moved his chair closer to the desk, concealing his lower body.

'Sorry I couldn't talk longer yesterday,' said Leo. 'I was in the middle of a client crisis meeting. You said you had more news?'

'There's been a development,' Nico confirmed, forcing his mind away from the sleepy, satisfied woman he'd left in his bed. He'd placed her chair within arm's reach, in case she wanted to get up, but he hoped she'd stay put. He wasn't finished with her yet.

He sat forward and gave a brief summary of the information Bruno had imparted yesterday. Late on Wednesday one of the two men they'd shortlisted as suspects had confronted Lina at the gallery and demanded to know Marietta's whereabouts. When Lina had claimed not to know he'd become aggressive and physical. Bruno was convinced they had their man. But now the guy had gone to ground.

Leo's expression was grim. 'Is the girl all right?'

'She's fine. I have a protective detail on her.'

'How will you find him?'

'We have the *polizia* fully on board now.' And his own men continued to work around the clock.

'Does Marietta know?'

'Not yet.' When the perpetrator was in custody—*then* he would tell her. In the meantime she didn't need to know about Lina. She'd only worry. 'I'll give her the details when the time is right.'

Leo dragged a hand over his face, pulled in a deep breath. 'Thank you, Nico,' he said gravely. 'I don't know how I can ever repay you for this.'

Nico shrugged. 'If our roles were reversed you would do the same, *mon ami*,' he said, tamping down on a flare of guilt.

Marietta was a grown woman, he reminded himself. She wasn't answerable to her brother—and neither was he.

He promised Leo to keep him updated and disconnected the call. When he returned to the bedroom Marietta was still in bed, early-morning sunlight streaming over her mahogany hair and golden breasts. He shed his clothes and climbed in beside her.

She stirred, blinked those beautiful dark eyes at him. 'I thought I heard you talking to someone...'

'Just a work call,' he said, cupping a soft, lush breast in his hand and thumbing its nipple. She moaned, and the little nub of caramel flesh peaked into a hard point that begged for the attention of his mouth.

A few more days, he acknowledged, his heart punching hard at the thought. That was all he'd have with her. Right then it didn't seem as if it could possibly be enough, but it would have to be. He had nothing to give her beyond these days on the island, nothing to offer, and she deserved more. She deserved a man capable of love. A man who would tear down the barriers she didn't even know she'd erected around herself and convince her she'd make an amazing wife and mother.

Nico wasn't that man. And for a moment, as he stared into her liquid brown eyes, the knowledge twisted his stomach into a knot of deep, gut-wrenching regret.

Marietta lay on her side on the soft beach rug and watched the steady rise and fall of Nico's magnificent chest as he slept.

He wore only a pair of swimming trunks and she trailed her gaze over his bronzed body, her belly twisting with a physical need she'd thought might have lessened over the last three days but had, in fact, only intensified.

They'd settled into something of a routine. In the mornings they'd linger in bed and make love, before indulging in a leisurely breakfast on the terrace, then Nico would work for two to three hours in his study and Marietta would paint. When her tummy grumbled she'd wash out her brushes and make them some lunch, and afterwards they'd swim and laze by the pool or at the beach. Dinner was usually a light snack, shared at the kitchen table or out on the terrace—and bedtime always came early.

It was indulgent and idyllic and it couldn't last.

Marietta knew that, and that was why she planned to enjoy it. Reality would intrude soon enough. For now she was going to accept these extra days with Nico for what she'd decided they were—once her anger over missing Ricci's birthday had worn off. A gift.

She traced her finger over the words tattooed around the emblem on his left arm. *Honneur et Fidélité.* It was the motto of the French Foreign Legion and somehow those words—honour and fidelity—fitted him perfectly. Because he *was* loyal and honourable. Her brother had said so many times, and Leo trusted him implicitly—as did she.

Her heart squeezed every time she thought about what he'd revealed of his childhood. She ached inside for the lonely boy he must have been, and she ached for the man he was now—a man who held himself aloof from the world. A man who seemed very much alone.

He was like a multi-layered gift-wrapped parcel, she decided. The kind that was passed around a circle of children at a party and when the music stopped another layer was unceremoniously ripped off. The excitement—and the frustration—was in not knowing how many layers there would be. Not knowing exactly when you were going to peel off the final layer and reach the heart of the parcel—the true gift beneath.

Nico had many layers—most of them deeply buried. His difficult childhood, the loss of his mother, his time as a soldier and the horrors he must have seen... But she sensed his greatest trauma—and thus the key to understanding him—had been the loss of his wife, and unfortunately that subject had been declared off-limits.

'Ready for a swim, *ma petite sirène?*'

She jumped, her hand jerking away from his arm.

Of course he hadn't been asleep.

She smiled at the endearment. *My little mermaid.* When she swam with him she *felt* like a mermaid, too. Graceful and elegant. Playful and sultry. For a while she'd forget all about her useless legs and simply revel in the freedom of the water. The exquisite pleasure of being skin to skin with him.

'In a bit,' she said, tracing her finger through the dark, crisp hair on his forearm.

Her mind toyed with the question.

*Did she dare?*

She looked at him, then took a deep breath and plunged in. 'Will you tell me about your wife?'

He tensed, and she held her breath.

He sat up, the lines of his shoulders and back rigid.

'I asked you never to speak about that.'

'I know, but—'

'Leave it, Marietta.'

She swallowed. 'I only—'

'I said *leave it.*'

And he lunged to his feet, stalked across the sand and dived into the water.

* * *

When Nico emerged from the sea he had no idea how long he'd been swimming. Fifteen minutes, if he hazarded a guess. Twenty at the most. Long enough for regret to outweigh his anger.

He had been too harsh with Marietta. These last few days they had been totally absorbed in one another, as physically intimate as two people could be. Her curiosity had felt intrusive, uncomfortable—more than uncomfortable—but it wasn't entirely unreasonable.

He padded across the sand. She lay on her back now, the awning shading her from the afternoon sun, her enormous dark sunglasses keeping her eyes hidden. A bright blue sarong draped her legs and she wore the yellow bikini top he'd enjoyed removing on numerous occasions. She must have heard his approach and yet she didn't move a muscle.

He dropped to his knees on the rug and shook his head, spraying droplets of seawater over her.

'Hey!' She whipped her sunglasses off and glared up at him.

He stared back, meeting that fiery little temper of hers head-on. 'You're upset,' he observed.

'You got up and walked away from me, Nico. How do you *think* that makes me feel? Knowing that I can't stand up and follow you?'

Shame pierced him, and he didn't like it. 'You pushed me, Marietta,' he said, taking a defensive tack.

'  'I asked you a question. That's all.'

Frustration needled under his skin. He grabbed a towel, dried himself off and sat down beside her. He stared moodily out at the sea. 'I don't talk about my wife with other people.'

A pause. 'Is that what I am to you?' she asked quietly. '"Other people"?'

He turned his head to look at her. 'No,' he conceded gruffly—because she wasn't. She was different—the only person he'd let get this close to him in ten years.

*Hell.* He pushed his hands through his hair, closed his eyes for a moment. Then he stretched out on his back beside her and took a deep, slow breath.

'Her name was Julia,' he began, 'and we met at a resort in Mexico when I was twenty-four.'

He could feel Marietta's gaze on him but he kept his own pinned on the blue and white stripes of the awning above them.

'She was vacationing with girlfriends and I was blowing off steam with some guys I had just completed a private security contract with.'

It had been a classic case of 'opposites attract'. He'd been a big, rough-around-the-edges foreigner and she'd been a pretty polished blonde from a privileged background. But Julia had been so much more than that. She had been sweetness and light—everything Nico had missed from his life since his mother had died.

Within six months they'd been married, despite her parents' protestations.

'It should never have worked,' he said. 'Our backgrounds were too different. And her father was running for the state senate.' He grimaced at the memory of Jack Lewisham's reaction to the man his daughter had declared she was marrying. 'I wasn't exactly desirable son-in-law material.'

He paused. Marietta was silent, but he sensed her listening intently.

'Things were rocky with her parents at the start, but eventually they accepted me.'

Nico had been determined to prove to Jack Lewisham that he was worthy of the man's daughter. He'd worked multiple day jobs and studied for a business degree at night, with the intention of starting his own company. In the end Jack had been impressed. He'd even loaned Nico a substantial chunk of capital to get the business started.

He closed his eyes and swallowed, his mouth going dry.

'Julia was kidnapped.'

Marietta gasped. *'Mio Dio...'* she breathed. 'By whom?'

'Opportunists. Criminals.' His jaw hardened. 'Her parents were extremely wealthy and high-profile.'

'Oh, Nico...'

He could hear the horror in her voice, blocked it out.

'Her father and I argued over whether or not to involve the authorities. The kidnappers had warned against it and Jack was terrified. He believed that his willingness to hand over the ransom combined with my military experience and resources would be sufficient to get Julia home safely.' He clenched his jaw. 'The man practically got on his knees and begged me to agree.'

'And you did?'

'Reluctantly.'

The absolute worst decision of his life. His biggest, most horrific failure.

She touched his arm. 'What happened?'

'Julia was shot.'

Marietta's hand tightened on his arm, communicating her shock, and somehow her touch grounded him. Kept him from sliding back to that dark place in his head where there was only that filthy ditch and Julia's cold, lifeless body.

'Were the kidnappers caught?' she asked gently.

'Eventually.'

He hadn't rested—not until every member of the gang responsible had been caught, prosecuted and imprisoned.

'They claimed her death had been an accident. Said she'd made a grab for one of their guns and it went off in a struggle.'

'Nico... I'm so sorry...'

Finally he looked at her. Tears streaked her face and he muttered a curse, gathered her into his arms.

'Please tell me you don't blame yourself,' she whispered, pressing her face to his chest.

In the silence that followed she lifted her head and stared at him.

'Nico! You can't possibly—'

'I can,' he said grimly. 'And so did Jack.'

'But that's crazy—how *could* he?'

'He was a man half-demented with grief.' It was something Nico had understood, for he, too, had almost lost his mind. 'He needed to lash out. To blame someone other than himself.'

Marietta put her head back on his chest. 'It wasn't your fault,' she said fiercely.

Nico tightened his arms around her. She was, he thought with an odd feeling of gratitude, the only person ever to try to absolve him of guilt.

For the first time in days Nico retired to his study after dinner, and when it got late and he still hadn't emerged Marietta went to bed alone.

She lay in his gigantic bed, thinking of everything he'd told her on the beach that day, and her heart ached for him.

How could he blame himself for his wife's death? And how could his father-in-law blame him for a decision the older man had essentially made himself?

It didn't make sense—but when did these kinds

of things ever make sense? It was the nature of tragedies. Of how people tried to cope. And she understood something about that. Her friends had died in the accident and she hadn't—how could she not have questioned that outcome? Not felt some degree of survivor's guilt? But in the end she'd had to let it go or it would have destroyed her. She had decided to be strong. To make something of her life—of the second chance her young friends had been so cruelly denied.

*And are you?* a voice in her head challenged. *Are you making the most of that chance?*

She frowned at the ceiling. She had tried hard for the last three days not to think about her conversation with Nico at the restaurant. He'd pushed some buttons she'd thought were no longer sensitive. Rekindled a longing for things she had convinced herself were out of reach.

But she knew that yearning for things that might never be was dangerous. A guarantee of heartache and disappointment. She had already travelled that road—with the experimental surgeries, with Davide... She couldn't set herself on a path of false hope again.

Which made the little daydreams she'd caught herself indulging in these past few days—silly fantasised scenarios of wheeling down a church aisle in a white gown, or holding a tiny sweet-smelling baby in her arms—all the more ridiculous.

The sound of footsteps coming down the hallway halted her thoughts. Quickly she closed her eyes, feigned sleep. If Nico had wanted to make love to her tonight he'd have joined her sooner; she had too much pride to let him think she'd been lying here waiting for him.

She heard the rustle of clothes being shed, felt the bed compress and then, to her surprise, the press of a hot palm against her breast. She looked up and saw the glitter of blue eyes in the semi-darkness before his mouth claimed hers in a hard, invasive kiss that drove a hot spike of need through her core.

He pushed her thighs apart, slid his hand between her legs and growled low in his throat when he found her wet and ready for him. He rolled away for a moment and then he was back, braced above her this time, his features stark, the glitter in his eyes ferocious as he entered her with a single powerful thrust.

She gasped his name, clinging to his shoulders as he drove deep, again and again. He had never taken her hard and fast like this before—as though he barely had control of himself—and she thrilled to the wild, primitive feeling of being claimed.

*Possessed.*

She dug her fingers into rippling muscle, feeling the tension and the heat building, spiralling, until a moan rushed up her throat and she crested that blinding peak at the same instant as Nico's big body tensed above her. He slammed deep into her one last time and pleasure pulsated from her core, obliterating every conscious thought from her head except for one.

One thought that stopped her heart as his weight bore down on her and she wrapped her arms tightly around him.

*She loved him.*

Marietta put down her brush and studied the canvas. The painting was finally finished and she was pleased with it. Her choice of colours and the way she'd illustrated the fortress's proud, crumbling ruins, with pale shafts of sunlight slanting through the old ramparts, had created the impression of something ethereal, almost otherworldly.

But she couldn't help but wish now that she'd painted something different. Something a little brighter, more uplifting. She had planned on leaving the painting behind—as a gift for Nico—but it seemed too haunting now for a man who was already haunted.

A shiver rippled through her. Their lovemaking last night had been so intense. So *silent*. Nico hadn't uttered a word—not before or during or afterwards—and yet he'd watched her the entire time he had been inside her, with that fierce intensity blazing in his blue eyes.

Her heart twisted painfully in her chest. The emotion she'd been wrestling with ever since her shattering revelation last night refused to be subdued.

She could *not* have fallen in love with him. Not so quickly. So hopelessly. So irrevocably.

Except she had.

And now her heart would break, because she wanted something she couldn't have. *A man*. A man too closed off from his emotions to ever be available to her or anyone else.

And already he was withdrawing.

He hadn't reached for her this morning…hadn't lavished her with kisses and caresses while the sun rose and then joined her for a lazy breakfast on the terrace. Instead he'd got dressed and gone straight to his study, emerging only for a quick lunch before disappearing again.

She put her paints away and folded her brushes into a rag for cleaning. The ache in her chest was her penance, she told herself harshly. She'd been a fool and now she'd have to live with the consequences— a concept she was all too familiar with.

She wheeled down the hall towards the utility room where she usually cleaned her brushes.

Nico stepped out of his study.

'Do you have a minute?'

She stopped and looked at him. He sounded so *polite*. The ache in her chest intensified. For the last three days she'd deliberately avoided asking about her stalker, assuring herself that Nico would tell her anything important.

He had something important to tell her now. Which meant this was the beginning of the end.

Her mouth drying, she nodded, and he stood back so she could wheel herself into the study. She stopped by his desk and he handed her a piece of paper—a printed digital photograph of a man.

'Do you know him?'

She studied the image. The man was clean-shaven, and he wore trendy thin-rimmed eyeglasses and a baseball cap. The photograph was grainy, as if it had been enlarged a few times, but the man's face was clear enough and... *familiar*.

She nodded slowly. 'It's Sergio Berardi. He's an artist.' She studied the photo again, an icy finger sliding across her nape. 'I exhibited some of his work at the gallery about a year ago.'

'Nine months,' said Nico.

The hairs on her arms lifted. 'I've met him a few times socially, through art circles,' she said, and suddenly it all made a horrible kind of sense. She put the photo down on the desk, not wanting to look at it any longer. 'He asked me out a couple of times but I declined.'

He hadn't been unpleasant, or unattractive, but she'd already decided not to waste her time on relationships. She rubbed her forehead. Thinking back, he *had* been intense. A little unsettling.

'*Santo cielo…*' Bile climbed her throat. 'I can't believe I didn't think of him before.'

Nico shrugged, as if it were of no consequence. 'Don't beat yourself up,' he said.

Did he sound distant, or was she imagining it? Being oversensitive?

Her heart lurched. She wanted to rewind. Go back to the beginning and relive her time with him. Relive the fantasy. Because she knew with utter certainty that her life wouldn't be the same when she got back to Rome. Not after Nico.

She swallowed past the lump in her throat. 'What happens now?'

'I'm leaving immediately for Toulon.'

She frowned up at him. 'Don't you mean *we* are leaving?'

'*Non,*' he said. 'I need to get to Rome as quickly as possible, to liaise with the authorities. I can travel faster if I leave at once and go on my own. I'll do a quick round trip and be back late tomorrow. We can stay here tomorrow night and then get you back to Rome on Wednesday.'

*One last night with him.*

Her heart somersaulted. 'Okay,' she agreed—too readily.

He glanced at his watch. '*Bien.* I'll call Josephine. See if she or Luc are available to come and collect you.' He started gathering together papers on his desk. 'You should go and pack an overnight bag straight away.'

Marietta blinked at him. 'Why would I do that?'

He paused. 'Because you'll be staying at Josephine's tonight.'

She blinked again. 'And why would I do that when I can stay here?'

He frowned. 'Because I don't want you staying here on your own.'

She stared at him. 'Why not? I live alone in Rome. You *know* that, Nico. I'm more than capable of spending a night here on my own.'

'Rome is different. You live in an urban apartment, with neighbours and people nearby. It's too isolated up here. I want to know you're safe while I'm gone.'

'You mean you want someone to babysit me?' Her face heated with indignation. 'I'm paralysed, Nico—not *useless*.'

His expression darkened. 'I did not say you were useless.'

'But you might as well have. Heaven forbid the poor cripple is left to fend for herself!'

Now his face turned thunderous. 'Don't call yourself a cripple!'

'Then don't *treat* me like one!'

'Marietta…' His voice was a low, warning growl.

She pushed her chin up. 'I'm staying here.'

He cursed loudly. 'I don't have time for this.'

'No, you don't,' she agreed. 'So I suggest you get a move on and go and pack *your* bag.'

A nerve flickered in his temple. He opened his mouth and closed it again, then scowled and stalked out of the room.

Nico sat in a leather recliner in his private jet and stared out at the thickening wall of cloud as the aircraft's powerful engines ate up the miles to Toulon.

It was twenty-six hours since he'd left for Rome and he was eager to get back to Île de Lavande. Leaving Marietta alone at the house had not sat well with him, but she was proud—stubborn as hell—and she'd argued him into a corner.

He stretched out his legs, rubbed eyes that felt gritty and strained. Dealing with endless police bureaucracy in Rome and the vagaries of the Italian legal system had been an exercise in frustration. But he'd called on some old contacts, pulled a few strings and in the end got what he'd wanted: a little one-on-one time in a non-surveillance holding cell with Sergio Berardi.

Nico hadn't laid a finger on the man and he hadn't needed to. Berardi had nearly wet himself the second Nico had locked the door, shrugged off his jacket and rolled up his sleeves. He intended to do everything within his power to ensure that the charges against Berardi stuck and he was locked up, but Nico had wanted to make certain that in the event the man was released he understood *exactly* what kind of retribution to expect if he went anywhere near Marietta.

He swallowed a mouthful of whisky.

He had missed Marietta last night. Missed her sweet, intoxicating smell, her soft warmth, the taste of her lingering on his tongue after making love. Even thinking about her now sent a powerful throb of desire pulsing through him.

*Mon Dieu.*

He'd crossed a line with her but he couldn't bring himself to regret it. Marietta had been a balm to his tortured soul. A ray of light in the sea of darkness that had closed over his head a long time ago.

He took another gulp of whisky.

Perhaps he was being hasty, confining their affair to these few days on the island? He couldn't imagine his hunger for her dying any time soon—nor could he imagine another woman satisfying him while his need for Marietta still burned in his blood. He could see her occasionally, could he not? A casual arrangement might be the perfect solution. Might suit them both until—

A massive jolt wrenched Nico sideways in his seat. His head hit the wall and the glass flew from his hand, whisky spilling everywhere and soaking the crotch of his trousers. He swore, looked up, and saw his flight attendant, Evelyn, clutching a seatback. He barked at her to sit down and strap herself in, then picked up the built-in handset that gave him direct access to the cockpit.

'Severe unexpected turbulence, sir,' his pilot informed him. 'It's the edge of a category three storm—coming through a couple of hours earlier than expected.'

*Expected?* Nico swore again. He always checked the weather forecasts when he was headed to the island. *Always.* But this time… This time he'd forgotten. He'd been preoccupied. Distracted.

'We have clearance from Toulon, provided we land in the next fifteen minutes,' the pilot advised. 'After that everything's grounded or diverted.'

Which meant he had zero chance of flying the chopper to the island. He stared grimly out of the window. The cloud was menacing and black, darkening the interior of the plane.

'What direction is the storm coming from?'

The pilot rattled off the latest update—and Nico felt the blood drain from his face.

The storm was headed straight for Île de Lavande.

# CHAPTER ELEVEN

THE PHONE LINE was dead.

With clammy hands Marietta put the receiver back in its cradle on Nico's desk.

*This is just some bad weather,* she told herself for the umpteenth time—then jumped as the entire house shifted and groaned under the onslaught of the powerful wind. She looked out of the window at the angry sky. *Dark.* It was so dark. Yet it was only late afternoon. She tried the light switch in the study, then a couple out in the hall—nothing. The house had no power.

*Dio. Please let Nico be safe,* she prayed. He wouldn't do anything crazy, would he? Like try to fly in this weather?

She wheeled herself to a window in the living room, looked out at the sea, which had been whipped into a seething grey-green frenzy, then back at the clouds—which looked wilder, even blacker now if that were possible.

No. Of course Nico wouldn't try to fly in this. He was too safety-conscious. Too sensible.

If only *she* had been sensible. If only she hadn't argued with him. If only she hadn't been so stubborn and proud and oversensitive about her independence. She could have been warm and comfortable with the Bouchards right now. Instead she was here. Alone and, yes—she'd swallow her pride and admit it—*just a tiny bit terrified.*

Rain came down—thick, horizontal sheets of it lashing the glass—and the wind roared like some kind of vicious animal howling for blood. It raised the hairs on Marietta's nape. Made her want to curl up in Nico's bed, pull the covers over her head and breathe in his scent. Pretend that he was there and she was wrapped in his strong arms, protected and safe.

She pulled in a deep breath.

Nico wouldn't travel in this storm. She was alone—at least for tonight. Which meant she'd need to be calm, practical. Prepared. She'd start by looking for a torch, she decided. Then she'd recheck the windows and doors to make sure the house was secure, and hunt out some candles and matches.

She found a lantern torch in the utility room and started her check of the house in the study. She wheeled to the window and glanced out—just as the large terrace table at which she and Nico had shared so many meals by the pool started to slide across the limestone pavers. Her eyes rounded with disbelief. The table was heavy—a solid piece of outdoor furniture—yet it might as well have been plastic for all its resistance to the wind.

Her heart surged into her throat as another wild gust shook the walls—and then the table simply lifted into the air like a piece of driftwood and flew towards the house.

Marietta backed her chair away as fast as she could and spun around. But the torch slipped off her lap and caught under her wheel. Her chair lurched and tipped and she threw her arms out to break her fall, crashing to the floor at the same moment as the table slammed into the study window. She locked her arms over her head, protecting her face from the splintered glass that showered all around her.

Fear clawed at her chest and a sob punched out of her throat. Clapping her hands over her ears, she tried to block out the violent cacophony of wind and rain. And started to pray.

Nico paced the floor of his hotel room in Toulon.

The room was tiny, compared to the hotel suites he normally stayed in, but the city was full of stranded travellers and last-minute accommodation was scarce. Not that he cared one iota about the room. He barely noticed the tired decor and frayed furnishings. Barely registered the cramped confines that forced him to spin on his heel every ten steps and pace in the other direction.

The floor beneath him shook and the glass in the windows shuddered. The wind was gaining strength, becoming brutal in its capacity for damage even with the full force of the storm yet to hit the mainland. Toulon and the other coastal cities and towns were in a state of lockdown; in this part of Europe storms of this category were rare and people were cautious and nervous.

A cold sweat drenched his skin.

*He* was nervous.

He stopped. No. *Nervous* didn't do justice to what he was feeling right now.

He picked up his phone from the floor, where he'd thrown it earlier in a fit of fury and frustration. But he still couldn't get a connection; the network was either down or overloaded.

He tossed the phone aside.

His house was strong, he reminded himself. Architecturally designed and built to withstand the elements. And yet bricks and mortar were no match for Mother Nature at her worst. If she was so inclined she would demolish everything in her path.

*Hell.*

He resumed his pacing. *Josephine.* Josephine and her family knew Marietta was alone at the house. He'd called his housekeeper yesterday, before he'd left, to let her know—just as a precaution. The

Bouchards would check on Marietta, wouldn't they? If they'd been forewarned of the storm...

But the weather predictions had been wildly off— the storm was hitting land two hours sooner than expected...

Nico's head threatened to explode. He felt useless. Helpless. And he knew this feeling. He *knew* it. Remembered it. Had sworn he would never feel it again.

Suddenly Julia's face swam in his mind—laughing, eyes dancing...and then glassy, lifeless, her pale skin streaked with dirt. And cold. *So, so cold.*

His legs buckled beneath him and his knees slammed into the cheap carpet, the impact jarring his entire body.

Loving Julia had made him weak, left him open and defenceless, so that when the worst had happened—when she'd been taken from him—he'd had nothing inside him to fight the pain. And the pain, the agony of losing someone he'd loved, had nearly destroyed him.

*Mon Dieu.*

He couldn't do this again.

His mother.

Julia.

*Marietta.*

A wild, rage-filled roar tore from his throat and he picked up an ugly vase from the coffee table and hurled it across the room.

* * *

Marietta navigated her chair around the tree branches and clumps of debris strewn across the Bouchards' front yard and cast yet another anxious look towards the hills.

She couldn't see Nico's house from the village, but every so often throughout the morning she'd taken a break from helping in the kitchen to come outside and scour the skyline for signs of his chopper. Thankfully power had been restored to most of the village, but the phone lines were still down and mobile coverage was intermittent.

A gentle hand squeezed her shoulder. She looked up, and Josephine smiled down at her.

'He'll be fine.'

Marietta nodded. 'I know.'

Josephine gave her an understanding look. 'It is too easy to worry about the ones we love, *oui?*'

Marietta felt her smile stiffen. Was it really so obvious that she loved him?

'How are you feeling?' asked Josephine.

'Fine, thanks.'

And she *was* fine. She had a cut on her forehead, scratches on her arms and some bruises from falling out of her chair. But otherwise she was healthy and safe—thanks to Luc and Philippe, who had driven into the hills as the storm had descended on the island and rescued her.

She cast another look at the sky—a clear vivid

blue in the wake of the storm—and then returned with Josephine to the kitchen. They'd been baking all morning, preparing a mountain of food to sustain the men who were tackling the massive job of cleaning up the village.

It was good to feel useful, to do something constructive, but her thoughts kept drifting back to Nico.

She wanted more time with him. Wanted to explore the possibility of seeing him once she was back in Rome. It was crazy, and extending their affair would only delay the inevitable heartbreak, but she wanted it all the same. Because as much as her feelings for him frightened her, the thought of tonight being their very last together frightened her even more.

A commotion outside the house pulled Marietta from her thoughts. She paused with a tray of pastries in her hand and heard car doors slamming, then male voices speaking in rapid French. She thought she recognised Philippe's voice, deep and firm, and then another, even deeper but louder—and agitated.

Marietta almost dropped the tray.

*Nico's voice.*

Josephine had hurried outside and now Nico appeared in the doorway. And he looked—*terrible*. Bleary-eyed and unshaven, his hair and clothes rumpled. A hint of wildness in the blue eyes that instantly zeroed in on her. He reached her in three strides.

She put the tray down. 'I'm fine,' she said, hurriedly, because she could see that he wasn't and it was scaring her.

He didn't speak. He just tipped up her chin and examined the cut on her forehead, then lifted her arms, one by one, scrutinising the many nicks and scratches she'd sustained when the window had shattered over her. His mouth thinned.

'Nico, I'm *fine*,' she repeated, wanting to erase the awful bleakness from his face.

Still he didn't speak and his silence unnerved her.

'I'm afraid there's been some damage at the house,' she said. 'Your study—'

'I don't give a damn about the study.' Finally he spoke but his voice was harsh. Angry, even. 'I've already seen the house. I thought—' He broke off. '*Mon Dieu*, Marietta,' he resumed after a moment. 'I thought…' He dragged his hand through his hair, stepped back, his expression shuttering. 'Do you have any belongings to collect before we leave?'

'Just my clothes,' she said, referring to those she'd arrived in last night.

There'd been no time to grab anything else. When the men had found her in the study, Luc had scooped her off the floor while Philippe had grabbed her chair, and then they'd driven at once to the village. The clothes she wore now had been borrowed from Josephine who, minutes later, hovered as Nico bundled Marietta into the Jeep, followed by her chair and a bunch of supplies from Philippe for the house.

Marietta thanked the other woman—for every-thing—then sat in silence as Nico drove them back up the mountain.

Several hours later Nico's gut still churned with a mix of emotions, some clear-cut—like relief and anger—others not so easy to distinguish.

It had taken him two hours to clear the debris from the pool and terrace, another two to get the study back into some semblance of order. The re-pairs he'd made to the house were only temporary; he'd need a glazier to install a new window, some furnishings replaced and the flooring fixed, thanks to a fair amount of water damage.

The antique desk that had belonged to his wife had survived mostly unscathed, but in truth he had barely spared it a thought when he'd arrived at the house this morning and discovered the carnage. And—worse—Marietta gone. The violent punch of fear and panic had almost doubled him over. Until rational thought had resurfaced and he'd realised the only logical explanation was that she was in the vil-lage with the Bouchards.

He'd felt raw, volatile with emotion. So much so that he'd struggled for words when he'd first clapped eyes on her in the Bouchards' kitchen. On the drive back to the house, when she'd asked him what had happened in Rome, he'd managed to clip out a brief, sanitised version of events, but then he had kept his jaw tightly locked, afraid of what would spill from his mouth if he opened it again.

Since then he'd largely avoided her, rejecting her offer to help with the clean-up and suggesting she pack her things in preparation for leaving tomorrow. The hurt in her eyes had cut him to the bone, but it was safer this way. If he got too close to her he'd drag her into his arms and never want to let her go. And that terrified him.

Now, showered, wearing jeans and a fresh shirt, he stood in the living room and studied Marietta's painting of the old stone fortress. It was a stunning piece of work. Beautiful and evocative, he surmised. Not unlike the artist herself.

'Nico?'

He stiffened... *God help him.* Even the sound of her voice challenged his resolve. Made him think twice about what he must do.

'Nico, please...'

Her tone was plaintive and it tore at something inside him.

'Talk to me.'

He turned, hands jammed into his jeans pockets. 'What would you like me to say, Marietta?'

Long shafts of late-afternoon sunshine streamed in through the tall windows, gilding her olive skin, picking out the amber highlights in her mahogany hair. She'd changed out of the borrowed clothes into long black pants and a sleeveless white blouse and she looked beautiful. She *always* looked beautiful. She rolled closer and he clenched his jaw, fisted his hands to stop himself from reaching for her.

'You could start by telling me why you're angry.'

He shot her an incredulous look. Did she really have no idea what she'd put him through?

'I went through *hell* last night,' he bit out, his resolve to remain calm, impassive, flying out of the window. 'Knowing the storm was approaching and you were here alone while I was stuck on the mainland—' He broke off, jerked a hand out of his pocket and thrust it into his hair. '*Mon Dieu*, Marietta!'

She pulled her lower lip between her teeth. 'I can imagine how worried you must have been,' she said, and for some reason her placatory tone of voice only riled him further. 'I was worried about *you*, too,' she added. 'But we're both fine—aren't we?'

He begged to differ. He did *not* feel fine. He felt as if someone had mashed up his insides with a chain-saw. 'You could have been seriously injured—you *were* injured,' he ground out.

'A few scratches,' she dismissed. 'Nothing more.'

'Thanks to Luc and Philippe rescuing you—which they wouldn't have needed to do if you hadn't been so damned stubborn and insisted on staying here by yourself.'

She bit her lip again, her eyes clouding. 'I'm sorry, Nico…'

She reached out, closed her fingers around his wrist, and he thought that simple touch might be his undoing.

He forced his hand to hang by his side. 'Forget it. It's over now,' he said. And he didn't mean only the storm. He watched Marietta's face, saw the flicker of understanding in her eyes.

She withdrew her hand.

'Does it have to be?' she asked after a moment.

He stared down at her. 'I told you—'

'I know what you told me,' she interrupted. Her chin lifted. 'And I'm not suggesting any kind of commitment. I'm just suggesting that maybe...once I'm back in Rome...we could see each other occasionally.'

An uncomfortable pressure built in his chest. Had he not contemplated that very arrangement just yesterday? He suppressed a humourless laugh as an even greater irony occurred to him—having Marietta on a casual basis wouldn't be anywhere close to enough.

He hardened his voice. 'I don't do relationships— casual or otherwise.'

'Why?'

Her soft challenge poked at something inside him. Something that already felt bruised. Raw. 'Don't push, Marietta,' he warned. 'I made it clear from the outset that I couldn't offer you anything more. I thought you understood.'

She rolled forward and he stepped back.

'I understand that you're afraid, Nico,' she said softly, and stopped in front of him, meeting his gaze with another firm lift of her chin. 'I understand that you've loved and lost and now you're afraid of getting close to people, afraid of caring for anyone— because if you do you might lose them.'

Nico's blood ran cold. He felt as if she'd crawled inside him. Into the darkness he tried so hard to keep hidden.

It was shocking. Exposing.

Anger rose, swift and defensive. He paced away, turned back. 'Are you calling me a coward, Marietta?' He stalked towards her. 'That's rich, coming from you.'

Marietta's head snapped back. Nico's comeback was harsh, unexpected, landing a sharp dent in her bravado. Not that her courage had been bulletproof to start with. Mustering the nerve to seek him out and talk so frankly with him after he had avoided her all afternoon hadn't been easy.

'What do you mean?' she said.

He shook his head. 'You don't see it, do you? You're so goddamned proud, so independent—you wear it like a suit of armour so that no one can get inside it.'

She stiffened. 'I've said I'm sorry about last night—'

'I'm not just talking about last night!' He cut across her, a vein pulsing in his right temple as he stared down at her. 'You accuse *me* of being afraid—'

'It wasn't an accusation!'

'But what are *you* afraid of?' he finished.

She gripped the arms of her chair, her heart hammering wildly in her chest. 'Nothing.'

'I think that you're afraid to admit you can't do everything on your own,' he carried on, as if she hadn't spoken. 'To admit that you might actually need someone.'

Her stomach twisted. His words sliced too close to the bone. Except she wasn't afraid of needing. She was afraid of *wanting*. Or was there really no difference?

She wheeled backwards, but he followed. 'You use your independence to isolate yourself,' he said. Relentless. Ruthless. On the offensive now because she'd pushed and he had warned her not to. 'To cut yourself off from what you really want.'

She balled her hands into fists. 'You don't *know* what I want—and you're a fine one to talk about isolation. This from the man who chooses to sit up here in his house all alone and wallow in his misplaced guilt.'

Fury darkened his features. 'You know nothing about my guilt.'

'Don't I?'

A fierce ache ballooned in her chest. This exchange of harsh, angry words wasn't what she'd imagined for their last night together. She dropped her shoulders, defeat and weariness washing over her. How had they ended up here? What were they *doing*? The sudden urge to retreat tugged at her, but she loved this man—too much not to serve him a final painful truth.

'I survived a car crash that killed three of my friends,' she said. 'So I *do* know something about guilt, Nico.' She paused, took a moment to choose her next words carefully. 'What happened to Julia was tragic and horrific but it wasn't your fault—and it wasn't your father-in-law's.'

His frown deepened ominously but she forced herself to finish.

'I think it's sad that you haven't spoken to each other in ten years, and while I never knew Julia I can't believe it's what she would have wanted—nor can I believe she would have wanted you to spend the rest of your life blaming yourself for not saving her.'

Nico was tight-lipped, but the emotion she knew he tried so hard to suppress swirled in his eyes.

'You need to let go of your guilt,' she said gently. 'And if you can't do it for yourself—then do it for her.'

*And for me.*

She turned her chair and wheeled away from him—before the tears threatening to overwhelm her could spill.

# CHAPTER TWELVE

THE NEXT MORNING they travelled in the helicopter from the island to the airstrip in Toulon, the entire journey conducted in tense, agonising silence.

Marietta's chest ached from the emotion she was bottling up inside. Tears threatened at regular intervals but she forced them back, determined to remain stoic. Even throughout the long night, as she'd lain alone in the guest bed, she'd refused to succumb, afraid that if the tears started to fall they might never stop.

When Nico carried her from the helicopter to the jet and lowered her into one of the soft leather seats she clung to him for a few seconds too long, desperate to imprint every detail of him onto her memory: his clean citrus scent, his hard male body, the bone-melting heat he exuded.

He straightened. 'Leo will collect you from the plane in Rome.'

She nodded; he had told her this morning that he wouldn't be travelling to Rome with her. Impulsively she reached for his wrist.

'Thank you,' she said. 'For...for keeping me safe.'

Flimsy, inadequate words—yet what more could she say? She couldn't tell him she loved him. Not when she knew she wouldn't hear those same words in return. And everything else—hurtful or otherwise—had been said the day before.

His gaze held hers for a long moment. Then he leaned down, cupped a hand around the side of her face and dropped a brief kiss on her mouth that brought those foolish tears springing into her eyes again.

'*Au revoir*, Marietta.'

And then he was gone.

A solitary tear escaped and she dashed it away, her insides twisting with the bitter irony of it all. Yesterday Nico had flung her fears in her face, and now he was validating them by walking away. Denying her the thing she wanted most. *Him*.

Twenty minutes later the powerful jet was soaring, and Marietta blinked as a glass half filled with amber liquid appeared on the table in front of her. She looked up. Evelyn stood by her chair, her mouth curved in a gentle smile.

'I know you like your coffee, but right now I figure you could do with something stronger.' She touched Marietta's shoulder. 'I'll give you some space, honey. Buzz if you need anything.'

Marietta murmured her thanks, then sniffed the drink and blinked at the eye-watering fumes. It was whisky rather than her favoured brandy, but she sipped it anyway, hoping the potent liquid would warm the cold, empty space inside her.

It didn't.


Nico swung the sledgehammer high above his head and smashed it down onto the centre of the beam. The wood split under the force of the blow and he finished the job off with the heel of his boot. The violent sound of splintering wood was gratifying, as was the burn in his muscles—the kind of burn only hard physical labour could induce.

It was almost a month since he'd been back here on Île de Lavande. After sending Marietta to Rome he had set himself a gruelling work schedule of back-to-back meetings and international travel, which had, for a time, kept him focused on work and nothing else. But in the end, no matter how deeply he buried himself in work, no matter how many meetings and travel destinations he piled into his schedule, he couldn't escape the simple truth.

He missed her.

'Nico!'

He looked up. Luc stood a few metres away, surrounded by the detritus of his family's boat shed. The storm had rendered the small building unsalvageable and the Bouchards had decided to knock down what remained and rebuild from scratch.

Nico had offered to help with the demolition. He

needed the distraction. Needed to escape the house he had once valued for its privacy and isolation but which now felt curiously empty and too silent.

'Break time,' said Luc, gesturing with a thumb over his shoulder towards the bistro. Josephine stood at the entrance to the courtyard, waving to catch the men's attention. Luc grinned and threw Nico a towel. 'Let's get cleaned up and grab a beer.'

Half an hour later the two men sat in the courtyard, along with Josephine's father Henri. Chilled bottles of lager sat on the wrought-iron table between them and appetising smells wafted from the kitchen. A middle-aged couple dined in the far corner of the courtyard and a small group of locals drank inside, but otherwise it was a quiet afternoon at the bistro.

Luc cradled his beer and tipped his chair back on two legs. 'How's Marietta?'

Nico's hand froze with the bottle halfway to his mouth. For appearance's sake he lifted it all the way and took a swig he hoped wouldn't choke him. 'Fine,' he said.

The younger man gave a couple of slow nods, exchanged a look with his *grandpère*, and then—to Nico's profound relief—switched the subject to football.

Ten minutes later Josephine dragged Luc away to help his father unload some supplies, leaving Nico alone with Henri.

The old man regarded him. 'You are troubled, *mon ami.*'

Nico tried to blank his expression. Henri might be long in the tooth but he was wise. Astute.

'I am fine,' he said.

Henri nodded slowly. 'So…you are fine… Marietta is fine…but things between you are *not* so fine, *oui*?'

Nico picked up his beer, realised the bottle was empty and put it down. He folded his arms over his chest.

'Things between us are…'

*Over. Forgotten.*

A peal of bitter laughter echoed in his head. Marietta *forgotten*? No. Far from it. She was in his mind every hour of every day, testing his resolve to forget. Only last week he'd been on the brink of flying to Rome. He'd travelled from New York to London for meetings and decided to spend the weekend at his penthouse in Paris. At the last minute he'd almost told his pilot to change the flight plan. Had entertained for a crazy moment the flawed notion that if he could have Marietta one more time, for one more night, he'd get her out of his system. His *head*.

Realising Henri was waiting for him to finish, he cast about for a suitable word and settled on, 'Complicated.'

Henri slapped his thigh and chuckled. 'Women *are* complicated, son.' He sat back, studied Nico's unsmiling face and grew serious again. 'You do not strike me as the kind of man to fear a challenge,' he said.

Nico's chest tightened. Henri's assessment of him was too generous. He feared a good many things—things Marietta had driven home to him, when she'd ruthlessly dished up a few unpalatable truths on that last night. Angry and offended, he'd accused her of labelling him a coward, but she was right. He *was* a coward. Because that night in Toulon during the storm, when he'd been out of his mind with worry, the truth of his feelings had struck with heart-stopping clarity.

He loved her—and the realisation had gripped him with unrelenting fear.

And instead of finding the strength to fight that fear he'd allowed it to control him. Had clung to his belief that loving someone again would make him weak because the fear of losing them would rule him, consume him.

But was it love that made him weak?

Or was it allowing the fear to win?

*Mon Dieu.* He had done exactly that. He had pushed Marietta away out of fear, to protect himself, and it wasn't only cowardly, it was selfish.

He swallowed. 'I have made a mistake, Henri.'

'Perhaps you should tell her that.'

Nico stood. *'Oui,'* he said, his thoughts clear, his mind focusing for the first time in weeks. 'But first there is someone I must see.'

* * *

The Georgian mansion nestled in the heart of the sprawling Hudson Valley estate was unchanged from the way Nico remembered it, its distinguished brick façade with its shuttered windows, columned portico and black front door as pristine and imposing as ever. The lawns were still manicured, the gardens meticulously kept, and as he walked up the white-painted steps to the door Nico's hands felt as clammy as they had the first time Julia had brought him here.

Before he could knock, the door opened and Barbara Lewisham stood before him.

A fist clamped tight around Nico's heart. Julia and her mother had always looked alike, both of them blonde and petite in size. Barbara's genteel face was older now, and lined with the remnants of grief, but still she reminded him of his late wife.

He braced himself, unsure of how his former mother-in-law would receive him in person. He had called ahead and, despite her obvious shock, she had been civil, polite to him over the phone. But then Barbara had always been a woman of manners and natural reserve. Even at her daughter's funeral she'd held her emotions in check.

She looked up at him and for a moment he thought her grey eyes glittered with anger. Then she stepped forward, took his hands in hers, and he realised it was tears making her eyes shimmer.

'Nico…' she said, her smile tremulous. 'It is so good to see you.'

The genuine warmth she conveyed threw him. He'd expected coolness from her at best. Hostility at worst. They hadn't spoken much in the days leading up to Julia's funeral, or afterwards. He'd assumed that she shared her husband's view of things. Had he been wrong?

'And you, Barbara,' he said.

She led him into the grand foyer and closed the door. 'Jack's in the study.'

'You told him I was coming?'

'He's expecting you.' She gestured towards the wood-panelled hallway that Nico remembered led to Jack Lewisham's study. 'Go ahead.'

The door was closed when he got there—which was not, he thought, a particularly welcoming sign. He took a deep, even breath, knocked once and entered.

'Hello, Jack.'

Jack Lewisham turned from the window where he stood across the room, and Nico kept his expression impassive as he registered the physical changes time had wrought in the man. He was still tall—six foot—and broad-shouldered, but the deep lines scoring his face and the grey streaking his hair made him look as if he'd aged twenty years rather than ten.

He didn't stride forward to shake Nico's hand. Instead he nodded a silent greeting, walked across the Persian rug to an antique sideboard and poured whisky from a crystal decanter into two cut-glass tumblers.

He took the glasses to a small table set between two deep leather chairs, and finally spoke. 'Will you join me?'

The invitation was stiff, the words wooden, and yet more polite than Nico had expected. Wary, his palms still clammy, he crossed the room and sat down.

Jack sipped his whisky. 'I see your company is doing well.'

Nico picked up his glass, inclined his head. 'It is.' He paused, then added, 'I'm not here to talk about my company, Jack.'

The older man eyed him for a long moment. He took a larger slug of whisky. 'I tried to talk her out of marrying you, you know.'

'I'm aware,' Nico said flatly.

'As a kid, she always had a thing for strays.'

Nico slammed his glass onto the table and stood. *Dieu.* What insanity had brought him here? He turned and started towards the door.

'Nico.'

Jack's voice halted him. He turned back. The man was on his feet, his mouth set in a grim line.

'I apologise,' Jack said hoarsely. 'It wasn't what I meant to say. Please…' He ran his hand through his hair. 'Stay.'

Nico hesitated, tension vibrating in every muscle, his gut churning with anger and indecision. After a moment he walked back, sat again.

'Thank you,' Jack said, lowering himself to the edge of his chair. He rested his elbows on his knees, scrubbed a hand over his face before speaking again. 'Julia had a good heart, is what I was trying to say. And she was smart—an excellent judge of character.' He paused, looked Nico in the eye. 'Despite my reservations in the beginning it didn't take me long to realise she'd chosen a good man.'

Emotion punched through Nico's chest, so swift and powerful his lungs were left airless for a moment.

'Losing her was the worst thing that had ever happened to me,' Jack went on. 'I didn't know how to handle it. The anger, the grief…' He bowed his head. 'I blamed you, but it was my fault…*my* fault,' he repeated, his voice bleak, filled with self-loathing. 'I was arrogant, stupid—'

He broke off, his body heaving with a sob that seemed torn from him, and Nico instinctively reached over, gripped the man's shoulder.

'You tried to save her,' he said. 'We both did—and we failed. But we are not to blame for her death. That responsibility lies with the men who took her.'

And for the first time in ten years, he truly believed that.

Jack looked up, his eyes deeply shadowed, his

face ravaged by years of grief and self-recrimination. 'I don't know how to move beyond it.'

Nico firmed his grip on Jack's shoulder. 'You have to let go of the guilt,' he said, his throat thickening as Marietta's voice echoed in his head.

Jack nodded and they sat in silence for a moment. And then they talked—until the whisky decanter was nearly empty and the shadows outside had lengthened across the manicured lawns.

Barbara ventured in to ask Nico if he would stay for supper. He accepted, and then excused himself to place a call.

Though it was already evening, his assistant at his New York office answered on the first ring.

'I need to travel on the jet out of LaGuardia first thing tomorrow,' he said.

'Yes, sir. Destination?'

'Rome.'

Marietta stared at the printout of the ultrasound image and felt all the same emotions she'd experienced the *first* time Helena and Leo had announced they were expecting: joy, excitement, happiness, and envy.

That last one she tried not to feel too keenly.

'Oh, Helena!' She leaned forward in her chair and threw her arms around her sister-in-law. 'I'm so happy for you. A little sister or brother for Riccardo.'

Helena hugged her back. 'I know—I'm so excited.'

Marietta was thrilled for her brother and his wife. They deserved every happiness. Their road to love had been rocky, and eight years ago their first child—an unplanned baby—had been stillborn. The tragedy had affected both of them deeply, even though Leo hadn't learnt about his son until some years after the event.

Ridiculously, her eyes began to prickle.

Helena looked at her. 'Marietta—what's wrong?'

'Nothing. I'm happy for you, that's all.'

She blinked the tears back and forced a smile. She'd left Île de Lavande over a month ago and still she was an emotional wreck. She needed to pull herself together, get back to being her old self, and yet she'd started to suspect with an awful sinking sensation in her stomach that her 'old self' was long gone and wasn't ever coming back.

Because her 'old self' would have celebrated the lucrative commission she'd recently landed with a night out with friends, instead of sitting at home alone with a glass of brandy and the DVD of a silly romantic movie—and, worse, *crying* over that movie.

Her 'old self' would have gone about her day with her usual vigour and would *not* have felt her heart surge every time she saw a tall dark-haired man, only to feel it shrink again when she realised it wasn't him.

Her 'old self' would have noticed the black vehicles with their tinted windows and the occasional watchful man in the shadows and felt outraged, instead of feeling her heart swell with the knowledge that he was still protecting her, from a distance.

And her 'old self' definitely *wouldn't* be sitting here feeling envious of her sister-in-law, wishing she had a handsome husband and children of her own to shower with love and affection.

Helena was still looking at her and she slipped her sunglasses on. They were sitting in the landscaped garden at Leo and Helena's Tuscan villa, enjoying the late morning sun and some 'girl time' while Leo entertained Ricci indoors. Autumn had arrived but the days were still warm, and the air carried the fragrance of flowers and fruits from the neighbouring orchards. Marietta had travelled up for the weekend, hoping a change of scenery would lift her mood.

'How far along are you?' she asked.

'Ten weeks.' Helena frowned. 'You know, you haven't seemed like yourself since you came back from the island.'

Marietta tried to keep her smile intact but the very worst thing happened—her lips quivered.

'Oh, Marietta.' Helena reached for her hand. 'What is it? Tell me.'

'I slept with Nico,' she blurted out, because she simply couldn't keep it secret any longer. She needed to talk about it with someone or she'd lose her mind. She stared at her sister-in-law, waiting for the look of shock. Of censure.

'Well,' said Helena, 'I can't say I'm surprised.'

Marietta's jaw slackened. 'You're not?'

'No. I'm not.' She let go of Marietta's hand and refilled their glasses from a pitcher of homemade lemonade on the table. 'I saw the way he looked at you on my wedding day, Marietta.' She picked up her glass, sat back and smiled. 'He couldn't take his eyes off you.'

Marietta frowned. She remembered Nico from the wedding day. He'd been impossible to miss. Aside from her brother he'd been the tallest man there, and by far the most eye-catching in his tux. But she'd taken one dry-mouthed look at his powerful body and his chiselled features, reminded herself that men like him were out of her league, and then steadfastly kept her gaze off him.

'I take it things didn't end well?' Helena said gently.

Marietta shook her head. 'I ended up wanting more than he could give.'

Helena exhaled on a sigh. 'Don't tell me he's one of those men who's allergic to commitment.'

'He's a widower,' she said, and this time her sister-in-law's face *did* register shock.

'I had no idea.'

'Leo doesn't know?'

'If he does he's never said anything. I'm guessing Nico has some issues, then?'

'A few.'

She wanted to share more with Helena, but Nico was an intensely private man and talking about his past—particularly the gruesome story of his wife's death—felt wrong. And then Leo appeared, carrying Ricci in his arms, and the little boy gurgled and squealed when he saw his mother.

Helena stood to take him, and he squealed again when she blew a raspberry kiss on his plump rosy cheek.

Leo put his hand to his wife's back, said something in her ear. Helena looked at Marietta and frowned. Her mouth opened, but Leo cut her off with a few quietly spoken words and then urged her indoors. Helena resisted, gave her husband a stern look and walked back to Marietta.

'I'll be right inside if you need me,' she said, squeezing Marietta's shoulder, and then she took Ricci into the house.

Confused, Marietta looked to her brother.

'Nico's here,' he said without preamble. 'He wants to see you.'

Her brain stalled. Nico was *here?* She blinked, trying to process the fact. 'How did he know where I was?'

'He called me and I told him.'

'Why didn't you say anything?'

'Because he asked me not to. And, frankly, he sounded…desperate.' Leo scowled. 'Do you want to tell me what the hell is going on, Marietta?'

She pulled in a deep breath, her heart pounding. 'Not particularly.'

A muscle flexed in her brother's jaw.

'Do you wish to see him?'

She hesitated. Briefly. *'Si,'* she said, and instantly her stomach quivered.

Leo strode into the house and a minute later Nico emerged. He walked towards her, smart and handsome in black trousers and a grey button-down shirt, his strong jaw clean-shaven, his dark hair cropped short. Her heart somersaulted. How could he look so good, so *unchanged*, when she felt so fundamentally altered? It wasn't fair.

*'Bonjour,* Marietta.'

His deep voice washed over her and just like that, with a few velvety syllables, all the heartache of the last month was swept away by a surge of heat and longing she was helpless to prevent.

*'Buongiorno,* Nico,' she managed, her voice cool. Composed. Silently she congratulated herself. No need for him to see how he affected her.

He gestured to the seat Helena had vacated. 'May I?'

She nodded, and he moved the chair closer to her before he sat. His proximity made her skin tingle. Her pulse race.

'I've missed you.'

Her insides clenched on another surge of longing. *I've missed you too*, she wanted to say.

'Did you come all the way to Tuscany to tell me you missed me, Nico?'

The corners of his mouth tilted, as though he were amused, and she wished he wouldn't smile. It weakened her.

'I did,' he said simply.

And that made her eyes sting, because she wanted so very badly to believe him.

Suddenly he moved, reaching towards her, and before she could stop him he'd pulled her sunglasses off her face.

His gaze narrowed. 'You don't believe me, *ma petite sirène?*'

'Please don't call me that.'

'Why not?'

*Did he really need to ask?*

'Nico, please…just tell me why you're here.'

He hesitated. 'I'd like to take you somewhere.'

'Where?'

'It's a surprise.'

Her stomach fluttered. 'I don't like surprises.'

'Please,' he said, and she heard the distinct note of uncertainty, of vulnerability, in his voice.

It weakened her.

Still, she made him wait a few seconds more. 'Okay,' she said at last, and his features relaxed a fraction.

He stood. 'Do you trust me, *chérie*?'

She nodded, because she did. She had always

trusted him and she always would. All the same, she wasn't expecting him to do what he did next—which was to lean down and scoop her out of her chair.

'Nico!' she exclaimed.

He carried her through the garden and round the side of the villa to the courtyard out front. A large black vehicle was waiting, a man dressed in black standing beside it. He opened the rear passenger door and Nico slid her into the back seat, closed the door, and a few seconds later climbed in beside her from the opposite side. He rapped on the dark glass partition that separated them from the driver and the vehicle started to move.

Nico reached across her—to strap the seatbelt over her, she assumed. But he hauled her into his lap.

'Nico—'

He kissed her, and shamefully, wantonly, she made no effort to resist. Instead she surrendered, snaking her arms around his neck and kissing him back.

It was a hot, hungry meeting of lips, and when they finally broke apart he was breathing hard. His large hands cradled her face, his blue eyes heated and glittering. '*Mon Dieu*, I missed you.'

Marietta trembled. 'Nico,' she pleaded. 'Tell me what's going on.'

He pressed his forehead to hers, the gesture so sweet that her chest flooded with tenderness and something else. Something she was too afraid to acknowledge.

'I don't know where to start,' he said.

'Start at the beginning,' she said softly.

He nodded, and took a deep breath. 'The morning after the storm, when I got back to the house and found the shattered window and you nowhere in sight, it was like Julia all over again—arriving home, finding her gone… I couldn't breathe… couldn't think…'

Marietta's throat ached. She laid her hand along the side of his face. 'I'm so sorry for putting you through that,' she whispered.

He placed his hand over hers, turned his head and kissed her palm, then tucked her hand against his chest and held it there.

'Losing her inflicted wounds I thought would never heal, and I was determined to never feel that pain again. To never feel that sense of loss and devastation.'

He fell silent. Marietta waited.

'You were right, *chérie*. I was afraid. Afraid to care for someone. Afraid to love again. But then…' He gave her a crooked smile. 'You came along.'

A jolt of warmth, of hope, went through her.

'And you were right about something else,' he said. 'I needed to deal with my guilt—confront the past.' He paused. 'I went to see Jack.'

Her eyes widened. 'And…?'

He grimaced. 'It wasn't easy, but we talked. Laid some demons to rest.'

'Oh, Nico… I'm so proud of you.'

'Don't be.' His mouth flattened. 'I pushed you away, and that's nothing to be proud of. I told myself it was the logical thing to do but it was logic driven by fear—a weak man's excuse.'

She frowned. 'You're *not* weak,' she declared. 'And you're not the only one who's been driven by fear.'

Nico shook his head. 'I shouldn't have said—'

She pressed her fingers to his lips. 'But you were right. I isolated myself, just like you did—but in a different way and for different reasons. I was afraid, too. Afraid of wanting what I couldn't have.'

Nico took hold of her slender fingers and kissed their tips one by one. He loved this woman. When he'd walked down that garden path and caught his first glimpse of her—beautiful in a simple white top and long skirt, her glorious hair flowing loose over her shoulders—he'd thought his chest might implode.

'And what *do* you want, *ma belle?*'

'You,' she said, a fierce light shining in her eyes.

He cupped her face in his hands. 'Marietta Vincenti, will you do me the honour of letting me love you?'

Tears welled in her eyes. She placed her hands over his. 'If you'll do me the honour of letting *me* love *you*.'

The car stopped and he kissed her, briefly, but with enough intensity to let her know there'd be more to come.

'I love you,' he said.

Then he lowered the window and pointed towards the middle of the large meadow by which they'd stopped. She blinked, and her eyes widened as she saw a fully inflated, brightly coloured hot air balloon.

'Will you come fly with me, *chérie*?'

Her mouth stretched into a grin. 'I thought you said hot air balloons are dangerous.'

He'd also said it would be a frosty day in hell when he flew in one. Well…today hell was having a cold snap.

A short while later the 'oversized picnic basket'—as Nico was fond of calling it—lifted off the ground. Marietta felt like a child. Breathless, giddy, excited. Or maybe like a woman in love. She sat on a special stool, high enough to enjoy the stunning view of the Tuscan countryside, with Nico's arms circling her from behind, his chest solid and warm against her back.

She jumped at the sudden loud whoosh as the pilot fired the burner, and Nico's hold tightened.

'I've got you, *chérie*.'

She smiled up at him. 'I know. I've got you, too.'

*For ever.*

# EPILOGUE

'*PAPÀ! PAPÀ!*'

A flash of pink and lime-green hurtled through the doorway of the study.

Nico swivelled his chair around. 'Amélie, don't run in the—*oomph!*'

His six-year-old daughter catapulted herself into his lap, and the moment she grinned up at him he forgot to finish scolding her. He closed his arms around her wriggling body and grinned back.

Amélie was a brown-eyed, dark-haired mini-version of her mother, and too damned adorable to stay cross with for very long—even when she pushed his patience to its limits. Which she did—frequently—because she'd inherited not only Marietta's beauty but a good deal of her stubbornness as well.

'Can we go to the beach now, Papa?'

And, like her mother, she loved to swim in the sea.

'In a bit, *ma petite sirène*.'

Her little lips formed a pout that was no doubt designed to weaken her *papà*. 'But I want to go *now*. Enzo's already there, with Remy. Why can't I go down the steps by myself like they can?'

'Because they are older and bigger.'

The tiny scowl on her face looked a lot like the one her mother occasionally wore when Nico earned her disapproval. Fortunately for him, those occasions were rare—and he always enjoyed it when they made up afterwards.

He scooted his daughter off his lap. 'Go and help *Maman* prepare the picnic hamper.'

He watched his daughter fly out of the room. Her energy was boundless, and these days it seemed she was incapable of *walking* anywhere. Enzo, his ten-year-old son, had gone through a similar stage, which had included climbing anything in sight that looked remotely scaleable.

Nico had been convinced he was destined for heart failure—especially in those first few years of parenting. On the day his son had been born he'd known fierce pride and elation, but also a sort of quiet terror. A fear that he would somehow fail to protect this tiny life in a world increasingly fraught with danger and risk.

Marietta had known. Whether she'd seen something in his face or simply sensed his inner turmoil, she had understood. And she had talked him down. Helped him to wrestle his fear into something less daunting, more controllable. And as their son had grown, she had insisted they did not wrap him in cotton wool. Had insisted that their son be allowed to experience the world. To grow up as safely as possible, yet with an understanding of risk and consequence.

It was Marietta, too, who had convinced him they should have a second child. Nico had been hesitant after her first pregnancy. Blood pressure problems and other issues related to her paralysis had dogged her from the second trimester onwards. He had watched her struggle with long months of enforced bed rest and vowed he wouldn't see her suffer like that again.

But she was resilient, and strong, and she'd set her heart on a little sister or brother for Enzo. And his wife had, of course, proved very persuasive in bed...

Nico closed his laptop. He had cleared enough emails and reports for today. Marietta growled if he spent too much time working during their family vacations on Île de Lavande.

He stood and his gaze caught, as it sometimes did, on the antique rolltop desk in the corner of the study.

Julia's ghost had been laid to rest many years before. Very occasionally the darkness and the guilt would stir in some deep corner of his soul, but the emotions never lasted for long—not in the face of the light and the laughter that his children and his wife brought to his world. He'd considered at one point getting rid of the desk, but Marietta had convinced him not to and he was glad she had.

He found his girls in the kitchen. Amélie launched herself into his arms again and he lifted her up.

'Now, Papa? Can we go *now?*'

He looked to Marietta and felt the familiar jolt in his blood. Her hair, still long and lustrous, was pulled into a ponytail and she wore a sarong and a crimson bikini top, ready for the beach. Into her forties now, she was as beautiful as ever—and she still made his body hum with desire.

'Are you finished with your little helper?'

She wheeled back from one of the low marble benches they'd had specially installed for her and smiled. '*Si*. And the hamper's ready. Take Amélie and the basket down—and don't forget to come back for your wife.'

He slid a hand around the back of her head and dropped a quick kiss on her teasing mouth. 'Funny, Mrs César.'

She grinned and his heart expanded—and he wondered, not for the first time over the years, how his chest could feel so full and yet so incredibly, amazingly light.

Marietta lay on a towel on the sand with her eyes closed, enjoying the sun on her face and the sound of her husband and children playing in the ocean. Nico had already taken her in for a swim and she was content now to relax and let the kids frolic under his watchful eye.

This was her reality now. The one that in the early years of her marriage she had secretly feared wasn't reality at all, but a fantastical dream of some sort. A great big bubble of joy that would sooner or later burst and send her crashing back to her *real* life.

But the bubble hadn't burst. It had only grown bigger and stronger—like her love for her husband— and eventually she'd stopped waiting on tenterhooks for the fairy tale to end and allowed herself to truly enjoy the life she'd never thought she'd have.

She smiled at the sound of Amélie's high-pitched squeal and guessed her *papà* was throwing her into the air. She could hear the boys too. Her son and Remy Bouchard—Luc's son—were firm friends, and Remy usually stayed with them for a few nights when they vacationed here.

She could not believe she and Nico had been married for almost thirteen years. They had finally settled in Paris, and they lived there in a beautiful home they'd renovated and fully modified for her wheelchair. They'd sold her apartment in Rome, but retained Nico's apartments in London, New York and Singapore, all of which he used when travelling for work.

Marietta happily divided her time between motherhood and her art career, which had flourished in the early years of their marriage and continued to keep her busy now, with several lucrative commissions each year.

She heard Nico's deep voice telling Enzo to watch his sister and then her son's obedient response. She smiled again. Enzo was becoming more like his father every day—serious and intense—but he also had a strong streak of curiosity about the world which showed he had something of his mother in him.

'What are you smiling about, *chérie*?'

She looked up through her sunglasses at her husband and her stomach clenched, because he was still the most magnificent man she knew. Dripping wet, he stretched out on a towel beside her and she marvelled at how hard and toned his body had remained over the years. Physically, he really hadn't changed. A few distinguished-looking grey hairs at his temples and some deeper lines on his face due to his secretly worrying about his wife and children, but otherwise he looked the same.

And he still loved her—as fiercely and passionately as he had in the beginning.

'I was just thinking,' she said, tracing her index finger along the strong line of his jaw, 'that Enzo is very much like his *papà*.'

Nico grinned—and she melted. She always did when her husband smiled at her.

His chest puffed out. 'But of course. He is good-looking, intelligent, irresistible—'

She slapped her hand over his mouth. 'And lacking in modesty!'

Her took her hand and pressed a kiss into her palm. 'And our daughter is very much like her *maman*.'

'*Si*. Beautiful, talented—'

'Stubborn, wilful—and her wish list is already longer than her mother's was!'

She laughed. 'A girl needs to dream.'

And yet her own wish list was practically non-existent now, because she had everything she could possibly want—and more.

All the things that had originally been on her list had been ticked off early in their marriage, before they'd started trying for children. Nico had taken her to Egypt to see the pyramids and the Valley of the Kings, and the trip had been magical—despite a team of his security men shadowing them everywhere they went. They'd gone up in a hot air balloon again—on their honeymoon—and eventually, after much persistence on her part, he'd agreed to her doing a tandem skydive. But not before he'd vetted the skydiving company and warned the operator that if anything happened to his wife he would personally throw the man out of a plane *without* his parachute.

The only things she wished for now were health and happiness for her family.

She looked at Nico, propped on his elbow, staring down at her. 'And why are *you* smiling, *tesoro mio*?'

He trailed a fingertip over her bare belly, inciting a flurry of goosebumps on her skin. 'Because I've arranged for Luc to collect the children in an hour's time and take them to his place for the night.'

A hot spark of anticipation ignited in her belly. She arched an eyebrow. 'And what will you do then?'

'Then, *ma belle*,' he said, his blue eyes smouldering, 'I will spend the night showing my wife how much I love her.'

\* \* \* \* \*

Keep reading for an excerpt of a new title
from the Modern series,
UNWRAPPED BY HER ITALIAN BOSS
by Michelle Smart

# CHAPTER ONE

MERRY INGLES STOMPED her way through the freshly laid snow from her chalet, tugging her woolly hat over the cold lobes of her ears as she went. The thick clouds that had obscured the stars overnight had cleared, leaving the skies above the Swiss Alps crisp and blue and with a sharp chill that fogged the breath. Further up the mountain, the Hotel Haensli rose like a beautiful majestic overlord peering down on its minions. In three years of working and living there, Merry had never lost the awe of her daily morning glimpse.

Ten minutes after setting out, and looking forward to the hot chocolate that would warm her frozen cheeks, she spotted a porter wrestling a huge netted Christmas tree that would be added to the twenty-four ornately decorated trees already placed throughout the hotel's ground floor.

'Want a hand?' she called, upping her pace.

Johann, one of the groundsmen who'd been tasked with chopping the huge Nordmann Firs the hotel grew specially for the festive period, put the base of the tree down and waited for her to catch up, a relieved smile on his face.

'You are a lifesaver,' he said. 'I need to get this to the spa lounge before it opens to the guests. Ricardo was supposed to help me.'

Up close, Merry's practised eye estimated the tree to be a good fifteen foot. Her nose wrinkled as she contemplated it.

They agreed that Johann would lead the way and in unison lifted the tree onto their shoulders. It was much lighter than she'd expected but the foot in height difference between them meant it slanted at a steep angle. Although her gloves prevented the stray pine needles poking through the netting from scratching her hands, to keep it stable she pressed her cheek to it and tried to ignore the scratching against her cheek and spectacles.

More through blind luck—and blind really was the operative word as Merry's hat sloped down and dislodged her glasses and she couldn't see anything past a blurry Johann—they manoeuvred the tree through the double doors of the staff entrance at the rear. Pausing to stamp snow off their boots and readjust their load, they then navigated their way down the long, wide corridor running the other side of the hotel's huge reception. By the time they reached the double doors that led into the spa, Merry's glasses had fallen down her nose again and were in danger of falling off her face.

'Hold on a sec,' she said, resting the base of the tree down. Hugging it tightly with one arm, she shoved her glasses back up with her free hand and tugged the zip of her snow jacket down a little. Wrapped up as she was, the hotel's warmth was stifling. Not wanting pine needles stuck in her hair, she kept her hat on.

'Ready?' Johann asked.

'Ready.'

'One, two, three…'

They lifted it back onto their shoulders. Johann opened the door. As he did, he twisted his body, forcing Merry to twist too, to keep the tree stable. She had no idea anyone was behind her until she felt a thud followed by a gasp of pain.

'Sugar! I'm sorry!' Setting the tree's base back on the floor, she turned to apologise to her victim, praying it was a member of staff she'd just accidentally bashed.

The tall man in an obviously bespoke navy-blue suit, handsome face wincing in pain as he rubbed his shoulder, was most definitely not staff.

'I'm so sorry,' she said, mortified at what she'd done. 'Are you badly hurt?'

Furious dark blue eyes ringed with dark lashes she'd give a kidney for set above cheekbones she'd give the other kidney for were fixed on her.

Repeating herself in German, she braced herself. There would be hell to pay for this. Only the super-rich and powerful could afford to stay at Hotel Haensli, and in exchange for the astronomical sums they paid for the privilege of staying in such a luxurious setting with some of the best views in the whole of Switzerland, they expected exemplary service. They did not expect to be clouted by a Christmas tree.

Giovanni Cannavaro stared at the horrified bright red face half hidden by a thick scarf, glasses askew and topped with the most ridiculous hat he'd ever seen worn by an adult. His flare of anger at being hit by a hated Christmas tree dissolved as he found himself smothering an extremely rare and extremely unexpected bubble of mirth.

It was also an extremely short bubble of mirth. He stepped towards the woman. 'Move.'

'What?'

'I will carry it for you.'

'But…but…you can't.'

'You hit me and now you tell me what I can do?'

What he could see of the tiny woman's red face instinctively recoiled in alarm at his words.

'I didn't…'

He pointed with his thumb to where the front of the tree was trapped in the door.

'You get the door,' he said, overriding her protest before nodding at the groundsman he suspected was trying to make himself invisible. 'I am tall, like him. Is easier. And safer,' he added pointedly.

She scuttled to open the door and pressed herself tightly against the wall as the two men carried it past her.

'All done,' Giovanni said when they'd placed it in the stand and the netting had been removed. He flicked stray pine needles from his shoulders and nodded at the two hotel employees. 'Next time, more careful, *si*?'

Then, in need of food and a cappuccino before he solved the mess that had seen him fly to Switzerland in the early hours, Giovanni strode to the breakfast room.

'Sorry I'm late,' Merry said as she hurried into the office she shared with her boss and Sasha, the other member of the hospitality team, only to find the room empty.

While she waited for Katja to come back from wherever she was—her computer was on, so she'd obviously been in—Merry put a hot chocolate pod in the snazzy machine and booted her computer up.

Where the rest of the hotel had been transformed into a Christmas wonderland, their office was devoid of decoration. Mostly. Merry had stuck a small plastic tree filled with tiny baubles on the corner of her desk and wrapped her monitor in tinsel. Katja had rolled her eyes at it, just as she'd rolled them when she'd seen Merry in her red woolly hat that had Rudolph the Red-Nosed Reindeer knitted into it.

She was finishing her hot chocolate and replying to emails when Katja finally hurried through the door, her face creased with worry. 'There you are. You're needed in the meeting room. We have a situation.'

Merry jumped to her feet. 'What kind of situation?'

'Everything will be explained... What's wrong with your face? Have you scratched it?'

'Pine needles. I helped Johann carry a Christmas tree to the spa.' She felt her scratched cheeks flame again, remembering how she'd accidentally bashed one of their esteemed guests with it. Another roll of dread played in her belly. The guest had taken it relatively well, all things considered, but she'd known staff to be sacked for less, and thought it best not to mention the incident to her boss.

That didn't stop the image of the guest's handsome face pinging back into her mind. He truly was gorgeous. Greek god handsome. Hair so dark it was almost black. Long straight nose. Chiselled jaw. And those lashes. Those *cheekbones*...

'That's why I was late. I couldn't let him struggle on his own,' she added as they strode down the corridor and she shoved Cheekbones from her mind. With any luck, she'd be able to avoid him for the rest of his stay there.

'I know,' Katja said tightly. 'You like to help people. That's why I chose you, remember?'

Merry had spent her first two years in Switzerland working as a waitress at Hotel Haensli, thrilled to have landed such a prestigious job in one of the world's top hotels. A year ago she'd been summoned by the management. Terrified she was about to be fired, she'd almost fallen off her chair when Katja, the Head of Hospitality, announced she was in need of a new assistant and wanted to offer Merry the role. Katja had read through the hotel guest book and online reviews and been impressed at how many times Merry's name was mentioned in them as someone who went above and beyond her duties. Returning guests often insisted she serve their table.

Overnight, Merry went from split shifts of six a.m. starts and midnight finishes to eight a.m. starts and, unless they had special evening events on, four p.m. finishes for double her waitressing salary. The job even came with its own two-bed chalet. No more sharing staff quarters with fifteen others! A career path had opened up for her and she was delighted to follow it.

The woman who'd made all this happen for her, Katja, hesitated at the staff meeting room door. 'Just…just think what this could do for your future, okay?'

And with those enigmatic words, Katja opened the door.

Seated at the oval table was Hotel Haensli's elderly owner, Wolfgang Merkel. The automatic smile of greeting on Merry's face froze when she saw the man beside him.

It was Cheekbones. The man she'd clobbered with the Christmas tree.

Heat flushed through her body like a wave. White noise filled her ears.

She, Merry, was the situation and she was about to be fired.

The noise in her head was so deafening that when Cheekbones rose from his chair and extended his hand to her, it took an embarrassingly long time for it to penetrate her brain that Katja had introduced him and she'd not heard a word of it.

Tremors raced through her fingers as she reached her hand across the table to her executioner.

It was the clumsy lady with the crazy hat. Giovanni, heart sinking, recognised her immediately. The large tortoiseshell spectacles gave her away. So did the horrified, gormless expression on her face.

A small hand and short fingers folded around

his just long enough for a brisk shake that sent an unexpected flash of heat through his skin. Disconcerted, he observed the movement of her slender throat, the flash of baby blue behind the spectacles and the flush of colour staining her rounded cheeks, and cast an idle sweep of his eyes over a body no longer bundled up in outdoor clothing.

Petite. A trim figure hidden beneath the hotel's standard black administrative uniform. Golden hair scraped back in a neat bun. Clear complexion. No make-up. Reasonably attractive without the stupid hat. How ridiculous had that been? He was quite sure Sofia, the younger of his sisters, had worn a similar one when she'd been a child.

Which of the Fates, he wondered grimly, had he angered that they would task this woman with rescuing the project he'd spent three years of hard work and planning on? The whole things was a cigarette paper away from being ruined and his hard-won reputation with it.

Twelve years ago, when his world had collapsed, Giovanni had left Italy and ended up in this very hotel. He'd worked as a porter until, months after starting there, the hotel owner had sought him out and, after a long chat, offered him a job as his assistant.

Overnight he'd become Wolfgang Merkel's protégé, had soaked up the man's knowledge of luxury and refinement and the art of giving the rich exactly what they wanted so they kept returning year after year. A year later, he'd received a small bequest from his grandfather's will and, with Wolfgang's blessing and good wishes, had left to form his own company, Cannavaro Travel.

In the decade since, his business had gone from strength to strength and Giovanni had joined that elite class, amassing riches beyond his wildest dreams. Luxury cruises, private yacht hire, private plane hire, road trips across continents, sumptuous hotels…his company specialised in all those things. Cannavaro Travel had become a byword for excellence and, with Wolfgang's wise words forever playing in his ear, he never let standards drop for a second.

He'd never doubted his mentor's judgement before but, staring at the woman Wolfgang considered capable of stepping in and saving the day, he worried for his old friend's mental faculties.

He waited until she'd taken the chair next to Katja before addressing her. 'Katja has explained the situation?'

She shook her head.

'Gerhard was taken to hospital last night. He has the…' He scrambled for the English word.

'Appendicitis,' Katja supplied.

Merry's hand was tingling so much from Cheekbones' handshake that she had to clamp her other one over it to muffle the sensation.

'Gerhard...?' The name rang a bell in her flushed mind and she tried hard to bring herself back to the present.

'Gerhard Klose. The man I've been training to run hospitality for the Meravaro Odyssey,' Katja explained.

Comprehension flooded her and she practically sagged with relief.

Cheekbones wasn't here to get her fired. He must be part of Cannavaro Travel.

He looked at her unsmiling. 'Now you understand the situation, *si*?'

Oh, yes, she understood.

Wolfgang Merkel had agreed to a collaboration with his good friend, the luxury travel specialist Giovanni Cannavaro. The two men, under Giovanni's direction, had spent the past three years partnering on a brand-new train service, one that would take their guests through Europe's most picturesque cities and landscapes directly to the train station a few miles from the hotel. The maiden journey departed in three days.

This wasn't just a maiden voyage. This was the social event of the year. Eighty of the world's richest and most powerful people would board the Meravaro Odyssey in Paris for a festive voyage of unsurpassed splendour. When, after two nights of glamour on board, the train the world's press were chomping at the bit to review finally arrived at Klosters train station, horse-drawn carriages would take its passengers to the hotel, giving them two days to luxuriate before the annual Hotel Haensli Christmas party. The party the world's elite would sell their kidneys for a ticket to.

As Katja had spent a decade working on the luxury train that had been made eternally famous in an enduringly popular crime book, she'd been tasked with imparting her wealth of knowledge to the gentleman hired to run hospitality on the Cannavaro Odyssey: the appendicitis-struck Gerhard. The role was simple—to ensure all guests had the experience of their lives and that all their whims, reasonable or otherwise, were catered for.

For Katja, training Gerhard had been a nightmare. Giovanni Cannavaro had insisted on frequent detailed reports about Gerhard's progress. Katja had been under no illusion that if the man failed in any way, her own head would be for the chopping block.

'Are you stepping in for Gerhard?' Merry asked her immediate boss, a wave of sympathy rushing through her for being shoehorned into a temporary role that might be a poisoned chalice.

Katja shook her head. 'Angie's on a week-long business trip in Frankfurt.' Angie was Katja's wife. They had a six-year-old daughter.

'Sasha?'

'She needs to be here for the Voegel wedding.' Katja's eyes were wide with apology. 'I'm sorry, Merry, but you're going to have to step in. There's no one else.'

Her chest turned cold. The white noise that had filled her ears at the sight of Cheekbones was now replaced with the drumbeats of doom.

Merry was working over Christmas and the New Year. Her new sister-in-law, determined to bring the Ingles family together, had insisted on hosting an early Christmas dinner for them to celebrate together. That dinner was in two days. Merry was flying home to England for it tomorrow.

No wonder Katja had been so uptight when she'd brought her into the meeting room. Katja knew all this. Knew how hard Merry had worked to ensure her diary was clear for her visit home.

It was ironic, really, considering Merry had been dreading going home. Thanks to her brother's hatred of it, the Ingles had barely marked the Christmas period since Merry was eight, but now he wanted to make his new wife happy and had badgered and bullied and emotionally blackmailed Merry for weeks, until she'd submitted and agreed to go.

On top of that, the day after the dinner her oldest and closest friend Santa was flying back to Switzerland with her for a long-planned stay in Merry's cabin.

She couldn't do it. Couldn't let her sister-in-law down. Couldn't let Santa down.

'You'll fly to Paris first thing in the morning,' Katja said, breaking the tense silence. 'The guests aren't due to board for three days, so you'll have two full days to iron out any potential issues and get to know the staff and the workings and everything.'

Wolfgang finally spoke, the first time in three years he'd addressed Merry directly. 'Katja tells me you are supposed to be on leave tomorrow. You will receive an extra paid week's leave in the New Year to make up for the time you are missing.'

This was a done deal, Merry realised with rising trepidation. No wonder Katja had warned her to consider her future before they entered the room.

Wolfgang Merkel paid generously, and gave perks that far exceeded the industry norm, but in return he expected complete dedication. He expected his staff to rally together in a time of crisis. The man was generous, but ruthless.

As Merry didn't have a six-year-old child who'd be left without care like Katja did, she had no reasonable excuse to say no. Saying, *But I haven't seen my family in six months and, much as the thought of spending a day with them creating a fake early Christmas fills me with dread,*

*I've made a promise*, would cut no ice but would certainly affect her future.

Even if she'd wanted to say any of those words, the moment was lost when Wolfgang groped for his walking stick and got to his feet. 'Now that everything is in hand, I will leave you to sort the details.'

Katja did likewise, minus the walking stick. Her stare was full of sympathy. 'I'll transfer the files to you while you two get acquainted.'

And then, while Merry was still trying to think of a way to get out of this emergency role without losing her job, she was left in the meeting room with Cheekbones and his piercing, astute stare.

'You not want the job, lady?' he asked coolly.

Feeling sick from the mingling dread and panic, she rubbed her face and managed a wan smile. 'I don't think whether I want it or not matters.' Then, fearing she sounded disloyal— if Cheekbones worked for Cannavaro Travel he would undoubtedly be reporting to Giovanni Cannavaro himself, whose reputation as a taskmaster was on a par with Wolfgang's. 'But I know how important this maiden voyage is, so I'll give it my best shot.'

What choice did she have? Accept the last-minute secondment or lose her job. Those were the only choices. If she lost her job, what would happen to her? She'd be forced to return to England while she sought another job. Forced to live in the bleak, unhappy home of her childhood. All the joy and light she'd experienced these past three years would be gone and she'd return to grey.

'What role do you play in it all?' she asked into the silence.

He raised a thick black eyebrow.

'Are you part of Cannavaro Travel?' she queried. 'Sorry, my mind went blank when we were introduced.'

The other eyebrow rose.

A tiny dart of amusement at his expression— it was definitely the expression of someone outrageously thinking, *How can you not know who I am?*—cut through Merry's guilt and anguish. The guilt came from having spent two months praying for the forthcoming trip home to be cancelled. The anguish came from her having to be the one to do it, and with just two days' notice. The early Christmas dinner her sister-in-law had spent weeks and weeks planning had all been for nothing.

Her brother was going to kill her.

The only good thing she had to hold on to was that she hadn't clobbered an actual guest with the Christmas tree, although, judging by the cut of his suit, Cheekbones was on a huge salary, so must be high up in Cannavaro Travel, and all the signs were that he had an ego to match that salary.

She'd get this meeting over and done with and then she'd call Martin.

With that set in her mind, she relaxed her chest with an exhale. 'Your role?' she asked again.

Dark blue eyes glittered. Tingles laced her spine and spread through her skin.

Cheekbones folded his hands together on the table. 'My role...? Think of me as the boss.'

His deep, musical accent set more tingles off in her. Crossing her legs, thankful that she'd come to her senses before mouthing off about being forced into a temporary job she'd rather eat fetid fruit than do, Merry made a mark in her notebook. 'I report to you?'

'*Si.*'

'Are you going on the train ride?'

Strong nostrils flared with distaste. 'It is no "train ride", lady.'

'You know what I mean.' She laughed. She couldn't help it. Something about his presence unnerved her. Greek god looks clashing with a glacial demeanour, warmed up again by the sexiest Italian accent she'd ever heard.

'I know what you mean and, *si*, I will be on the voyage.'

Unnerved further by the swoop of her belly at this, she made another nonsense mark in her book before looking back up at him and smiling ruefully. 'In that case, I should confess that I didn't catch your name. I'm Merry,' she added, so he wouldn't have any excuse to keep addressing her as 'lady'.

His fingers drummed on the table. 'I know your name, lady. *I* pay attention.'

For some unfathomable reason, this tickled her. 'Well done. Go to the top of the class. And your name?'

'Giovanni Cannavaro.'

All the blood in Merry's head pooled down to her feet in one strong gush.

He rose to his feet and stared imperiously at her. With ice-cool precision, he said, 'You have much to do. You will start by reading the files. We will meet later to discuss details and I will decide then if are you up to the job... Or not.'

He left the meeting room without another word.

# MILLS & BOON

# Book Club

Have your favourite series delivered to your door every month with a Mills & Boon subscription.

## Use code ROMANCESUB2021 to get 50% off the first month of your chosen subscription PLUS free delivery.

Sign up online at
**millsandboon.com.au/pages/print-subscriptions**
or call Customer Service on

AUS **1300 659 500** or NZ **0800 265 546**

**No Lock-in Contracts**

**Free Postage**

**Exclusive Offers**

For full terms and conditions go to millsandboon.com.au
Offer expires October 31, 2021

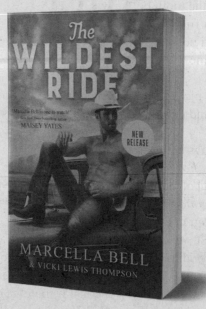